Dancing on the Whisper of God

A Novel

JEAN GILBERTSON

Order this book online at www.trafford.com
or email orders@trafford.com

Most Trafford titles are also available at major online book retailers.

© Copyright 2014, 2015 Jean Gilbertson.

All rights reserved. No part of this publication may be reproduced, stored in a retrieval system, or transmitted, in any form or by any means, electronic, mechanical, photocopying, recording, or otherwise, without the written prior permission of the author.

Dancing on the Whisper of God is a work of fiction. Names, characters, places, and incidents are the product of the author's imagination or are used fictitiously. Any resemblance to actual events or persons, living or dead, is entirely coincidental.
The only exceptions are names of renowned persons in the arts.

Printed in the United States of America.

ISBN: 978-1-4907-2161-3 (sc)
ISBN: 978-1-4907-2160-6 (hc)
ISBN: 978-1-4907-2162-0 (e)

Library of Congress Control Number: 2013922876

Because of the dynamic nature of the Internet, any web addresses or links contained in this book may have changed since publication and may no longer be valid. The views expressed in this work are solely those of the author and do not necessarily reflect the views of the publisher, and the publisher hereby disclaims any responsibility for them.

 www.trafford.com

North America & international
toll-free: 1 888 232 4444 (USA & Canada)
fax: 812 355 4082

Also by Jean Gilbertson

Nonfiction
> ***Two Men at the Helm: The First 100 Years of Crowley Maritime Corporation, 1892-1992***

In memory of my parents,
Geneva Lemmon   and   Carl Lemmon
(1907-1980)   (1905-1971)

*Cause me to hear Your loving-kindness in the morning,
for on you do I lean and in You do I trust.
Cause me to know the way wherein I should walk,
for I lift up my inner self to You.*

—Psalm 143:8 (Amplified)

Nine Weeks

Nothing about the day hinted change as Calvin Tropp headed along Market Street toward The Castro, except for the slow construction of the new streetcar line that was supposed to be finished in 1995, two years away. The Muni project appeared in disarray, but then maybe ballet choreographies in the making looked pretty rough to the untrained eye too.

A drag on the leash told him that Miss Agnus was showing too much interest in some scent along the way. "Leave it!" He tugged on the leather cord and the five-pound Pomeranian resumed trotting along beside him. Her tail fluffed forward, spreading across her back, and her pink tongue rocked against the bottom of her open mouth.

Extending blocks ahead and behind, the chaos of razing brought him back to the futile questions. *What has happened to me? When did I stop moving forward?*

The picture in his mind shifted to a day when, as a boy of seventeen, he had asked his mother, "But what if I choose wrong?"

Five freshly pressed shirts on hangers lined the straight-back chair beside her. The metal ironing board creaked every time she banged the hot iron down onto the cloth. He watched her finish both sides of a sleeve before she responded. "What does your heart tell you, Cal?"

"I want to be a dancer, Mom, but—"

"But you know your dad's against it."

"And you." He'd always felt closer to her, so it was harder for him that she too feared what he wanted for his life.

She slammed the iron down again, the ironing board shuddering. "We're just worried for you, is all. What do we know about dancing?"

"So you're as worried as I am that I might choose wrong."

Her hands stopped moving. "Everybody's bound to choose wrong sometimes. But you can't let that stop you from making the best choice you can, with what you know." The fingers of her left hand spread wide over the cloth as though at a keyboard, and she took up the iron again. "Then you trust that it will turn out right in the long run. There's bigger forces at work than we know."

Cal had taken her words as gospel. He had made the leap, left home with a one-way ticket to Chicago to find a place for himself in the dance world, and had danced with an experimental group for almost two years before his mother accepted his decision. His father never did. Then came Anne, the one big place where he had chosen wrong. And no bigger force had stepped in to make things right.

Later, when his mother passed and his father remarried within ten months, still no bigger force made itself known. As far as Cal could tell, he was alone.

Now, standing beside the disheveled construction site, he felt his heart constrict as, unbidden, an image of his lost wife stood in his mind. Their son, Jon, had her dark brown hair and her brown/gray eyes but apparently none—thank goodness—of her impetuosity or her ruthless disregard for the people she might be expected to love. "Maybe I didn't peak when you left, Anne," he said into the quiet afternoon, "but a big piece of me stopped moving forward."

That evening, as the sun eased behind the horizon and his living room grew noticeably darker each passing minute, Cal stood with Miss Agnus against his chest and drew the heavy drapes over the window. Instantly the room transformed to cavelike darkness, which he maneuvered by maintaining contact with the furniture as he moved toward a lamp. Having Miss Agnus in his arms ensured that he did not step on her in the darkness that neither had the vision to negotiate.

It was the very next morning—early, before dawn—that he heard:

We are going to make a new dance and the theme is prayer.

Cal's eyes sprang open to the dark room. No one had said it, yet he had heard it. He reached out a hand along the bedspread till he came to the warm, soft body of Miss Agnus, who was lying, as usual, on her back with her four paws in the air. Her undisturbed sleep was reassuring: if the vigilant and skittish Pomeranian had heard nothing, there was nothing to be heard.

Yet he had heard it, a pronouncement, in a voice not his own. Well, maybe not actually a *voice*, but he had heard *something*! Hadn't he? He tested his wakefulness, lifting his eyelids wide. No, he was not dreaming. What he had heard had brought him fully awake in an instant, sure with a certainty unlike anything in his usual world. He peered here and there, toward the closed closet, over by the window, by the door.

"But I'm not religious." At once he knew that the dance would not be about religion but something far more spiritual.

"Prayer is something different from religion?" His face twitched with the oddness of dialoging with the darkness. The bedroom would have been pitch-black were it not for the lighted blue face of the clock that kept him apprised of time's progress. The bedroom had little light; like the rest of his home, it emphasized dark woods and heavy furniture. Even the short set of steps he had built to enable Miss Agnus to climb up onto the bed was painted dark walnut.

After several seconds of silence, Cal concluded that it had been a vivid dream, and he started to roll over to go back to sleep. Then he saw a motion theme: a simple movement bringing both arms overhead, hands coming together and rising, energy expending upward, which would reveal itself in endless variations, all of them meaning prayer. He took a breath then and threw back the covers, winning a sleepy yip of complaint from beneath the rumpled blankets. Miss Agnus worked her forepaws in unison until she had uncovered her face, and then she rolled over and lay quiet, watching her master, in his pale briefs, as he switched on a nightstand light and stood before the mirror with his arms in an attitude of supplication.

In the shower, Calvin tried out some Bach in his head, some Stravinsky, some Chopin, some Handel, some Schoenberg. He thought of Purcell, Prokofiev, Wagner, Debussy. He thought of Duke Ellington. He couldn't remember whether he had shampooed his hair or not, but it was wet and the hot water was running cool, so he decided that he must have—possibly more than once. The fresh, sweet scent in the shower stall couldn't be from soap alone. He turned off the water and reached for a towel. His light brown hair (which, to be truthful, was beginning to thin as well as to gray) took only a couple of minutes to blow-dry.

He got to the dance studio early, thinking he might jot down some preliminary notes before the company had assembled for nine o'clock class, which he, as artistic director, taught twice each week. That is, half his mind was thinking about the notes; the other half was caught in a repeating helix of questions: What was that? Was it real? Was it a dream? Who's the *we*?

Behind those questions came others: Why me? Is my mind starting to slip?

He could hear dancers gathering in the building. A few were already in the main rehearsal hall, talking quietly as they warmed and stretched muscles. *Of course Deinken is here somewhere.*

Cal had got only as far as sketching the motion theme when Rob Deinken was at his door. Known for his no-nonsense, morning-person habits, the associate artistic director stepped briskly inside the office. "We need another piece for the October program. About thirty minutes should do it."

"Good morning, Rob."

The younger man smiled an apology, looking impatient with himself for having forgotten again that other people preferred some social interaction before getting to the point. "Sorry to intrude. Should I come back later?"

Cal put down his pencil. "No, now will be fine."

"Good. Well, I just wanted to say that we'll have to be choosing something. Opening night is only nine weeks away. I've come up with a list of everything in the repertory that's about that length." He leaned forward to hand the list to Cal.

Scanning, Cal saw twenty years' worth of his own shorter works, several by Ballanchine, others by Joffrey, Tharp, Tudor, Stowell, Cranko, Ailey, Feld. He raised three fingers. "We're already doing—"

Before he finished his sentence, Rob ticked off three choreographers' names, and Cal summed them up: "So we have a short classical ballet for the corps in tutus, a US premiere of a geometric work by the English choreographer, and a high-spirited production heavy on stirring music and flamboyant costumes."

"Right."

Adrenaline began pumping through Cal's body. He opened his mouth—and then clamped his jaw shut, turning his head to the side. When he could trust himself, he cleared his throat and opened his mouth again. "Let me think about it."

"We can't wait long to decide."

Cal nodded. "I'll let you know."

When Rob had gone, closing the door behind him, Cal sat waiting for his heart to stop pounding. He had nearly blurted out an announcement that they would tackle a new ballet on prayer. *Have I lost my mind?* He pictured how he must have looked early that morning, in only his briefs, arms raised over his head. Acute embarrassment swept over him in a hot tide.

Cal had spent a good portion of his life—certainly the last thirteen years since Anne left—avoiding situations that made him feel this uncomfortable. He shook his head, ejecting from his mind the loathsome memory of his early morning exercise, and hustled out of his office toward the rehearsal hall. He faced a full day of classes, rehearsals, and meetings with staff.

But on the drive home late that afternoon, his foot on the brake at a quiet intersection and no one coming up behind him, he heard it again:

Start the choreography. I'll help you.

Panic touched the top of his throat. This time there was no claiming it might be a dream. *Something* was talking to him. He jerked his head to the right and left, saw no one, and then leaned his forehead against the steering wheel. Almost at once he was jolted upright by a honking horn behind him. He drove around the corner, parked on a leafy side street, and sat with his muscles taut and straining. Nothing more came, and after half an hour he crept home.

Approaching midnight, Miss Agnus went to bed by herself, climbing up her stairs, scratching at the bedspread to bunch up a nest and settling down to sleep. It was nearly one o'clock before Cal came to the bedroom, too exhausted to continue on guard.

The next morning he awoke to silence, rolled over, and lay listening, holding his breath at first, and then relaxing when there was nothing to hear. Still he waited. *Maybe it's given up on me. Maybe I'm off the hook.* A little smile of relief formed as he left the bed and headed to the shower.

But then a faint twinge touched his heart, a small pang. *What? Now I'm wishing I could hear it again?* No, he and the entire troupe had plenty to do to get ready for the October opening as it was. An entirely new piece was too great a challenge to take on. It would be a huge, unnecessary risk. Why do that?

The day was nearly over before he and Rob had a chance to talk again. The last class of the day finished, Cal was sitting at his desk, flipping through telephone message slips. Rob's brisk double knock on the frame barely preceded the opening of the door.

"Did you have a chance to think about the repertory pieces yet?"

"Haven't done that yet, no."

"Maybe you and I could sort it out together tomorrow," Rob said. "According to the schedule, we should both have a little time around three. How 'bout it?"

We're going to make a new ballet on prayer.

Cal stared at Rob, holding himself rigid to keep from blurting "Did you hear that? Didn't you just hear a voice talking about making a new ballet?" But he could see that Rob had heard nothing. In fact, Rob, still standing in the doorway, was going ahead with the conversation: "I could even chart out what the best approach might be, if that would help."

Cal heard his own voice respond, "Sure, that would help." But he was not interested in a chart detailing the pros and cons of mounting any of the old works. Instead he was noticing a swelling in his chest, a rising confidence, excitement. "Second thought, Rob, no." He took a breath and out it came: "The fourth piece will be a new choreography. We need a world premiere for opening night, don't you think?"

He drew a breath and found that the air stopped at the level of his chest. He sat straighter and forced his shallow breath to reach deeper into his lungs.

Rob put his left hand against the tall bookcase that stood just inside Cal's door. "Uh, that would be nice, but I don't think we have one."

"I'm working on it."

He could see the suppressed flinch. Rob was accustomed to knowing everything there was to know about the company.

"It's called *Prayer.*"

Growing slightly red in the face, Rob asked, "Who's dancing it?" His fingers inched back and forth on the bookcase, as though measuring the depth of the sideboard.

"I don't know yet."

"What's the music?"

"I don't know yet."

Rob blinked and one corner of his mouth appeared to go into a spasm. He pulled his hand from the bookcase and buried it in his pants pocket. "We're going to do a world premiere in nine weeks, and we don't know yet what the music is?" Cal didn't answer. "What *do* we know about it?"

Cal took a deep breath and hoped that Rob couldn't hear his heart pounding. "Well, we know it's called *Prayer* and it's about thirty minutes long." The look on Rob's face was more than he could deal with just then. "How 'bout if we talk about it tomorrow? I should have more to tell you then."

For some minutes after Rob left the office, Cal sat immobile at his desk. He couldn't feel his feet. He couldn't even feel the padded, worn leather office chair beneath him. There was a loud churning noise in his head that he concluded was the sound of hot blood rushing in panic through his brain. *What am I doing? Of course Rob is right. This is crazy! The opening is nine weeks away and I don't even have a score. No score means no choreography. No choreography means no dancers lined up, no sets in design, no costumes being readied. And all of that means no lighting cues written, no orchestra in preparation, nothing built, nothing rehearsed.*

It means no performance. No possible way.

The churning in his head grew louder until it demanded his entire attention. He put his head back, closed his eyes, and took several deep, slow breaths until the noise in his ears lessened. Despite the fact that his desk was in its usual cluttered state, Rob's list of existing thirty-minute works was the first thing he saw when he opened his eyes. He read through them again. *There would be very little problem to get any of these up and running in nine weeks; why not just choose one? It would be a whole lot easier. The dancers already know them. Of course the audience has seen them all before, but anyone who attends the ballet knows you can't exhaust a piece without multiple viewings, with various dancers. And was there really any choice, with only nine weeks to go before opening night?*

Cal closed his eyes again, not wanting to see the nonsense he was contemplating, but then from somewhere a confidence stirred and with it came the challenge: Why couldn't a new ballet be done in that short a time frame? Why couldn't he do it? After all, he'd been choreographing for twenty years. He knew his dancers. His set, lighting, and costume designers were world class. The conductor and musicians could handle virtually anything. There was no one who would be involved who was new to the job or less than first-rate. The tricky thing was the time element. Could all of his people work at a creative pitch in the short time they would have?

Could he?

Well, he argued with himself, everyone in the company was accustomed to finding the reserves of strength needed to accomplish amazing feats of memory, creativity, and, on occasion, improvisation during performance. Maybe it wouldn't be easy, but it could be done if he got started immediately.

Cal looked at the clock. It was eight fifty. He punched a number on the telephone and Amelie Boiroux, the company's ballet mistress, answered. Her French accent evoked the assurance of cool, elegant capability.

"Amelie, I know it's awfully short notice, but I wonder if you would teach class this morning in my place. I need that hour and a half for something that can't be postponed."

"Of course, Cal. Is everything all right?"

"Never better."

Daring to put weight on his numbed feet, he sprang up from the office chair to lock his door and then returned to his desk. Without another glance at it, he put the list of finished thirty-minute ballets into a drawer. He piled into a heap the books, folders, letters, and sheet music scattered over his desk and cleared a sizable area to work. Then he pulled the pad of paper back in front of him. The music had to come first. That was how he had always started in the past: weeks or months—sometimes even years—of thinking about a piece of music, studying its structure, ferreting out its most subtle dynamics, settling on the best tempo. Inside himself, the roar had abated, and his consciousness sat on a floor of certainty.

But there isn't any music. The solid floor of his consciousness broke apart, and he felt himself slipping through.

He shoved the pad of paper away and abruptly rose from his desk, feeling as though he might burst if he didn't move. He went to the window and splayed the blinds apart, but he wasn't really looking outside. In three strides, he was at the door, and then he left the office, left the building, to walk. Outside, the fog was thinning, and the early morning August air provided instant solace. In another couple of hours, the sun would have heated the pavement to too hot, and the humidity would have packed particles of vehicle exhaust into every air molecule, creating a bad smell and a clear threat to health, but now the air felt good against his face and in his lungs.

He forced himself to think about the difficult facts. He was artistic director and chief choreographer of The Calvin Tropp Ballet Company—and it was no fly-by-night operation. After many years of hard work, not just his own, the company was not only firmly established but well respected. And here he was thinking of trying to develop a thirty-minute ballet—for which there was no score—in its entirety to open in nine weeks. From nothing. Sheerly on the basis of a couple of mystical experiences. Which might have come from anywhere.

He kept on walking, watching but not seeing the sidewalk, shaking his head again at how he had looked in the mirror. Maybe what was happening to him was a change-of-life thing, a willingness to take a risk even through appearing ridiculous was one of the possible outcomes. Stereotypically, men his age began propositioning young women who had previously been of only passing physical interest to them; some suddenly threw over years of marriage, family, and security to live reclusively and make their living by working with their hands; some were simply old overnight because they chose neither of the other options.

The thing was he had not felt so drawn by his work in years. The very thought of the new ballet made his steps quicker, made him feel alive in a way he had not felt in years. The moisture that stung his eyes surprised him.

But for the first time in his life he couldn't start with the music, because he had no idea what the music should be. This dance didn't start with music. This dance had to start with its theme, which was prayer, and he had only the vaguest notion of what prayer was. *I must be nuts. In the first place, there's not enough time, and even if there were enough time, I don't even understand my own theme!*

He stopped at an intersection and looked around him. Down the street to the left were a dry cleaners, a used-book store, a sportswear shop, a quick printer. To the right were office buildings, parking lots, restaurants. He could see a church steeple ahead. Back the way he had come were a drugstore, a bakery, a stationery store. He turned back to the stationery store, where he bought a pad of paper, an automatic pencil, and a dictionary. At the bakery, a warm, sweet, bready fragrance engulfed him as soon as he stepped inside, glad to see that he was apparently between the breakfast crowd and the midmorning-break crowd. He bought a cup of coffee and, after a few moments of consideration, a peanut-butter cookie dipped in chocolate. He chose a table in the corner, turned his back to the room, and sat down.

The dictionary definitions of prayer had to be reread several times: "a devout petition to God or an object of worship; a spiritual communion with God or an object of worship." Cal's frustration deepened with his realization that the phrases made no sense to him. Only after the fifth reading did he begin to hook into the words *spiritual communion with God*. He rolled the phrase around in his mind and then reread the full definition. Turning the page, he found a picture of a praying mantis, which he squinted at because it reminded him of the motion theme he'd sketched.

Finally he pushed the open dictionary to the side and opened the pad of paper. Across the top of the first page he wrote, *Why does a person pray?* He thought for some minutes, and then he began to list reasons: to ask for help, to ask for guidance, to admit a wrongdoing. Cal tapped the eraser end of the pencil against the pad. *How the hell should I know?* Then he scratched his thumbnail against his lower lip as he dredged up a few more: to ask forgiveness, to give thanks, to dispel loneliness. He ate the cookie and got more coffee but gave up on adding any more.

On the next sheet, Cal wrote at the top, *People might pray when they feel . . .* These came in a surge: scared, hurt, overwhelmed, inadequate—*like I feel right now*—alone, defenseless, lost, sorry, regretful, repentant, grateful, compassionate, joyous, awestruck.

So far so good. But we're nowhere near it yet, because I don't know what this *dance should be saying about prayer. What am I supposed to be communicating?*

He waited. Nothing came to him.

He sketched dance positions that incorporated his motion theme and the mood evoked by the different reasons and feelings associated with prayer. Then he turned again to the question of music and sat with pencil poised. Nothing came to him. Nothing! He stared into his coffee cup and saw his wan reflection in the shallow liquid at the bottom.

The clock above his head read five minutes after ten. Class would be over at ten thirty, and he had a rehearsal scheduled to begin a few minutes after that. By putting some speed into it and cutting through alleys, he figured he could be back at the studio in fifteen minutes. He turned to another fresh sheet of paper and wrote at the top, *Time Line*. Despite the boldness with which he penciled *Nine Weeks*, he felt a twist in his gut. Sixty-three days, give or take, and he was using up all of the first one trying to figure out whether he had anything at all to say about his theme.

Cal jotted down the elements that went into a production and began making notes. He could keep the costumes and set simple. That was appropriate, and there was no other choice anyway. Lights could be as complex as needed; he knew that Ned Freedman could deliver stunning visuals however this ballet developed. The choreography—well, the standard was an hour of work with the dancers for every minute of the dance, not counting subsequent revisions and rehearsals. Better plan on forty hours of choreography minimum, and of course that would be interspersed with the rehearsals and other preparations for the three works already planned for the October program. When it was all said and done, it would probably take four weeks to choreograph the piece. A sense that maybe this would be possible after all touched the back of his neck. A surge of wild excitement flashed through him, and he sprang to his feet to jog back to the studio.

The door of the bakery had just closed behind him, rattling with the sound of pane glass loose in its wood frame, when the realization hit him with a splash cooler than the air outside that this ballet would require *new* music. *Commissioned* music. A new composition for a thirty-minute ballet. *Now how the heck long will that take? And who will do it?* Cal swallowed back a curse as sweat sprang across his forehead and dampened the back of his shirt. As if under attack, he began to sprint.

* * *

Miss Agnus was already barking as Cal neared the side door to his home that evening. Her pom-pom tail swished as she bounced against his legs in ecstatic greeting. He microwaved some leftover Japanese food and opened a small can of pricey dog food. By the time he was seated to eat, she had left her bowl to sit beside him, begging for bites. It was their ritual that waiting with patience and no whining would win for her the last bite from his plate.

As darkness fell, he stood at a window that looked out on a small, sheltered, fenced backyard with a deck at one side and the rest amok with wild, growing greenery. Miss Agnus was in his arms, her head against his chest, and he thought about the new ballet. It was crazy; he had to admit it. There were mythical tales about composers creating long works in short periods of time. There must be dozens of stories about Mozart's ability to compose rapidly, and Beethoven is said to have written entire sonatas and sextets within a day. But such tales were always about dead composers; no living examples came to mind. The few composers he knew and trusted well enough to develop something he would want to work with were either overobligated already or out of the country. He stroked Miss Agnus until she squirmed, indicating that she had had enough, and then he touched the tip of his forefinger along her inch-long nose, kissed the top of her head, and set her onto the floor.

Maybe Deinken has another list up his sleeve. Cal sat down near the phone and dialed.

"Rob, you still up?"

"Yeah, Cal. What do you need?"

"A composer."

Rob was silent for several seconds, and for the first time in their two years of association, Cal was glad that the younger man had so little sense of humor. "You probably are hoping for someone who works fast, right?"

"That and real ability are the main requisites."

"Mmm. There's Hillbreet in Philadelphia."

"Not due back from Denmark for another six weeks."

"And that fellow you worked with, the one in Los Angeles."

"Yes, Richardson was good, but he's not quite right for this. But you're on the right track to be thinking of people we already know and can get to without too much difficulty."

Rob was quiet again, and Cal knew he was running out of names too. "I can make some calls first thing in the morning and get back to you."

"Great, Rob. Thanks." Cal hung up the receiver and sat staring into the dark sky. He had not turned on a lamp, so the room had darkened with the evening. After some time had passed, he heard Miss Agnus come back into the house through her dog door. She pranced into the living room, jumped onto his lap, and straddled his hand for a stomach scratch. When she had settled down and gone to sleep, he brought her up close to his neck and rubbed his chin against her soft head. Her ears twitched, but she didn't open her eyes. She was completely relaxed in his care.

Then Cal spoke into the darkness: "You said *we*. You said *we* are going to make a new dance." He gently stroked the sleeping dog and spoke aloud again. "I sure hope to God you *meant we* because this is not something I am going to be able to do by myself."

Miss Agnus was awake now, looking at him over her svelte red-gold shoulder. He carried her with him when he got up to close the drapes and get ready for bed. Always, the closing of the drapes brought a feeling of separateness, of safety from the world. He trailed his fingers along the back of a sofa until he reached the lamp switch, which he turned on, though the dark furniture in the room swallowed much of the light. "Another thing. If you want prayer for a theme, you'll have to give me a better idea what it is."

Cal finished up in the bathroom, checked the locks on the doors, and made sure the stove was off. Then he and Miss Agnus went to the bedroom. He was undressing when the phone rang.

"It's Rob, Cal. What would you think about Evana Arthur?"

Cal didn't need even a few seconds to think about it: "Too hard to work with."

"But good—and probably fast enough."

"No, no way." Cal was shaking his head with the receiver against his ear. "I worked with her years ago and—no, no, I can't even think about bringing her into this. Keep trying. I'm sure there's someone who could do this if we think about it hard enough."

Rob was silent.

Cal sat down on the edge of the bed. "I don't mean to stomp on your suggestion, Rob, but I don't know anyone who can get along with Evana Arthur. In fact, just about everybody I ever heard of who's worked with her ended up about half wanting to kill her!"

"Until the project is done," Rob said. "Then it usually turns out that she's the one who made it happen."

The two men were silent, thinking.

"I mean, what matters here, Cal? How well you get along with the composer during the creation or how the whole thing turns out?"

After some moments, Cal sighed. "Well, it's only nine weeks, right? Thank God we don't have more time." He coughed a dry laugh, but there was no answering chuckle from Rob. Still, Cal could not force himself to give a green light to Evana.

After a moment Rob asked, "How many dancers do you think you'll need?"

"Three: two women and one man."

"Who are you thinking of?"

"Alexandra and Matt and Katherine."

"That's good," Rob said, and Cal knew he meant that the three dancers were not only seasoned, quick learners but could also handle the stress that would certainly arise from the short time frame. Rob would schedule the dancers' roles in the other ballets on the program to accommodate their performances in the premiere piece. "So do you want Evana's phone number?"

"No way. I have the number somewhere, but we're not using her. Let's see who else we can think of."

"See you in the morning."

Cal set the telephone back on its stand and finished undressing, but his calm motions belied how stunned he felt. Rob had asked how many dancers, and he had said *three*—as though he'd thought it out ahead of time. In truth, he had been so obsessed with the theme and the music that he had not thought about the dancers at all yet. But somehow he had, or *someone* had, because now he and Rob both knew not only how many dancers but also who they would be.

He slipped under the sheet wondering just how he would use three dancers to present the theme of prayer. But before his head touched the pillow, he remembered the composer problem and his eyes opened wide. Sharp regret bit at the edges of his heart, creating a taste like metal in his mouth, and more than anything, he wished he'd never entertained the idea of a new world premiere, or at least never mentioned it to anyone. *I could back out—of course I could! Only Rob knows and he'd love to forget the whole thing.* The tiny start of joy survived only seconds before he realized that a small war had started up inside him. A big part of his heart did not want to do that. Hard as it promised to be, he *wanted* to do this ballet.

For hours he lay staring, unseeing, into the dark, going over and over every composer he'd ever worked with, no matter where in the world, and every composer he'd heard was good. Finally, the blue face of the clock told him that it was almost four in the morning and he had not slept. Worse, he had not come up with a better suggestion than Evana Arthur. *Damn, I hate it, but Rob is probably right. She'll be impossible to work with. I'm going to hate every second of it, but she's the only composer I know who might be able to do this. Damn!*

* * *

"Nice of you to see me on such short notice, Evana." Cal kept his voice even as he accepted the boiling-hot mug of coffee Evana's young secretary had handed him. On first glance, he'd taken the secretary to be about fourteen years old—someone's visiting daughter or maybe Evana's granddaughter. Then the hot mug demanded his attention. He wanted to set it on the edge of Evana's desk but was wary of any moves that she might interpret as presumptuous.

"I figured it must be something pretty extraordinary, Calvin. I don't think you and I have said three words to each other in five years, so I got all excited to see what this could be about."

Same old Evana. A familiar tremor rattled Cal's gut in response to Evana's sarcasm. *I hate this so much!*

"Well, actually—" Cal's voice cracked, and he started again, resisting the urge to close his eyes and shut all of this from view. "Actually, Evana, this *is* extraordinary, and it's something I find myself quite excited about." He had been refusing to look her in the face out of fear that his feelings might show, but he realized that not making eye contact would not serve him. Not only did it feed his demonization of her (which he did not need any help with), but also it surely made him less attractive to work with from her point of view. Setting his jaw, he brought his gaze up but found that all he could manage was to focus on the glinting metal where her half-lens glasses bridged her nose. "We're working on our October program, and we would like to include a new ballet—a world premiere— that I will choreograph and that will require a new composition. The piece needs to be about thirty minutes long. It will use three dancers, two women and one man, and the theme is prayer."

Calvin paused, surprised that he had managed to get it all said, but Evana made no response. He continued to stare between her eyes and went on. "My associate, Rob Deinken, and I put our heads together and decided to approach you about composing the music—so that's why I'm here."

"You mean October *next* year, I presume."

Cal's gaze slid to the left, and his insides quavered as he encountered the severity in Evana's right eye, peering at him above the sharp edge of glass. Involuntarily he compared it to the left eye—no difference—and then pulled his eyes back to the bridge of her glasses. *So much for eye contact.* It wasn't the sarcasm alone that was so unnerving, but her habit of slow, careful enunciation so that every drip of venom could saturate.

"No. This year." Cal forced a casual tone. He used both hands to lift the steaming mug to his mouth and, without thinking, took a large swallow, scalding his tongue and burning his throat. Against his will, his eyes teared at the pain.

Evana sat back in her chair and swiveled, turning her profile to him. Feeling released from scrutiny, Cal reached up to wipe the tears from his eyes. He drew a deep breath, for the first time since he'd entered the room, and felt sorry for himself that his tongue, now numb, also felt as if it might be coated with a layer of ash. He drew another breath but stifled it to prevent Evana from thinking he was sighing out of impatience. *You're gonna have to breathe normally.* For distraction, he let his gaze move right and left to take in Evana's office, which was vintage university in its décor. Dust on the ancient wood walls looked like it may have been there since the university was established in the early 1900s. Certainly some of those books on the shelves were from that era, as was Evana's leather office chair, which might have been a nice green color at some point but was now dulled by time and use. Still, it looked plenty sturdy to continue accommodating her small frame. The air in the room smelled like the windows had not been opened in decades. From the side, what was most noticeable about Evana herself was her hair: steel gray and cropped close to her head, accentuating her cheekbones. Behind her he saw a framed picture and realized after a moment that the woman in the picture had to be Evana, probably thirty years younger and in long hair, with two older men on a wintry beach beside the ocean. The two men resembled each other, probably brothers. He mused about who they might be; their affection for her, obvious in the old photograph, humanized her in his perception.

Coming back to Evana, he followed the line of her vision and saw that she was looking at a calendar on the wall.

"Late October, mid-October, what?"

"Early October. Opening night is the sixth, I believe."

She frowned at him. "What's the matter with Telemann? He did a lot of sacred music. You could use the second movement of almost anything baroque, couldn't you? Telemann or Handel or Bach, I should think."

"See, that's the problem." Cal leaned forward and claimed the right to set his coffee mug on the edge of her desk. He looked her in the eye and saw that she was indifferent to the existence, let alone the location, of his mug. "People think of prayer as related to some time in history like the seventeenth century. It's something the Pilgrims did. If I use a piece of music from that period, I'm just perpetuating the idea that prayer was an out-of-the-closet thing for those folks then, but not for people today. Can you think of anything recent that the arts have had to say about prayer?"

Without hesitation she said, "John Tavener and Arvo Pärt are doing some fine work."

He sat back. *Why didn't I think of them!* Immediately he knew. *Because I think of them as "religious" composers, that's why.* He nodded agreement. "But not quite right for this."

He thought he saw something in her eyes now. The severity had moved aside just enough to allow in a little interest.

"Where's the book?"

"The book?" His heart stopped with confusion.

She waved her hand. "The book—the whatyoucallit, the libretto. The thing that says what you're trying to communicate and the sequence you're saying it in."

He stifled both a groan and a grimace. "It's—not ready to show yet." Evana's scowl forced him to add, "But I'm working on it."

Cal took another searing drink of coffee to hide his face, ignoring the pain of hot liquid against his burned mouth. He hoped she couldn't see that he was fibbing. He hadn't used a libretto in years. Fifteen at least. Virtually all of his work had been choreographed out of the depth of his familiarity with an existing score and from a few notes and sketches.

"Let me see what you have so far."

He stared at her over the top of the mug. *She thinks my notebook is the libretto!*

Evana's hand shot toward him, the fingers demanding. "Come on! Let's see your notes so far. I have to be in the lecture hall in twelve minutes."

Cal handed her his notepad, his face stiffening, his chest feeling like an elephant had just sat on it, and watched her flip open the cover to his list of reasons under *Why does a person pray?* Despite his immense discomfort, he noticed that her face remained impassive as she read down the list and then flipped to the next page: *People might pray when they feel...*

It seemed to take a lifetime before she said anything at all.

"I'd add anger. I think people pray when they're angry." She pressed a button on the telephone. "At least I do." The childlike secretary appeared at the door, and Evana handed her Cal's notepad. "Make a copy of these two lists right away so Mr. Tropp can have his notebook back." She turned to Cal again. "When I'm composing, I'm usually mad as hell, pacing and swearing and cursing everything under the sun while I try to get the notes out and down on the paper. But that's a form of praying, I think. Don't you?"

Cal half nodded. "So you're saying you'll do the composition for us?"

She shook her head. "What you're asking is impossible, Calvin. There's not enough time. Surely you know that. You've only got eight or nine weeks total before your opening, not just for my work but yours and everyone else's, and I'd have to do mine before the rest of you could even start." Her voice had become angrier and she glared at him now. "That is, after you get around to doing the book. And it's not as though I could suspend the rest of my responsibilities, you know."

She stood up, so he did too. The secretary came into the room and handed Cal's notepad and two photocopied sheets to Evana.

"Well, thank you for your time and the coffee." Cal reached to shake her hand, remembering too late that Evana scorned such social practices.

She shoved his notepad into the outstretched hand and directed her attention to the photocopies. "I'll look these over again and call you after two o'clock. You get to work on that libretto. How's a composer supposed to do anything if she doesn't know what you have in mind?" She looked thoroughly disgusted.

"Right away," he heard himself say as he turned, dismissed, toward the door. He sensed that Evana wasn't listening to him, that her attention had been drawn away to be irritated by something else.

Cal got to his car, threw the notepad onto the passenger seat, and spun his tires, backing out of the parking space. At the first intersection he took a right because he remembered an ice-cream store near the university. He needed ice cream the way he had needed it to soothe himself as a child against the batterings of life. It had been years since he had had ice cream, but he was going to have some now. *Butterscotch should do it.*

* * *

It was just before two when the phone rang in Cal's office. *She's early*, he thought, closing his eyes in dread. *Maybe I'll just let it ring.* He groped for the receiver with his eyes still shut and muttered "Uh?" into the mouthpiece.

"Dad?"

Cal's eyes shot open. "Jon! So good to hear your voice, son! How are you?"

A pause. "Are you okay, Dad?"

"To be honest, I'm sitting here waiting for a call from the Witch of the West."

"And you thought this was it."

"Yes."

"I didn't know you had any witches in your life anymore."

"Just one, and I don't know yet whether she's going to be in my life or not—I'm really not sure which to wish for. What's up?"

"I was hoping to come up to see you on Sunday, and I wanted to make sure that would work for you."

Sunday was the ballet company's day off. "Yes, absolutely. Maybe I can get some steaks to barbecue."

"That'd be great. Should be there around noon."

"Jon, before you hang up—tell me, what do you know about prayer?"

"Prayer? Uh, gee, Dad, not much, I guess." He laughed. "They missed that in the law school curriculum."

Cal decided to persist. "Do you think it's something people can relate to?"

"Prayer?"

"Uh-huh."

"Well . . . I, uh . . . I think it's something everyone does, in their heart of hearts, but it's not something you go around talking about."

"But you think it's something everyone does—is that what you said?"

"Well, most people. At least once in a while. One way or another. What is this about, Dad?"

"I'm trying to get a handle on a new piece I'm working on. If any thoughts on prayer occur to you, I'd like to hear them."

"Okay, Dad." He laughed again, an embarrassed sound. "See you Sunday."

Cal hung up the receiver and reached for the notepad. He flipped to the third page and was writing down Jon's comments when the phone rang again. Evana's harsh voice blared into his ear sounding like someone trying to pick a fight: "I thought that if I spent more time with these two lists of yours maybe I could see what you're doing, but now it just looks to me like you haven't done any thinking about this at all. So now I'm trying to figure out if this is your idea of a joke."

Cal closed his eyes, a feeling of suffocation returning. *I was right: this is never going to work.* He wanted to hang up the phone and forget the whole thing. Instead, he sat up straighter and fought his way to a reply. "I'm not joking, Evana. I need a thirty-minute piece of music for a new ballet." He brought his teeth together then to keep from adding anything else. Those were the facts, and no excuses or apologies or explanations or pleading would further his cause. Either she would do it or she wouldn't.

The silence on the phone line went on so long he thought she might have set down the receiver to walk away. But finally she said in a low voice that might have meant anger or uncertainty, "You get that libretto finished up and get it over to me so I can figure out what the hell you're doing and what you need. Until I see that, I can't tell you anything. I'll expect it tomorrow."

Tomorrow! Cal opened his mouth to object but choked back the words. Evana would pounce on the slightest evidence of a lack of commitment, and he knew that if she would agree to try it, a huge task lay before her. It only made sense that she would need any guidance he could give her as soon as possible. Cal identified the buzz he was hearing as the dial tone. Evana had hung up without waiting for confirmation. He hung up the receiver and laid his forehead into his hand. He just wasn't at all sure that tomorrow was possible.

He wasn't at all sure that this entire project was possible.

Glancing up at the clock, he got to his feet to rejoin Rob and Amelie in the main hall, where a rehearsal for the whole company was underway. As he opened the door, his world seemed to fall back into place, and he stood still for a moment, eyes closed in gratitude for the familiar sounds, the calming, known scents of so many people focused on the same goal. Rob asked the pianist to try it a little slower, and forty sweaty dancers, dressed in a colorful array of tights, leotards, and T-shirts, mostly faded and all sweat soaked, sucked in air and got into position to run the sequence again.

After the rehearsal, Cal sat in his office before his blank notepad, and nothing came to him for the libretto. On the way home, he bought a fast-food sandwich for dinner, thinking that it made no difference what it tasted like, since his tongue had not recovered from the scalding that morning. He spent the early evening sitting in front of the blank notepad, and finally he said aloud in disgust, "I don't know what the heck I'm doing." Miss Agnus lifted her head from the top of his shoe and, ears alert, tilted her head first to one side and then the other. "Why don't we get out of here and take a walk, huh?"

One of the half-dozen words Miss Agnus recognized was *walk*. She sprang up from the floor and ran to her leash, turning a dozen complete circles en route. Outside, several quick snaps on the leather cord were required before she decided to remember that *heel* was another of the words she knew. She panted with excitement and stepped up to meet the world with enthusiasm and self-confidence. So what if she was only eight inches tall; Miss Agnus knew she was a match for anything.

To the open air, to the open sky, Cal said, "It would certainly be an advantage to know what it is I'm supposed to be saying about this. Okay, I acknowledge that in the first two days you've given me a theme, my dancers, and possibly a composer. That's a lot, but nobody can go a step further until we give them the libretto. Evana needs the libretto. *I* need the libretto." Finally he thought to add, "Please."

A strange thing happened then, less a thought in his mind than a sensation in his gut. A feeling of solidness came to him. The ground once again felt secure under his feet; his heart, clear and sure within his body; his mind, in a zone of detachment that he recognized as certainty. He took a deep breath of the growing dusk air, feeling it come inside him, and then he and Miss Agnus hurried home. There, he sat down at the table and began writing:

LIBRETTO FOR THIRTY-MINUTE BALLET
ON THE THEME OF PRAYER
First Movement (11.5 minutes)
Scene 1 (2.5 minutes)

Curtain opens to show a male dancer downstage right and a female dancer upstage left. They stand rigid with their backs to each other. As they begin to dance, their conflict is evident. They utilize the full stage because they generally dance apart, touching seldom, and when they do touch, there is distaste or irritation or anger in the touch. Recurring movements are a hand raised and becoming a fist, rapid turning of their backs to each other, and crossing the stage on the diagonal without looking at each other, passing without contact.

Scene 2 (2 minutes)

Female dancer alone on stage. It becomes apparent as she dances that the conflict and strife are within her as well as between her and male dancer. (Seeing Alexandra on the stage of his mind, Cal flipped to another page to make sketches of specific motions that would work well on her body.)

Scene 3 (2 minutes)

Now Cal paused to visualize his male dancer, Matt Wade, alone on stage, struggling with interior conflicts.

Despite the number of years since he'd written a libretto, he could feel his brain laying out the structure as familiarly as though he still wrote them for every ballet. He apportioned minutes for scenes and scenes into movements, determining that this thirty-minute ballet would have three movements encompassing a total of twelve scenes.

He rose from the table once to turn on the two nearest lamps and draw closed the heavy drapes. While he was up, he brewed a single cup of coffee, eating a handful of almonds as the hot caffeine filled a cup.

Toward the end of the first movement, the two dancers begin to turn toward each other with dance motions that introduce the prayer gesture, though insufficient trust and lack of humility prevent the coming together that each is beginning to desire. Even so, the rudimentary gesture of prayer is enough to cause the Spirit of Prayer—this would be Katherine—to appear upstage right, standing still, not noticed by the other two. By this point, Matt is dancing anger and frustration while Alexandra is lost in sorrow and grief. Cal sketched Alexandra kneeling, bowing low, with her head down, her arms crossed above her head, her hands open and drooping.

A small pressure against his right heel told Cal that Miss Agnus had curled up against him. Her presence was comforting. As he continued working, he was careful to keep his foot still and especially mindful not to move his chair.

From somewhere outside himself—or perhaps so deep within himself that he had never accessed it before—an understanding emerged and allowed itself to unfold on the stage of his mind. He knew, without knowing why he knew, just how his male and female dancers would respond to the advent of spirituality—the almost fright, the uncertainty and apprehensiveness, melting gradually into stubborn resistance, and then clumsy experimentation.

He could already see how he would choreograph Matt's sense of inadequacy and despair, Alexandra's shame and inability to forgive, and the elegant Katherine reshaping their fists into attitudes of prayer. Only when Miss Agnus moved away of her own volition did he get up to stretch and get some water.

He wrote as though the scenes playing out in his mind dripped into the muscles of his hand and became the ink flowing from his pen. Only twice he wadded up a half-written page and restarted a scene. He expected his hand to cramp, but it didn't, and even more surprising, his handwriting maintained a good level of legibility.

The twelfth and final scene included his dancers forming the prayer gesture together—Alexandra's left hand, Matt's right hand—and then Katherine shepherding them upstage right to their spiritual center. Cal looked at the clock. It was just past two. He took the time to go back over his nine or ten pages of paper and count, and then recount, the minutes he had allotted to each scene to make sure they totaled to thirty. Then leaving the papers spread out on the table, he went to bed, lying flat on his back with a cover drawn up around his neck and Miss Agnus against his left hip, and woke five hours later in the same position.

After a shower and shave, he called Evana and asked for a time when he could bring over the libretto. "Now," she replied and hung up.

Twenty-five minutes later he walked into Evana's office, declined an offer of coffee, and placed a photocopy of his scene notes on her desk. This time neither bothered with the niceties of social discourse.

"Sit down and listen to this." She handed him a set of earphones and pointed to the same chair he had sat in the day before. He saw the small tape recorder in front of him, and setting the earphones in place, he switched on the play button. What he heard was a snatch of piano music. It sounded somber; it sounded soulful; it sounded churchy. It was over in ten seconds.

He listened a second time and then asked. "What is this?"

"A music theme for your ballet."

He realized then that while he'd been writing the libretto, Evana had been composing. But the music theme was as wrong as it could be.

"It sounds like something for Mass."

She nodded. "Is it close to what you had in mind?"

He took a deep breath and shook his head.

She scrutinized him, the glints off the metal rims of her glasses almost blinding.

"It's too much like church music, Evana. I'm sorry—"

"Oh, don't start slobbering on me! I can tolerate rejection. I just thought it would be a good idea to start somewhere."

He nodded but kept his mouth shut.

She was glaring at him, but the sharpness in her eyes suggested not irritation now but analysis. "So you're doing a ballet about prayer, but it shouldn't have any relationship to religious music?"

"Well, not to what we commonly think of as institutional religious music. I'm not saying prayer doesn't happen in a church. I'm saying that that's not what this ballet is about. This is prayer as a personal thing, the kind of prayer that can have meaning to anyone, anywhere, not related to a typical religious setting."

She was silent, thinking.

He dared to add softly, "Like you praying when you're angry."

In the silence, he noticed again the old, dry, musty smell of her office and thought what a good idea it would be to open one of those windows. Better yet, open all of them. He glanced at the heavy metal apparatus around the ancient panes—the outside world warped by the old, filmy glass—and speculated how much strength would be required to open a window after all these years. Would the glass shatter in the effort?

When he brought his gaze back to Evana, she was still glaring at him. It felt like cold gel sliding down his neck, but he claimed the audacity to lock eyes with her and realized that the glare was not angry. She was assessing—whether assessing him or the ideas passing through her mind, he didn't know.

"Let me study over the libretto. I'm sure that will give me a better idea of what you want. Too bad you didn't have it ready for me yesterday." The last words were like acid.

On unfortunate impulse, he decided to push his audacity further. "So then you're saying that you'll—"

"No, Calvin, I am not saying anything! I am not promising you anything! You only just now handed me the damn libretto that you should have had done before you approached me in the first place. You don't get any commitments out of me until I've had a good chance to look this thing over, and right now, the smartest thing I could do is throw this back in your face. Now get out of here!"

Cal resisted the impulse to apologize. He clenched his teeth to make sure he didn't slip up and ask her when she might have a decision. On his way out of the university grounds, he also resisted the impulse to turn right to the ice-cream store. If there was even the slimmest chance that he was going to spend the next two months working on this ballet, he couldn't be going for ice cream every time he had an encounter with Evana.

* * *

Jon stepped into his father's hug with the ease of many years' practice. Coming apart, they looked each other in the eye with a smile and lightly slapped each other's right shoulder. Though Jon looked a lot like his mother—same dark brown hair, same brown/gray eyes—Cal rarely was reminded now of his former wife, Anne, when he looked at his son. Only occasional expressions on Jon's face, most commonly when he was surprised about something, bespoke the link to the woman long gone from their lives, and Cal never commented aloud about it when he saw one of those expressions.

"Come on out to the deck," Cal said. "The grill is fired up and Miss Agnus is guarding the steaks."

Jon laughed. "Who's guarding the guard?"

"Listen—hear that?"

From the deck came a distinct thud, followed every two or three seconds by another. Cal put a finger to his lips and motioned for Jon to follow. Easing their heads around the corner of the living room, they saw across the room the open deck, where the raw steaks sat on a platter in the center of a table, and the Pomeranian was thrusting herself upward in repeated leaps of sufficient height to bring her to eye level with the meat.

"That's Miss Agnus playing steak guard," Cal whispered. Immediately the dog shifted her attention and trotted to meet them.

"Hey, Miss A!" The tiny animal yipped and wheeled in circles at Jon's feet.

Cal had made potato salad and boiled half a dozen ears of corn to go with the steaks. As the thick cuts of meat sizzled and flared, he found a baseball cap like his own to shade Jon's eyes from the sun, and soon the two sat on the warm deck engrossed in the food. Miss Agnus sat, staring upward at Jon. She knew that Cal would reserve only the last bite for her, but Jon was a different matter. When too much time had passed since the last nibble, she let slip a tiny whine, and Jon cut another bite the size of a pebble for her.

In the next instant, Miss Agnus barked in fury and raced the twenty feet across the deck to the yard gate, where a large black Labrador—only now noticed by Cal and Jon—was easing its nose over the top. It peeked through the boards, and then reared up, throwing its forepaws against the gate and paying no attention at all to Miss Agnus as she threw her tiny body upward to snap at him.

"Holy cow! I've never seen that dog before," Jon said.

"It's a new one—couple of doors down. A pup, I think, even if it's the size of a moose."

Miss Agnus continued to bark and leap and snap, and the Labrador continued to ignore her. Then a sound came, of nails parting with wood, and Cal realized that the latch on the gate might not withstand the weight of the dog much longer. "I think I'd better see if I can get that dog back home before he breaks down my gate. I'll be right back."

Reaching the altercation, Cal picked up Miss Agnus and brought her back to Jon. "Mind holding the girl while I take care of this?" Then he slipped out and led the Lab away.

Jon shook his head at Miss Agnus. "You're not afraid of anything, are you? Don't you know he could have eaten you in one bite!"

But Miss Agnus would not have her attention drawn away from where the invader had so recently been. She growled and struggled in Jon's hands. When he was sure Cal and the Lab were gone down the block, he allowed her to break free, and she raced, snarling, toward an enemy now history.

"She's trying to be my role model," Cal said when he returned.

"How's that?"

"Miss Agnus. She's illustrating for me how to deal with the composer I'm trying to work with on this new ballet."

"Oh, yeah, you mentioned this composer in your phone call—the witch, I think you called her." Jon was gathering up the dishes from the table. "This new ballet—are you planning to use Alexandra in it?"

"Thought I would, if we do it. She doesn't know anything about it yet."

Alexandra Kreyling was one of the principal dancers in The Calvin Tropp Ballet Company, known in the San Francisco performing arts community as Tropp's Troupe. Jon had had a light crush on Alexandra since he'd first seen her dance in his father's company two years before.

Cal hesitated only a second. "Why don't you give her a call next time you're coming up? I'm sure she remembers you. Maybe you two could spend some time together."

"Oh, I don't think so."

His father's voice turned serious. "I hope there will come a time when you don't feel you have to judge every woman by what your mother did."

"I-I don't think this has anything to do with Mom. I never even think about her anymore."

"It was a big blow to both of us when she left. And you were only fifteen at the time, just starting to ask girls out. It seemed to me that you lost interest in girls after that, and I'm not sure you picked it up again."

Jon shrugged, his face already closed. "I do okay with women."

For several moments, Cal edited out comments that rose up in his mind. Finally he lifted a hand, palm open. "I apologize for butting in. This is your business." For some minutes the two of them stared into the yard. "The truth is, I think I'm only now getting over it myself. Thirteen years it's taken me." Then before Jon could feel obligated to reply, he stood up. "I'll get some tools. You'll help me take a look at that gate latch, won't you?"

They worked together in silence, sorting out that a new board was needed to replace the deteriorated one cracked by the weight of the Lab, and then unscrewing the latch hardware. In Cal's small workshop, they found a replacement board and cut it to fit. As they reassembled the gate, Jon asked, "So I take it the new ballet is coming together?"

Cal winced. "No, not at this point. I won't even know whether to move ahead with it until I hear from Evana Arthur. She's the composer. My guess is she's working out a musical theme this weekend, which maybe I'll get to hear tomorrow or Tuesday. It all depends on her right now—whether she decides to work on it at all, whether she likes what she comes up with, whether *I* like what she comes up with." He shook his head. "I've never approached a new work this way before."

"I didn't think you were in the habit of commissioning new music."

"I'm not. And I intend to go back to my old ways as soon as this is over."

Jon ran his fingers over the tops of the screws and then tightened them a final turn. "What made you want to do something on prayer?"

Cal decided to try the simple truth. "A voice woke me up Wednesday morning telling me that this is what we were going to do."

"A voice, huh?"

He thinks I'm joking. Probably best to leave it at that. "I'm sure glad that pup didn't wreck the hinge while he was at it." He tested the arc. "Speaking of Alexandra, she mentioned yesterday that she started TM several months ago."

"What's that?"

"TM? It stands for transcendental meditation."

"Geez, is there something in the water up here all of a sudden? You're doing prayer and Alexandra is doing meditation?"

Cal grinned at him. "No connection, as far as I know. But speaking of prayer, I don't suppose you've had any more thoughts about it, have you?"

"Well, actually I did think about it some on the drive up from LA this morning."

"And?"

"I remembered trying it back, you know, when Mom took off. At least I tried it for the first four months when we didn't know where she was or whether she was all right or what."

"That was a tough time."

"Then when we found out what was really going on, I was too angry with her and God and the world and everyone to try it anymore."

Cal nodded. "Evana seems to think that's a good time to pray—when you're angry." He pulled at the gate to test the repair job. "That should do it, don't you think? I'll find some paint for this later."

But as they returned the tools to the workshop, Jon said, "So seriously, Dad, why are you interested in doing a ballet about prayer?"

"It intrigues you a little bit, doesn't it?"

"I'm surprised, is all."

Cal nodded. "I really did wake up Wednesday morning with something telling me to do this ballet. And it made a strong enough impression that I've been trying to bend the world ever since to make it happen." Cal shrugged. "I already know it sounds unbelievable. Maybe even crazy." Another pause. "I don't know—I can't honestly explain why I am doing this."

Now Jon's expression was serious. "What did this *something* say exactly?"

"It said, 'We are going to make a new dance and the theme is prayer.' That was really all there was to it, but, Jon, something about it made me stand up, right out of bed, wide awake. It's like there is not another ballet I've made that means as much as this one. And something in me just wants to find a way to do it, no matter how impossible it seems."

For some moments Jon was silent, his expressions shifting with his thoughts. Finally he took a breath and said, "Well, it definitely sounds like instructions—but it's somehow collaborative too, isn't it?"

Cal nodded, noticing that what he felt now was relief. "It would seem so—at least, it had better be, or this will never happen in the time we have to do it."

* * *

Cal's schedule for Monday included teaching class; meeting with Ned Freedman, the set and lighting designer, on sets for the three works already on the October program; a lunch meeting with board members about funding; and lending a hand in five hours of rehearsals. But before any of that, Cal wanted to talk to Evana. He reached for the phone before even sitting down at his desk.

"She's not in today," the secretary said. "In fact, she'll be out of town for at least one week, possibly two."

Calvin felt the blood drain from his head like a receding ocean tide. "What? That's not possible!" He reached behind him for the chair and fell into it.

"Is there someone else in the department who might be able to help you?" The crisp tone contrasted with the youthful voice.

"Uh, no. She didn't leave a message for Calvin Tropp, did she?"

"Oh, you're Mr. Tropp? Yes, she left a recorded message for you. Just a moment."

A recorded message? A disconcerting image appeared in his mind of Evana throwing up her hands in rage, grabbing her small tape recorder, and yelling into it that he could just forget this whole idea and anyway he was a lunatic for even suggesting it! After several clunks and clicks audible over the phone line, the secretary said, "Here it is. I'm going to play it for you."

There was a rush of static, and then Evana's unmistakable, slow-paced voice came on the line. "Hello, Calvin. Now how did I know you'd be calling me first thing Monday morning, expecting me to be all ready to talk music?" The sound was tinny and remote but not enough to dull the sarcasm. "Two things got real clear to me after you left my office. One was that I wouldn't be able to handle much else, so I spent the afternoon reassigning my lectures."

She's going to do it! A surge went through him, only to be immediately blunted.

"The other was that I wouldn't have a hope in hell of figuring out whether to even try this if there was an eager choreographer ringing me up every other minute and destroying my concentration." Cal laid his forehead in his hand as he listened to the voice continue. "So I'm going off where you can't disturb me, and no, I won't be mentioning where. I'll call you in a couple of days when I have something ready for you to hear. Good-bye, Calvin."

There was a loud click in his ear, and then Evana's secretary asked him, "Did you get it? Should I play it again for you?"

"Uh, no. I mean, yes, I got it and I don't need to hear it again." His voice had trailed off, but he couldn't muster the presence of mind to care.

"Good-bye, Mr. Tropp." The phone went silent.

"Damn." *I'm completely at her mercy—and God only knows whether she'll come through or not.* Blood churned and roared in his brain, and he held his head with both hands. When he felt up to moving, he reached for his notepad and slowly opened the cover to his list of reasons why a person prays. He turned the page and looked at the second list. He had added *angry* at Evana's suggestion, bringing the list to twelve items. He let his eyes rest a moment on each item and realized that at the present moment he qualified under seven of them: the first six and the last.

"Well, I don't feel up to praying," he said aloud, hearing how irritated he sounded. "I just want to know what you're going to do about this damn composer you set me up with!" His body twisted in the desk chair as though it was being physically tormented.

But then a thought dropped into his mind:

Let it alone. Trust her to do her part. Go about your business.

It wasn't that calm settled over him exactly, and there was no fanfare. It was just that the urgency dropped away. Cal glanced at the clock, rose from his desk, and left his office for the main hall, where he found his forty dancers completing warm-ups in noisy conversation—most of it about their bodies, their aches, their massage therapists, who was injured, who was taking ultrasound. He clapped his hands once and said, "Good morning, people." In a jumble of sound, the dancers replied, "Good morning, Cal," and found places along the barres affixed to the walls around the room.

Cal looked toward the pianist, Judy Gordon. With snapping fingers and a gesture of his arm, he indicated a tempo, and she began to play a familiar theme she often used for barre work. He turned back to his company, and even though all of his dancers were already in first position, he called to them, *"Demi plié* from first position." He watched, letting his attention move from one dancer to the next, to the next. Alexandra's dark brown hair was already damp around her forehead; she probably had been in early to rehearse something or just to work by herself. The summer break often meant lapses in a dancer's strict regimen, and all the serious dancers—most of the company—wanted to restore their control over their bodies as quickly as possible. Cal looked for Matt and Katherine.

Katherine Melton was easy to find. At five nine, she was the tallest of the women, and her mastery of her dancer's space inevitably enabled her to look even taller on stage. She could be regal or lyrical or sultry or brazen, and Cal had always been grateful that she could command a stage, because there had been intervals during her ten years as a company member when there were no really suitable partners in the troupe. She had started as an apprentice at age sixteen and then quickly became a corps member, then soloist, then principal dancer. More than a dozen roles had been choreographed on her. Today her light auburn hair was bound up on top of her head, and a scarf was draped and pinned around it, leaving fully visible the balletic lift and line of her neck. A small tug in his heart reminded him of how beautiful he'd always found that line.

Matt Wade had apparently spent the summer in weight training. His muscular physique had made him a favorite of audiences for all of his five years with the company, and because he knew how to translate his strength into sureness and grace, he was also a favorite with the women dancers. More than one had commented to Cal that only Matt, among the male dancers, made them feel completely safe no matter how acrobatic the choreography became.

It was also apparent that Matt had been to a creative hair stylist. His initials were cut into the short hair on the back of his head: the *M* positioned above the *W*. *Well, it's not likely to become an issue.* Matt's shortcomings fell more under the categories of impatience and moodiness, not disruption of the integrity of an artistic production. Cal knew that the initials would be gone by October.

"Second position. *Grand plié*," Cal said, shifting his attention to other dancers and noting the degree of concentration on their faces. Sudden gratitude spilled like warmth inside him, and a little pinch came to the top of his nose. How welcome were the dedication, the intensity of these young people for whom the work in these rooms was as important as it was to him. How welcome the familiarity of the class, the barre work, the emphasis on line and technique. This was like breathing to him, like life breath. "Concentrate on your energy flow as you lower and lift."

He spent longer than usual on the *tendus*, slowing the accompanist once, then again, then faster, then faster still for multiple series of sixty-four. The dancers concentrated on his voice, the balance and control of their bodies, and the slide of their working feet in precise placement. With slight shifts of the head, they studied their reflections in the wall-sized mirror. Cal noticed an apprentice staring at the reflections of the older members of the company more than at her own. He went down on one knee to repair the alignment of her foot and then showed her with the tip of his shoe the exact spot her toe should reach in the *tendu*. Sweetly, like the tongue of a kitten, the tip of her pink ballet shoe slid precisely out to meet his, then back, then out, then back again. Her face was flushed and the eyes looked faintly frightened. He gave her a smile and a quick wink of reassurance before moving on to other dancers.

Rob and Amelie also moved about the large room, appraising the dancers as carefully as Cal did. It was not usual for all three of them to supervise class, but this early in the season it was good to have the entire company working together, and he knew they were all refreshing their own sense of what he, as head of the company, wanted to emphasize.

Without Cal's specific instruction, the older members of the company switched back and forth from a right working leg to the left, and the newer members followed this lead. Over the summer, three corps members had joined his company, along with two apprentices.

Barre work continued with *fondues, ronds de jambe a terre* and *en l'air, frappes, grand port de bras, developpes, degages,* and *grand battements.* The mental focus of the dancers was absolute as they endeavored to refine their technique and push the discipline of their bodies. With the conclusion of barre, the dancers turned toward the center of the floor and gave all of their attention to Cal's instruction for the first center exercise in *adagio* technique.

* * *

At the lunch table, Cal shook hands with three members of the board and accepted the sheet of paper from Mrs. Davenport. It was a list of a dozen events that had been arranged for raising funds to help cover the coming season's costs. "We're hoping you will be available to be the main speaker at these three," she said, pointing her gold pen at checked items on the list.

At seventy-something, Valina Davenport seemed to grow more elegant with each passing year. The matriarch was president of both the Tropp Ballet Guild and the board of directors. She was a tall woman who had learned early to use her height to her advantage; rather than shrinking to the expectations of others, she had embellished her looks to create an imposing persona.

Cal nodded. He thought of these speaking engagements as the "dancing bear" part of his duties. Sometimes he simply made himself available to answer questions from the ballet enthusiasts who frequented these events. Other times he told his own story, about growing up with Midwest parents who were against his dancing, taking dance lessons on the sly, and then leaving home with a single suitcase and a one-way ticket to make his mark in the ballet world. He had danced first in Chicago, where he had met Anne and where Jon was born, and then he had danced in New York, Houston, Montreal, London, and Copenhagen, gradually shifting his emphasis from dancing to choreography. Perhaps this time he would use one of the occasions to discuss what it means to choreograph and fully prepare a new ballet in nine weeks with a composer of extremely fine reputation but terribly uncertain reliability—and a mouth that could tear flesh from bone without making physical contact.

After the lunch meeting, he hurried back to the studio to check for messages from Evana before beginning rehearsals. There was no word from her.

* * *

That night he tried going to bed with a book to help himself think of other things and be more likely to sleep. He couldn't concentrate on the printed words though and didn't mind when Miss Agnus came walking up his body with a rubber mouse in her mouth. Lifting her chin as high as she could, she dropped the mouse over the top of his book and waited for him to play toss and catch and tug-of-war. Each time he allowed her to yank the toy out of his hand, she ran with it to the end of the bed and shook it violently before returning to drop it over the top of his book again. Soon he was tossing the mouse to the ceiling so she could try to catch it on the way down, and more times than not, it bounced against her tiny face and fell off the bed. She would chase after it, even though jumping off the bed meant having to run around to her set of steps to get back up. After several minutes she took the mouse to the foot of the bed, spread out panting on her stomach, and stared at Cal, who took advantage of the rest to stare back into the dog's calm, round, black-button eyes and to wonder again what the hell he was doing.

"Why me anyway?" he asked the room. "I don't know the first thing about prayer. I've never made a practice of it. I don't even know how to do it. For God's sake, I had to look it up in a dictionary!"

He was quiet, almost expectant, but nothing came. No voice but his own entered the silence; no calming thoughts dropped into his mind.

"What makes you think anyone *wants* to see a ballet about prayer? I mean, who's this going to appeal to—besides priests maybe, and they'll recognize right off that I don't know what the hell I'm doing."

There was no answer.

"And maybe this is a dead issue. How would you know whether anyone these days is into praying at all?" Miss Agnus cocked her head to one side, and Cal rethought his point. "Well, I suppose you *would* know that."

A sense of futility rippled over him. He got out of bed, went to the bathroom, and took a bottle of Excedrin PM from the medicine cabinet. Best nonprescription sleeping aid he'd ever found. He spilled two tablets into his palm and then reconsidered and shook out two more. He swallowed them with two glasses of water, shut off the light, and went to lie in bed, where he practiced very deep breathing until either sleep or hyperventilation overcame him.

When the phone rang at two o'clock in the morning, he had to struggle to rise out of the drug-induced slumber. While he fumbled for the receiver, his mind lurched from *Jon!* to *Anne?*

"I may have something here. I want you to cast judgment before I go any further."

Cal heard himself utter some sound, but he was too groggy to be coherent. Not that it mattered: Evana wasn't waiting. The next thing he heard as he struggled to read the blue face of the clock was a loud clunk, and then another, as Evana positioned the receiver. Then came several measures of piano. Despite his foggy mind, he knew that it was nice. Then there was another *clunk*, and Evana picked up the receiver. "Now hold on, Calvin. You have to listen to this too." *Clunk. Click. Click.* What came next was the same theme he had just heard, but now it was synthesized. As if by laser, the electronic sound pierced the grogginess and his mind came awake. His legs swung over the side of the bed, and he listened in amazement as Evana ran the tape back and played it again.

Then there was another *click*, another *clunk*, and then silence, but he knew she was there, waiting. When he found his voice, it said, "Evana, I think I'm in love with you."

She replied with no humor at all, "Oh, all you men say that sooner or later." A loud *clunk* suggested that she had put the phone down, but then her harsh voice returned: "I'm going ahead with this then."

"Yes. Yes—"

"That's all I needed."

Then the dial tone came, and then only silence, except for the thumping of his heart. *Damn, I didn't get a chance to ask her . . . She probably wouldn't have said for sure, but it* sounds *like she's in.* The churning of his blood receded in his ears. *Wish I knew for sure. Do I dare even start the choreography?*

Then he felt his mouth move into a small grin. Start it? He already had started it! He had already seen in his mind two of his dancers, Matt and Katherine, in wisps of choreography, and now it was Alexandra he was seeing in his mind's eye. Lithe, dark haired, beautiful, in the simplest of costumes, she danced in a diagonal across the stage from up left, with no movement at all in her body above her knees, which themselves revealed a soothing, tiny rhythm with the steady progress of her feet *en pointe*. She was one of his most dependable, unshakable dancers. No, it wouldn't be a bad thing at all if Alexandra and Jon were to become a pair. His reverie leapt from scenes of Alexandra on stage and in the rehearsal hall to scenes of her with his son, and he grew comfortable with the idea that she could become his daughter-in-law. Somewhere in the middle of those images, he managed to go back to sleep.

* * *

Eight Weeks

Alexandra Kreyling sat on a chair in her bedroom and felt the sun from the eastern sky blast into the room and strike the side of her face. Behind her closed eyelids, the darkness took on a golden hue. She continued to sit—easy, peaceful—and let her mantra repeat as easily as free thought. A "sound" never uttered aloud, little more than a mental impulse, her mantra was almost more familiar and dear to her than the sound of her name.

The window was open an inch to let in air still cool from the night, to offset the lack of air-conditioning in her apartment. Then outside, from the sidewalk two floors down, came the voices of two boys arguing:

"It's mine!"

"You said I could borrow it."

"That was *borrow*, not *keep*, stupid."

It sounded as though they had stopped under Alexandra's window on purpose to conduct their argument. It was impossible not to listen to them, impossible not to hear every word and anticipate the next.

"I'm not stupid—*you're* stupid, and so is this old skateboard of yours stupid. *Everything about you is stupid!*"

Now Alexandra was angry and fast getting madder. Her face felt flushed; her skin was hot to the roots of her hair; her eyes felt dilated and swollen with rage. *How can I be this mad? I've never been so angry in my whole life! There's no way I can meditate with this going on. What*

I really want to do is find a baseball bat and bash their heads in. Both of them. Kill them! Exterminate them! She stopped and inhaled. "Whoa!" she whispered. "They are just a couple of boys fighting. It's nothing to you. Calm down now. You're supposed to be meditating."

But then another surge of rage boiled up in her, and she shifted on the chair, bringing her legs up and folding her arms around them. *I'm out of control.* Tears leaked around the rims of her closed eyelids and felt cool on her cheeks as they slid down her face. *This is more anger than I can contain.* The boys moved on then, their voices receding until she could not distinguish words, and then she could not hear them at all. The rage within her eased to simple anger, then to vexation, then only mild irritation, until behind it she could sense her mantra repeating gently. She let her focus shift to the mantra, calming her heartbeat and the muscles of her body.

Was it always there, her mantra, behind and underneath everything in her daily life? Always available to her if she could still the rattle and clutter of her daily existence?

Perhaps some time had passed; she wasn't sure. She peeked at the clock through the lashes of her left eye and saw that twenty-four minutes had passed since she had sat down to meditate. She was supposed to meditate for twenty minutes and then rest. Rising from the chair with her eyes still closed, Alexandra crawled onto the bed and then rolled to her back, not bothering to brush her long, dark hair out of her face. The memory of the rage was a rock in her mind, a hard point of disturbance, but her body seemed to be relaxed. She lay quiet until she felt her conscious awareness gather. Then she rose from the bed and headed for the kitchen to make breakfast.

I've got to be doing something wrong. Maybe Janna can help with this. Janna was her transcendental meditation coach. From the beginning, TM had not been what Alexandra had expected. For the entire first month, she had sat on her chair twice a day, expecting bliss and finding mostly boredom, but then at night her dreams were more vivid, more colorful, more dramatic than ever before, peopled by persons she did not know and memorable for the emotions they evoked.

Now after many months of daily meditation practice, her dreams had settled back to normal, but she was finding that weird things occurred during her meditation sessions. One afternoon, her wrist had developed a tick that lasted most of the session. In an effort to ignore the tick, she had concentrated so hard on her mantra that a headache developed. She had wound up peeking every two minutes at the clock and felt only profound relief when the meditation session was over.

It would be nice to ask David. He was the only normal, everyday person she knew who practiced meditation. David was an electronics engineer she had met soon after she moved to San Francisco from New York four years before, having won a place in Tropp's Troupe during an audition Cal had held in New York City. Only twenty years old, Alexandra was grateful to find an older man who was so willing to help her get her bearings in a strange city. Then thirty-five, David was still looking for the right young woman, and he fell in love with her dancer's body and probably her youth too. He had moved her into his upscale, air-conditioned, high-security apartment within a week.

Two months later, the October 17, 1989, earthquake struck during an afternoon rehearsal. David was at Candlestick Park watching the third game of the World Series between the Giants and the Oakland Athletics. For the duration of the fifteen-second quake, she had prayed that he was safe. When the building had ceased to tremble and white-faced company members began to climb to their feet, someone turned on a radio, but there was only empty static until the broadcast stations switched to emergency power. Then the airways were full of news about lost lives, collapsed freeways, fires, and a massive public transportation crisis. At that point she began to pray that she and David would see each other again because she was now sure that no one would ever again be as important to her as he was.

They were six months into their relationship before she learned that he practiced transcendental meditation twice a day, every day, and had since the age of nineteen. "What's the big secret about it?"

"Nothing. It's just something I do. Makes my life run better, but it's not something I talk about much." Clearly he didn't intend to share much about it with her, and that made her uneasy. *Are there other things too, other important things that he doesn't share with me?*

Later he admitted that he saw it as a generational thing—something his generation had done but hers might find old-fashioned. The truth was, he said, none of his friends meditated; none of his co-workers did; none of his family members did.

"But have you told any of these people that you do?"

"No."

"So how do you know whether they are meditating or not?"

He didn't. But he was sure they weren't.

"But it must be a good thing—right?" she persisted.

"Yes, of course it's a good thing."

"Then when are you going to teach me?"

"I can't teach you."

"But you must know everything there is to know about it by now."

He had breathed a sigh of annoyance. "It has to be taught by someone trained to teach it. There is no sense doing it at all if you're not going to be doing it right."

They had let the subject drop then, but on her twenty-first birthday, among the pile of gift boxes was an envelope containing a certificate entitling her to TM training, paid in full. She had put the certificate away and forgotten about it for three years—until last May when, at his request, she had gathered her things to move out. More than anything else, she remembered the numbness with which she had responded to his sudden need for solitude. She'd been clumsy in the packing because even her fingertips were numb. She had longed for the daily discipline of ballet class, but when she'd tried to work on her own, she'd been unable to concentrate, unable to lose herself in the familiar regimen. Despite her hurt, her anger, her outrage at being asked so calmly to leave his life, she remembered the peace and groundedness that his meditation practice had appeared to give him, and now she desperately needed those in her life.

Alexandra pushed the kitchen chair back and put her breakfast dishes into the sink, washed them quickly, and left them to dry. She paused to stretch her inner thigh muscles, which were sore from Cal's class the day before.

It was partly her schedule, David had said. The relationship was no longer working for him. He had promised to help her find a new apartment, but she had found this place—such as it was—on her own. He'd said he'd be available if she needed any help at all, but she was certain she would never call him, no matter how urgent the need. It wasn't that he didn't still care about her but only that he didn't want to live with her any longer. It had nothing to do with love; of course, a part of him would always love her.

It was at this point in the memory that she always stopped. She would see how solemn his brown eyes had looked when he had told her this, and a feeling like choking would stop her from further replaying the memory in her mind.

She grabbed her ballet kit from the floor of the bedroom, took out the soiled leotards, tights, and socks, as well as two pairs of shot *pointe* shoes. She would later strip out the shank and insole and then use the shoes for class. Before they would be thrown away, she would remove and wash the ribbons and sew them onto new *pointe* shoes. Zipping clean clothes into the kit, she took a last glance around the apartment and left for the studio.

What he hadn't said, but what she had known anyway, was that he'd never had a relationship that had lasted beyond four years. A few more months and she'd have set a record.

Matt Wade caught up with her a block from the studio. He wore a tank top that set off both the blue of his eyes and the muscles of his upper body. "You picked up an earring over the summer," she commented.

"Like it?"

"Looks good on you." At some recent point she could not identify, at the beginning of the 1990s, a single earring on a man had stopped meaning *gay* and come to mean *macho*. "The initials are pretty interesting too."

He rubbed a hand quickly down the back of his blond hair. "It'll grow. Have you heard about Cal's new ballet?"

She glanced at him as they walked. "No. He's making something new?"

"Yeah, I heard it's for this season—though that seems a little absurd at this point. I thought maybe he's been working with you early in the mornings or at night or something."

"Not me."

They were silent, but Alexandra felt an edge of resentment: *If Cal isn't using me, he must have given the new role to Katherine—again! Why didn't he choose me! Why doesn't he ever choose me?*

"How did you hear about this?" She tried to sound casual.

"Someone overheard Rob talking to Amelie. It might be another piece for Katherine."

Damn! Even Matt thinks Cal would give it to Katherine! A picture of the long-legged, auburn-haired Katherine danced across her mind.

"Or maybe he's working with some of the new dancers on it."

"I can't believe he'd do that. Maybe it's a guest piece." The company sometimes invited a dancer from outside the company, often from New York City, to perform guest solos. These were usually single-dancer sketches rather than longer ballets.

Matt shrugged and held the door for her. "I guess we'll find out sooner or later."

"Looks like later."

A glance at the bulletin board told her that Amelie was teaching class that morning, which was a relief because it meant a traditional progression through the standard barre exercises, followed by *port de bras* and center practices. Class with Cal meant pushing her technique in some unanticipated direction and ending up with sore muscles for a day or two afterward. Cal thought as a choreographer even in class, always looking for ways to expand what the body could do, while class with Amelie or Rob meant refining and perfecting what she already knew.

But class was harder than expected because she couldn't keep from glancing over at Katherine Melton. She studied Katherine's placement and line, rather than watching her own. It became a kind of torture—like having a hangnail that one kept scratching at and teasing and pulling at and tearing until blood came and the soreness grew excruciating. Alexandra forced herself to look at her own reflection in the wall-sized mirror and saw that her face was red with emotion. *What is the matter with me!*

As soon as class was over, Alexandra took her can of fruit juice and sought out Katherine, who had put a red T-shirt on over her leotard and sat on the floor to remove the soft ballet slippers she'd worn in class. A well-worn white towel was draped around her neck. Beside her was a pair of new *pointe* shoes that she intended to wear in rehearsal. She'd cut the satin neatly off the tips to improve traction and sewn on ribbons. The box of each shoe had been flattened under Katherine's bare heels.

"Have you heard that Cal's working on a new ballet?" Alexandra tried for a small-talk tone of voice.

It was common company knowledge that Cal had choreographed more ballets on Katherine than on any other dancer in the troupe. But Katherine's eyebrows pushed upward even as she swallowed some Diet Coke. "No! Who's he using?"

"I figured probably you."

"I haven't heard anything about it."

"Matt mentioned it this morning. Maybe it's just one of those rumors."

"Maybe. I'll ask around."

By early afternoon, the word was well broadcast that a new ballet was in the works and that so far no one in the company was dancing it. Some had heard that Cal was bringing in guest dancers from the troupe's unofficial rival, the San Francisco Ballet. Some surmised that it might be an experiment in improvisation. Others had heard that it would be danced by some old friends Cal had known in New York. Two thought he was going to dance the new piece himself.

Alexandra was turning her face toward her upraised arm in *effacé devant* when it occurred to her: *Maybe I can use the anger. Maybe I can remember how this feels and use it in dance. At least then I might get something out of it.*

At three o'clock, Alexandra had a break for an hour before her next rehearsal. She picked up a sweatshirt and a towel and headed for the stairwell, still resenting Cal for always choosing Katherine over her, and Katherine for always being chosen.

In the studio basement, Cal and Ned Freedman kept old sets, tools for set construction, miscellaneous old furniture, and anything else that needed to be stored. The large room housed the history of the company, and many of the sets had not been touched in years. The air smelled of dust, old paint, and dry wood. With the beginning of the new season, Alexandra had searched the building from top to bottom, looking for a place to meditate without interruption. At first glance she had ruled out the basement as too creepy, but it was soon apparent that no other place afforded as much quiet and privacy. Closing her mind to the possibility of spiders and mice, she had explored the storeroom and discovered that the peace there was well suited to her purpose.

An old couch proved easy to separate from a pile of sets, and this she shoved into a corner under a lighted Exit sign. Every afternoon, when she could manage it between rehearsals, she made her way into the quiet, darkened basement for her afternoon TM session.

With her sweatshirt zipped to her neck and the towel around her damp hair, Alexandra settled into a corner of the couch, drew her legs up, put her hands into her pockets, and closed her eyes. She breathed easily, hoping she would not have a repeat of the morning's fierce anger. Soon her mantra came, repeating and receding, into her mind.

After a while, she thought to check the time and pulled a watch out of her pocket, peering at it one-eyed in the red haze from the Exit sign. Eleven minutes had passed. *Oh good, nine more minutes. I get to stay here just like this for nine more minutes.* Then, easy as thought, her mantra returned. She could see in her mind wisps of thought, but she gently rejected them, letting her mental screen go blank. Nothing. Nothing. The quiet was outside; the quiet was inside.

Then from somewhere the words settled into her mind:

The anger this morning did not belong to the boys; it belongs to you.

Her mind wanted to argue. *My anger? How could it be my anger? I'm not mad at anyone.* But her heart recognized the truth at once: of course she was. She gasped and tears came fast, falling in rapid succession from under her closed lids.

What? What am I so mad at? An image of Katherine dancing came into her mind. She compared it to the truth in her heart, and she knew this wasn't it. Katherine might always be chosen, always be graceful and beautiful, always be perfect. But these were only resentments, close to the surface. No, what she was so angry about was much deeper, so deep as to be hidden from awareness, smoldering there inside her, eating at her confidence and sense of ease in the world.

A fresh wave of tears came as she felt within her a tarp being lifted, the edges loosened and peeled back to reveal the black froth of her rage at David. A sob rushed up inside her, exploding in a noise of pain from her open mouth. Words came then into her mind, urgent, ramming against each other: *How could you! How could you ask me to leave with such indifference, such coolness that made a lie of every moment of love and passion we shared? How could you so completely reject me when I would have loved you for the rest of my life? I was so willing for you to be everything to me. How could you have loved me so little after all?*

Her mouth still open in anguish, Alexandra felt the words stop within her. The muscles of her face relaxed, her mouth closed, and the tears all but stopped, hanging onto the lashes of her closed eyes like single drops of rain along a roof's edge after the cloudburst has ended. Not bothering to check her watch, she stretched her legs out on the couch and lay back, letting her whole body rest from the expunging of the pain. She lay spent, with her arms stretched above her head. Her mind stayed quiet now. An image of David's face came, but she felt too weary of it to linger.

After full awareness had returned, she opened her eyes but continued to lie still for several more minutes. When she was willing to move, she sat up, took off the towel and shook out her hair, and then wiped the remnants of tears from her face. Her steps felt only a little unsteady. The venom of her rage was not entirely gone, but what remained felt under control. She hoped there was time to get something to eat before the next rehearsal.

* * *

It was Friday, August 13. Cal stared at his calendar. Not so many years ago, he had found ridiculous people who were superstitious about Friday the thirteenth, and now here he was under a pall of foreboding that had deepened when he had noticed the date on the calendar. *Could this all be some kind of cosmic joke? Is this what Mom meant by a bigger force at work? Or am I simply crazy—an insane man, hearing things in the night and then designing my life around them? Phantom whispers from unknown sources? Phantom phone calls?* Cal had not heard from Evana since two o'clock Tuesday morning.

"I *know* she called! I'm just *sure* that she called," he had said to Rob during a program status conference that morning. "I just wish I had a witness or a recording or something. *Anything* to prove that that call actually happened!"

Rob had shifted in his chair and crossed his legs. "I'm sure you didn't dream it, Cal."

But what if he had? What if Evana was not working on the short score at all? What if he so much wanted her to be working up usable music that he had dreamed the whole conversation? He struggled to remember what the music had sounded like, but all he remembered was a piano and a synthesizer. He damned the Excedrin PM that he'd used as a sleep aid. If he hadn't fogged up his mind with the pain reliever, maybe he could remember the music. He recollected that at the time the music had seemed exquisite, perfect for his new ballet, and in his drugged state he'd thought Evana was the most wonderful person on the earth. *Damn that Evana! How could she do this to me?* She had to have known how difficult he would find being left in the dark with no way of contacting her. He'd lost count of the number of times he had reached for the telephone during the last two days. Finally he decided he had waited long enough. He reached for the phone and made the call. Evana's secretary answered.

"No, I'm sorry, Mr. Tropp. Mrs. Arthur hasn't called in since Monday, so I don't have another message for you." She sounded even younger on the telephone than she appeared in person.

"But you can get a message to her, right?"

The secretary hesitated, and Cal became aggressive. "What's your name, dear?"

"Teresa."

"Teresa, I would give almost anything to have a secretary with the competence and skill you've shown. Evana has no idea how fortunate she is."

"Thank you, Mr. Tropp." Wariness had entered her tone.

"And I know you're called upon to use your own discretion and good judgment a hundred times a day."

As if proving the truth of his words, she made no response.

"Teresa, what I have here is an emergency. What I think—or hope anyway—that Evana is doing, wherever she is, is composing a score for a ballet I'll be choreographing for the October program. Opening night is eight weeks away, and I'm getting desperate for something to start with. This really is an emergency, Teresa. I wouldn't ask you if it weren't. I really need for you to give me Evana's telephone number."

"I can't do that, Mr. Tropp." Teresa sounded annoyed now and a bit frightened. "Mrs. Arthur told me that you'd be calling me up and using the *E* word."

The E *word?*

"And she said I was just to ignore you. She said that at this point in the project, she's in a much better position than you are to know whether it's time to use the *E* word."

"She actually said that?"

"In so many words."

Cal paused for several seconds, collecting himself, struggling to put himself in Teresa's place. Twice his mouth formed words that he squelched. Then, "I imagine the truth is that she said a lot more than that."

"That's right, Mr. Tropp."

"Well, never let it be said that I don't recognize a brick wall when I'm hit in the face with one. Will you at least give her a message from me when you hear from her again?"

"Yes, Mr. Tropp."

"Tell her I begged. Tell her that I was down on my knees begging for some little piece to start with. Twenty bars. Say that I begged on my knees for twenty bars. Will you tell her that?"

"Yes, Mr. Tropp, but—"

"I know. I know. It's hopeless, right? The . . . the *H* word. I get it."

"Yes, Mr. Tropp." She giggled. "Good-bye."

* * *

During the performance part of the season, Saturday matinees were scheduled for two o'clock, followed by an evening performance at eight. On those days, class was less rigorous than usual, even when Cal was teaching, and rehearsals were by request of dancers who wanted additional work on particular sequences. The idea was to help dancers save their energy, especially dancers who faced the strain of double performances. Over the years, Saturday had become accepted as the company's casual day, even when no performances were slated and regular rehearsals were scheduled.

But this particular Saturday, there was a buzz about the dancers. It didn't take long to figure out that the buzz was about his new ballet. He had not mentioned the world premiere to anyone besides Rob, but somehow all forty dancers seemed to have heard that he was working on something new. Cal tracked down Rob. "Did you have to tell the whole company?" He didn't bother to hide his annoyance at having lost his shield of secrecy. The more people who knew about it, the less avenue of escape.

Rob stared at him wide-eyed. "I said not a single word to anyone!" But his expression turned almost at once from wounded innocence to guilt. "Except Amelie. But she wouldn't—" Shame took over his face.

"I'll talk to Amelie." By the time he could fit in a short conference with Amelie, she'd already noticed the whispering among the dancers and figured out what it was about. She spoke first when Cal approached her. "I sure hope that wasn't a secret, Cal. When Rob told me the news,

I didn't know until he'd left the studio that one of our corps girls was in the room and heard the whole story."

Cal squelched the words he had intended to say. "You didn't know she was there?"

The ballet mistress shook her head. "She was sitting on the floor on the other side of the piano, prepping her feet, and neither of us saw her. It sure didn't take her long to get the word out."

Cal nodded. "What ballet company isn't a hothouse for gossip?" He felt sick to his stomach. With a weak wave to Amelie, he headed toward his office, even though he was much too restless for paperwork. As he passed the set designer's office, Ned Freedman's rasping voice called out: "Hey, Cal!"

"Morning, Ned." Cal backtracked to the open doorway and leaned a shoulder against the frame.

"Say, what's this I've been hearing about a fourth ballet for the October program? Nobody in sets or costumes knows anything concrete." Ned stretched out an arm and began to roll up a sleeve of his flannel shirt. He habitually wore flannel shirts, winter or summer, but he rolled the sleeves up in summer. In his left pocket was an open but full pack of cigarettes.

"There's nothing concrete to know yet. I'm trying to commission some music, and if I can get it soon enough, I'm going to try to choreograph a new piece." He'd said the whole thing without grimacing.

"And it's really for the October program? *This* October?"

Cal nodded and Ned whistled. "That's impossible, Cal. There's not enough time." He reached to his left shirt pocket—a sure sign of sudden nervousness—but changed his mind and left the pack intact.

"It won't be anything elaborate. Simple sets. Simple costumes."

"Is there anything I can see on it?"

Cal shook his head. "You'll have to wait till we start making it. I firmly believe that Arthur is out doing the score right now."

"Arthur who?"

"Evana Arthur, out at the university."

From the sudden change in the expression on Ned's face, Cal knew that Ned had worked with Evana before. He didn't want to hear what threatened to come next. "Catch you later, Ned." He moved on down the hall, nearly diving into his office for peace behind the closed door.

When he felt up to venturing out again, he went to the main rehearsal studio to watch his dancers warm up. A few whispered conversations indicated that the rumors were still making the rounds, but mostly the snatches of conversation he overheard as he moved around the room had to do with how Sunday would be spent. It was the dancers' one day off each week. In a corner, two of the men teased a third about his car as they bobbed slowly up and down at the barre, and two women sat in full splits on a mat, chatting as they stretched the muscles of their legs, hips, and backs. He stopped to talk with Katherine Melton, who sat on the floor, wrapping her toes for another new pair of *pointe* shoes.

"I thought you used brown paper. Now you're using lamb's wool?"

Katherine smoothed a small piece of wool around a toe. "Oh, brown paper was two seasons ago. I've gone through brown paper, Kleenex tissues, newspaper. The *Chronicle* worked pretty well for a while. Then I hit on paper towels. I thought they might do better soaking up sweat instead of wrinkling and causing blisters."

"And the lamb's wool?"

"Seems to be working for now. My feet keep changing though, so nothing seems to be permanent."

He watched as she finished positioning the wool and then picked up a shoe, pulled it on with both hands, and began aligning the ribbons. "How many ballets have you and I made together?"

She looked up in surprise. "Fifteen." When it appeared that he wasn't going to say anything further, she continued. "There's a rumor that you're working on a new piece now."

"I wish I were. I have to wait for the music before I can do much with the choreography."

"Is it for this season?"

"Well, I had hoped so."

"What's it going to be?"

"I was going to do a short ballet on prayer."

"Really? That sounds wonderful!" Her lovely face was turned upward toward him now and shone with enthusiasm.

He looked at her, amazed by the warmth that touched his stomach. "You think so?"

"Oh, absolutely! You could do a beautiful job with a theme like that."

He smiled then. *How many days since I felt like smiling?* "Are you a spiritual person, Katherine?"

She raised a shoulder. "More than a lot of people are, I suppose."

"Then maybe you can tell me what prayer is."

She turned her attention back to her ribbons, which she tied and then tucked in the knot at the back of her ankle. "It's talking to God, isn't it?"

"Yes, but how do you do the talking? And who or what is it you're really talking to? And how do you know if God is listening? And does God talk back?"

Katherine laughed. "Is that what you're going to deal with—all in one ballet?"

He shook his head and shrugged. "I don't know."

For several moments, neither said anything. Katherine slowly stretched her hips and back. "Who says you have to wait for the music?"

He tried to smile again, but his stomach was twisting. A feeling of light dizziness poured over him. "Because that's how choreography is done, Katherine. You know that. At least, that is how *I* do it. I have to have the music to work into. You dancers have to have something to move to. I've never choreographed without the music first. I doubt that it's even possible. The music drives my choreography." He could hear how defensive he sounded.

"But if this is a ballet about prayer, maybe prayer should drive the choreography. Sounds like *someone* is talking to you."

Cal stared at her, panic rising. "I'm getting out of my depth real fast. I think I'll go teach a company class, where I know what I'm doing."

But in class he had to struggle to concentrate. His mind bounced around the room without settling on anything useful. *What's happening to me!*

That evening, he reached for Miss Agnus's leash as soon as he was home, finding it urgent to do something not connected to choreography. Immediately the tiny Pomeranian began to bark and turn circles on the floor, punctuating her dance with jumps against his leg. Outside, the air was beginning to let go of the worst heat of the day. Cal stuck a baseball cap on his head and pulled down the bill against the sun and then set out for the fast-food outlets two miles away. "If you get tired, you just let me know."

Miss Agnus strained so hard against her collar that she was choking herself. They had gone two blocks before he commanded her to heel and she settled down to walk beside him, her tongue flipping up through what appeared to be a big grin. He was complimenting her for maintaining her good manners when they turned the last corner onto "fast-food row."

Just then a city bus wheezed up behind them, coming to a stop twenty feet away. Miss Agnus leapt into the air and threw herself toward the bus, barking in high-pitched fury. The leash went flying out of Cal's hand, and the tiny animal raced, snarling, at the bus. Dodging the feet of people getting on and off the vehicle, she went for the tire of the huge beast. By the time Cal caught up to her, every red-gold hair on her body stood at attention as she struggled, eyes wild, to open her tiny mouth wide enough to get a grip on the edge of the hard rubber.

Feeling Cal's hands about to close on her, she squirted to the other side of the wheel, under the bus, and resumed her snarling attack on the vehicle.

Cal stood up, frantic, calling, "Wait! Wait!" to the driver, who caught his eye without moving another muscle of her face, and then nodded once. "My dog! I have to get my dog!" Cal yelled. Another single nod—that was all.

The metal side of the bus was like the sun-hot wall of a building. The heat and glare coming off it struck his face and forced him to squint. The pungent smell of hot pavement, tires, car exhaust, and metal only added to his distress. Then Cal noticed that the loop of the leash handle had caught under the tire. Getting the tiniest grip on it with his fingertip and thumb, he teased the leash out until he could grasp it with his whole hand. He wadded the leash into both fists as he pulled the snarling Miss Agnus out from under the bus. Bundled under his arm, she flailed with all four feet against his body, propelling herself by sheer determination. Exploding herself free, she was for a split second loose in the air, five feet above the ground, before he caught her again and closed both arms tight around her wiggling, shuddering body.

Immediately the bus pulled away from the curb, and Miss Agnus claimed the victory, barking triumphantly as if to say, "And don't come back around these parts or I'll run you off again!" Her tiny body quivered with adrenaline and joy.

Cal was trembling too. He turned back to the sidewalk and saw several half smiles of sympathy directed his way from people who had stopped to observe the drama. He secured Miss Agnus with one arm around her body, the other hand holding both leash and collar.

Walking only a few more yards, Cal realized that the bus episode had cost him his appetite. He turned around and headed back toward home, crossing streets for the quickest access to quiet residential sidewalks. All the way, he lectured her: "You don't have an ounce of good sense, that's your problem. What in the hell made you think you could tackle something the size of a city bus? Don't you have any sense of proportion at all? You're just a *little dog*! You could have been killed—flattened—without the driver even noticing a bump! If I hadn't been there—" Miss Agnus turned her head to his face, darting her small tongue over his nose and mouth. It was six blocks before he put her on her own feet, and even then he tested the security of the leash clasp and threaded the leash loop onto his belt for safety.

At home, he fed Miss Agnus, made a grilled cheese sandwich and a salad for himself, and then settled down on top of the bed with a book. It was just before three o'clock in the morning when he awoke, switching to a fully conscious state, eyes alert and focused on his mental picture of Katherine dancing. Despite the darkness of the bedroom, he could make out, by the light of the clock, where Miss Agnus lay, on her back with her paws in the air, the back ones splayed out straight, the front ones bent forward. She was snoring. Cal slipped out of bed one limb at a time to keep from disturbing her, though he knew she had awakened with his first movement. A natural mind reader, she would know he wanted her to stay where she was.

In the living room, he reached for the lamp and then changed his mind and sat down in the dark. He saw Katherine in his mind. He played bits and pieces of all fifteen ballets he had choreographed on her, plus snatches of dozens of other ballets in which she had performed. In the years-long progression of dances, he saw her clarify her technique and grow more sensitive in her interpretations as she came to understand her capacity for motion. Her concentration was invariably absolute.

As he watched, he became aware that the music had fallen away. The only melody was the flow of her line. He watched it rise and fall, become quiet, then loud, slow, then fast—a continuous line as of notes and phrases following each other in song. In silence she asserted rhythm and created the form and intensity of sound. With her whole body, she expressed a music that somehow his soul perceived, and he felt throughout his mind that peculiar, singular response his body normally reserved for symphonic sound.

Maybe it would be possible.

Then he saw her upstage right, dressed in a long, diaphanous gown to which a shawl of the same light material was attached. Her auburn hair hung straight down her back, caught by a single jeweled clasp high up at the back of her head. She was on stage in performance, and he knew he was seeing his Spirit of Prayer. His breath caught and held as she began to dance. Immediately a large repeating pattern emerged, with short rhythm phrases within it.

Cal ran the scene again in his mind, refining the large pattern, adding variations to the rhythm phrases. In silence. Finally Katherine moved to where Matt was slumped to his knees, his fists together against the top of his head. Matt, who was dressed in rehearsal clothes, rose to his feet but then stood waiting for instruction from Cal, who now saw himself on stage too. He moved to a position beside Matt, knelt in Matt's previous posture, and then came to his feet and proceeded into a phrase of movement. He stopped and looked to Matt, who knelt, then stood in a replica. They repeated the sequence, and Cal told Matt, "Don't smudge the line of dance—don't sacrifice a single detail." Alone in his home, more a witness than a creator, Cal watched the ballet come into reality in his mind.

The phone rang. Simultaneously, Cal on the imaginary rehearsal stage and Cal in his living room chair reached for the receiver. He murmured a greeting.

"This is a hell of a way to create! And don't you dare say that God did it in six days, so why can't I—I'd gladly give this job to God."

"Hello, Evana. How's it going?" He was caught in a wonderful, serene place, from which he could respond only in peace.

"I called to give you a piece of my mind about calling my secretary and harassing her."

"Yes, I knew I was making a mistake by pressuring Teresa, but I was feeling some discomfort about—"

"Discomfort!" She screamed the word. "You'd be in a whole lot more discomfort if I called you up every time I was struck with uncertainty about this project! Right now, the less you know about how it's going, the better for you."

Cal turned to read a clock. It was almost six in the morning. He noticed now that thin lines of light were visible at the edges of the dark drapes. "Evana, when was the last time you had some sleep?"

There was silence on the line, and then she said, "Uh, Thursday, I think."

"You need a break, Evana. I want you to take the day off and get some sleep."

"What the hell do you mean? I thought you were rearing at the bit to get something to work with. I thought you were begging on your knees for twenty bars."

"I *am* rearing at the bit, but I want you to get some sleep. Then starting tomorrow, I want you to work on this composition no more than a normal workday at a time. Doesn't matter whether you work at night or day or some of each, but no more than ten hours in twenty-four."

Evana made a noise but no identifiable words.

"You got a dog there?"

Another pause. "Huh?"

"I, of course, have no idea where you are, but if you can borrow a nice dog for a few hours a day, spend some time walking the dog or just playing with the dog—or see a movie or just get an hour of fresh air."

Evana made another noise followed by what sounded like a sniff.

"And I want you to eat right—nutritious stuff three times a day—and sleep seven or eight hours in every twenty-four."

She sniffed again, and with a horrifying rush of compassion, Cal realized that she was crying. Another sniff and she found her voice. "I don't think that's going to get this composition written."

His voice softened. "Well, I'm paying for this piece. That makes me the customer, and that's how I want you to work."

He held his breath and squinted in anticipation of an onslaught of sarcasm, but what came, after another silence, was a quiet, muffled sound that might have been 'kay.

"Go on to bed now, and maybe you'll call me—what? Say Tuesday?"

He was hanging up the receiver when he heard her voice calling him back. "Cal? Cal?"

"Yes, Evana. I'm here."

Her voice was restrained, barely recognizable. "I forgot what I called you for. I've put twenty-some bars on a cassette that I'll send out of here Monday by Federal Express. It should be on your desk Tuesday by ten."

His breath caught in a gasp, fully in present time, no longer caught halfway in his vision.

"It's not the beginning. I'm having problems with the beginning. If you look at your libretto, this is the end of scene 9 when your Spirit of Prayer dances for the second time, plus a bit of scene 10. This is the only part of the composition that feels ready to give you, and even the end of this, where there's that first connection with your male, it's still rough, but it's firm enough to choreograph."

Evana hung up before Cal could manage a response. His voice, when it came, was a bare whisper that didn't quite form words for the "thank you" in his soul.

Then a sudden, sharp wave of heat poured over him. The music Evana had described was the music for the scene he had seen Katherine dance, without music, in his mind. His heart began to pound, and he looked around the room to make sure of where he was. A movement at the doorway caught his eye. Miss Agnus peered around the corner, watching him. He stretched out a hand toward her, and she ran to him, jumping into his lap, and he embraced her. "Girl," he whispered to her soft ear, but he kept himself from saying aloud what was in his heart: *I'm starting to think this might be okay.*

* * *

There was virtually no furniture in Matt Wade's apartment. The small single bedroom contained a mattress on the floor with a blue blanket folded neatly across the bottom. There were no pictures on the walls. Clean practice clothes, underwear, and socks were kept in a cardboard box; dirty laundry went into the laundry basket. The closet held one brown-tone sports coat, a tan lightweight jacket, four ironed shirts, two pairs of pants, five brightly colored tank tops, three pairs of jeans on hangers, and several pairs of shoes matched up, two by two, on a shoe rack. In the back of the closet, stored in front of the ironing board, was a lined brown leather jacket sealed in a plastic bag and reserved for winter.

The living room was a rectangle featuring a tidy composition of weight bench, incline board, treadmill, and free weights. A pair of well-used weight lifter's gloves rested on top of a fifty-pound dumbbell, and a folded white towel lay at one end of the incline board, perfectly square with the board's edge. A dancer's barre was affixed to one wall where the bare floor afforded a small practice area. The single image on the wall was a framed poster promoting one of the Tropp Troupe's recent seasons; in the poster Matt held Alexandra above his head, and stage lights glistened in an aura around them.

Matt stopped to look around the kitchen, where he had just finished washing his breakfast dishes, and turned out the kitchen light. In the bathroom, he used a hand mirror to check the progress of the hair growing where his initials had been shaved in. He rubbed his hand briskly up and down over the initials, a daily practice he had initiated in case stimulating the blood flow would encourage the hair to grow in faster.

"Why I ever did that—"

At nine thirty he locked the apartment door behind him and set off at a jog to keep his every-other-Sunday-morning appointment with Stephen Marksman. The two men had been meeting for almost two years. Matt both hated and loved therapy, which he had entered into to try to understand the dreams that plagued his nights and interfered with his sleep. He knew that the process was good for him, and when he followed Stephen's instructions, he invariably learned something about himself that lightened the interior load he carried. But individual sessions could feel like torture.

As usual, there was no one in the waiting room when Matt arrived. Stephen hadn't wanted to schedule the Sunday appointments, but Matt had convinced him that no other day of the week would work when the company was in the performance season. Precisely at ten, Matt heard a door close upstairs where Stephen lived, and the therapist came to the top of the steps. Matt stood up, cleared his throat, and started up the stairs.

"How are you this morning, Matt?"

"Fine. You?"

"I'm so happy to be living where the nights are cool, even if the days are hot. The older I get, the sweeter a night of sleep is."

"Tell me about it." Matt followed Stephen into the office, where they sat down in facing chairs.

"What would you like to talk about today?" asked Stephen.

"This." Matt sat forward and turned his head so that Stephen could see the initials.

"Ah. Did you have that the last time you were here?"

"Yes, I'd just gotten it."

"How do you suppose I missed it?"

"I wanted you to miss it, that's how." Matt sat back in the chair. "I wore a cap, and when I took the cap off I made sure you saw only the front of my head."

"Ah. What is it you want to discuss about the haircut?"

"I want to know what ever possessed me to have it done."

"Does this feel like possession to you? You feel like some devil made you do it?"

Matt looked quickly at Stephen to make sure he wasn't joking. "I just mean that it's not like me to do something like this."

"Something like? How would you characterize it? What kind of act is it to have your initials shaved into the back of your head?"

"Well, it's radical . . . it's juvenile . . . it's rebellious."

"And you're not any of those things?"

Matt shook his head. "I'm certainly not radical, and I've never thought of myself as juvenile. If anything, I never had a childhood to be juvenile in. And the last thing anyone could ever legitimately accuse me of is rebellion."

"Mm, that's a mouthful: not radical, no childhood, no rebellion. Well, why do you think you had it done?"

"I don't know."

"But if you *did* know, what would you say?"

Matt rolled his eyes. "You've tried that with me before."

Stephen laughed. "I guess we did go through that once before, didn't we?" But he waited.

"I still don't know."

"Okay. Let's go back to what you said about no one *legitimately* accusing you of rebellion. That sounds like someone accused you illegitimately at some point."

Heat started upward from Matt's chest, up his neck, into his face. "Yeah, I've been illegitimately accused of rebellion."

"Tell me about that."

Matt was aware that he had begun breathing a little more quickly, that his face had reddened. Still, he made the effort to stifle his emotions. "I had this jackass for a stepfather, and he accused me of that once."

"You haven't told me a lot about him yet."

"He's not one of my favorite subjects. He came into my life when I was six. He'd already fathered my sister before my mother married him. For the first couple of years he lived with us, I kept waiting for her to see what she'd done and make him go away. It took a long time to grasp that she actually *wanted* him there. By the time I got clear on that, I was about twelve or thirteen, and I had already decided that my main job was to forget about her and concentrate on protecting my sister."

"Protecting her? From your stepdad? From her father?"

"Yeah, and from our mother. By then I'd decided that her judgment pretty well sucked too."

"Go on."

"Anyway, I was having trouble with grades, couldn't seem to get my homework done at home, that kind of thing. Then a friend of mine got caught coming to school with drugs in his pocket, so my stepfather decided that I must be using too. Which I wasn't. But between that and the problem with grades and a few other things he dreamed up, he decided that I was rebelling against them and that the rebellion had to be put down."

"How did he go about that?"

"I was grounded to my room except for taking care of my sister. The only things I was allowed out to do were to go to school and to take my sister to her dance lessons three times a week. I even ate meals in my room. Usually Laney brought hers in to eat with me. Laney—that's my sister. Elaine."

"How long did this go on?"

"The grounding was for three months—until the end of the school year. Taking my sister to her dance lessons lasted longer because when the dance teacher saw that I was coming every lesson anyway, she kind of pulled me into joining in. Gave me lessons for free."

"That was how you got started in ballet."

"Yep."

"So the point is that you were being punished for rebellion when you weren't rebelling."

"Right."

"How did that make you feel?"

"I thought it wasn't right."

Stephen nodded. "That's what you thought, but how did you feel?"

Matt blinked twice and sat up straighter. *Here we go with this feeling thing again—like I have any idea what he's talking about.* "I thought—it seemed to me that the whole thing was unjust."

"Did you feel angry?"

"Not really angry. More . . . uh, I don't know." The chair where he sat was too hard; the edge of it was cutting into his thigh muscles.

"I think I would have felt pretty angry myself. Did you feel insulted?"

"Insulted?"

"At having your integrity and honesty questioned?"

Matt tilted his head to one side, then back. "Probably some of that."

"Betrayed? Disrespected?"

Matt's face grew warm again as, inside, something clicked into place. "Yeah. I felt betrayed."

"By whom?"

Matt rubbed a hand over the back of his head. "More by my mother, I guess, than by him. My stepfather and I never had any relationship in the first place, so there wasn't anything to betray. I knew he was a jackass from the first time I saw him. But my mother. She knew I wasn't doing drugs. She knew I would never do that. Yeah, I thought she was betraying me."

"And how did that make you feel?"

Matt stared at Stephen. The seconds passed. There was nothing inside him, nothing moving, nothing noticeable, mostly a kind of numb silence, a learned hardness. Then he entwined his fingers, popped a knuckle. "I don't really remember feeling anything about it."

"Was that the first time she betrayed you?"

"No. She betrayed me by bringing him to live with us and by marrying him."

"You look surprised."

Matt shifted, seeking a more comfortable spot in his chair. "It never occurred to me to look at it that way before."

"You never saw your real father alive. Isn't that what you've told me?"

"That's right. He was killed in Vietnam when I was still a baby. First he was an MIA, then when I was about three, Mom got the word that his body had been found. He'd been killed in some jungle and had actually been dead for quite a while."

"How did your mother handle all that?"

Matt took a deep breath and leaned back to look at the ceiling. *Man, this is one of those sessions I hate—and this chair is giving me a backache! How long before this is over?* "Well, all I remember from when I was real little was that she cried a lot when she was home. I got left with a sitter a lot. Then after she found out that he was dead, she was really bad off for a couple of years."

"What do you mean *really bad off*?"

"Well, she was drunk most of the time, and looking back on it now, I realize she was probably doing drugs too. She'd be asleep on the couch or in a chair all day and all night, and there was no waking her up."

"Who was taking care of you?"

"I was. I mean, I could make peanut butter sandwiches if I was hungry, put on a sweater if I was cold, go get into bed if I was tired. Pretty soon I could heat up a can of soup. You know."

"You were how old?"

Matt stopped to think. "I guess I must have been about four when this started. For a while before she got pregnant with my sister, I was also feeding her and sweeping up the place as much as it was ever swept. When Laney was born, Mom straightened up some at first, but it wasn't long before a lot of taking care of Laney fell to me too."

"But you were only a child yourself."

"Well, I was almost six when Laney was born." *I wasn't a baby, for Chrissake!*

"What do you suppose the other six-year-olds were doing while you were cooking and cleaning house and taking care of your mother and a baby?"

The words hit Matt like a heavy medicine ball had just landed in his gut. His breath caught, and for a terrible moment, he thought he might cry. He held his face still; his torso felt rigid, as if it were made of concrete. The left half of his upper body seemed to be a hard, dense block of cement. Finally he realized that he had to answer. "Don't know."

"So here we are twenty years later. Are you any closer to understanding why you might have suddenly decided to have your initials carved into your haircut?"

Matt cleared his throat before he trusted his voice to work right, to sound calm and under control. "You're saying this stems from all that back then?"

"I don't know, but if I were you, I'd certainly consider it."

"Is that my assignment for the next time?" Matt shifted to the edge of the chair. *I've had enough of this. I have to find a way to get out of here.*

"That and see whether you can come up with what your feelings might have been while all this was happening to you." They talked for several more minutes, winding down the therapy hour on less volatile themes, then—as early as he could get away with it—Matt got to his feet. As he escaped through the door, Stephen added, "Oh, and, Matt, you can call me anytime, you know—set up extra sessions or just talk by phone. Okay?"

Matt didn't answer, didn't turn around, but raised his left hand in a quick wave to acknowledge that he had heard.

He turned toward home as usual when he left Stephen's office, then changed his mind and headed toward the bay. He knew an overlook that reminded him of how Puget Sound had looked from a spot near his childhood home in West Seattle. And if he could find some fish and chips for lunch, that ought to really put him in the mood to remember—not that remembering was his favorite thing, but he liked to try to do whatever Stephen asked of him, and it was better to do it sooner rather than put it off and stew about it, maybe end up never getting it done.

The sun was soon too hot for his shirt. He took it off, twisted it into a rope, and slung it over his shoulder with one end under the strap of his red tank top. Breathing in, he thought he could already smell the tang of bay saltwater, even though he was a good ten or twelve minutes' walk from his view point. He began to walk faster and detoured to another street to beat the Sunday lunch crowd at the seafood takeout stand.

Reaching the overlook, he gulped the large soft drink that had come with his meal and chose a seat on one of the park benches, laying out the fish and chips beside him. He ate the chips first, saving the salty, firm slices of deep-fried fish for last. That gone, he took a moist fingertip after the stray bits and pieces of salt and fried breading in the bottom of the fish carton. Only when the carton was clean and his paper waste discarded did he finally turn his eyes toward the water. There it was again—that same unbelievable stretch of water diffusing to the right and left till stopped by the abrupt and irregular green and brown shoreline and far ahead to where haze blurred the horizon. The air was warm and smelled of the sea. If he listened closely, he could hear the gulls, though they stayed near the water's edge, seldom flying so high as the overlook where he sat. Two tugboats, like toys, were bringing in a containership, and other vessels lay at anchor here and there.

If this were Puget Sound, then my house would be four blocks down that street to the left and five blocks in.

Then a scene sprang into his mind, crowding out his physical sight and replacing the sunny day with an aura of darkness and squalor. He saw the little house, saw the small porch, saw the front door open, saw the dirty front room with the broken-down couch and his mother's back as she lay on her side, still, sleeping—drugged. He pulled his gaze away and it lurched, as if stumbling, toward the back of the house. Then he saw the kitchen, saw the table, saw slices of white bread and open jars of peanut butter and jelly, saw a small blond-haired boy struggling to climb onto a chair at the table. The boy was so little. The boy was so little. *The boy was so little!*

Then he heard a choking sound and the picture vanished from his head, leaving an afterburn against his eyes, as though he had been staring straight into the sun. All he saw now was the bay. He choked again and realized that his face was tight and contorted, and tears were falling in whole drops. He put a hand to his chest, where it felt as though something large and dense and compacted was breaking apart.

Then he was running, running hard until his lungs hurt so much he had to slow down. Then he was running again. There was only one goal, only one thing he wanted: to get back home to his apartment, where everything was neat and clean and in its place. Where the kitchen held two dishes, two sets of silverware, two glasses, four mugs, a skillet, two cooking pots, an espresso maker, a small table, and two chairs.

And nothing—nothing—in the whole apartment was bigger than he was.

* * *

Evana awoke with a start and a headache. In a second, her feet were off the bed and on the floor, but the sudden movement made her head pound worse. She swore aloud and pressed her hands inward above her ears.

She looked at the clock, which read five after seven, then looked at it again and groaned aloud as though there were someone there to hear her. "I don't know whether I've slept an hour or thirteen hours. Or it could be Monday morning, for all I know." She closed her eyes against the pain behind them. "I feel like I've been dead a long time."

She pulled on a robe and left the bedroom. The Pacific Ocean spread itself out in leisurely undulations, filling the large windows at the front of the cottage. Evana walked barefoot across the main room and out the door to the elevated porch and stood leaning against the railing, breathing in the salt air. The weathered boards were cool and rough under her feet. The crash and roar of the water provided thematic melody for the improvised ornaments of the seagulls.

A cool breeze blew steadily, stiff enough to ruffle her short hair. Evana breathed in, held the breath for a count of ten, then let it go and repeated the exercise several times until her headache lessened. Then she noticed the sun, on its downward journey toward the ocean. "So it's evening then. Well, eggs would be good anyway." She headed toward the kitchen—that part of the cottage's main room where one wall was given over to the stove/microwave, refrigerator, sink, and cabinets. She added cheddar cheese and canned mushrooms to the eggs as she scrambled them and put two slices of sourdough bread into the toaster. *Martha wouldn't have forgotten the orange juice, would she?* Nope, there it was, cold and sweet, waiting in the back of the refrigerator where she hadn't thought to look before. *What would I do without Martha?*

The cottage belonged to Martha now that Frank, Martha's father (and brother to Evana's deceased husband), was gone. She had aired and dusted the place, made up the bed, and stocked the kitchen with food immediately after Evana had called to ask about using the cottage for a couple of weeks.

"You still have the piano there, don't you?"

"Yes, and a lot of Dad's electronic gear is still there too."

"Like what? Do you recall?"

"His polyphonic synthesizer and a sequencer, I think, along with the stuff that goes with them. That old synthesizer, the little one that he built himself, is there somewhere."

"Mind if I get them out and see what I can make them do?"

"Experiment all you want. It's all just sitting there."

"Oh, and, Martha, get the piano tuned right away, will you?"

"I doubt that I can get anyone out there before next week." Annoyed resignation edged Martha's voice.

"No. I need it done today, tomorrow at the latest. Pay him extra, promise him whatever you need to—I'll cover it. Just get the piano tuned by tomorrow."

So the piano tuner had been there on Saturday, and Evana had filled the time he worked by dusting off and looking over the electronic equipment.

The eggs and toast made, Evana set the cassette tape player on the table to listen to her developing composition as she ate. She made a sour face a couple of times, got up to get her sketch sheets, and noted some revisions before returning to her breakfast.

The headache was still not gone after she had eaten. *Water. I'm probably half dehydrated.* She drank three glasses from the tap and then finished off half of another with some aspirin. Then she changed into jeans and tennis shoes, grabbed a small pad of staff paper and pencil to stuff into her jacket pocket, and left the cottage to walk the beach. Finding the log that she had come to consider hers, she sat down to take stock of where she was, now that she'd had a week of work and a glorious thirteen hours of sleep.

The piece was going to be a variation of a sonata: two participating instruments, just like prayer, the three movements progressing in key from D minor to B-flat major to D major. Only after some struggle had she decided that the basic ABA form would have to be altered to ABC, with the third movement not so much a recapitulation of the first but more of an evolution of themes and phrases. *I presume the point of this ballet is that the individuals involved don't end up where they started.*

She had sketched rough melodic portions of all three movements, concentrating on the formal shape and phrase structure. Now she was building melodic detail and harmony, keeping in mind the interplay of the two instruments. Then one day the previous week, it had occurred to her that if her two participants represented the two parties in prayer, then perhaps the piano should be reserved for the human element and the electronic sounds should be used for the spiritual element. But that gave her another problem: did that mean that she could use only piano for the first seven or eight minutes before Cal's Spirit of Prayer showed up, or could she use both instruments throughout the sonata, on the theory that the spiritual element is a part of the human even when it isn't recognized or acknowledged? She had added this to her list of questions to be resolved and still wasn't sure how to handle it.

The sun was riding low over the water when Evana noticed that she was having difficulty seeing to scribble note values onto the pad. She had formed a habit of walking and humming until she'd come up with a bar or two she liked, then standing still long enough to jot them down or returning to her log to hum and sketch several tentative bars. Sometimes her humming swelled into a kind of angry scat singing, a kind that made loose dogs shy away from her with tails tucked in and heads lowered.

The phone was ringing when Evana returned to the cottage.

"Hello, Aunt Ev. It's Martha. Are you about due for more provisions? I thought I might drive over tomorrow and restock your refrigerator, since I'm sure you're not paying attention to details like that yourself."

Evana was silent for a moment, adjusting to the irritation of an intrusion into her work time but also thinking it could be useful. She made up her mind. "Yes, that would be good. What time are you coming?"

"When would be good for you? You know when you're taking breaks—if you're taking any—and I can make it anytime."

"Well, come for early lunch then, and maybe you can help me get an overnight package out of here and on its way to San Francisco. I've promised it for Tuesday."

"Yes, I know places here in Portland if we can't find one there. What kind of food do you want to stock?"

"More of the same: breakfast stuff, salad stuff, just like you had it when I got here. Oh, and, Martha? Do you still have that dog? What was his name?"

"Charley? Yes. He's right here. His muzzle is a little grayer than the last time you saw him and one leg seems to bother him now, but I still have him."

"Bring him along. He likes the ocean, doesn't he?"

"He loves the ocean—but I never had the sense that you thought much of him."

"Nonsense. I'd like to see him."

Martha chuckled in disbelief. "We'll be there in time for lunch."

Hanging up the phone, Evana sat down at the piano and played the bars she had noted on the beach and added to her working sketch sheets the ones that still seemed acceptable. Soon she was lost in it: playing, sketching, playing, revising, humming, playing, recording, listening, revising, playing. When at last she decided to stop, the unattended moon—what there was of it—had left a thin drizzle of stain on the ocean surface.

* * *

Evana was towel-drying her hair when Martha and Charley arrived on Monday. She looked through the back-door window at the golden retriever, who was prancing in excitement to be out of the car and near the ocean. *What was I thinking of, listening to Cal? That dog may be older, but he looks as obnoxious as ever to me, and Lord knows how he must smell!*

Charley burst into the cottage as soon as Evana opened the back door to the driveway. He smashed into Evana's knee on his way past her, his toenails like a burst of tin sheet percussion on the tile floor. His tail slapped her as he spun around, despite a brief problem with traction, and ran back to Martha. Now he was barking and panting, and after throwing his forepaws against Martha's shoulders once, he went racing off around the cottage to the beach.

"I thought you said he had a bad leg and was getting old."

"He'll calm down in a minute. The ocean reverts him to puppyhood. Here, help me with these bags."

The women carried in the groceries, and Evana made a salad while Martha set a large pot of water on the stove to heat. "Thought I'd make up some spaghetti for you to have to eat for a couple of days. You can just heat it in the microwave."

"Why are you so nice to me, Martha? I know I never did anything to deserve it."

Martha laughed. "You remind me of Dad, that's why. He was just like you are when he was composing: demanding this, needing that, never taking time to eat right, working around the clock, forgetting to sleep, being a grouch and a half."

"I'm like that whether I'm composing or not."

"Yes. You are. So was Dad."

"Your father and I used to agree—just between us—that composing is just like constipation. You sweat and push and swear and you think you're never going to get the music out of you, and then finally it starts to come and you know there isn't a better feeling in the world."

Martha cleared her throat. "Yes, I'd heard that."

After lunch, Evana gave Martha the cassette tape for dispatch to San Francisco, and the two of them took Charley for a short walk along the ocean before his trip home. Evana listened closely to commands Martha gave to the dog and watched as she found a stick to throw repeatedly into

Evana nodded. "Just give me a kiss before you go, and don't bring Charley back here again." She watched Martha back out and drive off and then returned to the cottage, limping and swearing.

* * *

By Tuesday, Evana's sketch sheets were becoming illegible again, the numerous revisions having left erasures, cross-outs, arrows to revised bars several staves down the page, and occasional confusion, even for her, about the exact placement of some of the notes. It was time again to sit down and write out a clean and current sketch. The job by itself would take several hours, but adding in the revisions and expansions that would inevitably arise, it was realistically an all-night affair. The music took over her conscious mind as she strove for the inner logic that would express within the bounds of musical proportion what Cal seemed to want to say. Her photocopy of his libretto was ragged and stained from the dozens of times, now, that she had reread it, scribbled and crossed out notes to herself, and tried to draw the lines of connection that would result in passages of music with suitable structures and evolving themes.

After writing out a clean sketch of her progress on the first movement—an exposition full of ferocious discords and offbeat sforzandos, she had realized that she would need at least four additional bars in order to strengthen the relationship between this passage and the second-movement section that she had already developed and sent to Cal. She had noted the new bars on a yellow Post-it note, and now it was gone.

Again she went through her pages, the smeared and curling pages of previous sketches and the fresh pages of newly written notes. She cursed herself for not leaving enough empty staves on the page. She cursed herself for relying on a flimsy Post-it note and then losing it. She tried to recall the four bars, but couldn't and cursed herself for that. Why hadn't she at least put it on the tape recorder or taken the time to write out another fresh page incorporating the additional bars?

Maybe the thing is that I am too old to be doing this composition anyway. There was a time when she and Frank could work and keep on working without the need for sleep or food, and the ideas seemed to never stop coming—and no bars were ever lost. *But Frank is dead now.* The thought hit her in the stomach. *And Jack is dead now.* Two brothers: one, her closest friend and composition partner; the other, her husband. Tears the waves for Charley to race after and retrieve. He appeared to love the ocean and was undaunted by the rolling water.

"What would you think about lending Charley to me?"

"Aunt Ev, you *hate* Charley. You've *always* hated Charley. In fact, as far as I've ever been able to see, you hate all animals. And Charley in particular. What makes you think you would want him here with you?"

"Somebody told me it might be good for the composition. I'll bring him back to you after a couple of days."

"Ha! Dog hair in *your* car? I'm sure! Besides, why would I trust to leave him here with you?"

Evana's eyes narrowed. "I won't abuse your dog, Martha. What do you take me for?"

"I take you for exactly what you are. That's why I'm having a problem with leaving Charley here."

Evana stood looking at Martha in silence and then called, "Come, Charley. Come, boy." Even Charley was surprised, but he came running, stopping within a yard of her to give in to his urge to shake the saltwater out of his coat. Bracing his feet in a wide stance, he lowered his neck and let the shudder overtake him until his body became a blur spewing fat water drops all over Evana, who realized too late that it was up to her to get out of his way. Having shaken himself, Charley sat and threw a wet, sandy paw up for her to grab, leaving a long smear on Evana's pant leg. His tongue fell out of the side of his mouth as he gazed up at her.

Martha was laughing again. "This is the *real* Charley, Aunt Ev. Today it's your pant leg he muddied. Tomorrow it might be your sketch sheets."

Wavering, Evana bent to pet the dog, who threw his nose up suddenly and hit her in the chin. Her teeth clicked together audibly.

"And you'd have to go to the store to buy him food. And remember to feed him every afternoon."

Evana opened her mouth wide to test the hinge of her jaw. "Maybe you're right, Martha. I guess you'd better take him back with you."

Martha opened the car door. "Get in, Charley." As the dog spun around, his back foot and all sixty of his pounds came down onto the arch of Evana's foot, leaving mud on the white shoe, a bruise on the foot inside, and a toenail scratch on the ankle. "I think it's only true dog lovers who compose better with dogs around." Then Martha smiled. "I love you, Aunt Ev."

were stinging her eyes, and she reared up from the piano bench, creasing the side of her leg on a sharp corner, and went to stand at the window. But the ocean may as well not have been there either. She scanned the sky, but the moon had turned its dark side, and there was no light visible anywhere.

She was pacing and swearing, far past any ability to perform productive work, when the phone rang. It was Cal.

"How the hell did you get this number?" Her voice was shrill with fury and pain.

"It was on the airbill."

"What airbill?"

"The package, Evana. You sent me a cassette by overnight service, and your phone number was on the airbill."

She paused, shocked. *Martha.* "Well, what the hell are you doing calling me at this hour anyway? I'm trying to get some work done!"

There was silence on both ends of the line for a moment. "Actually, I have no idea, Evana. I just woke up out of a sound sleep and dialed your number. I didn't even realize I'd memorized it from the airbill. Do you know it's almost two in the morning?"

"I've got a clock here!" The words felt like fire in her throat. "I don't need you to call me with the time. I suppose this is your way of trying to push me along a little faster. Let me tell you something, Calvin. You think composing is like choreographing, and when you haven't worked out a transition you can tell your dancers to improvise. Improvise! Make it up! Well, let me enlighten you just a trifle. A composer does not have the liberty to tell an orchestra, 'I haven't quite worked out this part, so for the next four or five bars, just improvise!'"

Cal appeared not to notice her anger searing the phone line. "Since I have you on the phone, I can tell you that the part you sent is exquisite. It's perfect, Evana. It's beautiful and heroic and inspiring. It's exactly what I would have written if I could have composed it myself."

Evana said nothing. A strange pumping started up in her chest, and her breath threatened to turn to gasps. She put a shaky hand over the receiver to keep Cal from hearing.

"And I would guess you're having trouble with the composition now, so maybe I called to tell you that what you've composed so far—I don't see how it could be better. And maybe I'm supposed to remind you that you told me once that you pray when you're angry."

There was again silence on both ends of the line until Cal said softly, "Get some sleep, Evana. Good night." Then he hung up.

Evana put the receiver down and stood at the window, looking out where the Pacific Ocean should have been. All was dark, though she could hear the waves coming in and coming in. The only light was a blue flasher on a distant buoy marking a rocky outcropping on the irregular shoreline. *How long has it been since I prayed?* She couldn't remember praying since Jack had been so sick and she had begged God to spare his life. But he had died, leaving her with a destructive loneliness and so many bills that she was forced to sell the home they had shared and move to an apartment. At least she'd had the professorship at the university.

"God?" Her voice quavered. Only her reflection showed in the window glass. She closed her eyes, and into her mind came her vision of Cal's Spirit of Prayer. *He probably intends to use that tall girl, the one with auburn hair.* Then her mind was blank; she had no idea what to say next. She looked toward the piano and saw the chaos of sketch pages scattered in disarray, wads of paper on the floor. No order. No logic. No structure. No Post-it note. "I-I don't . . . I can't do this by myself." Now she was trembling from head to foot.

No more words came. She took a jacket from the hook and closed the door behind her, finding herself at once enveloped in a chill of blackness that pushed in at her from every side. The tart salt smell felt cleansing, and she sucked it in, letting the mist coat the inside of her. She made her way mostly by memory to the log on the beach. Here she sat with her hands in her pockets and looked out at the point where there should have been a horizon, but now the dark sky blended as one with the dark ocean. The longer she sat, the calmer she felt, and now she could make out a star—then another—faintly visible in the sky. She could tell by the sounds and by the brisk waves of air against her face that the ocean was there. "Evidence of things unseen," she whispered to the night. Then she tried again to pray, but as before, the only words that would come were, "I can't do this by myself."

Composure settled over her, and with it a sureness that felt foreign—so long had it been since she had felt it—a sense of certainty that she would finish the composition and that it would be right. Not thinking, only doing, she stood up to return to the cottage. She shook off her jacket as she climbed the steps to the door. Inside, she went immediately to the piano and began organizing the sketch sheets, filing the early versions in an accordion file, out of the way; ordering and numbering the new pages; discarding wadded-up sheets and unusable papers. On the back of a crumpled sheet she found the lost Post-it note and stuck it with Scotch tape to the appropriate new sketch page.

Then she sat down with the new pages and the keyboard in front of her and began to work, balancing the contrasts between sections of melody, adjusting phrase lengths, canceling bars here and adding bars there, varying pitch and rhythm, studying placement of climaxes to adhere to Cal's libretto, and at the same time building relationships and evolution among and between the three movements. Through the remainder of the night she worked, all through the next day and into the next night, with twenty-minute catnaps and occasional platefuls of cold spaghetti.

By the early hours of Thursday, the rough composition was down on paper, minus dynamics and other articulation marks. Additional arrangement would come later. She turned back to a place that had been bothering her: bars 204 through 206. She added a series of syncopated *F*s, followed by rests. Then she closed the piano keyboard, put her arms down on it, laid her head on her arms, and slept.

* * *

Seven Weeks

"All right, people, listen up," Cal said at the end of class on Wednesday morning. "I want to see Alexandra, Matt, and Katherine Melton in Studio C at four today. Judy, you need to be there too," he said to the accompanist. "The rest of you, be sure to check the bulletin board for your rehearsals."

Cal noticed Matt and Alexandra turn to look at each other from across the room. Matt's eyebrows were up, and Alexandra winked at him with a wide grin. They both turned to find Katherine, but her attention was still focused on Cal. Katherine had gained her reputation for aloofness in part from her regal five-foot-nine-inch stature but even more from the way she aligned herself in the company with Cal and Rob, rather than with the other dancers, no matter that she sweated right along with the rest of them. Now she was moving smoothly toward him, her walking steps as much like dance as her stage work. "So what happens at four?" Neither Matt nor Alexandra would have dared to ask so boldly.

"Well, I thought we'd try to get a start on choreography for a new piece."

"The much-rumored new ballet for the October program?" Before he could reply, she went on. "Is this the one on prayer? I thought you didn't have music for it."

"We're still short on music, but I think we have enough to start with."

Her blue eyes seemed to appraise him, and then a smile broke over her mouth. "Good! Can't wait."

Studio C was a high-ceilinged room with windows on one side, a thirty-foot mirror across the front, and barres the full length of two walls. The awning-style windows had all been pushed open, and the stale smells of sweat, rosin, and carbon dioxide were being washed along by the warm, fresh breeze that flowed through the room. Outside, cars passed in the street at the slowed speeds acceptable for the largely residential neighborhood. Katherine entered the room at four, with Matt and Alexandra behind her. Cal turned from his conversation with Judy and Amelie to watch his dancers. *This is going to stretch them.*

The three dancers had changed into dry rehearsal clothes. Katherine was wearing a pink camisole over a white leotard and pink tights; she was twirling and pinning her hair up off her shoulders as she entered the studio. Alexandra was dressed in a silver unitard and powder-blue T-shirt but held a shawl drawn around her shoulders. *She's just emerged from one of those meditation sessions she thinks I don't know about. Can't believe she can tolerate that stale old storeroom.* Alexandra sipped a cup of something hot enough to steam. Matt had changed into a red tank top with black cutoff sweatpants. He pressed a small white towel against his face.

Out of habit, they had converged near the piano, but Cal held up a cassette tape. "Listen, people, it's going to be frustrating to work with this until we can get Judy up and running with sheet music, but for now this is all we have." He turned toward his accompanist. "I'll get you a piano score as soon as I can." He slid the tape into the player. "What we have is about twenty-five bars so far, but the rest is coming." *I hope.*

All eyes on Cal, no one said anything in response. Then the music began: Evana's simple piano playing both parts. Even in the short sample there was the promise of a theme. Cal played it through three times without comment and then turned from the buttons on the player. "This drops you in the middle of the composition—actually near the end. It's in the ninth scene of a twelve-scene ballet." He looked from one dancer to the next. *Whoa! Slow down and start at the beginning. They don't have a clue what we're doing here!* He took a breath and started again. "We are going to make a dance on the theme of prayer. Matt, you and Alexandra represent a male and a female in the world today, a couple really, but a couple on the rocks, and I suppose you're sort of human beings on the rocks too. In the early scenes of the ballet, you fight a lot with each other, but it becomes clear that each of you is really fighting with himself—and herself.

"When the fighting and discontent begin to wear thin, each of you—first one, then the other—begs for some sort of reconciliation with the other, and even though it doesn't work, since there's no basis in trust, it evokes what I am calling the Spirit of Prayer to appear on the stage and in the lives of these two people. Katherine, you're the Spirit of Prayer, and your home base is upstage right. That's where you materialize, and that's where you return when you have occasion to wait and see what these two misguided humans are going to do next."

The dancers listened, perhaps picturing Katherine "materializing." They let Cal talk without questions.

"What's basically happening in the ballet is that a sort of spirituality, which I'm thinking of as a spirit of prayer, is taking root in these people's lives and teaching them how to reshape how they live. There's lots of room for dancing emotion in this. Just about every emotion in the book comes into it, at one point or another, and I'm going to want every drop of it out of you."

Cal moved to Katherine and reached to take her hand. "Now the snippet of music we have here begins with the Spirit of Prayer hanging out at home base." He led Katherine to a position at upstage right and then turned her to face downstage, toward the large mirror. "Judy, will you let about three or four bars of that play."

As the music started, he dropped Katherine's hand, rose to the balls of his feet, and took the first six steps of a large repeating pattern. He stopped, nodded to Judy to cut off the music, and turned to look at Katherine. This was her cue, and without waiting for the music, she stepped off the same six steps *en pointe* and then stopped as if frozen in place. Cal returned to her side and stepped off again in silence, a series of small steps this time with expansive arm movements and slight turns of the body. When it was Katherine's turn, she *bourreed en pointe* toward center stage but missed some of the subtlety of the body turns. "Try it again," Cal said. "More *efface devant*. Judy, can we have the first three or four bars again?"

Cal added arm and body movements, changed the direction of a turn, and then they ran the two combinations together. First Cal performed the series, and then Katherine followed, adding the balletic positions and flair that came naturally from her training. He had already known how it would look on her, but he asked to see it again and again anyway, making repairs and adjustments as they went. Then they listened to more of the tape. "Going on," he said, leading her in the next series of steps, which he had first seen danced by her in his mind in the silence of his living room before a recent dawn. Through it all, Amelie took notes on a yellow pad of every step, turn, and floor pattern. When Cal changed his mind, she drew a single line through the old steps, knowing that Cal might return to his original idea. Under it she indented to record the refined idea. Matt and Alexandra sat beside each other with backs against the mirror and watched, soaking up the mood and intent of what Cal was doing and waiting their turns.

It didn't take long to reach the end of the music on the tape. "That's all you have here, Cal," Judy said.

"I know. But I think we can go on with this anyway." For half an hour more, he connected movements with theme and ideas in silence, knowing that when the music arrived, he could cut or reshape or expand to make the dance fit. His mind and his body felt in sync with the work so that with each step he modeled, the next motion was waiting when he was ready for it. *It's as though I already know the music and am merely staging someone else's choreography!*

By the end of the session, Cal and the three dancers had put together twice as much of the dance as what they had music for.

* * *

That evening, the doorman of the condominium building where Katherine lived with her mother greeted Katherine with a salute. "Your mother's keys, dear. She asked me to give these to you when you came in." He handed her keys that fitted the little yellow 450 SL. "She had me park it for her when she returned this afternoon. It's in her stall downstairs."

"Thank you, Mr. Hooper."

The condominium on the fifteenth floor gave a broad view of water and, in the distance, the Oakland Bay Bridge, but the drapes were usually drawn to discourage sun-fading of the carpets and upholstery. By many people's standards, there was a lot of what could be considered "wasted space" in the eight-room, two-thousand-square-foot condo, but the space was artfully filled with sculptures from various artists whom Mrs. Melton admired, as well as expensive mementos from lengthy visits in sundry parts of the world.

As was her practice, Alice Melton came to the door to greet her daughter as soon as the key sounded in the lock. "Hello, sweetheart!" She enfolded her daughter, who was several inches taller than she, into a hug. The gold tones of her perfectly coiffed hair exactly matched a strand of threads woven into her silk scarf.

"Hi, Mom. Mr. Hooper says the car is in its stall downstairs." She handed her mother the car keys.

"Well, of course it is. Where else would he have put it?"

Katherine's mother held a teacup by its slender handle in her left hand. She was rarely without a teacup as she went about her daily affairs, which seldom required her to leave the condominium. She could keep up with her investments, do most of her banking, maintain an active correspondence on a variety of political issues, help raise funds to support Katherine's ballet company, and carry on other private interests all from the little desk in the third bedroom. When she wasn't at the desk, she was often at the grand piano, which held a prominent position in the large space they considered their living room. Mrs. Melton took particular interest in obtaining sheet music and learning to play the scores to which her daughter danced.

None of these activities took her more than a few steps from her teacup, which was refilled uncounted times each day with a special blend of caffeine-free green tea that she purchased monthly from a small shop in Ghirardelli Square.

"I thought I'd poach that salmon for dinner. Any objections?"

"No, that's fine. I'm just going to work on a pair of *pointe* shoes. We got in a new shipment, and I think the tips of the shanks are going to hit too high."

"Well, send them back!"

Katherine shook her head. "Then I wouldn't have enough shoes to get by till the next shipment. I think I can fix them."

"Can you do it here? How am I going to talk to you if you're back in that room where you normally do your little chores?"

"Sure, I can do it here." Fortunately, the kitchen was plenty spacious. Katherine got a small hammer from the utility room and spread a towel in a corner of the kitchen floor. After wetting both shoes under the tap, she sat down on the floor, inserted a last in one, and proceeded to hammer first the pleats and then the tip of the shoe. She took her time and tested the wet shoe with her hands, inside and out, until she was satisfied. Then she smoothed out the satin, removed the last, set the shoe to dry, and began on the other one.

At the same time, Mrs. Melton wrestled with the salmon, turning it to first one side, then the other to slice away the layers where bones lay together like piano keys. She had put a full-length apron on over her slate-blue sweater and slacks. The color of the fish was nearly the same shade as the woodwork in the kitchen, where the rows of cabinet doors were white against maroon. Finally she put the salmon into a pan with water, fresh ginger, orange wedges, garlic, and lemon juice. They talked comfortably as they worked, each of them familiar with the details of the other's life. Mrs. Melton had heard step by step about the rumors of a new ballet for the October program; she'd heard about all the surmises floating around the company about who the dancers would be; she knew that Cal wanted to do something on prayer. Now she celebrated with her daughter the leading role in the new ballet.

"The best part this time is how well Cal knows what he wants to see," Katherine said. "Sometimes, in the other ballets he's choreographed on me, I've felt like he was kind of floundering along, not really knowing where he was going with the thing, but this time he's so definite. I mean, he does a step for me, and that's exactly what he wants and nothing else will do."

"What's the music?"

"It's being commissioned, and apparently there's not much of it even composed yet. And that's part of what I mean, Mother. Cal has only a little snatch of the music, but he's choreographing as though he already knows what the whole thing will sound like and look like! Today we did easily twice as much of the ballet as what we have music for."

Mrs. Melton smiled to hear her daughter's enthusiasm as she kept track of the progress of dinner in three pans on the stove.

* * *

If the dancers were elated with the first day's progress on the new ballet, Cal was euphoric. Driving home that evening, he realized that a fine dust had long ago settled on that keen excitement he could feel when a new dance took shape in his mind, and then on his dancers. Though he had continued to make new works through the years, the dust had become thicker, and now he could feel it being shaken off. He felt pierced through with joy, certainty, solidity, the perfection of what he was doing. "My God, how long has it been since I felt this way?" He hadn't meant it to be a prayer, and he definitely was not expecting an answer. But one came: *not since Anne.*

Cal's foot came off the gas pedal in his surprise, and he gasped with the discovery that she could still command such power over him: a woman he had not seen in thirteen years. A woman who had abandoned not only him but their fifteen-year-old son too. A woman he had loved with every particle of his being because he hadn't had a clue that he could lose her until the day she was gone.

Their apartment, from which she had fled thirteen years before, had been a cramped little duplex with cheap furniture in Houston. The ceiling had stains from water leaks, and he had felt so bad that he could not afford to replace carpets that were worn in all the traffic paths. Still, he had had no idea that her unhappiness had reached such a depth. He and Jon had stayed up all night waiting for her, the night she disappeared, telling each other stories about where she might be, reporting to each other every time another phone call to friends or relatives failed to turn up any clue, struggling to hold down their terror about what might have happened to her. The next day he had called a long list of people who were unlikely to have heard from Anne but who were the only people left he could think of, and then he had called the police. Three days passed before the horror of her absence became commonplace enough that he finally went to bed and tried to sleep. For years afterward, just thinking of those days brought quick, stinging tears; now here they were again, coursing down his face.

As he had learned to do back then, he wadded up the picture in his mind and mentally threw it away: a bank shot, into a hoop, and then straight down into a black trash can that had no bottom, and neither did the hole in the earth over which the can sat, so the wadded image would continue forever to fall farther and farther away from him, toward where he imagined hell to be.

Cal cranked the steering wheel to pull the car into his driveway. His shirt stuck to his armpits and back and felt cool across his shoulders, and he realized that he was sopping wet from the heat and energy of reliving that pain. *No! I'm not giving you this!* He pulled his mind back to Katherine and how she had looked hours earlier in her pink and white rehearsal clothes, dancing as his Spirit of Prayer. He sat in the car and watched her dance. A dog was barking somewhere: a small dog's voice, more Donald Duck than canine, and he realized it must be Miss Agnus, coming outside through her dog door at the sound of his car. Still he sat, determined to fully recover his equilibrium before leaving the car.

Then, as Cal sat with his hands clenched on the steering wheel, into his mind came an image of Matt dancing pain. He transposed the images to picture Matt in that shabby, tiny duplex in Houston, dancing out the hurt and loss, sorrow and disbelief, shock and anger, fury and pain of that awful time. It was Matt and it was himself, and the dance was the dance of a man whose life is broken and in need of prayer. He watched the dance, studied the motions, and let Matt's movements contain and express all that he had felt then, until into a separate level of his consciousness came the familiar excitement of creation and the satisfaction of giving articulate expression and valid form to what cannot be said as effectively any other way than through dance.

* * *

Alexandra flung her bag of soiled practice clothes as soon as she had closed the door of her apartment. It hit the wall across the room and rebounded into a glass lamp, which, in the fall to the hardwood floor, was reduced to shards and splinters. She stood looking down at the mess, which caught the early evening sun and resembled jewels thrown by mistake into the trash. Her face contorted then, her lips flaring into a snarl as her eyes darkened with jealousy. "Why her! Why is it always her! Tall, perfect Katherine! If her damned legs were any longer, we'd have to get a bigger stage!"

She let herself fall to the couch in a plop, bringing her knees to her chin and folding her arms around her legs. Her nose found its nook between her kneecaps as she let her head down to rest, cradled into herself. She closed her eyes as self-disappointment flooded her. This was the very thing she tried so hard never to do: letting the envy get out of control. It hadn't happened more than a handful of times in her entire professional career, but it seemed to be harder lately to keep down. It was as though she had somehow reverted to those terrible days in ballet school when everyone was jealous and distrustful of everyone else. She was every bit as good a dancer as Katherine was—she knew that. Surely everyone in the company could see that. But Cal seemed always to prefer Katherine, not only for the special roles he choreographed but also for the little chats he had with dancers sometimes before class and during rehearsals.

And it wasn't only that. It was the ease with which Katherine did everything. It was the communication and understanding she and Cal had built up between them so that Katherine appeared to read his mind and could produce a gesture or a movement or a look that was exactly what he meant even when he hadn't quite said it. It was the devotion between them. And then there was the rest of it: this perfect family thing Katherine seemed to have with her mother.

Everyone in the company knew that Mrs. Melton was a key donor for Tropp's Troupe; everyone had seen her waiting backstage at the end of Katherine's performances. It was common knowledge that she was intimately involved in Katherine's career. Something like homesickness stung Alexandra's nose then, and she had a harder time than usual pinching down the urge to cry. In truth, it was homesickness for the family she would have liked to have had, not for the one she had fled from when she'd been accepted into The Calvin Tropp Ballet Company. The last time she had seen her parents was at the going-away party they had given for her. About two dozen people had shown up: some of her mother's friends, some of her own friends from high school, a few people from her ballet school, and several dancers from the small company with which she had danced for a short time before Cal's New York audition. During the festivities, her father had never surfaced from the basement where he was watching television and "imbibing a few," and her mother had made a little speech that had burned Alexandra's ears for its lies. *Did she think that none of these people knew?*

"We're so proud of our Alexandra. We've all watched her progress and held her hand in the hard times, and now she's going off to dance with a big established company on the West Coast."

Held my hand in the hard times? Whatever are you referring to? Do you mean like that time when I fell during the ballet school recital and was so ashamed that I didn't leave the building? She had spent another whole day and night at the ballet school, hiding out, and when she finally did go home, her mother appeared not to have even realized she'd been gone. *Or maybe you mean my little bout with bulimia, when it took someone else's mother to notice what I was doing and help me get straightened out?*

Her mother's comments, like the going-away party itself, came under the heading of "doing what was expected" and were unrelated to real emotion or their real lives.

The truth was her parents' emotional connection to each other and to the rest of the family had been suspended ever since Ricky had died. It had suddenly become too risky to be invested in the lives of their remaining son and daughter.

Alexandra snapped her head up and took her feet off the couch. "I have my own life. I do just fine in my own life." She got up, pulled a paper grocery sack from the narrow niche alongside the refrigerator, and began to pick up the larger pieces of glass from the broken lamp. Next she swept up the small pieces and then finally went over the area with damp paper towels to pick up chips and slivers too tiny for the broom. Having started to clean, she was energized to keep going, noticing a film of dirt here, a dust ball there, a torn bit of paper to be picked up. The rug needed vacuuming; there was a thin layer of dust under the countertop microwave; the hardwood floor could use a wet mop; and the books in the bookcase needed to be cleaned off and realigned on the shelves.

It was after eleven when she quit, her frantic, compulsive energy reduced at last to exhaustion. She lay on the couch, looking around the apartment and feeling in control of things again.

The next morning, Alexandra crawled out of bed, took a quick shower, and then sat down on the straight-backed chair in her bedroom to meditate. After a few deep breaths, she sat quietly, letting her mantra come repeating into her mind. When she caught herself a few minutes later, her mind was at the studio, going over the working relationship between Cal and Katherine. She was busy watching how they moved, how the choreography appeared to grow out of their interaction, rather than out of Cal's mind alone. Giving an impatient shake of her head, she brought herself back to the mantra, forcing her attention to stay focused on it. But after some time had passed, she realized that once again her attention had gone from the mantra to something Matt had said the day before, then to more of the choreography, then to a ballet teacher she'd suffered with in ballet school, and finally to the first boyfriend with whom she'd had a sexual relationship. It was the evocation of sexual feelings that brought her suddenly back to the room where she now sat and was supposed to be meditating.

If I'm not going to do this right, I might as well not waste my time doing it at all! When the twenty-minute session was over, she lay on the bed for two minutes—only because she was disciplined enough to do so—but her body was impatient to move. She got up, jammed some clean clothes into her ballet bag, and rushed to the studio.

After lunch, Cal conducted another choreography session on the prayer piece without music. All three of his dancers were in the studio, but he began with Matt and Alexandra in the opening scene. "We'll do about two and a half minutes for this first scene. At this point, you two really hate each other, but the truth is that both of you hate yourselves too. You are tortured, unhappy people for whom life is not working out, and right now the easiest thing to do is blame each other." Cal stepped off into a demonstration of Matt's first running movements, full of gestures that were not the least vague in their sharp, angry lines. At the conclusion of the first series, he stopped and turned to Matt, who immediately executed the steps. "Not on the balls of your feet though, Matt. That will come in later. Right now you don't want it to look so light and effortless because that's not how life is for you now. Try it again."

Over and over Matt repeated the running steps, which were harder with his heels hitting the stage. Soon his shirt was stained dark with sweat and beads ran from his short, blond sideburns down his jaws. The air in the room grew dense.

"Rest for a few minutes," Cal said to Matt and turned his attention to Alexandra, whose early movements revealed similar emotions but emphasized her refusal to look at Matt. "Let me see more tension in your body. Let me see the rage and frustration you're feeling." He adjusted her left elbow to a sharper angle and turned her head farther to the right. She danced the sequence he had given her and then danced it again as he watched. "Good. Good facial expression. But you have to count it, Alexandra."

"I *am* counting it."

"You are? Then why do you and Matt keep getting off from each other?"

"Because there's nothing to count to! There's no music, no beat to count against! I'm probably counting faster than he is—or slower maybe—I don't know!" She stopped, hearing how bitchy she sounded. She took a deep breath and, in a calmer voice, asked, "How are we supposed to count the same when there's only silence in here? We're not hearing the rhythm that's in your head. We need some kind of musical marker."

Cal popped the heel of one hand against his temple. "Of course! I'm sorry I didn't think of that before!" He turned to Matt, who squatted on his haunches, rubbing a towel against the back of his neck. "Will you go get a metronome—I'm pretty sure there's one in Studio D."

When Matt returned, Cal started the instrument to ticking and then adjusted it to match the tempo in his mind. "This will all be easier when the music finally arrives. Your patience will be rewarded."

Alexandra found her towel, where she'd left it draped over the barre, and wiped down her face, neck, and arms. Then she let her face rest in the towel. *What's wrong with me? I'm mad at Cal; I can't stand Katherine; even Matt seems like an idiot to me today.* She hung the towel over the wooden barre again, took another deep breath, and pulled her composure together to turn toward the others.

Metronome ticking, Cal asked them to dance the first scene straight through. "I won't interrupt, no matter what. I just want to see how we're doing on the minutes." He nodded toward the clock on the wall. "Do you remember all of it?"

They walked to their positions—Matt downstage right and Alexandra upstage left. "I guess we'll find out," Matt said.

He and Alexandra turned their backs to each other and tightened their bodies into rigid form.

"Begin on the count of five." Cal snapped his fingers in time with the rhythm of the ticking. "Two, three, four, *five.*" When they had run the sequence, he said, "So we need another twenty-five seconds for this scene." He raised his arm and wiped sweat from his forehead onto his shirtsleeve. "Katherine, you can go, if you want. I'll use the rest of the time today with Matt and Alexandra."

"If you don't mind, I'd like to stay and watch." She sat down against the wall, bundling her knees and ankles inside her loose-weave sweater.

Cal went to stand beside Matt, assuming his concluding position. "Going on." He stepped off into a new sequence, right hand raised and immediately becoming a fist. For another hour they worked together, with Cal constantly creating short sequences and then revising and correcting as he saw the motions translated on his dancers.

"Matt, I know it won't feel quite right, but you'll have to put your weight on your back foot there or else you won't be where you need to be for the next step. Let me show you." Again Cal demonstrated, and when Matt had done the movement correctly, he added, "But I don't want to hear the stomp. I just want to see it."

Finally at four o'clock Cal said, "We have to stop for today. It's looking great, kids." Matt reached down and pulled Alexandra to her feet, briefly embraced her, and kissed her wet forehead.

The next day, Cal began working with Alexandra and Matt on the partnering in scene 4, which brought in echoes of movement themes from scene 1. The first minute and a half of the scene continued the conflict and strife. "That's right, Matt, you have to let her foot come right up against your throat, almost smashing into your Adam's apple." For just a moment, the look on Matt's face broke the tension of the session by causing the other three to laugh, but Cal returned at once to the work at hand. "Alexandra, go a little bigger on the *assemblé*." But when she focused on the leap, which came halfway through the scene, her timing was thrown off. "You have to be there by three, Alexandra. Begin standing on two and be there by three. And squeeze all you can out of that jump."

In the story of the scene, each dancer reached out to the other, attempting reconciliation that ended unsuccessfully. "When she's there on her knees, Matt, and you reach down to her, keep your hand in a fist. You thrust your arm down and hook your fist over her shoulder, like this." He demonstrated and watched again. "Let's work on that release. What you want to do, Matt, is grasp her, and then we want it to look as though you are literally throwing her out away from you." The tired, dripping wet dancers ran the scene again. "That's better. Do it again."

* * *

After one of these grueling rehearsals, Alexandra, feeling wound tight, threw on a shawl and took a can of grapefruit juice from her ballet kit. Then she ran for the stairwell door and down the steps to her basement retreat. The heavy door creaked as she opened it, and the cool, musty smell was like a welcoming embrace. She breathed it in, not caring that her deep breath assuredly sucked in ancient dust. By now she could ignore the light switch, preferring to feel her way to the couch as her eyes adjusted to the dimness of the large room. Faint, murky light came in toward the back, probably through a basement window that had not been cleaned in decades. The pale light diffused over the odd shapes and draped forms in the room. Against a wall, under the red glow of an emergency exit sign, sat the old couch, now with one of her blankets folded at an end. She sat down and pulled the blanket over her legs, bunching it at her calves, and then took a few minutes to quiet herself. All in the world she wanted now was the bliss of peace that she knew was possible in meditation.

But no sooner had she begun to repeat her mantra than her mind was again drawn away into thoughts and memories and pictures. It was as though her meditation sessions had become a time to process whatever was upsetting in her life. Again and again she tried to keep herself easy in her mantra, only to find, after lapses of several minutes at a time, that her mind had been off tending to other things. Then—her body knowing before her mind—the hair on the back of her neck rose with awareness. *Oh my God, I'm not alone in here!* Full consciousness slammed back into her mind, bringing her instantly alert and dizzy. Her eyes flew open, but all she saw in the dim light was the pile of old furniture a couple of yards away. Her stomach reacted with a sharp twist. She stopped breathing to listen but could hear nothing but the banging of her heart. Her eyes darted to the left: nothing but the usual dusty sets, descending away into the darkness of the corners. There! To the right! A pair of eyes looking at her! Despite the iciness that spilled through her insides, she threw up a hand to the light switch by the emergency door and flipped it on.

With a startled yowl, an orange striped cat turned swiftly, jumped down from a sawhorse, and fled.

Nauseated now from the sudden spurt of adrenaline and return to alert consciousness, Alexandra looked at her watch. Seven minutes remained of her session. She held her head in her hands for a moment. Closing her eyes, she slowed her breathing and brought her mantra back to mind. After a few minutes, her stomach grew calm, but despite the steady underlayer of the mantra, her mind went tripping off pell-mell. *Mother's birthday's coming. Wouldn't it be nice to fly her out to San Francisco for opening night.* Then on its heels: *why would I have a thought like that?* Irritation returned with her rise out of the meditation session. *Why am I thinking about my family at all when I'm supposed to be meditating!* Alexandra did not take the full two minutes of rest she was supposed to take but instead refolded her blanket quickly and ran to the stairway that returned her to the active world. Moving directly to the telephone that all the dancers used for local calls, she dialed the number of her transcendental meditation coach and asked for a private consultation—as soon as possible!

* * *

That evening, Alexandra opened the door of the TM Center and stood waiting. "Hello?"

"Oh, you're here!" Janna called back. "Have a seat in the main room. I'll be right down."

She found a dozen chairs set up, their order disrupted into odd angles by the recent departure of Janna's evening meditation group. The air in the room smelled used, and Alexandra went to the window to let in some freshness.

"You're right on time!" A bit breathlessly, Janna entered the room.

"Well, I appreciated your agreeing to see me on short notice like this."

"Let's sit down and talk about it." She pulled a couple of chairs to one side, positioning them to face each other. "What's happening with your meditation?"

"It's driving me crazy—that's what's happening. I sit down to meditate, and all I do is think about this and think about that, and I start remembering this thing that happened years ago, and then I'm off remembering that thing. And worst of all, I get into these insane jealousies about other dancers that I haven't had for years, and I can't get my mind off them! I can't seem to stay on track."

Janna had been nodding through the entire recitation. "But you *are* on track as long as you're not trying to control and direct it all. If you're having thoughts, just remember that that's how TM releases stress that you've stored down there inside you probably for years. In your case, it sounds like some of this stuff has been down there for a decade."

"But I thought the goal was a quiet mind."

Janna's blonde hair swung when she nodded. "But you're not going to get a quiet mind by trying to command it or by trying to control and direct your meditation. You get to it by letting the meditation release stress in its own way."

Alexandra closed her eyes and put her head back. "Okay. I mean, it sounds like you don't think this is something I should be so worried about."

"No. It sounds to me like part of the normal process. The key is not to give up and stop just because it gets uncomfortable. Look, why don't we go ahead and meditate together for about ten minutes. I'll keep track of the time. Let's see how you feel at the end of it."

Maybe it was Janna's presence or just having a master meditator in charge. By the end of the short session, Alexandra had come to the peace she had craved all day. She felt light, almost pure. Janna encouraged her to continue what she was already doing, twice a day, twenty minutes for each session, and not to fight whatever came up for her.

Alexandra said good night to Janna, but as she turned from the door to the street, into her mind flashed a scene from the ballet session with Matt and Cal. *Maybe it's not just the meditation that's causing all this emotional upheaval. Maybe it's this new ballet.* The thought resonated inside her. *Maybe I am turning into the woman I am dancing—every negative emotion possible coming to the surface.* From the peaceful place her heart had finally reached, she began to think about Katherine and realized that peace had taken the edge off the jealousy. *I wonder if Matt and Katherine are being affected by this too.*

* * *

Evana awoke to find sunshine blasting into the bedroom, coming at her from a side of the room where there were no windows. The confusion frightened her, until she realized that she lay crooked across the bed, her head nearly hanging over the side. She was fully clothed except for shoes and her feet were entangled in a green blanket near the pillows, which were still folded inside the bedspread.

Wonder what day it is. She had arranged to have two weeks off from her lectures at the university, and it must be nearly two weeks by now that she'd been at the cottage. A cold thought gripped her: *What if I've gone over time? What if it's Monday and I'm due back at the school?*

She scrambled off the bed, tripping in the green blanket that was twisted around her left ankle. With the blanket trailing like a demoted veil, she moved to the main room to stare at the wall calendar. Then she blinked and swore. "What the hell good is a calendar that doesn't tell you what day it is—only what all the possibilities are? I *know* it could be the nineteenth or twentieth or the twenty-first or the twenty-second. Or even the twenty-seventh. What I want to know is *which* one of those it is!"

She looked at her watch. It was five to ten. "That helps me a lot. I've located myself in time at five to ten."

Evana went to the sink and poured a glass of water to give herself time to think. Then she filled the kettle and set it on the burner to heat for coffee. Finishing her glass of water, she went to the telephone and dialed her office in San Francisco.

"Mrs. Arthur's office," said a child's voice.

"Teresa, what day is this?"

"Oh, hi, Mrs. Arthur. Um, it's Friday, the twentieth . . . of August . . . 199—"

"Okay, okay. Teresa, is it this coming Monday that I'm due back there?"

Teresa was silent a moment, confused. "Yes, Mrs. Arthur. Don't you remember? You have the first lecture at nine thirty, another at eleven thirty, and a staff meeting at three thirty, plus the private lessons. Then on Tuesday, you have—"

"Okay, Teresa. I just was confirming about Monday. I'll see you then."

"Don't you want your messages?"

"No!" Evana hung up. "Better overeager than undereager, I suppose." Evana knew the child was grateful to her, and for the entire six months that they had worked together, she had kept expecting the gratitude to wear off. It never did.

So relieved was Evana to know that she was not overdue at the university, that in fact she had the whole weekend before returning, she decided to luxuriate in a large breakfast. Why, she actually had three days, since it was only ten in the morning on Friday. Despite herself, she glanced again and again toward the piano as she prepared the food. It seemed haloed by the sun coming in, reflected off the ocean, but she knew it was more than that. She felt good about the work accomplished, the short score she'd developed, sitting at that piano, playing those keys. The new composition was perhaps the best thing she'd ever done, and the neat stack of sketch sheets seemed to glow. It was as though the piano itself had given her the gift of its collaboration, and she was pleased just to be in the same room with it. *I'm getting carried away here.* But the hard part was done, she was sure; what was left to do hardly fell into the category of work at all. She would be ready to give Cal a large section on tape on Monday and probably the rest by Wednesday, along with sheet music for the accompanist. After that, it was a matter of clarifying the two-part arrangement, last-minute revisions, supervising Cal's people on the interpretation, perhaps helping to select the musicians.

Having eaten and washed her dishes, including those that had accumulated during the previous days and nights, Evana turned with satisfaction to her sketch sheets. She sat down at the piano and began to play the whole thing through. By the second sheet, however, a slight frown had begun to form across her forehead. She kept going. She wanted to hear the whole thing. In the middle of the third sheet, she winced and tucked her lower lip between her teeth, but again she continued. Before reaching the fifth sheet though, Evana pulled her hands from the keyboard and let them drop into her lap. It was dreadful! It was appalling. The music she had written—that she had thought was so good, perhaps her finest work ever—was terrible! There was no way she could give this to Cal. Her face suddenly hot and flushed, she hoped that no one had passed the cottage on the beach and heard her playing this mess. *What in the hell have I been doing?* At the moment, she wasn't sure that any of this material was salvageable.

It was not a good time for the phone to ring. It was an especially bad time for the caller to be Cal.

"What are you doing calling me?" There was none of her usual fire; a close listener might have identified her tone as meek.

"We had such a nice chat the last time I called I decided to check in again."

"This . . . this is not—can I call you back, Calvin . . . sometime?"

"I just wanted to tell you that we're progressing on the choreography. The piece you sent gave us a good idea of what you're doing with the music, and we're going ahead, just sticking as close to the libretto as we can. If you're doing the same thing—following the libretto, I mean—we should be fine. I'll be able to make what we're doing fit what you've done once we get the music."

Evana took a breath. "I don't think this is going to be possible, Calvin. There just isn't enough time—and . . . and maybe I'm not the right composer for this, in any case."

Cal paused. "How about if you send me another tape of what you have, and we'll keep going on this end. You're probably just overdue for a rest again—"

"I've just had a rest! That's why I know this isn't going to work! I've worked on this goddamned thing for two weeks, and this morning I get up and try to play it through and I finally have to quit because it's just shit! Is that what you want me to send you, Calvin? A bunch of shit disguised as music?"

"Please, Evana, my imagination—"

"Shit, shit, shit, shit! I can't believe this is what's been coming out of me when all this time I thought I was composing something your people could dance to!"

"Well, now, you know, that early section of the music might actually *need* to be a little bit rough, because that pretty much sums up how these two people are living their lives at that point, right? Evana?"

Evana didn't answer, and for some moments the line was silent. "I think we'd better forget this, Calvin. Use something from your rep."

Numbness paralyzed Cal's hands. "Listen, I'll call you again tomorrow. You'll feel better about—"

Evana broke the connection and laid the receiver on the desk, letting the dial tone waste itself into the room. Long before the phone began its *subito crescendo*, leading up to the indignant recording—"If you would like to make a call . . ."—Evana was out of the cottage, hurrying out to the refuge of the beach.

* * *

Cal sat staring at the receiver. He wasn't surprised that Evana could hang up on him, but he was astonished beyond words that she could think of dropping the composition after she'd let him come to count on it, even make headway with the choreography. Absently he put the receiver into its cradle and sat forward to put his elbows on the desk, his hands at the sides of his face. There it came again, that churning in his head that sounded in his ears like the boiling of his own blood. No doctor was necessary to tell him that this was not a good sign. He let his face fall forward into his hands, taking deep breaths, eyes closed. "I'll deal with it," he whispered. "I'll find a way to deal with it. I'll find a way."

Eventually the churning abated, taking with it the tightness around his hairline and inside his ears. He opened his left drawer and rummaged through the papers until he came to Rob's list of thirty-minute ballets in the company's repertoire.

Systematically he went through the list, jotting notes about what each piece required in terms of dancers, sets, and costumes. In a couple of cases, the sets had been appropriated and altered for other ballets and would have to be rebuilt. Those he crossed off the list. Three of the ballets required set materials that would have to be special-ordered from New York, and since there wasn't time now to be certain of receipt, he crossed those off the list. The costumes for another ballet were on loan; he drew a line through that one. Another was eliminated because it required special permission, under contract, with the choreographer. Three had themes and styles too much like other pieces already slated for the October program, so they were crossed off. Another was scratched because he had always meant to change the costumes and there wasn't time to have them all redesigned and sewn up. Four more were quickly lined through because—well, he just had no interest in doing them.

He ended up with five that might be remounted in the time available with a minimum of confusion and pain for all persons concerned. Then he reached over to the bulletin board and pulled down the list of three works already in rehearsal and preparation. His mouth drew to one side, then the other, as he considered the list and how the ballets would look on stage. *At least we have a US premiere—that's not so bad.* Then he closed his eyes. "Not so bad! Just the kind of summation a ballet company director wants to have about the first series of a new season." Cal rubbed his forehead and temples and then got up and walked down the hall to Studio E. Instead of entering the room, where Amelie was conducting a rehearsal for six corps members, he stood outside at a window and watched. The double-paned window and soundproof walls muted the music and Amelie's shouted instructions. His main sensory impression was the sight of dancers in motion.

Maybe we can go ahead and finish it and just perform it without music. It would be a matter simply of continuing what they were already doing: sticking close to the libretto, choreographing the themes, without musical cues or any substructure of sound. Other companies had done pieces in silence.

Yeah, silence—except for the sounds of toe boxes hitting the floor and the squeaking and squawking of rosin. Pretty undesirable distractions. And wasn't it funny how even he, when watching a soundless dance piece, had been distracted by the heaving chests of the laboring dancers—something he rarely noticed when there was music behind the movements.

Well, then, how about doing it barefoot? No rosin, no toe boxes. But he didn't even need to think about that. It was impossible to consider having his Spirit of Prayer *sans pointe*.

That afternoon he worked with Alexandra, choreographing the movements of conflict and strife that were principally within herself in the role. Matt and Katherine stood at the side of the room, leaning against the barre, watching. Judy, having no music to work with, had stopped attending the sessions.

"Good use of the face. You're doing a fine job of making me believe." Cal had noticed that Alexandra approached every session as if it were a performance, giving everything she had to give. Even in rehearsals of finished ballets, she rarely marked steps but endeavored to dance every motion at performance pitch. He didn't recall that she had done that in previous years, and he wondered where she got the energy to do it now.

Back in his office, Cal stared at the calendar. He had forty-five days till opening night. Forty-five days, and it looked as though—in terms of music—he was right back where he started when he had sixty-three days. He'd lost more than two weeks because of Evana. Anger flared up in him again at the thought that Evana could leave him in the lurch like this. He rubbed one hand down over his face and then sat with his hand covering his mouth, waiting for some thought to come to his mind. But none did. For two days now, and half of the third, he'd been choreographing without music, and even though he felt that the choreography was coming together, the finished work would be seriously diminished without music. It would not have near the impact. He shook his head as the decision crystallized: he would rather not do it at all than have it come off so flat.

Again, he pulled from his drawer the list of thirty-minute rep works, now rumpled and annotated. It took him a couple of seconds to reorient himself in the scratchings and find the five pieces that he had thought might be possibilities. He read their titles, then read them again, pictured how they looked on stage, then sighed: yes, they could be done, any one of them, but he could muster no enthusiasm for them. He was left with the third option: no fourth piece for the October program. Just go with the three already in preparation and ignore the fact that the evening would be a bit short. Maybe they could do longer intermissions. *Maybe we could offer short appearances by two or three dancers in costume in the lobby during intermissions.* He dismissed that thought immediately as unfair to the dancers and disillusioning to the audience. It was unthinkable to ask that of a dancer about to go on stage, and a dancer who's just finished a performance would not want to appear in a sopping wet costume in close proximity to members of the audience. For balletomanes, part of the mystique and romance of ballet was that it appeared to be completely effortless—a myth that would be dispelled at the sight of winded, sweating, often limping dancers at the conclusion of a difficult piece.

I sound desperate. He again crammed the list of thirty-minute ballets back into the drawer. *Hell, I am desperate. I'm going insane with this.*

* * *

That night in his dark bedroom, with Miss Agnus already snoring at the foot of the bed, Cal lay on his back with all three of his unattractive options swimming through his brain. He'd reviewed them over and over, and none of them was acceptable. Finally, as he was falling asleep from exhaustion, he dreamed that he heard himself say, "Okay, I need help with this. What do you want me to do?" And as if to torment him further, the whisper came:

We are making a dance and the theme is prayer.

In the anguish of his dream, he had thrashed and flailed as though caught in a large trap.

At four thirty in the morning, he awoke, feeling that no time had passed, that he had only dozed for a few seconds. What sat in his mind was the airbill from the package Evana had sent him earlier in the week. As though the sheet of thin pink paper floated in the air above his bed, he could see the telephone number—and an address! Cap's Landing, Oregon.

He jostled the bed in his eagerness to get out of it, and Miss Agnus growled softly as if to say, "What's wrong with you—it's still night."

"We have to get moving, Aggie. I need to get gas in the car and we'll need a map of Oregon."

Miss Agnus yawned so hard she squeaked.

"Breakfast? Did you ask about breakfast? Well, I thought we'd swing through McDonald's and get a bacon, egg, and cheese biscuit for me and dog biscuits for you. That way we can eat on the road. Okay?"

He picked her up, petted her tiny head, and rubbed his index finger up and down her nose, which was barely larger than his fingertip. Her dark eyes stared up at him.

"All right, all right. You drive a tough bargain. I suppose you can have some of my bacon, egg, and cheese biscuit, but you'll have to run off the fat on the beach." Leaving the bedroom, he spirited her through her dog door to do her business outside while he did his in the bathroom.

The sky was beginning to lighten when Cal unlocked the ballet company door to leave a note for Rob, asking him to cover the day's class and rehearsals. Back in the car, Cal opted for Interstate 5, thinking it would allow them to make better speed than the coastal highway. He gave Miss Agnus almost all of the bacon from his bacon, egg, and cheese biscuit, which she consumed on the passenger-side floor mat, leaving only little circles of wetness where she had daintily licked up every crumb. Right after breakfast, Miss Agnus settled down on top of Cal's jacket in the passenger seat and went back to sleep. For the next three hours, she slept peacefully except for two occasions when first a car horn and, second, the rushing sound of oversized truck tires brought her awake and on her feet barking. Each time, Cal reached over to pet her soft fur and encourage her to lie down again. By noon she was sitting up, still on Cal's jacket, nodding as she maintained balance in the moving vehicle, her eyes glazed by the continuous hum of the car and her limited view.

They stopped once for food and gas and twice to stretch their legs. At two thirty in the afternoon, they reached the city limits of Eugene, Oregon, where they got gas again and turned left on Route 126 to the ocean.

It had not occurred to Cal that he might have trouble finding the address, but once he reached the small village, from which seaside houses, A-frames, and small cottages spread forth at irregular intervals up and down the beach, often down obscure sandy lanes, he realized that it might not be so easy. Putting Miss Agnus on a leash so she could get some exercise but not be tempted to run too far from him, he walked down the single street of the small town, considering the café, boat repair shop, gasoline station, church, and combination grocery and hardware store. Every structure had the same gray, weather-beaten look. What trees there were had been driven into odd shapes by the ocean winds.

A bell clanged over his head as he went into the store.

"Yup!" The man at the counter greeted him, standing straight and turning from where he had been bent over a newspaper. His unshaven cheeks and briskly cropped hair were both gray. "What can I do for you, young man?"

Cal smiled back, thinking perhaps the other man *was* old enough to be his father. "I'm looking for a friend of mine who's staying in one of the houses along here. She's a composer. Her name is Evana Arthur."

The storekeeper stared at him. "Cute little dog ya got there."

"Thanks."

"Arthur, huh? Don't know any Evana Arthur. That what you said? Evana? Kind of a queer name, ain't it?"

Cal shrugged and waited.

"But now, I do know a *Frank* Arthur. Least I did. Dead a long time now. His family still has a cottage on the beach here. I see his daughter every now and then, but her name is—let's see, I believe her name is Martha. She's been in a couple of times lately." He thought some more. "Nope. Don't know any Evana Arthur."

"Maybe you'd point me toward the cottage? Sounds like it's worth a try."

The storekeeper was still lost in his own thoughts. "Now Frank Arthur was a musician, if I remember right." He thought some more, his eyes looking off toward some memory. "Yeah, yeah, that's what he was, all right. Kept a piano at his cottage and used to play all the time."

"That sounds like the place."

"Well, it's down the beach quite a ways. You could take the road, but you'd probably miss the driveway. It's not marked. You and your dog probably want to just walk down the beach. Close to a mile probably. Look for a cottage with a deck on the front of it. About as close to the tideline as they get."

They set out walking, opting quickly for the wetter, better packed sand closer to the water's edge. Exacting her solemn promise that she would come when he called her, Cal released Miss Agnus from her leash, and she began to run at her top speed, barely leaving tracks. Every beach-bound log drew her up short to sniff and explore. Seaweed was a particular mystery, as were recently broken crab shells. Anything especially interesting got urinated on. Again and again, Miss Agnus ran close to the water's edge and stared as it came racing toward her on a thousand tiny toes. She barked at it, raced off, and returned to challenge it again. The grin on her face was unmistakable, and every time she came running toward Cal, her face was a tiny red/gold orb, apparently earless, of three black dots amid slicked-back hair.

Cal kept his gaze on the land and the near-water houses as they walked along. Any cottage set back from the sandy shore was ignored. Cottages not fully visible were given only a second glance, and that was only to make sure there was no front deck. Full-blown houses and other large structures were also passed over.

As it turned out, he heard the music before he saw the cottage. He stopped in his tracks upon hearing the piano, and now he moved closer, careful to avoid coming in view of any windows. After some minutes, he looked around for something to sit on, found a log, and sat facing the cottage. He listened to the labor, listened to the corrections, listened to the starts and stops, heard what he thought might have been Evana cursing. But finally it began to come, and he was sure that what he was hearing was Matt's solo—the "lost" Matt, given over to his isolation and misery.

Miss Agnus continued to run and explore, never quite out of sight of Cal and returning every few minutes to his side. At last, panting hard, she trotted up beside him and plopped down with her belly on top of her leash.

Having listened to the fits of music for perhaps an hour, Cal got to his feet and began to create Matt's first solo. When Evana started again, so did he, over and over. Despite the jeans he wore, he traveled in Matt's *glissades en arrière*, struck positions and balances, leapt in Matt's *jetés*, and explored ways to use aberrations of the prayer gesture to express dispirited agony. It took a couple of seconds to realize that the music had stopped. At that moment, he swung his head toward the cottage and saw that he was within view of the large picture window—where Evana stood staring at him.

Each of them was frozen in place. Evana was the first to move. In the next instant, the cottage door sprang open, and then Evana's mouth sprang open too, but before she could speak, he called out, flinging out both arms for emphasis, "No! No! Go back to the piano and play that again before you lose it. It's perfect, Evana. You have to write it down. It's perfect!"

Evana's mouth closed, but she stood looking at him for some moments longer before she turned back inside, leaving the door standing open—which he chose to see as an invitation for him to follow. She was seated at the piano, erasing and rewriting notes as he entered the cottage.

"That's for Matt's first solo, isn't it?"

"Who's Matt?" Her head was bent toward her sketch sheet.

"The male dancer. In the libretto."

"Yes, that's what it is." She turned now on the piano bench to look at him. "What are you doing here?"

He was suddenly struck by the absurdity—that he could have made such a long drive, hours and hours on the highway, without having once asked himself that question. He looked to the left, where wadded sheets of paper extended from the foot of the piano all the way to the picture window; he looked to the right and saw dirty dishes stacked on the floor. "I-I guess I came to talk you out of dropping the composition."

Evana drew a deep breath and let out a long sigh. "I didn't drop the composition."

"I can see that. But you said on the phone—"

She looked at him with a tired expression. "This is just one reason why I didn't want you to have my phone number. In the last two weeks I've decided a hundred different times to cancel out on you, and a hundred different times that I couldn't do that, that I had to produce *something* for you." She shrugged and turned back to the piano. "You caught me in the middle of the process."

Cal dropped his gaze to the floor at his feet, but before he could speak, she turned back toward him. "Do you mean to say that in your choreography you don't come to places where you think, 'This can't be done,' and you throw up your hands and quit—just for the moment?"

Surprised, Cal met her eyes across the room. He wanted to be sure before he answered. "No. No, I always know there's a way, somehow, to do it. I always know I'll find a way."

She stared back and then snorted, "Well, aren't you lucky?" There was a scratch at the door then, followed by a tiny whimper. "What the hell?"

Cal was already turning to let in Miss Agnus. "Oh, it's my—" He reached down to pick up the Pomeranian and turned back to find Evana on her feet, her eyes and mouth open wide.

Her voice traveled upward half an octave: "You brought a *dog* here?"

Cal scooped Miss Agnus into his arms as if to protect her from Evana. "She's just a little dog, Evana. She doesn't make any trouble."

Evana brought her mouth closed by apparent effort and then opened it again. "You'll have to keep it outside or in your car—it can't be in here."

Cal looked at Evana for a long moment. "I'll just fasten her leash to the deck out here. She'll be all right for a while on the porch."

When he came back into the cottage, Evana was seated at the piano, her back to him. She played a short section, then played it again, then stretched the fingers of her right hand to play a major seventh, then tried the minor seventh, compared that to a perfect octave, played the minor seventh again with the left-hand notes added in. Then apparently accepting the discordant interval, she jotted notes onto the sketch sheet in front of her and returned to the keyboard to play another short section. The look of concentration on her face was absolute.

The baby grand piano took up most of the room, but a sofa separated it from the kitchen area, and squeezed against the inner wall was an electronic setup consisting of two keyboards and a box with a mass of buttons and dials. Cords connected the three pieces to each other, and the stool at one keyboard was pulled out for ready use. Despite an itch in Cal's fingers to touch the keys and hear what the setup could do, he was unwilling to disturb Evana.

He glanced out toward the deck and was relieved to see that Miss Agnus had settled down on her stomach with her head resting on her front paws. She was probably napping after her long romp on the beach. Then he looked toward the sink and thought about how much he'd like a drink of water. Probably Miss Agnus could use one too. It seemed apparent that Evana intended to ignore him until he went away, and he wondered if maybe that wouldn't be the best plan, since she *was* working on the composition. Of course he had no idea where he could go, around here. It was already evening, and what he was really thinking about was food. He looked out at Miss Agnus again and saw that the sun hung low over the ocean, casting the beginnings of a golden patina around the edges of everything it touched.

Grabbing a glass from the shelf he ran water from the tap, noticing that Evana appeared to have forgotten his presence. He drank the water and ran another glassful, which he carried to the deck and poured slowly into his palm for Miss Agnus to drink. She rose to her feet and stretched her back legs out straight behind her, one at a time, and then dipped her tongue into his palm to lap. Leaving the glass on the deck by the door, he unfastened the leash and walked with Miss Agnus to the rear of the cottage and then headed up the road toward the village, glancing behind him to memorize landmarks. At the village, he put the dog into the car and went into the store.

"Find what you were looking for?"

"Yes, and thanks for the directions. You don't carry fresh meat and produce here, do you?"

"The meat was fresh when they froze it, I reckon. Sure, I got steaks, lots of good cuts, and as much fresh produce as you could want as long as you want lettuce, tomatoes, and apples. Got some mushrooms in a couple days ago that are pretty good."

Cal went to look at the mushrooms, decided they were passable, and began to consider his small repertory of familiar recipes. He scooped up a sackful of the mushrooms, added an onion and some garlic cloves, and took them to the counter. Next he chose a pound of frozen beef sirloin and found a can of beef broth and another of tomato paste to add to the pile.

"You don't carry sour cream, do you?" He knew that the gray-haired man had watched his progression around the store.

"Yep. Dairy's right back yonder." He stood straight briefly to point toward the rear of the store.

Cal chose a cup of sour cream and grabbed a stick of butter. At the counter, he stood looking at the supplies, wondering what he was forgetting.

The store owner looked them over too. "What ya making?"

"Stroganoff."

"Ya got noodles?"

"Noodles!"

"Back there." A straight arm pointed toward one of the wood-floor aisles, where the walkway was as tilted as a raked stage, and Cal hurried along the short row of shelves until he came to the pasta section: two bags of noodles, three bags of spaghetti, and two boxes of macaroni and cheese mix. He took one bag of noodles. On the way back to the counter, he passed a half-dozen cans of dog food and picked up two small ones. He also grabbed a bag of rolls.

"Ya got flour?"

"Oh, surely she's got flour." Then Cal wavered. "Everybody's got flour, don't you think?"

The old man shrugged. "No telling how old it is."

"Well, it doesn't take but just a little bit of flour."

Another thoughtful nod. "Could be someone bought flour to make a cake back in 1970, and that's the flour you're planning to use for your stroganoff."

Cal's gaze swung toward the shelves of canned and packaged goods. The pointing arm came up again into view. "Back there."

The sky was beginning to darken as Cal drove the short distance from the store back to Evana's cottage. He heard the piano as he pulled into her driveway. Leaving Miss Agnus in the car, he took the sack of groceries to the door and knocked three times before Evana left the piano and came to glare at the intrusion.

"How about if I make us dinner?" He held up the sack. "That way you can go right on working."

By way of an answer, she left the door standing open when she turned her back and returned to the piano.

As he thawed the meat in the microwave, Cal picked up the dishes from the floor beside the piano, washed them, and set the table with them. Outside, he fed Miss Agnus beside the car and then carried her into the cottage, gave her a hug, and set her on the rug by the deck door. "Stay!" He reinforced the verbal command by holding his flat palm in front of her face.

Evana's tortuous process of composition continued as Cal made the meal. She could not have avoided seeing Miss Agnus when she came to the table, but she sat down without comment and allowed Cal to serve her stroganoff. As they ate, the Pomeranian remained on the rug by the door, and only Cal knew that she was performing her best begging behavior, sitting with ears up smartly and eyes so intent she was almost squinting.

"Do you ever use that setup on the side there?"

"Of course I use it."

Cal ignored her brusque tone, determined to have a pleasant conversation with dinner. He was sure that the home-cooked food would mellow her mood. "Are you still planning to use electronic sound in the new piece?"

Evana nodded but took another mouthful of stroganoff and chewed it thoroughly before continuing. "I had to make a trip to Portland to upgrade the sequencer."

"But you still compose at the piano, I notice. Why not on the keyboards and that electronic gear over there?"

"There aren't any distractions at the piano." She took another bite of noodles and beef and chased it with a roll.

"Miss Agnus has been very well trained. Watch this." He looked past [Eva]na toward the dog. "Miss Agnus, come!"

The tiny dog got to her feet and trotted to Cal's chair.

"Sit!"

The little red/gold haunches hit the floor. Soft-furred front paws [plant]ed, Miss Agnus stared up at him.

Cal offered her the bite of meat. Instead of wolfing it down, she [sniff]ed it before daintily opening her mouth to receive the bite. When she finished, she remained sitting, her eyes on Cal.

"Down, Miss Agnus." He pointed an index finger toward the floor.

Miss Agnus collapsed to her stomach, watched Cal a moment longer, then put her head on her paws and regarded with upraised eyes first [Eva]na, then Cal, then Evana, then Cal again. As she looked from one to [the] other, what appeared to be tiny soft eyebrows raised in turn.

Evana, Cal noticed, had not taken her eyes off the dog. Finally, with [wha]t sounded like a satisfied sigh, she rose from the table and returned to [the] piano. Cal stored the remainder of the stroganoff in the refrigerator [and] washed up the dishes again, all the while seeing in his mind the [step]s and movements Matt and Alexandra could do to the music Evana [was] creating behind him. Sometimes she stopped playing and apparently [liste]ned to the music in her mind, murmuring short sketches that [sou]nded like "ya ta ta da ta ta da" as it came to him from across the [roo]m. After a series of these murmurs, she said to him, "I imagine you're [tire]d. Better take the bedroom because I'll be at this a while yet."

Cal squelched his impulse to refuse the offer of the bed. Since the [sofa] was only a few feet from the piano, he was sure he couldn't get to [slee]p with her working so close, and he was in no shape to get into the car [and] try to find somewhere else to sleep. "If you're sure."

"I'm sure. Most nights I just take catnaps on the sofa in here anyway."

"Uh, Miss Agnus usually—"

Finally she swiveled to look at Cal and then at the dog, which still [lay] where he had ordered with his "down" command. In a slow drawl, she [sai]d, "Don't tell me you and the dog sleep together!"

"That way I can make sure she doesn't disturb you."

Evana thought this over. "I guess you'll be responsible for her."

"Completely."

Evana turned back to the piano and went back to work. After a moment, [Ca]l picked up Miss Agnus and her leash, and the two of them set off down

Cal pushed ahead. "But I thought that the poi[nt] gear was the ease of composing and putting together composition."

She shook her head. "Not for me. The piano is l[ike] me, and I can hear what I'm doing more efficiently. On[ce] worked out the way I want them, then I put them on the I can add in the parts, harmonics if I want that, all kin[ds] when I can pay attention to all those connections and dia[

"How did you get involved with this electronic teaching that at the university, are you?"

Just as he had hoped, Evana's mood had softened. "[I had] private instruction in it, but I'm not doing it. The ke[y was] to my husband's brother. You may have heard of hi[m]. Anyway, he was one of the early enthusiasts for electr[onics,] his own synthesizers. Of course it was not well accepte[d by] musicians, but he loved to come here and sit at those k[eyboards] with the sounds all night long."

"Private jam sessions."

She nodded. "He soon got his brother, Jack, and [me into] what he was doing. Jack was my husband. We were all e[xcited about] computers could do for music. So the three of us spent [especially in the early 1980s when there were suddenly instruments being made that would connect up with ea[ch other."]

"So the three of you composed music here?"

"We composed it, we arranged it into parts, we put layers of sound until we created entire orchestras playin[g. We could do high school bands playing Sousa marches and sound effects. There just didn't seem to be a limit t[o what we could] do with that equipment."

"Sounds like those were the days."

She nodded again, but her expression grew somber[. Her] eyes made the cheekbones seem more prominent.

Finished eating, Cal saw that Evana had noticed the on his plate. "That's for Miss Agnus."

"Who?"

He tipped his head toward the small dog sitting patien[tly]. "I always save the last bite for her."

Evana looked at the Pomeranian. "Seems pretty well b[

the steps of the deck and onto the beach, where the air was cool and fresh after the warmth of the cottage. The moonlight was almost nonexistent, but what there was cast an irregular silvery sheen on the incessant motion of the ocean. No one else was out walking as far up and down the beach as he could see, but a hundred yards farther on, Miss Agnus barked once at a dark form that he'd taken to be a stump but which now moved and spoke and turned out to be a young couple sitting embraced with their backs against a log. Finally Miss Agnus found a tangled mass of seaweed suitable for relieving herself, and then they headed back to the cottage.

In the bedroom, Cal spread one blanket on top of Evana's bed to sleep on and pulled a second blanket up over himself, placing Miss Agnus on her back near his feet. He scratched her stomach for some minutes and told her what a good girl she was, and then he lay back and fell asleep listening to the piano.

* * *

In the morning, the cottage was quiet. Cal was still on his back, in the same position in which he'd settled down the night before, but Miss Agnus wasn't. After taking a few moments to remember where he was, he lifted his head to check on her, but she wasn't on the bed. Not worried yet, Cal sat up in the bed and looked all around the room. No Miss Agnus. He whispered her name and looked around the room again, but there was still no dog. Now Cal was on his feet. He rushed to the window, but it wasn't open wide enough for her to have squeezed through. Next he went around the bed, flipping up the skirt of the bedspread, but she wasn't hiding there. Abandoning the whisper, he called her name aloud. He tried the closets; he looked behind the dresser; he jerked back the bedsheets. No Miss Agnus. He yanked his pants on and then pulled open the bedroom door and went charging barefoot into the main room. There on the sofa Evana lay sleeping fully dressed, with one arm curled around Miss Agnus.

The dog lay perfectly still; she hadn't even lifted her head when Cal rushed into the room. But her eyes were turned toward him and the expression on her face told him, "Keep it down, will ya? People are sleeping in here."

For a few long moments Cal was completely at a loss as to what to do. He stood in his bare feet, looking from Miss Agnus to the front door best sounds for his new ballet. She had not played the sequencer to let him hear how the electronic harp sounded with the piano, and he was sure that she hadn't really intended to; she didn't want him to hear anything that she felt was not completely ready. He hesitated near the door but realized that she had already said her good-bye. He picked up Miss Agnus and eased the deck door shut behind them.

* * *

Six Weeks

Matt checked the bulletin board first thing, as usual, when he entered the studio on Wednesday morning. Anyone coming up from behind him would see that almost all traces of the initials at the back of his blond hair had been clipped away.

"Cancelled!" he said in surprise.

"What's cancelled?" Alexandra asked, joining him at the board, dropping her ballet bag at her feet.

He turned to her, a quick smile for hello. "Our session on the new piece this afternoon."

"Really? Well, I don't know about you, but I could use a break from that anyway."

"Yeah, I don't know which is worse: trying to learn a dance in silence or trying to do it with that metronome." They studied the big board for messages.

"It's more than that. This choreography is starting to affect my *life*, and not in such good ways. I've even started to dream about it."

Matt looked at her. "What do you mean?"

"I think it must be all these negative emotions we're dancing. Aren't you noticing any changes since we've been doing this?"

Matt shrugged. "Nothing like you seem to be talking about." He turned his attention to the lists of rehearsals on the bulletin board, finding his name and noting time slots and studio numbers.

"Wonder why it's cancelled though," Alexandra said.

"Maybe Cal's getting sick of this too."

"Maybe Cal's given up ever getting the music."

Matt nodded. "I've been wondering how far he's going to go with this, I mean trying to choreograph without music. Seems kind of—"

"Kind of stupid?"

Matt felt himself blink and hesitate. "I was going to say inefficient. I mean, if the music ever does come, we'll have to redo half of it. Seems like it's just going to result in a lot of confusion for everyone. And we have only, like, six weeks."

"I guess we'll muddle through," said Alexandra, turning toward the main rehearsal hall.

"Like always." He headed away from her, and then twenty feet down the hall, he turned back. "Hey! You want to go see Ricardo Vitale tonight? I think I can get us tickets."

Her dark brown hair swung out from her shoulders as she faced him, eyes wide and a grin on her mouth. "Sure! That would be great! He's in town guesting for the San Francisco Ballet, isn't he?"

"Yeah. They're opening their fall season tonight and he's the main draw. Brandon—remember him?—is a soloist now. I'm pretty sure he can get a couple of tickets into will call for me. They'll probably be second balcony, but at least we can see him."

"Sure, I'd love it. Where should I meet you?"

"I can pick you up. About seven, okay?"

"Okay."

* * *

It was a few minutes before seven when Matt rang the buzzer to Alexandra's apartment, but she had only to grab a shawl to finish getting ready. They crossed town with a minimum of traffic tie-ups and arrived at the will-call line ten minutes before curtain. The lobby of the War Memorial Opera House was a noisy circus of glittering ballet-goers eager for the midweek opening. Some of the women were in long gowns, some in short party dresses, some in slacks. Some looked as though they were about to attend a business meeting—and may well have come directly from the office. Most of the men were in ties and suits, with the occasional fellow in jeans and no socks. Mothers held the hands of young dancers who wore stiff dresses, patent leather shoes, and hair pulled back into buns. People hurried here and there in unmistakable excitement. Several stood just outside the door taking last puffs on cigarettes or glancing from their watches to the onrush of last-minute arrivers.

The seats Matt's friend had provided were, indeed, in the second balcony, so far to the side that upstage left was lost to view. Most of the people seated in this section were young families with children. He pulled a pair of opera glasses from his pocket. "I'll share these," he offered, but Alexandra pulled out her own miniature pair.

"I was hoping you'd bring your own, so *I* wouldn't have to share!"

Matt's friend Brandon danced in the first two pieces, and Ricardo Vitale appeared alone on stage just before the second intermission. The Italian dancer, on an eight-city tour of the United States, danced a long classical solo, full of *sautés, elances,* and *glissades*. He was like a foreign bird darting over the stage in *pas de basque elance,* and the set of his dark head made his *grand jeté en tournant* even more striking.

"That's some elevation," Alexandra whispered to Matt.

"He's stealing time from the prep steps so he can stay up longer," Matt whispered back. "Watch the next one, and you'll see."

They joined in the standing ovation when the Italian took his second bow, tucking their opera glasses under their arms as they rose from their seats clapping. The house lights came up for intermission and Matt said, "I'm going to see if I can find Brandon. He's done for the evening, and I want to catch him before he leaves. Want to come?"

"No, thanks. I'm going to get something to drink."

Matt was stopped by the stage manager as he approached backstage. "I'm sorry, sir." Despite the man's khaki pants and denim shirt, his English accent made him sound like a diplomat. "You can't come back just now. If you'll just wait until the end of the program."

Beyond the stage manager's shoulder, Matt saw several dancers dressed in a mix of street clothes and costumes, nearly all in stage makeup, amassed near Ricardo Vitale, who was bent over from the waist, breathing hard with his face in a towel. Two men in suits stood next to him, talking to each other.

"I was hoping to thank Brandon Wickem for the tickets he got for me for tonight," Matt explained, feeling formal despite himself in response to the Englishman.

"Maybe after the program, sir?"

Then Matt spotted Brandon among the dancers who were huddled close to Vitale, waiting for a chance to speak to him. "There he is! Wouldn't it be possible to just call him over here for a moment? I'm a dancer too. In Calvin Tropp's company."

The stage manager looked back toward the gathering uncertainly, and Matt took advantage of the opportunity to wave both arms over his head. Several of the San Francisco company dancers noticed, and just then Ricardo Vitale lifted his head from the towel. His dark eyes settled on Matt and held. Instantly Matt's heart struck his breastbone powerfully, and his breath caught in a gasp.

The Englishman's face showed instant concern. "Are you all right, sir?"

"Matt!" Brandon called, breaking from the group to come at a trot to the side. "What'd you think, man? Wasn't he *great*!"

Matt stared back into the dark eyes of the Italian, ten yards away, and could only mumble, "Yes, yes, he was."

Then Brandon grabbed Matt's shoulders and pulled him aside with a nod and a "Thanks, man" to the stage manager.

"Listen, we're having a party tonight at one of the dancers' houses, and we're going to try to get him to stop by. You want to come to it?"

Matt's eyes were drawn irresistibly back to the guest dancer, who had turned now to talk to the others. "Uh, I've got a friend with me."

"That's cool. Bring her too. Sheryl and I will be there. You got something to write on? I'll tell you where it's going to be."

Matt pulled out his ticket stub and an ink pen and wrote down the address.

"Hey," Brandon said. "Can you imagine how great that'd be if Vitale did show up?"

Matt nodded. "Thanks, Brandon, and thanks for the tickets too."

"No upstage left though, right?"

Matt shrugged. "That's no problem. I'd better get back—they'll be flashing those lights any minute now."

"See you at the party, man."

* * *

After-performance ballet parties typically progress just the opposite from standard parties. While the latter begin somewhat sedately, moving toward jubilation and frenzy with the increases in noise, familiarity, and substance levels, after-performance ballet parties begin at a high pitch of jubilation and frenzy and then often back down toward tranquility as performance highs wear off. As a result, since they were early to the party, once they found the right street, Matt and Alexandra had no difficulty locating the house where the party was. Music, laughter, and loud voices spilled out from the open front door and open windows despite the late hour. Inside, fresh-scrubbed, bright-eyed dancers hugged each other with enthusiasm, screamed congratulations to dancers across the room, eagerly scanned the table of food, loaded up their plates, and convened in groups to talk about the evening's performances.

Though the house was plenty large, the party spread to additional rooms as more and more people arrived. Moving toward the den for a place to sit down, Matt and Alexandra found Brandon and Sheryl.

"Hey, did you see him out there?" Brandon asked.

"No," Matt said.

"See who?" Alexandra asked.

"Vitale, who else!" Brandon frowned at Matt and then said to Alexandra, "I can't believe he didn't tell you! We invited Ricardo Vitale to come!"

"Wow! You mean he's here?"

"Not yet, but we're hoping. He's known to be quite a party guy, so he'll probably show up."

"No wonder this place is packed. At least the decibel level isn't so high in this room. Out there everyone is shouting."

They ate and shared dance stories, discussed diets and body aches, new dancers and old injuries for perhaps an hour, when the noise level from the living room suddenly subsided to near silence. "He must be here!" Brandon squealed. He and Matt were on their feet at once, rushing out of the den and leaving Sheryl and Alexandra to follow. Brandon babbled, "I can't believe it! I can't believe it! I'm so excited that he actually came!"

They rushed down the short hallway and found the living room twice as stuffed with people as it had been earlier. A neat semicircle of bodies had formed at the perimeter of the room, and in its cup stood Ricardo Vitale with one of the two suited men Matt had seen backstage. Vitale wore light gray slacks and a brown leather jacket as light and soft as his eyes were dark and blazing. He cast his smile in an arc that took in

With that Katherine turned her head away and eased into a deep stretch, folding her upper body until the side of her face touched the floor in front of her.

"Everyone seemed pretty impressed by him," Alexandra added, pressing into her own deep stretch. "Do you think we're *ever* going to get music for the *Prayer* ballet?"

"We'd better! I think the programs are already being printed." Katherine pulled upward now, her back straight and slim, only to slide back down until her other cheek touched the floor. Sitting straight, she wiped her face with the corner of a plush green towel draped around her neck.

Earlier that morning, during her meditation session, Alexandra had found herself thinking about Katherine and realized that the jealousy had receded. Into her mind dropped the idea:

Talk to her. Get to know her better.

She wasn't sure how much stock to put in ideas that came to her out of nowhere when she was meditating, but this one—like the one about flying her mother to San Francisco as a birthday present—just seemed right. She felt good, whole, light just thinking about it. "Well, I hope it all comes together in time."

"I'm sure it will. If he has to, Cal will reach into his little bag of miracles and pull out another one. I've seen him do it lots of times. You probably have too."

"Well, you've had a lot more years with him to see that than I have." This was by way of an apology, even if Katherine had no idea that one was in order. "Not to change the subject, but I'm thinking of sending my mother a plane ticket to come out for opening night."

Now Katherine interrupted her floor work. "That's a wonderful idea! She's back in New York, right?"

"Yes. It's for her birthday. We haven't seen each other in four years."

Katherine's blue eyes widened. "Four years! My God, I can't even imagine not seeing my mother for four years!"

"You two are really close, aren't you?"

Before Katherine could respond, Candace Bennington clapped her hands and called, "Okay, dancers. Let's have a go again." Candace had traveled to San Francisco from England to teach her father's choreography of "Angles and Intersections" to the company. "Let's have the gentlemen on stage, and we'll start with the entrance of the eight ladies. Everyone in place, please." Sixteen dancers scurried, crisscrossing the main rehearsal hall into proper places. Cal and Rob stood at one side of the room, watching.

Candace nodded to Judy, who began playing midscore. The women dancers entered one by one in rapid succession while the men pared a square formation into a triangle, but Candace clapped her hands. "No, no. The diagonal must be much steeper." She waved with a rigid forearm the angle she had in mind. "Much steeper. And you there in the braces," she called to the group of men, who looked in confusion at each other. "You in the red—" She looped her thumbs at her shoulders and looked in question toward Cal.

"Suspenders."

"Yes, you there in the red suspenders, you're anticipating the beat a bit. Count it more carefully. Precision is critical to this ballet."

Bradley Eaton ran his thumbs up and down the inner side of his suspenders, which he'd thought till now were a cool addition to his practice wardrobe.

"And make sure your braces are straight, Brad," Nick Taylor teased. The dancers who heard him grinned, but everyone was ready when Candace asked them to start the sequence over again. Cal moved in closer, and when Brad again slipped in his timing, Cal began dancing with the group, counting aloud for Brad to hear.

When the rehearsal broke for lunch, dancers hurried about, pulling on sweaters and leg warmers, leaving the large room in twos and threes. Katherine stayed behind to practice a section of "Angles," and Alexandra decided her sandwich could wait. She went to a position two paces from Katherine and picked up the movement, practicing along with her. Candace, Cal, Rob, and Judy formed a knot at the piano, and along one side of the room, two men stretched leg muscles at the barre. In another rehearsal studio down the hall, Amelie worked with ten dancers on a corps section of another ballet.

"I've decided to give up being jealous of those long legs of yours," Alexandra said.

Katherine looked at their reflections in the mirror and then smiled at Alexandra. "Then I guess I'd better give up being jealous of that perfectly proportioned body of yours."

The surprise on Alexandra's face caused both of them to laugh.

At four o'clock, Cal entered Studio C waving a cassette tape high above his head. "We've got music, people! We've got music!"

"You're kidding!" Alexandra said.

"Nope, and you're gonna love it!"

"In that case," Matt said, "we're chucking this!" He picked up the metronome, carried it to the trash basket by the door, and set the instrument into the can.

Alexandra clapped and Cal said, "Just don't forget to take that out of there later."

"We have *all* of the music?" Katherine asked.

"No, not all of it, but we have a big piece of it here, from the beginning, and for the first time I have faith that the rest of it will come."

Cal put the tape into the cassette player. "Let's just listen to it once or twice, then we'll see if we can fit the choreography into it." Finally, he turned to Alexandra and Matt. "Let's take a look at what we've got."

"For some reason, this makes me very nervous," Matt said.

Cal nodded. "You and me both." Once they were in position, he pushed the button on the cassette player, and Evana's music started. A rush of joy swept Cal as he watched his dancers step off perfectly and begin their first combinations. Perhaps eight bars of music had played before first Matt, then Alexandra, sneaked swift glances at Cal as the steps fumbled and bounced against the music.

"Keep going. I want a feel for just how off we are."

"Hello!" Matt said at one point when a phrase of choreography happened to end perfectly with a phrase of the music.

Cal watched with one hand at his chin and the other arm folded across his waist. When the two dancers reached the end of the choreographed material, they stood with mouths open to take in air, listening as the music continued. Cal shut off the sound, rewound the tape, and scratched at the top of his head. "It might be helpful to think of this as a conversation of sorts. Actually two conversations. First there's the one going on between you two, and that's pretty much an angry conversation early on, with hostile gestures, both yelling at once, so to speak, and no ability to hear what each other is saying. The second conversation is in the music, between the piano and what will be an electronic harp. That represents a conversation between the human plane and the spiritual plane, but in the first part of the score, the piano is so predominant that the harp won't be audible anyway."

He walked toward them. "My point is that these are two different and pretty much unrelated conversations at this stage in the ballet, so I don't think we *want* you with the music necessarily. The music tells us that you are trapped in the human plane with virtually no access to the spiritual element, and the dance tells us that on that human plane, you two get along about as well as trapped, enraged animals."

Matt was nodding. "So what you're saying is that we probably won't be changing much of the choreography up front."

"I know it's going to feel like you came to dance a tango and someone has switched the music to a polka. It just means you both will have to count carefully, and we may smooth out the phrasing here and there where it looks really awkward, but the movements you're making in this early part are not a representation or a pantomime of the music. You have a separate meaning to convey."

"Will the whole piece be like that?" Katherine asked. She was seated, back against the wall under the barre. Her light auburn hair was still damp from a rehearsal just prior to the choreography session, but she'd taken the time to change to dry clothes. The same green towel was draped around her neck, over a light blue leotard and black tights.

"No, as the music progresses, there's more of a balance between the human and spiritual planes, and the dancing will gradually reflect that growing harmony. And since you are pure spirit, Katherine, your steps will always fit closely with what the harp is doing."

Cal moved back toward the cassette player. "Let's go through it again from the beginning, as far as we have choreography."

Matt and Alexandra scrambled into position, rigid backs turned to each other, and Cal punched the start button. This time they weren't more than a minute into the music when they both lost the thread of the choreography, first Matt, then Alexandra. Since they were not dancing in coordination with the music, there were no musical references for their movements, and they were unable to pick up the steps a moment later. They stood, looking lost and confused, on a diagonal near the center of the rehearsal hall.

"But you just did it!" Cal said.

"I know. I'm sorry. I can't remember what comes next," Matt said.

"Alexandra, you too?" Cal said in disbelief.

Her voice sounded muffled. "When he wasn't where I thought he'd be, I lost—"

"Well, let me think." Cal turned slightly away from them. He rubbed his forehead and then moved to where Matt stood and recreated Matt's steps just before the lost phrase. "You're here, then a turn on your left foot, a kick of your right, and out toward Alexandra, arms out, then crossed overhead, fists, then—what comes next?" He and Matt looked blankly at each other. "How can you not be where you're supposed to be?" *I can't believe I've forgotten it too! Is this whole thing going to come apart now?* Cal returned to the same starting point and began the sequence again. Alexandra found a starting point for her sequence center stage left, but she again lost the steps in the same place and stood with both hands in her hair.

"Do you remember, Katherine?" Before she could get to her feet, he demanded, "Where's Amelie?"

"She had another rehearsal for 'Angles,'" Katherine said.

"Well, go get her, will you? Tell her to bring her pad. And if you see Rob out there, grab him too."

Katherine went at a trot toward the studio door, and when she returned with Amelie, the two men still stood in the center of the floor, their bodies bent with their struggle to remember the lost steps, while Alexandra whirled toward them from center left, counting audibly.

"We're lost," Cal said to Amelie, who crossed the floor in jazz slippers, a black leotard, and a full cotton skirt. "I sure hope you have good notes."

"I have great notes. Show me where you are." She scanned the sheets of her yellow pad as Cal started the score from the beginning and the two dancers began again, nervous now and distracted. When they stopped, she moved to the center of the room.

"Matt, you've added a step and that's causing you to be on the wrong foot for your *piqué en arrière*, and that means that when you come out of that, you can't get to where you need to be. You're even headed off in the wrong direction." She held the pad in one hand and stepped through Matt's sequence. He watched, standing with his hands on his waist, and then he moved to a position beside her and stepped through the movements too as she did them a second time.

"Sure, I remember now."

"Well, thank God," Cal said. "Katherine, did you find Rob out there anywhere?"

"Didn't see him."

"We need to get this videotaped as we go. We can't risk losing what we've already got done, and Amelie might not be so available the next time. Katherine, have Cindy at the front desk page him and send him here right away. Amelie, let's make sure that while we're building this thing we don't have you scheduled in other rehearsals—at least for a few days until we get this down."

"Okay, Cal. Shall I stay today or go on back to the 'Angles' rehearsal?"

"No, go on back to what you were doing. Let's just clear up the assignment sheets for a week or so, so you're free at the same time we are."

Amelie was at the door to leave the rehearsal studio.

"Oh, and, Amelie? Thanks for taking such good notes."

She smiled, opening the door wider. As Katherine reentered the room, the page came over the intercom system: "Rob Deinken, you're wanted in Studio C at once. Rob Deinken. Studio C at once, please."

A further half hour of rehearsal time was lost while Rob was briefed on the problem, went to locate the video gear, and then got the handheld camera ready to tape. Alexandra and Matt spent the time running through the trouble spot over and over, imprinting the movements on their muscles to override the faulty version.

Katherine and Alexandra were just finishing up in the women's dressing room when the telephone call came. Instead of paging, Cindy came looking for Katherine in person and found the two out of the shower but not quite dressed. It was Alexandra who noticed how white Cindy's face was.

"Cindy? Something's wrong—what?"

"Katherine, I'm sorry. We've just had a call from Mercy Hospital. Your mother's been taken there. She's been in a car wreck."

For a couple of seconds, Katherine went on fixing her hair and adjusting her clothes, and when she stopped, it was as though she had lost her ability to move at all. She stood staring into the mirror at her reflection. "What did you say?"

"I thought maybe—would you like me to call a cab for you?"

Still Katherine stared into the mirror. Alexandra looked from one to the other and knew that the only thing to do was take charge. "Yes, call a cab for us, and call the hospital back. Ask them where we're supposed to go."

In the cab on the way to the hospital, Katherine's face changed from white to red, and her breath began to come in urgent gasps.

"Try to stay calm," Alexandra told her. "We really don't know anything yet. Your mother may have just been shaken up some."

"Admittance or emergency or what?" the taxi driver asked.

"Follow the signs for the emergency room," Alexandra said. Leaving the freeway, the cab followed a narrow route with high concrete walls that curved quickly to the right and proceeded under the highway and then, perhaps a quarter mile later, into the hospital grounds. Once afoot, Alexandra led Katherine onto the walkway toward the emergency room. Inside, she spoke to the woman behind the admittance desk. "We're here to see Mrs. Melton. This is her daughter. Can we see her?"

Putting her glasses on top of her head, the triage nurse looked at Alexandra and then turned to talk to someone else in the room before turning back and saying, "Who was it now—what is it you want?"

"Mrs. Melton. She was in a car accident and brought here."

She typed in letters and brought her glasses back down onto her nose to read the screen. "Milton, did you say? We don't have—"

"Melton, with an *e*."

"M-i-l-t-e-n?"

"No! M-e-l-t-o-n."

"Oh, Melton." She typed again and stared at the screen. "And who are you to her?"

"I beg your pardon?"

"What is your relationship to her?"

"My friend here is her daughter. Someone from here at the hospital called her to come."

"Well, you can't see her right away. She's still in Trauma. Go take a seat, and if I don't call your name in thirty minutes or so, then you can come up and ask me about her again."

Now Katherine spoke up. "All I want to do is see her. She's my mother! Can't I just see her?"

The nurse put her glasses on top of her head and looked placidly at Katherine as though she might start the line of routine questions again. Alexandra put her hands on Katherine's shoulders and turned her away. "Let's sit down for a few minutes. I'll check back after a little while."

In a room that could seat sixty people, only a few small clusters of two or three people each sat waiting. It felt more like a train station than a hospital waiting room. Katherine started up out of her chair every time a white uniform entered the room, and if she was seated, she clawed and bit at her fingernails and cuticles.

"So did you grow up in San Francisco?" Alexandra asked finally.

"Huh? Uh, yes."

"When did you start ballet school?"

"Uh, when I was five my mother started me in a lot of different kinds of classes." She turned to look at the double doors leading to the hospital rooms and then made an effort to settle down in her chair. "Uh, she had me in ballet, tap, violin, fencing, riding."

"Fencing? For five-year-olds!"

"Well, the epees aren't sharp, of course."

"The what?"

"The epees—the fencing swords. And even at that, the instructors put these round things like ping pong balls on the blunt tips, so we couldn't have hurt each other with them very easily."

"What good does fencing do for a child that age?"

Katherine shrugged. "It helps balance and poise. And it teaches how to pay attention and stay alert."

"And no one got hurt?"

"One kid got a concussion from tripping over his epee, but no, no one got stabbed or had an eye put out or anything like that."

Alexandra resisted the urge to smile. Katherine's attention was pulled away when a doctor in a white jacket walked into the room, looked around at the people waiting, and walked toward an older couple.

For the first twenty minutes, Alexandra tried first one topic, and then another, in an effort to keep Katherine distracted and talking. Then she returned to the admittance desk and again asked for word about Mrs. Melton. The triage nurse pushed her glasses up on top of her head and looked Alexandra over for a second or two before putting her glasses back on and checking her computer screen. "M-e-l-t-o-n," Alexandra said.

"Give us another thirty minutes, maybe forty-five."

Alexandra was walking back to join Katherine when the streetside door opened and Cal rushed into the room. He spotted Katherine at once and went quickly to her. She stood up to give herself entirely to his embrace. She was gasping again, and her tears washed down in wide swaths that wetted her cheeks and dripped from her chin to Cal's shoulder. Her height came within an inch of his.

"Have you heard anything yet?" He was looking over Katherine's shoulder to Alexandra.

She shook her head. "They say it'll be another half hour, forty-five minutes before they can tell us anything."

He held Katherine for a few minutes longer, saying twice, "We'll see you through this. You're not alone." Finally the three of them sat down to continue the wait. After another hour had gone by, the admittance nurse could only tell them, "She's still in surgery. At this point there's nothing more I can tell you. You're welcome to wait, or I can telephone you if you want to go on to your homes."

"We'll wait," Cal said.

"I'm going to find us some food." Alexandra headed off down a long hallway, branching off first right and then left and hoping she could find her way back. When she found the hospital cafeteria, warm smells of food greeted her, but only sandwiches were portable. She gathered up three—all of which turned out to be tuna salad—and poured coffees to take back to the waiting room. There, she pulled up a small magazine table to set out the food. "Katherine, you should eat something."

But Katherine was staring at Cal. When he noticed, he leaned toward her to take her hand. "What is it, Katherine?"

Her eyes looked sore and frightened. "I don't know what to do. I guess I'm waiting for you to tell me what to do."

He closed his other hand on top of hers. "Alexandra is right—first, what you need to do is eat something. You've worked hard today, and it's been a long time since you've eaten. And then what we'll do is wait here together until they come to talk to us. I'll be right here. Alexandra, how about you?"

"I'm staying right here too." She handed a sandwich to Katherine and was relieved to see her open the cellophane and begin to eat.

It was three more hours before a doctor came into the waiting room, looked around, and finally chose their group. "Miss Melton?" He looked from Alexandra to Katherine. Katherine stared silently, her soul in her face. Cal and Alexandra spoke at the same time: "This is Miss Melton. She's right here."

"I'm sorry you've had such a long wait with no word. Your mother's out of surgery and in recovery. From what we can tell now, she should pull through fine, but I think it would be better for all parties if you didn't see her tonight." The doctor, a middle-aged man, looked tired. What may have been only fatigue on his face communicated as worry.

"No!" The pitch of Katherine's voice sounded like panic. "I have to see her tonight. I can't just walk out of here and go home without seeing her! I can't do that. She's my mother!"

"I understand." The doctor looked at Cal and then turned his attention back to Katherine. "I want to emphasize that we've done all we can for now, and we think she'll be fine. Seeing her tonight would not do her any good, and it probably would not do you any good either."

Katherine looked as though she might scream.

"I suggest that you plan to come back in the morning. We're keeping a close eye on her, and we can let you know if there's any change."

Katherine turned pleadingly to Cal.

"Look, Doctor, I know that you know what is best and that you think Katherine shouldn't go into her mother's room right now. And you might be right—you probably are. But couldn't she at least *see* her mother, maybe from the doorway of the room? Just so she can see with her own eyes that her mother is really there?"

The doctor heaved a sigh but nodded assent and led the way to the inner floors of the hospital. His footsteps were somewhat plodding, and he shook his head more than once. At Mrs. Melton's room, he stood so that his body blocked entrance. "She can't hear you," he reminded Katherine. Mrs. Melton lay on the hospital bed fifteen feet away.

Alexandra couldn't see into the room, but she could see the doctor's weary face, which seemed to soften as he watched Katherine. Tears were coursing down Katherine's face, and she whispered, "Mother . . . Mother."

After leaving Katherine's telephone numbers with the hospital staff, the three left in Cal's car.

"I don't want to be alone," Katherine said.

"I'll stay with you," Alexandra immediately volunteered, and Cal said, "Let's go by Alexandra's first to get whatever she needs, then I'll drive you both to Katherine's."

"Miss Melton." The doorman touched the bill of his cap as Katherine stepped out of the car in front of the condominium building. Katherine nodded to Mr. Hooper; she would tell him later about her mother but not tonight. He held the door open for the two women to enter. As soon

She nodded, fighting down the lump in her throat in order to speak. "I wouldn't be able to concentrate at the studio anyway."

"I know. So you stay here, and I'll check back with you around noon."

"Do you want me to stay with you?" Alexandra asked Katherine.

Katherine took a moment and then shook her head. "I'll be okay here today, but could you spend the night with me again?"

"Sure."

"Well," Cal said. "We'll go ahead then and see you later today." He took her hand and leaned toward her to kiss her forehead. Her arms closed around him, and she pressed her face against his shoulder.

On the drive to the studio, after several minutes of silence, Alexandra asked Cal, "What will this mean for the new ballet?"

"That's what I'm wondering myself. We'll just have to give it a day or two to see how things are."

"It's a good thing you started with her solo."

"I guess it is, but there's a lot left to choreograph." He took a deep breath. "And we're certainly not going to be able to do the ballet without that role." Cal fell silent and Alexandra didn't press further. The worry was on his shoulders, not hers, and now was not the time to force him to think about that.

For three days Mrs. Melton remained in serious and guarded condition. Katherine spent the days at the hospital, though her mother was heavily medicated and not lucid when she did awaken. Nurses came and went regularly, allowing Katherine to stay in the room while they monitored fluids and machinery and added injections of medications but asking her to leave when they changed bandages or bedding. Alexandra spent the nights with Katherine in the fifteenth-floor condominium. She slept on a cot normally stored in Mrs. Melton's office. They had wheeled it down the hall to Katherine's room.

"This isn't any of my business," Alexandra began as they got ready for bed on Sunday evening. "But I've been wondering about your father. Do you think you should contact him and let him know about this?"

Katherine had made a pot of her mother's tea, and now she held a cup of it near her mouth, blowing gently on the surface. "I wouldn't know how to contact him. And even if I did, I don't think I would."

"You don't know where he is?"

"Oh, I think he's in LA. He used to be head of some large stockbroker firm down there. Maybe he still is. I guess I could find him if I had to. When I turned eighteen, I had a choice finally about his visitations and I put a stop to them."

Alexandra pulled a nightshirt over her head and slipped under the light cover of the cot. "Do you know why he left your mother?"

"I'm sure I don't know the whole picture. Basically he wanted a new life, and he paid my mother a whole lot of money to go away so he could do that."

"How old were you when they broke up?"

"Seven. What about your parents? Are they still together?"

"Well, they live in the same house, but I can't say there's really much togetherness between them. My family went to pieces in 1984 when my brother Ricky died. Everybody sort of withdrew into themselves and away from everybody else in the family."

"How did he die?"

"He—it's strange to say this about a kid who was only a young teenager, but he actually drank himself to death. It was an overdose, I guess. My mom and dad have never come to terms with it."

"My God, that's horrible! How did you cope with that?"

"I was sixteen and in ballet school at the time. I guess I coped by putting all my energy and time into ballet. It's been harder for my older brother, Daniel, I think. They were really close. Ricky worshipped Daniel, and Daniel liked being worshipped. It was hard on both of them when they grew in different directions and the brother bond didn't keep up. Daniel thought he should have been able to protect Ricky from getting involved with alcohol like he did."

"So you've been pretty much on your own since you were sixteen?"

"I guess you could say that. I mean, I still lived in my parents' house, but none of us had much contact with each other. We all came and went and barely spoke if we happened to pass each other at the door. It's not so hard to avoid people when you know their routines."

Katherine was silent for some moments. "I can't imagine trying to live my life or make decisions for myself or do much of anything without my mother." Tears came rushing to her eyes, but she grabbed a tissue and caught them just as they spilled to her cheeks.

Alexandra raised up onto an elbow. "They say it's best to just let the tears come."

"I know. But I'm trying not to give in. I'm trying to give her all the support I can, and that means not giving in. She's *got* to come out of this. She just has to." Katherine blew her nose, dabbed at her eyes, and blew her nose again. "Let's talk about something else."

"All right."

"How's it going at the studio?"

"Well, 'Angles' is looking good. Candace has Rebecca standing in for you. And the three of us keep on working on the *Prayer* ballet."

"Is it coming together?"

"It feels like a circus sometimes because Cal has Rob in there with the video camera and Amelie with her pad and pencil, but you know how it goes: Cal barely gets a movement down before he's changing it, so Amelie is scratching out her notes and drawing arrows and making new notes. Then Rob is running over to the camera bag to get a fresh battery or a new film cassette. And Judy is there listening to the tapes because he keeps promising her that the sheet music is going to come any day now."

"This can't be very easy for Cal either."

"No. But you know he would not want you to be worrying about that. It's just a ballet. We'll work that out however we have to. You have more than enough to deal with now. And the best thing at this moment is to get some rest."

"I know. It's just—I feel tired but then my eyes fly open as soon as I start thinking about her."

"Well, let's just try something. Okay?"

Katherine looked uncertain but then nodded her head.

"Go ahead and close your eyes and take a deep, slow breath. Hold it for a moment, then breathe out slowly." Alexandra slowed and softened her voice. "Open your eyes about halfway, close them, take another deep breath, and hold it." She lay back on the cot, letting her own breath slow down. "Now breathe out slowly." She paused and then spoke again, more quietly. "Let your eyes open just enough to barely see through your eyelashes now, then close them again, and take a deep, slow breath. Hold the air inside you." She paused again. "Breathe out slowly. Go on now, breathing slowly and deeply. See in your mind your mother walk into the room, smiling at you." Again she paused and then spoke even slower. "Hear in your mind your mother's voice, telling you that no matter what happens, it will all be all right. Everything will be exactly as it should be. Feel your mother's hand lightly touch your face as she smooths your hair and runs her fingers gently over your forehead—once, twice, again, gently soothing you to sleep. Notice in your mind your mother's fragrance in the air. Take a moment to breathe in your mother's fragrance. And feel the peace of knowing that she is here with you and both of you are safe and everything is okay. No matter what is ahead, everything will be as it should be."

Alexandra's voice continued, with longer pauses and quieter tones until she was sure that Katherine had fallen asleep.

* * *

On Tuesday afternoon, Katherine sat near her mother's bed, watching her mother's face. It seemed to her that her mother was lucid. Suddenly Mrs. Melton opened her unbandaged eye and looked at her daughter. "Pet," she said, "why don't you bring those shoes into the kitchen so you can talk to me while I make dinner? I got a great piece of salmon today."

Katherine looked back at her mother, struggling to clear a passage for words in her throat. "Sure, Mama," she said, feeling her face crush inward as her mother's unbandaged eye closed. "Sure, Mama. That's a good idea. Salmon would be—" But her voice failed.

* * *

Five Weeks

Alexandra awoke to find Katherine sitting cross-legged at the end of the bed, staring through the window as dawn grew over San Francisco.

"I'm going to the studio with you today. I can't take any more of sitting there seeing her like that and not being able to do anything about it."

"I think that's a good idea. We can let the hospital know where you are and ask for a phone call if there's any need. The nurses would do that, wouldn't they?"

Katherine nodded. "Yes, I'm sure they will." En route to the studio, she said, "I'm actually excited to be getting back to work. My body feels like it hasn't had a decent workout in a month!"

But at the studio, Katherine's ability to concentrate was so limited that she continually lost steps and once collided with a dancer traveling in a light, rapid *pas de bourrée couru*, sending them both bouncing to the floor.

That night, Cal lay on his back on his living room sofa with his bare feet buried in a wadded-up afghan and Miss Agnus curled up asleep on his shins. *She was one rattled ballerina.* He pictured Katherine in the studio that day: stiff, distracted, barely able to keep a string of three steps in mind. He couldn't bring himself to test her during the *Prayer* choreography session to see whether she remembered any of what they'd already worked out. *If her mother doesn't make it, this role is down the tubes.* "And probably the whole damn ballet with it."

Miss Agnus raised her head and looked back at him. Then she rose to her feet, stretched her front legs and her back legs, turned in a full circle, and lay down again, facing him this time.

"Miss Aggie." He touched her tiny black nose with his fingertip. "Do you know you're only three inches taller when you're standing up than you are when you're lying down?"

Miss Agnus blinked at him twice and then put her head down on her front paws and closed her eyes.

He'd made the mistake of pulling Katherine to the side after class and offering to give her time off, even replace her in the Spirit of Prayer role, do whatever she needed to make it easier. "Whatever you need," he had emphasized. And she had looked at him—her blue eyes nearly on a level with his own—and said, "What I *need* is not to lose this too!"

He had recoiled as if from a slap in the face, and all he could manage to say at first was, "No. No." What he had meant as a gesture of support she had heard as a threat. Now remembering the pain of the moment, Cal reached down with both hands and pulled the Pomeranian onto his chest, stroking her fur. Miss Agnus grunted in brief complaint and then snuggled her tiny, cold nose against his neck. Her breath was only faintly perceptible on his skin. *What if she can't handle this? She's never faced anything in her life without her mother, and now it's facing life without her mother that she has to deal with. She might not be strong enough to do it. She's rattled; she's insecure; she's acting like the solid ground has evaporated out from under her feet.* Cal pressed his head back into the sofa pillow and closed his eyes to prevent his anxiety from carrying him completely away. As he did so, a moment of quiet, like the break between movements of a symphony, occurred in his mind. Slowly it came then, a sense of sureness settling over him like calming water. Into his mind came the thought:

She's strong enough. Give it some time. Everything will come together.

Cal pushed his head further into the cushion, wanting to soak up the tenuous peace and reassurance until it became substantial enough to fully support him, and when he finally raised his head, he found that a tear had leaked through at the corner of his eye.

* * *

On Saturday, choreography sessions on the *Prayer* ballet were divided up: an hour in the morning after class and two hours in the afternoon, starting at three o'clock, after most of the troupe had gone home for the weekend.

"Katherine, you're on stage for the first time during this scene, but you're not doing much but standing by and observing. And you don't actually walk on. We'll do it with lights, probably. Upstage right will be in total darkness, then suddenly—or maybe gradually, we'll figure that out later—a spot comes on and there you are.

"Remember our story, people. You have this unfortunate, unhappy couple struggling and all but defeated by the conflicts between and within them, and finally by scene 4 it's beginning to dawn on them that this way of life isn't working. First Alexandra, then Matt, tentatively reaches out to the other with this gesture"—he touched his palms to each other, fingers straight and together—"and even this unskillful, undeveloped gesture of communion is enough to cause the Spirit of Prayer to appear. Let's listen to a few bars." He turned to Judy, who stood by at the tape player. "Judy, I promise you the sheet music is coming." He smiled weakly.

"Have you noticed how blue I've become from holding my breath?" Her smile softened her sarcasm.

"I have, yes. The tape is at the right spot, if you'll start it, please."

They listened to several bars of music, and as Judy rewound the tape to the counter mark, Cal instructed his dancers, "Katherine, you're at upstage right. Matt, you're downstage right. Alexandra, center left. This will start out a lot like scene 1 but not so harsh. Matt, here's yours." Cal danced Matt's part of the first sequence with the three dancers watching.

* * *

That afternoon, after lunch and a short rehearsal with Candace Bennington on "Angles and Intersections," Alexandra ran to the stairwell and down the steps to the basement. She entered the large darkened room, feeling gratitude for its musty familiarity. Draping the blanket around her, she sat down on the couch under the fading red Exit sign. As she sat quietly, tingling sensations occurred here and there as her body settled and relaxed, and then she let her mantra come repeating into her mind. It was as though, without any pictures of it in her mind, she somehow left a surface of rough waves and bobbed beneath the turbulence into a peaceful place. She may have continued to sink as if in quiet waters, or she may have found a level of serenity and remained there. Time passed as if there were no time. A gentle pressure on the edge of the couch reminded her briefly that she was sitting in a blanket in the basement, and then she drifted away from this realization back to a place of no realization.

When her consciousness rose to the surface again, she opened one eye just enough to see her watch through her lashes and saw that nineteen minutes had passed. *Oh, good, one more minute.* She let her body and her mind slip away again.

Two minutes had gone by when she looked at her watch again. A sweet sense of pleasure filled her at the thought that she had in pure innocence stolen an extra minute of peace. She closed her eyes again and let her head back to rest against the couch. After a few minutes, during which her consciousness slowly returned to a waking state, she opened her eyes. The darkness of the room was not so impenetrable now. Calm and relaxed, she looked at the room, the piles of furniture, the old sets leaning against the walls. Then she grew aware, without the slightest fear, that a form sat on the couch with her, and she recalled dimly the pressure on the couch that had roused her during her meditation. She slowly moved her head to look to the left, and there was the orange cat, sitting at the far end and staring intently at her. "Hello there." The cat continued to stare, alert and ready. For some seconds, they remained looking at each other, and then Alexandra carefully lifted a hand to reach out, and the cat turned and sprang away into the shadows.

* * *

They were a half hour into the late-afternoon session of *Prayer* choreography when Cindy came to the door. The hospital had called for Katherine: Mrs. Melton's condition had been downgraded back to critical. Katherine got to her feet, her dread apparent.

"Should I go too?" Alexandra asked Cal. She hoped she was the only one who had noticed his flinch.

"Do you want Alexandra with you?"

"No, I'll be fine. I'm starting to know how to do this now."

When Katherine had gone, Cal stood looking at the floor, hands on his waist. Cheeks inflated, he blew out a heavy breath. Then he looked at his remaining two dancers. "Let's see if we can go on. Matt, you're offstage now. Alexandra, you're here. Coincidentally, what you're trying to portray is sorrow and grief. Put as much into it as you feel up to."

He led her to a tape mark on the studio floor. With his head turned sharply to the left, he shielded his face with his right forearm. The fingers of his left hand extended at his right side from behind his back. He lifted his right leg parallel to the floor and held the position for some seconds before turning the leg in the hip socket fully open, then back, fully open again, then back, and then he let his body crumple as if it had been hit in the stomach by a blow. Then he looked to Alexandra.

"*En pointe?*"

"Try it first flatfooted. Let's see how it looks." She ran through the sequence, and he walked to her. "Let's try the left hand here." He moved her arm from behind her back and, opening the palm wide, fingers spread, at her left hip. "Up." He gently bent her wrist.

"It won't go straight up." Irritation stirred inside her.

"Then let's try turning it out." He manipulated her wrist. "Run the steps again." When she had done so, he approached her again. "When you crumple, close the left hand in against your stomach, like you're protecting your midsection."

Moments later, he showed her a *jeté* and then asked her to change the direction of it. She heard Amelie's pen scratch the revision onto the yellow pad. "I'm not sure I can do that. It'll look awkward."

"It might. Just try it."

She tried the jump, which went against the technique her body knew, and she landed off balance. She turned to Cal, suppressing the urge to say, "See!"

"Don't worry. We'll use that off-balance energy. Trust me. Try it again."

She tried the *jeté* again, with the same awkward finish, and looked at Cal in frustration.

"That's good. Grief is off balance and awkward, isn't it? You're dancing sorrow."

"It won't look right on me." *Shut up! You can't keep letting your frustration be so evident.* It wasn't Cal's fault that her nerves were stretched taut by the schedule she was keeping with Katherine. Then into her mind flashed a picture of Katherine, how patient she was during a choreography session, how ready to do whatever Cal asked without ever showing any annoyance with the process. *No wonder he always chooses her.*

"We'll do it twice so everyone will know that you didn't make a mistake."

She rolled her eyes toward Matt, who winked at her and nodded.

Later they left the studio together. "Want to catch a bite to eat?" he asked her.

"No, thanks. I've barely been in my own apartment for two weeks. I think I'd like to go there and just crash for a few hours."

"Are you staying with Katherine again tonight?"

"Probably. Especially if her mother is worse. I'm going to try to track her down as soon as I get home."

"It really doesn't look bad on you, you know?"

"What?"

"That jump Cal wants you to do. It just *feels* awkward. It looks fine."

She sighed. "This ballet has been so difficult. I mean, first no music and then that metronome, and now Mrs. Melton. It seems like there's been one thing or another to be upset about since we started it. The whole thing has been off balance."

"I know, but we have to trust Cal and go with that he says to do. Most choreography is trying something one way, then revising that, then revising the revisions."

"No wonder some dancers end up resenting the whole thing."

Matt laughed, but then his face became serious. "Are you *resenting* this?"

I can't answer that. "At least we have tomorrow off. I hope I can have a few hours to myself to take a walk or something. Thank God for Sundays!"

* * *

Matt had felt his face grow tight at Alexandra's mention of Sunday. *Stephen!* It would be his day to see his therapist for the first time since he'd spent that amazing night with Ricardo—the most wonder-filled experience of his life. *What am I going to tell Stephen about this?*

The question didn't leave him all night long.

"Good morning, Stephen," Matt said when he heard footsteps nearing the top of the stairway. He had arrived ten minutes early, but Stephen always unlocked the door to allow Matt to wait inside. The entryway had little natural light—only what crept in through the narrow, green glass panels around the door—but there was a lamp on a small table beside a padded straight-back chair. This setup passed as Stephen's waiting room for the therapy practice he conducted from his home. The chair creaked when Matt sat down and every time he moved.

"Hello, Matt." Stephen stopped his descent halfway down the stairs. "How are you?" He motioned for Matt to come up.

"Fine. You?"

"Well, I'd be happier if the sun were shining this morning." Inside the therapy room, Stephen sat down in his usual chair opposite Matt's and looked at his client closely. "What would you like to talk about today?"

"Why don't you pick something this time?"

Stephen smiled at him and then shook his head. "I have a whole list of things we could discuss, but the bad news—which is really the good news—is that you get to choose what we talk about." Matt sat with his left knee swinging rhythmically back and forth. His mind was completely blank. Finally Stephen asked, "How about the initials?"

"Huh?"

"In the back of your haircut?"

"Oh." Matt put his left hand to the back of his head, feeling the kiss, not the initials. "They're almost gone."

"So that's not troubling you anymore?"

"I'm pretty much past that."

"Ah." Stephen became silent, but his eyes remained on Matt's face.

He's going to wait me out. "It's just—" Matt thought of a different starting point and sat up straighter in the chair. "We've been having a terrible time at the studio. This new ballet we're putting together, one of the gals, Katherine—her mother was in a bad car wreck, like, two weeks ago, and yesterday she was put back on the critical list, so Katherine's been out most of that time, and when she was there on Friday and Saturday, she was really having a hard time."

"How do you mean?"

"Not able to concentrate, not able to remember what she's supposed to be doing."

"That's understandable, isn't it?"

"Oh yeah, sure. It's just—"

After a long pause, Stephen asked, "Do you think she should be handling it differently?"

Matt glanced quickly at Stephen and then away. "I don't know. There's something about it that's really bothering me."

"Have you ever been in Katherine's shoes?"

"Oh no, no. My mother was never in a car wreck."

Stephen thought about that for a moment. "Well, maybe not a *car* wreck."

"Why did you say it like that?"

Stephen lifted one shoulder. "Your mother was never in a *car* wreck, but she was incapacitated for periods of time, when all she could do was lie unconscious on the couch while you fended for yourself."

Matt blinked.

"Maybe you're feeling that if you could manage in those circumstances when you were only a small child, Katherine ought to be able to manage better than she's doing."

Matt shifted in his chair and rubbed his eye. "I don't know. Jeez, that makes me sound like a jerk."

"What have you noticed yourself feeling toward Katherine since the accident?"

Matt looked to one side, thinking back. "Well, I was shocked, just like everyone else was, when we heard about it and how bad her mother was." He heard his own words. "I mean, how bad her injuries were." He paused then, thinking. "Mostly I felt sorry for Katherine. She's always been really close to her mother, and this is probably the first thing she's ever had to do on her own, without her mother there telling her what to do."

"Are you and Katherine friends?"

"Well, yeah, we're friends. I mean, we've known each other for five years, as long as I've been with the company. We've danced together, seen each other six days a week at the studio."

"You said a moment ago that this is probably the first thing Katherine has ever had to do on her own."

"Yes."

"Does that make you feel . . . anything?"

Matt shook his head. "Should it?"

"It occurs to me that here Katherine is an adult, probably somewhere in her twenties?"

"Late twenties, I think."

"So she's maybe a couple of years older than you are, and this is the first time she's ever had to handle something without her mother. But you've had to handle nearly everything in your life since you were a child, without much help from your mother—or a father either. I just thought you might have some feelings about that."

"This isn't about me. It's about Katherine."

Stephen's neutral tone of voice turned gentle. "No, my friend. This is about you. How you're reacting to what's happened in Katherine's life is about *you*, not Katherine."

Why did I have to choose this for a topic! This isn't even what we need to be talking about here. Matt felt perspiration gathering at his hairline.

"This isn't unique to you, Matthew. The same thing is true of all of us. How we react to life says a lot more about us than it does about what we're reacting to."

"But I don't really feel that Katherine isn't handling this as she should. This is a terrible blow to her. Her world is turned upside down and none of it is her fault. She's just having a hard time getting her feet back under her."

"Uh-huh. And what if Katherine's mother dies?"

"That would be terrible."

"And it's a real possibility, isn't it? I mean, there's a chance she might not make it?"

"As of today anyway, she's not getting better. She's getting worse. Yes, she could die."

"And what does that mean for you?"

Matt blinked again. "It doesn't have anything to do with me."

"Sure it does. Because then you're going to see another woman—probably about the same age as your mother was then—going through the grief of losing someone who's vital to her. This could be a replay for you, and something inside you sees it coming."

Matt stared at Stephen. Dread was tightening his breathing space.

"And maybe you're afraid that if she can't do any better than she's doing now, when her mother is only injured but at least alive, she'll fall completely apart if her mother dies—just like your mother fell completely apart when she learned that your father was dead."

Matt's face was white now. He didn't need a mirror to tell him that, because he had felt the blood drain from his head. Everything about him felt constricted: his face, his muscles, his mind. Through a narrowed windpipe he said, "Not everything that happens in my life is related to my mother."

Stephen shifted in his chair and set the ankle of his right foot on his left knee. "No. No, that's right, and this may be one of those things that aren't. Breathe, Matthew." He linked his fingers together and studied his thumbnails in the silence. "On the other hand, it's worth considering. The very thought of it seems to be pretty upsetting to you."

Matt sat up again, looking first to one side and then the other. "Okay, I'll give that some thought sometime."

"How about right now?"

Deep breath; let it out slow. Into Matt's mind then came a picture he'd seen of himself partnering Katherine. Flatfooted, she was an inch taller than he was; when she was *en pointe*, the difference in their heights appeared dramatic. "Katherine is not my mother. She's definitely not anything like my mother."

"Why do you say that?"

It took no effort to come up with the answer. "Katherine is disciplined. She's strong. She's capable. She's only thrown by this temporarily. She'll be fine."

"And you're saying those are all things that your mother was not."

Matt nodded.

"On the other hand, they both are grown women dependent for their equilibrium on someone else."

Matt's voice rose. "Katherine is not curling up on a couch somewhere with booze and pills. Look, Stephen, couldn't it just be that I'm concerned about a friend of mine who's going through a tough time and it has nothing—nothing!—to do with my own goddam mother?" He held his breath, willing himself to calm down, wishing the cursing hadn't come out.

Stephen steepled his fingers and let the steeple slide up and down his nose. He did not raise his voice. "Yes. It could just be that. The only thing is you arrived today all knotted up inside yourself over something. It feels to me like more than simple concern for a friend who's going through a tough time. It feels more like there's something going on that's upsetting you as much as this thing with her mother is upsetting Katherine. So if it's not a question of how Katherine's situation bears on you, then I'd say you're smoke-screening us and there's something else going on that we should be talking about."

"I spent a night with a guy."

The steeple stopped moving up and down the nose. "Why don't you tell me a little bit about that."

Matt's head waggled from one side to the other as he described seeing Ricardo Vitale backstage at the opera house and then Vitale's advances at the party and his own decision to follow up on the invitation to Vitale's hotel room.

"And you've never had a sexual experience with a man before?"

"Never. Well, I mean, you know how kids are in grade school. Some of us fooled around some, but no, nothing like this." He couldn't stop squirming.

"Why are you so uncomfortable about it?"

"Well, because!" Matt gestured as though the thing should be obvious. "I never . . . this isn't . . . I didn't—"

"You don't think you're gay."

Matt nearly leapt out of his chair. "Of course I don't think I'm gay!"

"And you're having trouble reconciling that with the fact that you were attracted to this man Ricardo."

Matt slumped down in his chair again, with his eyes closed and his face partially hidden by one hand. In his misery, he could only nod an affirmative.

"All your other sexual experiences . . ."

"Have been with women," Matt finished quickly.

"I won't ask you how Ricardo compared. I think I can see." After several seconds had gone by, he added, "Would it be so terrible if it turns out you are gay?"

"I would . . . just hate to fit that stereotype: gay male ballet dancer. I've never particularly cared when people made dumb comments about that because I knew it didn't fit me, but now I'm thinking what if it does!"

In his struggle to find a comfortable way to sit in his chair, Matt inadvertently shoved backward, lengthening the distance between himself and the therapist. At once he grasped the arms of the chair to move it back so that Stephen would not think he had moved away on purpose.

"So I take it you're having a difficult time fitting this encounter in with the idea you've had of yourself, who you think you are."

Matt stopped fidgeting and sat still for a moment. "Yes."

"So this is something else that isn't 'like you.'"

"What do you mean, something else?"

"Well, the last time you were here you were upset about the initials in your haircut because you said that it wasn't like you to do something like that."

They were both silent for some moments and then Matt said, "So you think there's a pattern emerging here? Like maybe I'm just starting to find out who I really am?"

"I'm not sure that either event is a reflection of who you really are. I'd guess that maybe this is the first time in your life that you've let yourself experiment a little. Maybe something inside you is giving up its insistence that you do everything perfectly by the book and according to the rules."

Calmer now, Matt rested his cheek against his right index finger. He was able to look Stephen in the eye.

"And if that's the case, you can expect some repercussions."

"Like what?"

"Well, maybe you won't—let's hope you won't—but some people in this situation find themselves bumping into things, dropping things, making mistakes they normally don't make. Some people start forgetting things, losing things. It's their subconscious way of punishing themselves for breaking the rules, since no one else is punishing them."

Matt's eyes widened. "That's weird. I forgot the choreography the other day on this new ballet. It was awful. I put in an extra step, and then I couldn't get to where I needed to be, and because I had fouled up, everyone else forgot how it was supposed to go too."

"And that's not like you either, is it?"

"No. I don't forget anything. I can still dance the first ballet I ever learned." He shifted in the chair and added, "So you don't think I'm gay after all?"

Stephen's right hand rose in a gesture that suggested the answer was inconsequential. "I don't know whether you are or you aren't. I don't think that you can determine that from one experience."

A scene flashed across Matt's mind of Ricardo and himself in the hotel room, bringing a twinge at the base of his abdomen.

"It sounds to me as though you found it very exciting, but that could have as much to do with what Ricardo Vitale represents to you as it does with your true sexual orientation." Stephen's tone changed again. "There's no reason to be flushing and squirming, Matt. Look, this isn't confession here. We talk about what's going on in your life to see what we can learn from it so that maybe we can make your life better."

Matt stared at his knees and nodded.

"Why don't you tell me a little bit about who Ricardo is? When did you first hear of him?"

"I've known about Ricardo Vitale about as long as I've been in ballet. He's famous, not just here in America but all over Europe. There was a poster of him on the wall where I took my first dance lessons."

"Ah. So he's quite a bit older than you then?"

"Not that much. He's probably midthirties, I guess."

"Isn't that old for a dancer?"

"Somewhat. It depends on the dancer. He mentioned that he's thinking of becoming less active."

"And how does one get to be famous in ballet?"

"By being good, really, *really* good."

"What was that like to actually meet the man who was in that poster you saw when you were just beginning?"

Matt shook his head, lost for a moment in awe. "I can't even tell you. I felt like the whole night was just not quite real. I won't ever forget it."

Stephen was silent, his eyes on Matt, and then he said, "An older man, someone you've looked up to for years, professionally your superior, and here he shows up in town and takes an unusual interest in you."

Matt caught on quickly. "You're trying to say I turned him into some kind of father figure?"

Stephen shrugged. "You never had a father. Your real father died before you ever saw him. Your stepfather was a jackass. I believe that was the word you used."

Matt's anger flared. "Well, no thanks for that idea, Stephen! Whatever that night was, it wasn't incest!" Now there was insult and outrage in his squirming.

Stephen took a deep breath and leaned back in his chair. "Probably not," he said, without a trace of irritation or apology in reaction to Matt's indignation. "I don't know if this might be a key, but I gave you an assignment that had to do with feeling. Remember that from last session? You were supposed to feel something, and the last time you were here, you were having some trouble even identifying what that meant. So what did you do? You went out and had a one-night stand with a guy whom you admire, and—no question about it—he made you feel something. Look at what you got out of that one experience: you got intense excitement, you got fear, you got dread, you got some emotional connection of some kind, and now it looks like you even got some shame and anxiety. That's a hell of a lot of feeling!"

When Matt finally smiled, he ducked his head without comment.

"What?"

"That's what Cal wants too. Feeling, lots and lots of feeling. That list you just ran through sounds like the list I'm supposed to dance in this new piece we're trying to put together."

"And how's that for you? Can you dance those feelings?"

"Sure. I don't have any trouble *dancing* feelings." He grinned, anticipating what Stephen would say.

But Stephen saw the grin and nodded. "And how about your night with Ricardo Vitale, could you have danced it better than you can live it?"

"Funny you should make that parallel because that kept occurring to me too. That night when I was driving to his hotel, I kept thinking, *This is just like before a performance.*"

"How do you mean?"

Matt looked to the side, seeking the words. "Well, before a performance, particularly an opening night, which I guess you could say this was, there's this real keen awareness, like all your senses are on alert. You know there's an audience out there with a lot of expectations, and that only increases the level of alertness because you already have your own idea of what you're supposed to do and what you expect to happen, and most times—unless you're really having an off night—there's this massive energy available to you that you have to somehow put across through your body out to the audience. It's not like rehearsal. It's not like class. It's not like any day-to-day thing. When you're on stage, everything is suddenly bigger than life, and the only thing on your mind is contributing to that without letting it get away from you."

"Get away from you?"

"You have to stay in full control of where you are on stage and what your body is doing, and this can be difficult when you're out there, doing a lot of high-energy movements, and your emotions are pulsating, and there's the audience out there, and the lights might be in your eyes. When you're new at it, it's hard to keep your head."

"And that's what it was like to go meet Vitale?"

Despite the red flush he knew was spreading up his face, Matt smiled as he nodded again.

Stephen opened his mouth but appeared to edit his words. "Do you think you'll see him again?"

"I don't know."

"But if the opportunity arose?"

"Then I would." Matt cleared his throat and said more firmly, "I most certainly would."

* * *

"Hello, Mother?"

"Who is this?"

Alexandra swallowed before she could respond. She'd actually had to call directory assistance for her parents' telephone number, and she would not have gotten that far if she hadn't felt a strong push during her meditation session that *today* was the day to call her mother.

"Uh, it's Alexandra, Mother."

"Oh! Honey! Oh, I'm sorry! I thought it must be a wrong number. I didn't dream it would be you."

Alexandra swallowed again, surprised both by how painfully familiar her mother's voice was and by the warmth in it.

"Well, how *are* you?" her mother said now. "Are you all right? Is everything okay?"

"Yes, everything's fine. I called because it's your birthday in October, and I want to send you a ticket to come out to San Francisco for our opening night."

Mrs. Kreyling caught her breath. "I—hardly know what to say."

"Just say you'll come and I'll get a ticket for you."

"Well, of course I'll come!" There it was. Alexandra recognized the lie under the words: the fragment of hesitation, the creeping reluctance. It was this coldness, this unwillingness to be involved, this desire for lack of contact on her parents' part that had caused her withdrawal in the first place. Despite the promise, Alexandra knew that there would be a return call next week or maybe just a note in the mail: "Sorry, something's come up at the office, can't possibly get away just now, but thanks *so* much anyway, very touching of you to offer—really." An impulse rushed forward to simply hang up the phone and resume life as usual, but a larger urge came in behind it, dominating with a foreign strength, and this urge said, *Talk to her, give her some time.*

She chose the one subject that was always safe. "How's work going?"

"Oh, work is just fine." Her mother drew out the last word, obviously relieved to be in more comfortable territory.

Alexandra struggled to remember. "Are you still in the transportation end of it?"

"Yes, but I oversee all the documentation now." The lilt had returned to her mother's voice.

"And are you still putting in sixteen-hour days?"

There was pride in her mother's chuckle. "When I need to."

"And you need to most days, right?"

They shared a knowing laugh, and then her mother asked about her dancing, and Alexandra described the *Prayer* ballet.

"I haven't learned how to be a good subject to choreograph on yet," Alexandra admitted. "I tend to get frustrated and impatient with the process, but the parts that Cal—Cal's the artistic director of the company—the parts he considers done I really love. So far it's mostly high-energy moves, and we have to be aware every second of what we're doing because we're counting against the music, and sometimes the phrasing of what we're doing has no relation to the phrasing of the music. You can't be just a hoofer and do this."

Her mother laughed again, and Alexandra realized that this was part of her mother's defense, always laughing, always socially graceful, always ready to put a lighthearted brush to everything. "I gather you haven't forgotten how Daniel used to tease you about being a hoofer."

Daniel! Maybe we can talk about it after all. "Have you heard from him?"

"He calls me now and then at the office, never at home. The last time, let's see—it's been five, maybe six months ago now. Never volunteers where he is or what he's doing, and he never quite answers when I ask him." Mrs. Kreyling's words were coming faster; she was impatient to be done with this topic.

Not yet, Mother. Alexandra took a deep breath and closed her eyes, knowing the risks of bringing up her brother's death. "It nearly killed us all when Ricky died, didn't it?"

In the silence that followed, she bowed her head and waited. Finally her mother's voice came back, thin and choked, the initial words unrecognizable.

"I'm sorry, Mother. I didn't hear what you said."

Another choked sound, and then her mother cleared her throat twice and tried again. "I said that I still can't talk about it."

Compassion nearly swept her under, and over the lump in her own throat Alexandra said, "You know, Mom, it's been nine years. Sooner or later, we're all going to have to start talking about it. Ricky's gone, but the rest of us are all still alive."

A stifled sob, and then another, less stifled, broke across the phone line, and then silence.

"We all did the same thing," Alexandra went on. "I guess we all did the only thing we could to survive, but it meant that we withdrew from each other. I buried myself in ballet, you did it with work, Dad turned to drinking, and Daniel—I guess we don't know what Daniel turned to, except that it wasn't to the rest of us."

"Well, your father's still drinking," Mrs. Kreyling said, sniffing loudly. From familial instinct, Alexandra knew that her mother had latched onto the bitterness as a lifeline, finding in it a way to return to strength and composure.

"How is he?"

"Just pretty well pickled. He stays home all day now, in the basement for the most part, and what with my schedule, I barely see him from one day to the next. I can't remember the last time I saw him sober."

"He doesn't work anymore?"

"Lost his job a few years ago and won't leave the house, or his booze, to find another one."

"Isn't there any way to get him some help?"

"He doesn't *want* help." Her voice was louder, angry. "He just wants to drink! He's perfectly content to stay home with his bottle."

"And all you and I have wanted was our work and our dancing." There was silence on the line for some moments. Then Alexandra said, "Mom, I would really like you to come. You can be here for opening night, see the new ballet, and we can celebrate your birthday together. I know you have vacation time long overdue. Just think it over, okay? I'll call you again next week before I get the tickets."

After a few seconds, the quiet voice on the other end said, "I-I've really got to get off the phone now, but I'll think about it. I promise to think about it, honey."

* * *

Monday was Labor Day. Except for everyone involved in the *Prayer* ballet, the company had the day off. But Cal surprised the three dancers, plus Amelie, Rob, and Judy, inviting them to a party at his home early that evening. "I figure we'll knock off here about two, two thirty, and all convene at my house around five. What do you think?" The faces turned toward him looked as though they could not have understood him right. *Haven't I ever invited my dancers to a party before?* "Yeah, a party! We've all been working hard on this new ballet. I think we ought to take a little break and have some fun."

Rob's face looked worried. "I don't know if we ought to be letting up on the pressure just yet. We have a long way to go on this."

"It's just this one evening. We'll come back to it fresh tomorrow morning."

Except for Rob, everyone warmed to the plan.

Late that afternoon, Miss Agnus started barking and running in circles every time someone new came to the door. Her pitched-forward ears, bright eyes, and eager grin declared her certainty that all the visitors and excitement were somehow in her honor and for her enjoyment—a perception that was confirmed over and over as Cal's guests exclaimed, "You are so cute!" and reached to pet her before saying hello to him or anyone else.

Cal had also invited Candace Bennington and Ned Freedman and, with some hesitation, Evana Arthur. Jon was up from Los Angeles too. Out on the deck, Candace and Judy were talking with Ned, who hovered over several items that smoked and sizzled on a large grill. By the time Alexandra pushed open the front door, calling "Hello!" Jon, Matt, Rob, and Cal were sipping at sweating glasses, waiting for Ned's grilling operation to produce dinner. Jon jumped up to greet her, beating Cal to the door. "I'm Alexandra." She reached a hand toward Jon, who grasped it with his left before switching to shake with his right hand. She turned a quizzical look on him.

"I know. I've seen you dance."

"You're—"

"Jon. Cal's my dad."

"Jon! We've all heard fine things about you. First the law degree and then a good spot with a big LA law firm." She paused to give him a chance to respond, and when he didn't, she went on. "Well, your dad is really great to work with. I'm glad to meet you."

Cal watched the exchange. *He can't be this awkward with all women, can he?*

"Uh, what will you have?" Jon asked her. "We've got Coca-Cola, sparkling water, and iced coffee. There's some wine—both red and white—and beer."

"Iced coffee would be perfect."

"Find a seat, uh, on the couch and I'll get it for you."

"Thanks. Let me make the rounds first."

Cal went with her to the deck, where Candace was finishing up a story: "So that's how I wound up taking my first ride on your delightful trams. It was just ripping. Can't wait to take another."

Everyone on the deck watched Ned poke and prod at the grill.

When Alexandra had greeted everyone, Cal asked, "Do you think Katherine will be here?"

"I expect she will, though she said we shouldn't wait for her. I talked to her a little bit ago. Her mother isn't any better, but at least she isn't any worse." She turned to accept the iced coffee from Jon, taking a sip and raising her eyebrows with a smile to let him know the coffee was fine. He escaped to the kitchen, where he began turning salads out into bowls.

Miss Agnus scurried from the scents near the grill back to the front door at the first sound of footsteps. This time it was Evana, who confirmed all of Miss Agnus's perceptions by scooping the tiny dog up into her arms. She held the dog as she trailed from the kitchen to the living room and out onto the deck. Two of the men rose to offer her a seat.

Amelie arrived, carrying flowers.

"You didn't have to—but I'm glad you did," Cal said, thanking her.

While Jon poured sparkling water for her, Cal found a vase large enough to accommodate the ample arrangement. She busied herself near Jon, chatting as she cut the ends of the stems with a knife and arranged the flowers. "You two haven't already met, have you?" Cal asked.

"No," they said at the same time and smiled at each other as Cal made the introduction. "There!" Amelie said, finishing with the flowers. "Where do you think we should put them?"

Cal started to answer, but Jon took the vase. "They're beautiful," he said. "Let's put them on the coffee table where we can all enjoy them. Don't forget your glass." He nodded toward the sparkling water he'd poured for her. Cal watched Amelie reach for the glass. *He thinks she's going to follow him.* She did.

Ned called from the deck, "Five minutes!"

Cal relayed the message to the group in the living room. "Jon, you want to help set out the rest of it?"

"Okay, Dad." Jon returned to the kitchen and began pulling salads and desserts from the refrigerator, Amelie peeking over his shoulder. Rounding the corner on his way to the deck, Cal heard her say, "Well, I know Cal didn't make all of this, because he was working today. Does that mean you did it all?"

"Who cooks these days? Delicatessen down the street."

"Of course. Let me help." She took up the bowl of potato salad. "Where does it all go?"

"There's a side table on the deck just outside the door."

"I'll show you," Cal said.

Amelie and Cal carried several dishes to the table, arranged stacks of plates and silverware, and uncovered the prepared food. They returned to the kitchen to find Jon tying on an apron. "I thought we were done," Amelie said.

"Oh, no. I have to whip the cream for that blackberry torte you just carried out." He reached for the electric mixer. "Somehow if I don't have an apron on—" He shrugged and grinned at her again.

Cal rolled his eyes. "I'll be on the deck, if anyone wants me."

On the grill were fish, chicken, and small beefsteaks. Cal watched, deflecting the thanks and compliments to Ned, as plates were filled and everyone found places to sit to eat. Miss Agnus settled herself beside Evana's deck chair, one in a circle around a shaded round table where Candace, Judy, Ned, and Cal also gathered. Rob and Alexandra sat in the early evening sun on the steps leading down into the yard, and Amelie, Matt, and Jon chose the relative cool of the living room.

"I'm curious, Candace," Cal said. "How does your father go about it when he choreographs?"

Candace held her knife in her right hand and her fork in her left as she ate. She cut a tiny piece of chicken and pierced it with the tines of the fork, the outer curve faced upward. "He's actually quite cerebral about it. In the studio, that is. At home he throws himself about a bit while he's working it out in paper diagrams, but at the studio with his dancers, he's very collected, almost scientific in how he goes about getting what he wants."

"How do you mean?"

"I'm saying that the overall design is what he's after. I've always thought his ballets should be seen only from the back of the theater or, better yet, second balcony, where the audience can get back far enough to follow the overall shape from one form to the next. When he's choreographing on the dancers, he'll experiment with how to move them from one shape to another, but he's really not terribly concerned with the transitions. Just that the resulting shapes have to be perfect."

"But doesn't everyone sitting in the second balcony bring a pair of opera glasses?" Judy asked.

Candace nodded. "They think the thing to see is every little step and position. There ought to be warning notices posted for Dad's ballets: Leave your opera glasses at home!"

"How does he deal with those days when he just seems to be cold?" Cal asked. "Or doesn't he have any?"

"A lot of people have accused my father of being cold by nature."

Cal smiled back. "What I mean is, doesn't it happen this way a lot? You've been working on a piece for days on end, but one morning you try to get into the creative process and it's as though you've never been there before. So you try not to panic. You try to coax it along, press in here and there for an idea. The dancers are surly and you secretly guess that they think everything you've done so far is insipid. You just can't get into it somehow. And just at that moment it all seems pretty empty to you too. You're just—cold."

Using her knife, Candace had layered the back of her fork, still with the bit of chicken on the tines, with small portions of two kinds of salad. She was just opening her mouth to answer when Evana broke in.

"Oh, come off it, Cal!" Evana's face bore the contemptuous frown he knew so well. "If you have a job to do, you sit down and do it. You knock heads with the piano or the orchestra or the dancers or whoever you have to, to get it done. I've never had any patience for the creative types who think every little note or brush stroke or dance step they put down comes from some muse. There's nothing magical about what we all do. It's just work. You sit down and do it, whether you're cold or hot or what."

In the jarred silence that followed, Cal stared at Evana and then noticed that the others were staring at her too. Suddenly Candace laughed. "You'd get on great with Dad!" Then she turned to Cal. "And even if you don't quite espouse the philosophy, I've seen you practice it too. Look at what's been happening with your new ballet just in the weeks I've been here. You've had heads to knock, and you've been knocking them, in your own nonviolent way." Candace glanced back toward Evana. "And I think Dad rather relishes that stage when the ballet's a bit messed about. I think he finds his best pleasure in ironing out the disorder." Finally she took the layered bite into her mouth.

The telephone rang and Cal excused himself to answer, relieved to leave Evana to the rest of them. In the silence, even those on the deck heard him say, "Katherine, is that you? Good Lord! Oh, I'm so sorry. I'll be right there."

Alexandra was at his side by the time he hung up the receiver. "What's happened?"

"She died."

He was dizzy for a moment, staring into Alexandra's eyes, and then she said, "Let's go."

Cal turned toward the small group in the living room. "I'm sorry to abandon you like this. Katherine's just lost her mother. Jon, will you take over here?"

Almost unheard in the exclamations from the group, Jon said, "Sure, Dad. You go ahead." Then he called after them, "Call me later."

The drive to the hospital was in silence. Once there, Cal parked in the spot he had come to think of as his own parking space, and they rushed inside. They found Katherine sitting alone in an alcove down the hall from what had been her mother's room. When she saw them, she rose to be embraced by first Cal, and then Alexandra. The hysterics Cal had secretly feared were nowhere in evidence; she was calm, and the first thing she said was, "It's over." And again, even quieter, "It's over."

But then it seemed to hit her. Her long, graceful form folded itself into the chair, her face against her knees, and she gave way to the realization of loss. Cal knelt beside her and took her hand in both of his.

Alexandra stood on the other side of Katherine's chair, bent over with her face against Katherine's hair.

Once the funeral home had been called, then Mrs. Melton's lawyers, there was nothing more to do at the hospital. "I really don't want to go home, but I suppose I should," Katherine said.

"If the funeral home needs to contact you, that's where they'll call. But there's no reason we can't stay with you, if you want us to."

Katherine nodded.

At the condominium, the first thing Katherine did was take down her mother's favorite teacup and put it into the trash, and then no sooner had she walked away than she returned, took the cup out of the trash, and set it on the counter. She moved it to the window sill and then back to the counter and left it there while she led Cal and Alexandra to the living room.

"How was the party?" Her voice was a monotone.

"We missed you. And Evana was in one of her ornery moods." Cal thought about the abundance of food. "Have you had anything to eat?"

Katherine shook her head. "After the rehearsal, I went straight to the hospital, thinking I'd get some food there and see Mother, then leave a couple of hours later to come to your place. But then nothing in the cafeteria looked appealing, and I was barely back in the room when Mom started to fail. She looked at me, and then it was like she just gave up." Tears came quickly to her reddened eyes, and though her mouth opened again, there seemed to be nothing more she could say.

"Maybe it was taking all the energy she had just to stay alive," Alexandra said.

Katherine nodded, and the tears went sliding down her face.

Cal rose from his chair. "One thing I know is that you need to eat, and that's something I can take care of. Do you have any druthers about what you'd like, or shall I just put together what I can with what I find in the kitchen?"

"Anything's fine. Thanks, Cal."

He found eggs, fresh mushrooms, cheddar and Swiss cheese, green and red peppers. As he put together a large omelet, Katherine returned to the kitchen, picked up her mother's teacup, and placed it on a cabinet shelf, out of sight.

In the late evening, Alexandra elected to stay overnight with Katherine and send Cal back to his party. When he reached home, he saw

Jon's car still there, and Amelie's too; everyone else had gone. He walked in to find them laughing together in the living room over dance steps Amelie was trying to teach to Jon. Miss Agnus watched from the sofa. All the party leavings had been cleaned up and put away. "Well. What are you two up to?"

"She can't believe I could be your son and not have an ounce of dancing ability in me."

Cal turned a weak smile toward Amelie. "I've always loved him anyway."

"Yes, that can't have been very hard." Amelie looked from father to son and back. "How is Katherine?"

"Not as bad as you might expect. Alexandra is staying with her again tonight. I don't know if either one will make it to the studio tomorrow." He heaved a sigh. "That poor girl."

A somber mood settled over all of them. "I hadn't realized how late it must be getting," Amelie said. "I'd best go on home. I'll see you at the studio in the morning, Cal."

"Good night, Amelie."

Jon walked Amelie to her car and said his good-bye there, a process that took over half an hour. Returning to his father's house, he had barely closed the door when Cal said to him, "Jon, what are you thinking? She's old enough to be your mother!"

Jon looked too stunned to reply. Finally he sputtered, "In the first place, she's only ten years older than I am. And in the second, I can't believe you'd consider referring to Amelie and my mother in the same breath."

Cal flinched and dropped his head for several moments. "I'm sorry, son. I don't know what's the matter with me. This thing with Katherine's mother—" He rubbed both hands over his face and through his hair, and then he apologized again. "To be honest, I guess I'd thought that you and Alexandra would, you know, decide you liked each other, even become a couple maybe. You and Amelie just took me by surprise."

"I think we took ourselves by surprise. And as for Alexandra, I couldn't manage to form three sentences with her, and she didn't seem interested in saying more than about that much to me."

Cal made another unsuccessful effort at smiling. "I guess there's no accounting for these things. It's been a hard day. I think I'll turn in." He felt tired and beaten.

"Dad, there's ice cream in the freezer. I thought you might need it, so we went out and bought some for you this evening."

Cal looked at his adult son, feeling for the first time a hint of reversal of roles and was a little pleased to notice that he didn't mind. He smiled now and said, as a much-younger Jon had said to him so many times, "Better be butterscotch!"

* * *

Four Weeks

"Oh boy!" Cal didn't realize he was groaning out loud. A chill sat in his gut, and he was trying to warm it with hot cocoa. He took another gulp, counting on the mix of heat and milk and chocolate to ease the terror in his belly.

Just like that morning exactly five weeks before, he had called Amelie and asked her to take his place in the morning classes. Just like then, he had headed out into the air in a rush, trying to walk faster than the panic that was overtaking him. Just like then, he wound up at the bakery with the rickety door but with such pleasant smells it was hard to imagine that things couldn't be made to work out somehow. He nodded to the slim, middle-aged woman behind the counter, who looked at him expectantly. "How's your day going?" she asked him.

"Fine," he lied. At the counter, he looked over the sweet things and chose a chocolate-dipped peanut butter cookie but decided on hot chocolate rather than coffee and then returned to the same table where he had sat before. The rough chair legs grated against the flooring when he pulled out the chair to sit. The notepad was not new; it was the pad he had purchased five weeks before, and it was now worn from frequent revisiting.

What was not just like that morning was that now he had not sixty-three days but only twenty-eight before opening night. Twenty-eight! Bending over the notepad, he drew out a chart with one square for every day remaining. It was something he could do at this moment: take stock, get it down on paper, refuse to go completely crazy until he had captured on one sheet all the steps that had to be taken. He knew what stood between this moment and that moment: so many decisions, so many obligations, so many fine points to smooth out—so much depending on Katherine.

He whispered her name as his hand stopped charting. His muse of fifteen previous ballets, the ballerina he had trained and shaped and made into a star, his free and elegant bird—but she was wounded now. He saw her in his mind as she had been in class the day before, trying so hard to take refuge in normalcy but unable to find the reassurance and steadiness of routine. At one point she had started a *glissade*, brushing one leg gracefully outward from her body, but then she apparently forgot what she was doing, forgot to shift her weight and stumbled in a most basic step that should have taken no thought at all. What if she had been landing from a *grand jeté* and suddenly was confused about which foot went where or when to be *en pointe* and when not? Cal had realized then that she could hurt herself if her mental focus was not fully in the studio. But, of course, how could it be? And what could he do about it anyway, except keep watch and be as supportive as he could?

He shook his head and doggedly returned his attention to the chart, filling in meetings to schedule with Ned Freedman regarding sets and lighting, with Natalie Stevens about costumes, with Evana about fine-tuning the music, with the stage manager regarding the landing lights, with the fund-raiser Valina Davenport who had asked him to keep specific dates open for talks before groups, with the publicist who had been begging him for program notes. He blocked out whole afternoons for work with Alexandra and Matt—and Katherine. At least no orchestra was needed but just two musicians, one on piano and one on a synthesizer creating the electronic harp. It would be up to Charles Good, the troupe's music director, to get the musicians to the place they needed to be.

He closed his eyes, and into his mind's ear came the music, Evana's triumph, completed in an amazing three weeks. He had glimpsed the cost to her, knew that she had had to push past a multitude of physical and psychological barriers, but she had done it. In the space of a half hour, the music grew by subtle increments from discord and unhappiness to peace and resolution. Evana was still breaking out the parts for the two instruments and sheet music was yet to be finalized, but the elusive music had been captured. He had cassettes of Evana playing a piano arrangement of the whole thing, straight through.

Noticing how calming it was to think about the music, he decided to list what else had been accomplished. If he could see in one place all that had been done in thirty-five days, he might feel better about what had to be done yet in only twenty-eight. Cal held his pencil over the paper and for a terrible moment, he could think of nothing at all that had been accomplished. He took a deep breath and then grabbed for the cup as though taking a swallow of cocoa was the most critical thing he had to do in that moment, as though one of his serious tasks was draining the hot chocolate from the cup.

"Okay," he said in a whisper, fighting the noise of confusion that had grown louder in his brain. "Let's just start at the beginning. We have the theme. That's one thing we have accomplished. We are going to make a new ballet, and the theme will be prayer." Then he grimaced. *And we have a thin idea of what our theme means.*

Quickly then he listed: music, dancers, more than half the choreography—then his eyes slipped back to *dancers*. Though he so much did not want to, he could not keep himself from drawing a question mark next to the word. The feeling of disloyalty was overwhelming; he immediately scratched three thick lines through the question mark. His eyes closed again and from within his heart arose, *Oh, God! God. God, you have to help her.* Tears formed and moisture seeped from under his eyelids.

Then another thought came, this one from his head. *Ohmigod*, it said, *you're praying!* It was surprise more than disbelief. A feeling as of old concrete crumbling came over him as he witnessed the argument within. He could not remember that this had ever happened to him before and fleetingly wondered if this meant that his mind was splintering.

Not the least intimidated, his heart spoke back. *Yes, I'm praying. I'm praying, and not even for myself.* Then he reached out with his prayer again. *God, God, she's just so lost! Even if we never get this ballet on stage, you have to help her. You have to make her understand that she's not as alone as she feels.* For some moments then he sat in silence, thinking nothing, praying nothing, as calmness gained a fragile foothold in his heart. His breath came with a start, as though it might have been suspended for several seconds. He straightened his back and, on purpose, took a few deep breaths.

Cal flipped back several pages in the notepad and read through his lists: "Why does a person pray" and "People might pray when they feel . . ." To the latter he added "powerless to help someone they love." He sat back in the chair then, reading and rereading the addition, surprised by the realization that as deeply as he wanted divine help with the progress of the *Prayer* ballet, even more he wanted divine peace for Katherine. That had been his prayer.

He took another drink of the cocoa and let the sweet smoothness rest against his tongue. The chocolate was a bit cool now, certainly no risk of scalding his mouth, and the change of temperature had changed the texture. For some seconds he let his tongue be bathed by the sweetness. Finally he brought his attention back to the chart and the practical issues before him. He studied the question mark he had scratched through. *If I were to use another dancer*—he forced himself to consider it—*who would it be?* He paraded three of his leading ballerinas across his mind, but one by one, the images dissolved. The idea of replacing Katherine wouldn't even take root. Katherine was his ballerina for this ballet. Another surprise hit him: he realized that he was dedicated to her. When had she become so crucial to his choreography? *Okay, then my Spirit of Prayer will be Katherine and no one else.* A picture of the grief-distracted dancer leapt to his mind, and he had to say it again—this time half aloud: "My Spirit of Prayer will be Katherine and no one else. Decision made."

He closed his eyes then and simply sat, waiting to remember what else had been accomplished so far. Nothing came to him. With impatience, he brushed the tears away just as he heard the glass rattle in the frames of the bakery door.

"Thought I might find you here!" It was Ned Freeman's rasping voice.

Cal looked up in shock. "You did? Why did you think you might find me here?"

"Deinken said you come here sometimes."

Cal blinked. "Rob said that! How would he know?"

"I don't know, Cal. Maybe the guy's been following you." He took off his cap and automatically ran a hand over his balding head, but a few golden hairs stood upright until he replaced the cap. He yanked a chair out and sat down. "All I know is I asked him if he knew where you were and he said you might be here."

"Then he *must* have followed me." *Hard to blame him. He must think I've gone completely nuts.* "Well, he probably—" *But, geez, I've been here exactly twice in my life!*

"Look, Cal. Natalie and I are both about to bust a gut waiting for something to work with on this new piece you put on the October slate. Neither of us thinks there is anywhere near enough time—in *any* case—and here you are stalling on us! It's past the place where we can stand it now. This is just not like you, Cal." Pleading came into Ned's eyes for a moment before the anger resumed. "It's just not fair to us and our people, so either you come up with something for us now—and I mean *today*—or you might just find yourself trying to do the piece without sets or lights or costumes." Ned's face had become redder the more he spoke; he hurried on before Cal could open his mouth. "Now I know this might sound like insubordination to you, but we don't care even if it sounds like insurrection. I'm representing all of us here, Natalie and her people and all of mine. We've talked about it and we're all on the same page. We can't do the kind of work we are expected to do if you keep holding out. You've pushed us too far. We know there are some problems—" For the briefest moment a look of compassion washed over his face, followed by renewed anger. "We know you've got something because you've been working with those dancers, so why aren't you working with *us*?" He stopped, his eyes fierce now, demanding a response from Cal.

"Well"—Cal hesitated—"I'm not interrupting, am I?"

"No! Talk to me, man!"

"Hearing you say that I might have to do the ballet without sets made me visualize what that would look like—and I realized that it's not *sets*, it's *set*. Just one. And very, very plain. We'll need a drop across the entire rear of the stage, something dye painted and a little translucent that will reflect color well."

The red began to leave Ned's face, but he still stared hard at Cal, demanding more. "Normal flat stage, no rake? No arches, no props, no walls dividing the stage?"

Cal shook his head. "Normal stage." But he was thinking about something else. "But probably something at up right. I don't know what—maybe a short set of steps or maybe just a scrim. Upstage right needs to be set off but not by walls or anything substantial. You'll need to come up with an idea for that."

Ned was nodding. Cal continued, "But lights, now, Ned, the lighting is critical. Coloration is going to change a lot and keep changing in a progression through the whole ballet. The piece is thirty minutes, and I have the music now, so I'll get a copy of it for you this afternoon. And I have a libretto." He watched Ned's face, but there was no sign that Ned found anything unusual about Cal's using a libretto, though this was the first time the word had ever been used between them. "That will walk you through every scene and exactly how long it is and what sort of mood is going on in it. I'll get a copy of that for you this afternoon. The main thing from you is going to be the lights."

A that's-more-like-it expression had settled on Ned's face. "Sounds simple in scenery but complex in optics. We can do that. You'll have your lights."

"I'll get in touch with Natalie right away when I get back to the studio," Cal said. "Maybe she can meet this afternoon too."

"She'll want to do that. Anything I can tell her when I get back, just to take the edge off her worries?"

Again Cal had the sensation that decisions were being made almost without his conscious attention. "The costumes will be just one for each of three dancers and really simple. Two of the dancers will be in black and white, and the third—well, a little less simple for the third. Something diaphanous, probably long, a contrast from the other two. I'll go through the racks with Natalie. We probably already have something that can be easily modified or even work just as it is."

"I'll tell her so she can start thinking about it." Ned wiped a hand over his forehead, and his voice became scratchier. "I'm sorry, Cal. Natalie has been pretty upset, and so have I."

Cal waved away the apology.

"And we've been worried about the Melton girl. She's in this new piece, right?"

Cal nodded. "I'm worried about her too. But I'm leaving her in." His tone was defensive; Ned raised both palms as though to say, "Hey, no fight from me!" Cal went on, "We'll all just have to help her as much as we can."

"But she's going to lose pretty much all of this week too, isn't she? I mean, what with the funeral and burial and all those arrangements. That all takes time, let alone the grief part."

"The shock and grief are the worst of it now. It's really hard for her to concentrate. Her entire world has been knocked off-kilter. She needs some time to adjust, and with opening night so close, she doesn't have that luxury." He corrected, "*I* don't have the luxury of giving her that time. And the truth is, she doesn't want the time off anyway. She insists on being at the studio and trying to carry on." Cal looked around the bakery as though there were answers somewhere in the room. "I understand that though. I'd be doing the same thing. I think that with her mother gone, the troupe is her family and she'd rather be with us than be alone."

"I suppose the funeral will be this weekend? What do you know about her plans for that?"

"I don't think there's going to be a funeral now. She said something about a memorial service in a few months when she has a chance to let all the family and friends know and can sort that out. She's decided on cremation, so that will mean a lot less in the way of immediate arrangements."

"But, Cal—I mean, how is she going to focus on dancing?"

"I know. It's going to be hard. But even if I wanted to or thought I could, I wouldn't have the heart to take this away from her too." He cleared his throat and shifted in his chair. "But Katherine is a professional. She'll pull herself through this."

"What can we do to help her?"

"Just go out of your way to make sure she knows you're there and you care about her and what she's going through. Alexandra Kreyling is spending a lot of time with her, staying at her place with her."

Ned nodded and then pushed back his chair. "I'm going to get back over to the studio." He looked at his watch. "I'll be at your door in about two hours for that libretto and a copy of the music, okay? That way I can get going on it yet today."

"That will be fine, Ned. I'll have them ready for you. And ask Natalie if she can see me around three."

* * *

That evening Cal drove into his driveway, hearing through the open car window the sound of Miss Agnus barking in greeting. He fed the Pomeranian and then found some leftovers from the party to heat up for himself. As usual, Miss Agnus sat on the floor beside him, her single-focus intensity making her eyes appear even darker and rounder, but she didn't make a sound.

"And how was your day?" he asked her.

Miss Agnus's head tilted ten degrees to the right, her eyes fixed even more intently upon his.

"Any neighborhood pooches come calling?"

Her head tilted another five degrees.

"How about that brown Lab—any more run-ins with him?"

Now her head tilted the other direction as she strained to hear a word she knew. As her head straightened again, her tiny mouth opened to pant, and her tongue slipped over the edge of her teeth. She looked like she was smiling. Nothing would draw her attention away from Cal and the food on his plate.

"Here you go, girl." He reached toward her with a small piece of meat on his fork—the last bite. Delicately, she put one front paw against his leg and stood up on her hind feet to sniff the bite before pulling it off the fork. He rose from the table to take his plate to the kitchen.

Later he sat in his living room as the evening darkened. The heavy drapes were still open. After eating, he had sat down on the sofa and had not moved since. No reading, no phone calls, no music playing, not even any thinking. He simply sat. After an hour Miss Agnus jumped from his lap to the floor. She chose a hardwood spot to lie on, stretching out to her full length for as much coolness on her belly as possible, but she still watched him. He winked at her and she looked away and then brought her eyes back to his. He winked again, and this time she decided it must be an invitation. She got to her feet, came to him, and sat. Intentionally or not, her tiny butt had landed on his right shoe. He smiled, feeling her five-pound weight on his foot.

Then she pulled her front paws off the floor and, rising up, balanced herself on his shoe as she began waving her front paws together. Over and over she touched her paws and then let them drop an inch or so before bringing them up together again. "I haven't seen you do that since you were a puppy!" This resulted in her speeding up the motion, never once dropping his gaze.

Careful not to upset her balance on his shoe, he reached down to scratch her belly. Miss Agnus relaxed her forepaws as long as he scratched but began waving again if he stopped. There was no variation in her routine. "Who's your choreographer for that move?'

Perhaps it was his own question settling into his mind or perhaps something else, but into his heart came the secret of what he must do to help Katherine. The choreography for his Spirit must be refined until it was elegantly simple, with the subtlest evolution of poses, not difficult to remember, and flowing inevitably from one motion to the next, something she could learn with minimal effort yet still dance with grace. *That's how spirit functions, isn't it?* The revelation took form within him.

It's not about complicated steps or acrobatic moves. It's about who she is, not what she does, about being, not about doing. A deep breath came into him, and then out, and he reached with one hand to scoop Miss Agnus up into his arms as his mind went to that blessed place from which all dance comes. Holding the Pom against his chin, feeling her fine red/gold hairs catch in his stubble, he saw the dance in his mind, saw Katherine gliding from one gentle, serene movement to the next.

It was almost completely dark outside when Cal next became aware of the room. Moonlight gave what illumination there was, and that brought a whitish sheen to everything it fell upon. He pushed the backlight on his watch and saw that it was after midnight. At some point Miss Agnus had again left his lap for the cool hardwood boards. She lay sleeping, her tiny face turned toward him and resting on her front paws. He felt peaceful himself—so peaceful that he could finally notice that something waited at the edge of his awareness, something not yet pondered, not yet addressed. *I was actually praying in that store today. Purposefully praying.* His eyes came open. *I prayed to God to help Katherine.* It was so unusual, so atypical for him, that he had not even permitted himself to remember it until now, when no other distraction could be mustered to deflect his attention.

He remembered the calmness that had settled over him, the way his terror had subsided, and the difficulties of the coming weeks had begun to feel manageable. He had prayed for Katherine not to feel alone, and in his heart he had sensed with a deep assurance that Katherine *would* come through this blow, that she also would understand that she was not alone. But there was more, and this was the part that made his heart stand still in awe: somehow the sense of not being alone had come to *him* at the same time. He had prayed for Katherine, and through the prayer, he had been touched too.

Then his heart began beating a little faster as a new realization came, and he whispered to no one in the room, "I think I finally understand my theme." Keen excitement pushed a smile onto his face.

* * *

"Hello. This is Matt." The perspiring dancer rubbed a worn white towel against his forehead and then tried to grip the studio phone and still wipe sweat from his hands. Cindy, the studio receptionist, had paged him at the close of a rehearsal to say there was a phone call for him. No one had ever called for Matt at the studio before.

The gentle voice on the line said, "There you are."

Matt's leg muscles felt suddenly dead. Squeezing his voice past his now-tight throat, he barely breathed the word: "Ricardo?"

"I've been working on my English. Can you tell?"

Matt tried to swallow but found that his mouth was too dry. He struggled again to swallow.

"I see I have surprised you." Ricardo laughed. "Well, I confess, I wanted to surprise you. I went back to Italy, but I could not forget the blond boy I met in San Francisco."

Matt winced. *The blond boy?* The flirting tone felt belittling and annoyed him. "Where are you?"

"On the other side of the world, I'm afraid."

For a curious moment, Matt felt both relieved and stricken. "You sound like you could be right next door."

"I want to come to see you."

The image of dark eyes looking straight into his own from the bathroom mirror filled Matt's mind, followed by the image of Ricardo, smiling, in the open hotel room door. "Uh, the thing is, you know, we have the fall season opening in less than four weeks."

"Yes, I know. Are you saying you don't want to see me?"

"No. No, I want to see you." He paused, hearing his own heart pound. *Do I really? If I want to see him, why am I more scared than excited?* He was aware of Ricardo waiting on the other end of the line. "Sorry, the truth is I haven't been thinking about anything but the opening next month. There's a premiere—that we're still learning the choreography for. In fact the choreography is still being worked out."

"What are you afraid of, Matt?"

Oh shit! How can he tell I'm scared! He pushed the thought away. "I'm not afraid of anything."

"Didn't we have a good time when I was in San Francisco?" Ricardo's tone still sounded like flirting; Matt still didn't like it.

"Yes, we did. So, are you doing a guest spot for another US troupe somewhere, or why are you thinking of coming back to America?"

"You're the whole reason, Matt. I want to see you again."

Matt felt his face grow warm: *A world-famous dancer interested in seeing me?* "I-I find that hard to believe."

Ricardo sighed into the phone. His accent seemed to become stronger in the absence of the teasing. "Look, Matt, I'm not going to try to talk you into this. I thought there was something good between us, but maybe I was wrong."

"No—" Matt struggled for more words but could think of nothing to say. In the same instant he wanted to shove Ricardo away and yet pull him closer. The dichotomy paralyzed him.

After a few seconds had passed, the soft voice calling from Italy said, "I'm sorry I bothered you." And the phone connection was broken.

Matt's eyes widened in shock and sudden disappointment. "Ricardo, no!" But it was too late. Now his stomach felt sick and fainting seemed a real possibility. He slid his back down the wall and sat down, staring at the phone receiver. *How can I get him back?*

"Matt? Are you all right?" Alexandra stood in front of him, but he couldn't raise his eyes above the shabby, stained ballet slippers she wore for class. The end of one of the ribbons had come loose from where she'd tucked it at the back of her ankle, and he focused on the wispy threads.

"Matt! What's wrong?" She squatted down next to him and took his face in her hands. "What's wrong with you? Are you sick?"

He took a breath and shook his head. "Nothing's wrong, Alex. I'm okay."

"You look like death. What happened?"

He shook his head again and held up the receiver. "That was just a really important phone call, and I blew it."

"Well, call whoever it was back!"

Tears came to his eyes. "I can't! Sometimes you don't know you're having your one and only chance at something until you've just blown it."

Alexandra stared at him. "Who was on the phone?"

"It was Ricardo."

"Ricardo?"

"Vitale."

She blinked—that was all—but Matt could see that she understood the implications. He grabbed the towel from the floor, reared to his feet, and turned away, heading down the hall. Behind him, he could hear Alexandra call out, "Matt, come back here. It's okay."

But he rushed into the men's room, turned on the cold tap, leaned over the sink, and repeatedly threw water into his face. He was playing the brief conversation with Ricardo over and over in his head when Rob Deinken walked in.

"You okay, Matt?"

Matt found Rob's reflection in the mirror. "Uh, I was about to come look for you. I'm not feeling up to any more today."

"Okay, okay, no worries." The concern on Rob's face deepened. "You look like you need to go home and get into bed." When Matt said nothing further, Rob went on, "Maybe we've been pushing too hard on the new piece. I'll make sure Cal and Amelie know you went home sick."

Matt nodded.

"Just call us if you can't make it tomorrow."

But Matt didn't go home; he headed for Stephen Marksman's office, running the ten blocks' distance. There was a strange car parked in front of the house that served as both home and therapy office. Matt took the steps two at a time, let himself into the narrow entry that served as the therapist's waiting room. Inside, he closed the door quietly and stood in silence, listening, and could just hear the murmur of indistinguishable voices on the floor above that meant Stephen was with a patient. He sat down, but almost at once he was on his feet again and began to pace, replaying Ricardo's voice in his mind. After about twenty minutes, a door on the upper floor opened and a man dashed down a hall, down the stairs, and out the front door with only a nod at Matt. Within minutes Stephen appeared at the top of the steps.

"Matt?" He looked confused. "Did I make a mistake—?"

"I'm sorry. I know I'm not supposed to be here today."

"That's okay. I have a few minutes before my next appointment. Come on up." Matt rushed up the steps and followed Stephen into the office. Instead of sitting, Stephen turned and peered into his face. "What's going on, Matt?"

"I need to see you. I need to talk to you about something."

"Can you give me some idea what it's about?" Stephen continued to watch Matt's eyes.

"I-it's—I-I'm sure the whole thing will sound silly to you."

"I guarantee that it won't."

"It's just I heard from Ricardo—"

"The Italian dancer who was in town last month."

"He was calling from Italy, but I kind of freaked, didn't know what to say to him. He said he wanted to come see me, but I didn't know if I really wanted that or not—"

"I see."

Matt's voice dropped and he stopped meeting Stephen's eyes. "Anyway, now I know I really *do* want that, but he hung up on me since I was being a total speechless idiot, and I don't know how to reach him, and I'm afraid of what it means—that I want him to come back." Matt's eyes felt sore and so did his stomach.

"Okay, I understand." Stephen turned to his desk and pulled his calendar around so he could read it. "Listen, I don't have an opening until five, but I could see you if you want to talk then." Matt nodded, and Stephen came back to stand near him. "You'll be okay till then, right?" Matt nodded again. "I'll see you at five then."

"I'll be here."

Stephen did not accompany Matt down the stairs, so he was self-conscious of the sound of his footsteps through the hall and of every creak in the stairs. He was grateful that no one sat waiting in the narrow entry, because he did not want anyone, not even a stranger, to see his face. It would have been nice to be invisible.

As the front door closed behind him, Matt stared at the steps down to the street. What could he possibly do to fill up the hours before he could come back to this very door? First he paced the sidewalk, some twenty feet, then back, then back again. In his anguish, both of his hands rose to his head, and his mind split along two lines of awareness: one part engulfed in the loss and confusion of the moment, the other recognizing the gesture as the same as a moment in Cal's choreography for the *Prayer* ballet. His mind pulled away into the choreography then, and he pictured himself dancing the steps up to that moment; he saw his hands rise to grasp his head in the balletic move.

What was I dancing? What was Cal expressing? Matt's body was trained to achieve and hold artistic positions and move from step to step with little rational thought. He relied on body memory to take him through choreographies. But now he watched himself and Alexandra dance on the screen of his mind and thought about the meaning behind their postures. He saw conflict and anger, irritation and strife, beseeching that led nowhere, frustration and sorrow, fear and resistance—these until Katherine began to dance, and then gradually the change. Now he sat down on the step as the point of the *Prayer* ballet spilled over him: *It's about people who feel as lost as I feel right now finding the way out! What I am feeling since Ricardo hung up on me is the sort of pain Cal has in mind for the early scenes—before Katherine comes in.*

He brought his hands back to his head and began to let himself make the connection between what he was feeling in his life and what he was expressing through the dance. What was it Cal had said? Something like, "The music tells us that you are trapped in the human plane with virtually no access to the spiritual element, and the dance tells us that on that human plane, you and Alexandra are getting along about as well as trapped, enraged animals." *What did he mean by "no access to the spiritual element"?*

"Hello? Are you okay?"

Matt was jolted out of his thoughts. A woman stood in front of him, looking at him in concern—Stephen's next patient probably.

"Uh, yes, I'm okay. I'm sorry. Let me get out of your way." He moved on then, from in front of Stephen's house, but he wasn't seeing the sidewalk. He was seeing the scenes of Cal's ballet, which now made sense to him in a way it never had before. It seemed like the most important ballet he had ever danced.

He came to a small park where he chose a space under a tree and began marking his steps, pausing often to think about what they meant. Then he saw in memory the steps and moves Cal had choreographed for Katherine—how she looked, how she moved, how peace was the main theme she danced. He knew her steps as well as he knew his own. *And she's the Spirit of Prayer.* Getting used to the idea for the first time, he sat down under the tree, watching Katherine dance, noticing that the longer he watched her, the more peaceful he became.

* * *

When Matt had rushed off down the hall at the studio, leaving her calling after him, Alexandra realized that her acceptance of him as a gay man had come a fraction of a second too late. *Well, he could have let me know at some point.* Then she understood. *He didn't know it either. He's as shocked as my face must have said I was.* "Oh, Matt."

"Something wrong with Matt?" It was Rob, coming toward the reception desk.

She swung around to him. "I'm not sure, Rob. Maybe you should see if he's all right. He's in the men's room."

Alexandra had a half hour before her next rehearsal. She grabbed a sweater and ran to the door leading to the basement. The cool of the building's recesses became more noticeable as she moved from one floor to the next down the stairs to the dim storeroom. She had come to feel that this space was her own, having never seen another being down there except the orange striped cat. But no cat's eyes glowed anywhere in the darkened room today.

She settled into a corner of the sofa, spread the blanket over her legs, and began the quieting process. In her mind she saw Matt, swamped in shame, speechless with distress, and started to let the scene dissolve, as fog in sunlight, but then stopped herself. *I wish I could bring Matt with me into the meditation.* But already her mind was giving up its control as her thoughts lagged to a slower pace. She held onto the image of Matt a few moments longer and then let that go too as her body relaxed and she descended deep within herself.

She hardly needed the peek at her watch after twenty minutes. Her body knew that it was time for her return from the level of quiet universe where her spirit had gone. Despite the blanket, her body felt cold. She sat for several minutes with her eyes closed and gathered herself fully back until she could feel her blood coursing warmly again. She sat up straight from where she had slumped into the corner of the sofa.

It was her mother she was thinking about now as she emerged from the meditation session. Somehow the focus had shifted from Matt. She was remembering her mother's choking tears at the memory of Ricky. The phone conversation the previous week had been the first time they had talked about his death and how everyone in the family had reacted; in fact, the call was the first time they had talked at all for a very long time. *I promised to call her this week. But if I call, that will give her a chance to make a lame excuse and refuse to come.*

Walking up the steps, which she did slowly to let her leg muscles warm up gradually, she felt the decision become firm: *I'm not going to call. I'm just going to buy the ticket and mail it to her.* A pleasant sense of certainty rested on her heart.

* * *

At five on the dot, Stephen Marksman appeared at the top of the stairs and said, "Matt, come on up."

Heart beating faster and mouth growing dry, Matt rose from the straight-back chair in the entryway and went up the steps. At the top of the staircase, Stephen reached to shake his hand—*Probably an excuse to look me in the eye*—and then Matt followed Stephen into the therapy room. "It's warm in here."

"Mm," Stephen answered, and Matt understood that it wasn't really warm in the room—he was overheated with his emotions. "So Ricardo Vitale called you."

"He was talking about coming back to San Francisco to see me, and I just . . . froze up at the idea. I guess I convinced him that I'm not interested, and he hung up on me."

Stephen said nothing, waiting for Matt to go on.

"But it turned out that I am a lot more interested than . . . than I want to be—because it nearly killed me when I realized he'd hung up and I had no way to call him back."

"What would you say to him—if we could get him on the phone right now?"

"Well, I-I . . ." Matt looked to one side of his chair and then the other. "I guess I'd be just as tongue-tied as before."

"Stop and think about it a second. After all, he might call again, and this time you won't have to be caught off guard."

Matt took a breath and sat up straight, his back pressed against the chair. "He could teach me a lot about dance, you know, with the career he's had." Stephen's expression was bland, so Matt went on. "He knows things about technique that I've never been taught, and I could learn a lot just being around him—you know, talking to him."

For a moment longer Stephen was silent, and then he opened his hands: "So you're saying that the whole reason you were desperate just a few hours ago over his hanging up on you is because you see him as someone who can help your dance career?"

Matt felt his face go hot and he squirmed in the chair. He stared at the windowsill, then at the design in the rug, then at the crease in his pant leg. A noise, like the sound of air rushing past his ears, confused him.

After a silence, Stephen asked, "Are there any *personal* reasons you want to see him?"

"Yes. No, not like—yes."

"No, not like what?" Stephen pressed. "Matt, this is a man you've already slept with. How would you keep any relationship with him strictly professional after that?"

The pitch of the rushing air became more intense. Matt could not make himself look at Stephen. His mouth was so dry he could hear his tongue move. "But what if it means I'm gay?"

The therapist sat with his posture open, receptive. When at last Matt's gaze rose to meet his, Stephen shrugged and repeated the question. "What if it means you're gay?"

Matt looked away again and squeezed the words out in a whisper. "I couldn't stand that."

This time Stephen answered at once. "What's the alternative, Matt?"

The abrupt question shocked Matt out of the quicksand of misery, and he raised his head. "Alternative? What do you mean?"

"What are the other ways to look at this?"

Matt's eyes shifted away again, but he had regained a tiny measure of self-control. "I don't know."

"I don't know either." Stephen's voice was nonjudgmental, matter-of-fact. "It seems to me that you've reached a point where you need to think about that question."

Silence descended between them, but the quiet felt nonmalignant. Matt had stopped squirming. Perhaps a minute passed, possibly two. Matt knew that Stephen would not rescue him. "Stephen, if I promise to think about that question and deal with it next session, will you let me change the subject?"

"Of course."

"Because there's something else I want to talk about, and I need some input."

"Okay."

"What do you know about the spiritual element?"

Stephen smiled. "That's a surprisingly good question, Matt. But it's one I want to think about a little bit before we take it up, and I'm sure you will too. So we both have a little homework before our next session."

* * *

Three Weeks

"You can't be serious!" Despite his outrage, Cal still noticed the tug at his heart at the series of expressions following each other across Jon's face: surprise, hurt, disappointment, irritation, anger.

"Well, yeah, Dad, I am, actually." Jon's brown/gray eyes held his father's gaze without flinching.

Cal bit down hard to keep his mouth from opening, at least long enough to regain control of what words might come out. He couldn't quite do it though. "But you only just met her!"

It had started as a nice weekend, with Jon driving up from Los Angeles on Friday, though most of his time in San Francisco had so far not been spent with Cal. The two had always been easy with each other, and disagreements were rare.

"Look, I know Amelie is a nice woman—she's a *good* woman. I know that—she works for me after all. Why wouldn't I know that? But—"

"But she's ten years older than I am?"

Cal shook his head. "No, that's not it. At least, that's not the main thing. It's what I said: you only just met her. Has it even been two weeks?" In spite of himself his voice rose nearly an octave. "For crying out loud, Jon!"

"Some people get married right after they meet when they just know it's right. Some people do that, Dad, but we're only *talking* about it."

Disappointment chased the exasperation on his face. "I thought you'd be happy for me. For both of us."

A slight yelp from the doorway caused both men to turn their heads. Miss Agnus peered into the room, her red-gold ears pitched forward as if to demand, "Why are you two making such a ruckus?" Cal stretched out his hand toward her, and she scampered to him. He sat on the sofa and held her on his lap.

After regaining his composure, Cal said, "I guess what you're telling me is that you're in love."

"Yes, that's what I'm telling you. This is the best thing I've ever felt, and you're acting like I'm a fourteen-year-old who has no clue about the real world."

Cal stroked the tiny dog without reply, not trusting what he might say if he spoke to his son.

"We're not kids, Dad—and do not say, 'Well, *she* sure isn't' because that would make me furious. Neither one of us is a kid."

Now Cal broke his resolve to silence. "I just think you haven't had nearly enough experience with women to be talking about marrying one."

"How the hell would you have any idea about how much experience with women I've had? Do you honestly think I've told you about every skirt I ever chased?"

Cal made a struggling attempt at a grin. "Okay, how many skirts have you chased?"

"None of your business!"

Cal raised both hands in surrender and then ran them through his hair. "Of course that's none of my business, Jon. But I'd like to think I have a right to be concerned if it looks like you might be rushing into something as serious as marriage."

"My point, Dad, is that we're not rushing anywhere. I just wanted you to know that Amelie and I are both committed to this relationship."

"Have you set a date?"

"No, not really, but we're both thinking six months."

The relief that poured over Cal was followed at once by panic—relief that at least they weren't planning on next week but panic because six months was still far too soon. How could either one really see and come to know the other in only six months, especially with the distance between Los Angeles and San Francisco?

Jon sat down at the opposite end of the sofa, and Miss Agnus left Cal's lap to sit in Jon's. She began licking his hand. Jon took a deep breath. "You don't have to tell me why you're having such a fit, Dad. I already know. But how long did you know Mom before you married her?"

"More than two years."

"And, really, how well did you know her after all that extensive research? Did you have any idea she would abandon us?"

"Not a glimmer."

"So, if I'm not going to really know Amelie until I've been married to her for sixteen years, why wait two years to start the marriage?"

Cal succumbed to the tidal wave of certainty that he would have to give it up. "You make a good point, Counselor."

"And besides, Dad. You're my ace in the hole here. *You* know Amelie. You said yourself that she's a good woman."

"I did. She is. I've worked with her a long time. I would trust her with anything at all having to do with the troupe or the studio. I just never envisioned having to trust her with my son's heart."

At long last, Jon grinned. "And just think what a good daughter-in-law she will be." He looked at his watch. "And I have a date with her right now. Do you want to join us to get something to eat?"

"No, thanks, son. You two go ahead, and have a good time."

When the door had shut behind Jon, Cal stared after him. The oddest urge came over him. For half a minute, before he got hold of himself, he thought he might start bawling. He closed his eyes and was profoundly grateful when Miss Agnus climbed back into his lap, reared up on her hind legs, and licked his face. He wrapped both arms around her. "What's wrong with me, Aggie? How come joy is the furthest thing from my heart right now? I should at least feel some happiness for the fact that he's so happy—shouldn't I?"

The little dog looked directly into his eyes and tilted her head to one side.

Despite the pain in his heart, he could not help smiling at her. "Ya got any ideas about that?" He watched as she tilted her head to the opposite side, as he had known she would.

"Well, do ya?" Back turned the little head, but now she was more intent, because *do* was a *D* word—just like *dinner* was. Miss Agnus truly loved the *dinner* word.

"Does this mean you want your dinner?"

As though she'd been hit by electrical current, Miss Agnus jumped straight up. Her enthusiasm said "Yes! Dinner! Yes! Oh boy!" She jumped to the floor and raced to the kitchen where her empty bowl waited. There she yipped twice and then tried to sit, couldn't manage it, and tried again. Finally she sat, licking her mouth and quivering as she watched Cal get her bag of food out of the cabinet and put an eighth of a cup of kibble into her bowl. To this he added a little canned food.

Cal watched her eat. "You really must teach me how you live in such a constant state of pure happiness."

Returning to the living room sofa, he sat down and let his mind go to that ancient source of his pain: his wife, Anne, and the history they had created. Grief as raw as when first endured flooded him, shocking him by how undiminished it was. *One would think that time would have healed this.* But it appeared that no healing had taken place. None at all! Burying himself in his work had not done the job. Refusing to talk about Anne had not done it. Refusing even to think about her had not done it. The grief was a giant that had merely stood by, waiting for vulnerable moments like this one to spring forth and overcome him. "My God, this is too big for me." Years of unshed tears burned his eyes. His face contorted so fiercely that he felt shame at being unable to control it, and he knew that it would relax only when he had let some of the grief expend itself. "My God," he whispered again. "Help me."

Did he really think someone out there somewhere was going to help him?

Yes, he did. By now he had had evidence that somehow help was available to him. It didn't even matter that he had no idea how. So he was not surprised when the intensity of the pain subsided to a manageable place, where the tears could stop splashing down his cheeks, where his face could calm to its normal configuration, where his hoarse gasps could ease up and his chest stop lunging. Into his mind dropped the thought:

Amelie is not Anne. It is safe to be happy for them. You'll see that it is safe.

What he felt then was a strong sense of peace, followed very soon by gratitude, and he remained with his head bowed in a silence of thanksgiving for several minutes longer. When he raised his head and opened his eyes, he saw that Miss Agnus had rejoined him on the sofa, lying with her front paws just barely in contact with him, her head resting on the paws. Her eyes were lifted toward his in complete peace. He smiled at her. "Next to Jon, there's no one in the world I'd rather have here beside me than you." He blinked and cocked his head a bit. "Did I just say that? No offense, Miss Agnus, but that's kind of a sad state of affairs, don't you think?"

She brought one paw to rest on top of his hand.

* * *

The next morning, a Sunday, Jon slept in and Cal drank a second cup of coffee at the kitchen table, thinking about his son, who was certainly an adult now and no longer needed his supervision. In past years, the two of them would have spent this last day of Jon's visit together, maybe visiting antique shops or hanging out at home trading sections of *The New York Times* or the *Chronicle* or even catching a game. But things were different now. Cal knew he would have to let a new way of being emerge. All these years he had thought of Jon as an extension of himself, and that could no longer be. He found a notepad and scratched out a quick note: "Hey, son. I hope you won't mind, but I need to spend some time at the studio today. How about if I leave you free to spend the day with Amelie? Have fun. Love ya! Dad." Then he grabbed a jacket and hurried to the door, wanting to be certain of escape before Jon was up, now that his resolve was made.

The drive passed without his conscious thought, and at the studio, he paced, stalling, dreading that he might be making a mistake. Finally he reached for the phone and dialed the only principal dancer's phone number he knew by heart.

"Hello?" The voice on the other end sounded hesitant.

"Katherine?"

"Oh, Cal! I'm glad it's you." Then panic entered her voice. "Isn't today Sunday? Have I missed class or something?"

"Yes, yes, it's Sunday. No, you're not missing class. Not to worry." He paused and cleared his throat. "You're sort of monitoring your calls, huh?"

"Yes, it's just—"

"I understand. You feel okay about talking now?"

"Sure." But then she fell silent for a long moment. "Since Mom—I've been really worried about today, what with no classes, no rehearsals, no reason to go to the studio."

"You were wondering what you were going to do with yourself."

"Yes. Sunday used to be the day she and I would go somewhere for brunch and then figure out something we both felt like doing for the day."

"Sounds nice. I know you miss her terribly."

Cal heard Katherine stifle a sob, and it took a few seconds before she could say, "I'm sorry."

"No." He was wary of taking the next step. "It's good, you know, not to bottle up your grief but to let it out."

She didn't answer, so he went on, feeling clumsy, feeling his way. "Actually I have that on firsthand authority. You probably don't know this, but when Jon was a boy, his mother left us, abandoned us, and I could never let myself grieve the loss. She never came back, and I never grieved. And it still catches me off guard now and then." *Reduces me to raw meat, if you want the truth.*

She murmured the appropriate things: "That's terrible! No, I didn't know that. I'm so sorry." He heard her draw a breath then and recognized the determination when she spoke. "Listen, how about if we meet at the studio and do some work on the *Prayer* ballet. You saw me dance this week—you know I could use some extra work."

Cal hesitated. "Wouldn't that be just the opposite of the sage advice I just gave you?"

"I know. I suppose it would be—and I heard the advice. I really did. But I've already cried my eyes out today, and I know I'll be doing more of that tonight and tomorrow and the next day. But just at this moment, I'm feeling that a little work might be the best thing. Of course, I don't want to take away your Sunday if you have other plans."

He smiled. "Jon's in town, but he has things to do today, so no, I have no other plans. The truth is I'm already here at the studio. I guess I was going to get around to asking if you wanted to come in—once I was finished giving the sage advice."

She laughed. "See, this is why I was glad it was you on the phone. I'll be there as soon as I can."

She walked into the studio a half hour later looking, at a distance, poised and collected, as if her world had not been turned upside down.

She wore a white oversized sweatshirt over a black leotard and tights with a long red scarf.

"I have us set up in Studio C," Cal said.

When she had changed into old ballet slippers, they began, as if they were beginners, with basic warm-up exercises at the barre. The scarf and sweatshirt were soon discarded. When she was ready to begin rehearsing, Cal helped her relearn the count and the cues before her first dance in scene 6. First he let her dance it from memory, and where she faltered, he looked to see what he could simplify so the steps would flow more naturally, one to the next. They drilled the steps, making each motion part of Katherine's body memory, steps she would dance automatically no matter what her frame of mind during performance. The grace and line of her body were already so much a part of her that no amount of distraction would unsettle them. Watching her now, his heart rose with pride in her ability and awe at her beauty. Her light auburn hair swung free, and when she stood *en pointe* with her head back and arms angling downward, he noticed that her hair reached nearly to her thighs. *Has her hair always been so long?* Usually pinned into a bun for performances and arranged in some short fashion during class, her hair had never fascinated him quite so much. He should have been watching her feet, her arms, the line of her body, but all he could see was her hair.

He remembered his prayer, just a few days earlier: *Even if we never get this ballet on stage, you have to make her understand that she's not as alone as she feels.* "Do you feel alone?"

She stopped in surprise, dropping five inches from *pointe* to flat feet and looking as though he'd jolted her out of a trance.

"I'm sorry. I shouldn't have asked that."

"It's all right." She touched her fingers to her forehead. "Right now, no. Here with you I don't feel alone at all."

A look of distress crossed her face then, and he knew he'd broken a spell of some kind. He hated himself for reawakening her pain. She had felt safe in forgetfulness, lost in the familiarity of working on a dance sequence in the studio with him. But now she was remembering, and he could see the sorrow hit her. She half turned, as though to hide her tears and crumpling face, but of course he could see everything in the all-revealing, wall-sized mirror. He even saw himself stepping forward, reaching for her. Then she was in his arms, her weight collapsing into him, her tears wetting his shoulder, her sobs loud at his ear. He held her lightly and spoke quiet words to her, encouraging her to grieve, reminding her that she wasn't doing it alone.

Then he stared at his own reflection, into his own eyes, because it felt so right to hold her and share this pain with her. Not only did he want her not to feel alone, but he wanted to be the person who shared her experience with her—all of her experiences from now on.

They stood in the embrace until she grew calm. At the same moment, he felt her back straighten and saw her in the mirror as she regained composure and eased herself out of his arms. She wouldn't meet his eyes. "Please don't be embarrassed. I understand." Then he stepped back too, not forcing her to look at his face. "Listen, that's probably enough work on the ballet today. You made good progress. Why don't we go get something to eat?"

Katherine nodded and reached for her sweatshirt and scarf. He drove her to a small restaurant where no one would mind her leotard and tights, even less the obvious fact that she had been crying. They ate and took a walk afterward. "This has helped me so much, the way we have spent today," she said.

"Maybe we can make it a Sunday pattern for a while then."

She took his arm. "I would like that very much."

* * *

By ten that evening, Cal's living room had grown dark, but he sat on the sofa without turning on a light, thinking over his hours with Katherine. Miss Agnus lay beside him, sleeping. She started up instantly when they heard Jon's key in the lock.

"Home early?"

"I have to get up to drive south in the morning. And I was hoping to see you for a little while tonight."

"How was your dinner with Amelie?"

"Oh, it was great, Dad. You know, you're not going to talk us out of this."

Cal held up both hands. "Don't want to. You're right—you're both adults and old enough to decide your own lives, including when you marry."

Jon looked surprised. "Hold that thought while I get something to drink. Want a Coke or something?" He started to move toward the kitchen.

"No, thanks. But, Jon, this time I want *your* two cents on something that's happening with me."

Jon stopped and turned around. "I'm not certain, but I think that might be the first time you ever said that to me. What's going on? Something legal?"

Cal laughed out loud, startling Miss Agnus, who had just settled down again. "No, son, I'm not being sued as far as I know, but you're right that you're the first person I would come to if I were. Maybe I'll take a Coke after all."

Jon came back with two bright red cans, handed one to his dad, and popped the other. They both took a long pull on the Coke, their cheeks puffing out and lips compressing in identical fashion. "So what is it then?"

"I want to ask you what you think about Katherine."

"You mean estate stuff? I know her mother was a wealthy woman."

"She was. She's been a good donor. No, I mean what you would think about Katherine—and me."

Jon blinked. "You mean you and Katherine—like as a couple?"

"Like as a couple."

Jon hid his face behind the red can, pretending to rub the cold metal against his forehead for some seconds. "You can imagine what's going through my head, can't you?"

"No, son, I really can't. What *is* going through your head?"

"My first thought was, *You can't be serious! She's way too young for you*, but then I realized that sounded a lot like our previous discussion and probably doesn't make much more sense in this conversation than it did in that one." Jon took another swallow. "Then I thought about asking if you're really over Mom yet and knew right away that that was ridiculous. Of course you are." He got up to pace, and Cal knew that he was about to hear the hard truth that he was already thinking himself. "So then I settled on, 'What are you thinking? The poor girl just lost her mother!'"

Cal leaned forward to set his Coke can on the coffee table. "That's the one I'm struggling with."

"Well, what *are* you thinking?"

"I'm not actually thinking anything. I saw her today at the studio, and the next thing I knew she was sobbing and in my arms, and I realized that I've been in love with her for a long time." There. He'd said it to another person, to Jon, which meant fully admitting it to himself.

"It's Sunday—what was either one of you doing at the studio on a Sunday?"

"I called her because I knew this was going to be a tough day for her, and then all of a sudden we were agreeing to meet at the studio to do a little work on the new ballet."

"Convenient." At once Jon apologized. "Sorry, Dad. You really didn't go there with any—"

"Of course not!"

"I knew that. I knew that." Jon took a breath. "You're just—you're just going to have to take it really slow. That's the best two cents I have for you."

Cal nodded, rubbed a hand through his hair, and then reached to gather Miss Agnus onto his lap. "That's my best two cents on it too." He found it impossible not to smile.

* * *

It was morning. The chill of the San Francisco night clung to the room like a damp sheet. It would take the purposeful effort of the sun, coming in soon from the eastern sky, to dry the fog and warm the air.

But Alexandra Kreyling was not thinking of the September coolness. She sat fully encased in a blanket on a straight-back chair in her bedroom. Even her head was enshrouded. A small lamp on her bed table was lit to enable her to peek at the clock, though by now her body knew when twenty minutes had gone by. The quiet was outside; the quiet was inside. Even her mantra had receded. No thoughts, no sounds, no mental impulses.

When the soft awareness came, it bypassed her rational mind, as it always did, and centered itself at a depth under her heart, where it waited quietly. She did not notice it in every meditation session, but it never came to her outside of meditation. In fact, between sessions, it was completely forgotten, unknown to her mind and completely out of her spiritual awareness until, like now, in the deep silence, she was aware of its presence again. It rested. She rested. It was a familiar, sweet, shared peace.

Perhaps thirty seconds went by—it could as well have been thirty minutes; there was no reckoning of time in the spiritual awareness—but at the end of it she felt her mind stir and knew that her meditation session was coming to a close. Like a snuffed candle flame, the heart awareness disappeared and her thinking awareness began to hear traffic outside on the street. Eyes still closed, she rose in a crouch from the straight-back chair, moved in two short steps to the bed, and let her body fall onto the bedspread. She noticed her heart gradually speed up to resume its normal pace and felt warmth spread through her limbs. Finally she rolled onto her back, pulled the blanket away from her head, and opened her eyes.

After a couple of minutes more, Alexandra began thinking about the ballet studio, about Cal, about Katherine, about Mrs. Melton's death, about Matt. When scenes from the *Prayer* ballet entered her thoughts and her muscles began to respond with the urge to move, she felt compelled to get up and get dressed. Wide awake now and rested, she poured cereal for breakfast, eating spoonfuls from a bowl in one hand as she went about the apartment replacing the towels and clothing in her ballet bag, making a sandwich for lunch, and checking to be sure that she had everything she would need for the day. What lingered from the meditation session was a peaceful sense of being all right in the world.

At the studio, she moved toward the rather noisy main hall, where the entire company had gathered for class, which would start in another ten minutes. Rob and Amelie were at one side, probably discussing the day's rehearsals. Amelie, she noticed, looked smiley and energized.

The forty dancers displayed every possible color of T-shirts, leotards, and tights. Some had towels around their necks. There were dancers at the barre, others seated on the floor to wrap their feet and put on ballet slippers, and others stretched out on floor mats. She scanned the group twice before spotting Katherine off by herself, seated on the floor with her back to the room. She hurried over, dodging dancers' limbs.

"Hi, you!" When Katherine looked up, Alexandra scanned her face and surmised, "Bad day, huh."

Katherine nodded and then shook her head. "It's getting better."

"Takes time."

"Takes time," Katherine agreed. Her eyes glistened.

Alexandra extended a hand to Katherine. "Come on. Let's find a place at the barre together."

Katherine swallowed and then let herself be pulled to her feet. By habit, Katherine headed toward her usual place and settled her hand in the very same spot on the wooden pole that it had been in thousands of times over ten years. Alexandra took a spot next to her, after glancing around the large room to make sure that the dancer who usually warmed up at this place had already left the barre for center floor exercises. It was a courtesy; no one actually "owned" any particular place along the bar, but everyone knew and respected who was generally where. They began the gradual warm-up exercises, saying nothing now, letting the mastery of their bodies take over.

* * *

At the university, the new fall classes would be starting in a few days. Freshmen were already on campus, doing their best to look like they belonged and knew what they were doing, but just behind their eyes lay the fear that they were out of their depth and might drown before Thanksgiving rescued them from this alien place.

Evana Arthur hastened from her car to her office along a path that was still sun-dappled. In another month the fallen leaves would obscure the sidewalk, but at the moment, it still looked like summer. The reason she hurried was to ensure that no lost new student would ask her for directions, mispronouncing the names of buildings and in general begging to be taken under her wing. Her petite stature combined with her age could mislead students into thinking of her as potentially motherly, perhaps even grandmotherly. Her unflinching, steely gaze was meant to cause a rethinking of this assumption.

Gaining the entrance to the music building, she kept her head up and eyes focused straight ahead as she sped up the stairs to her office. Only when she was safely inside did she let slip her vigilance, scowling in disgust that the general ineptitude of students nowadays forced her to go to such lengths. She smoothed her clothes before sitting down at her desk.

Of course, it was nice to be back at work, and a new school year was always exciting. It was a tension she liked: everyone a bit on guard. In general, the world, especially American students, had become far too casual. It was nice, each fall, to see the students step a little more briskly.

She turned her attention to her inbox, which had filled in the short weeks she had taken off between quarters. There were class rosters, new policies the university regents had established for the new school year, notices of welcome-back meetings scheduled by various groups and organizations. At the bottom was a single sheet of staff paper with musical notes she had penciled in and comments in her handwriting along the side. She looked at it, blinked, and felt her eyes grow wide.

"Oh no! *Teresa!*"

In the next office, a chair pushed back, scrapping the floor, and a childlike voice answered, "Yes, Mrs. Arthur. Coming." Then the waif was at the door.

"What is this?"

"Well, I-I don't know."

Evana felt her blood pressure rise a few points. "Of course you can't tell what it is from over there, Teresa. Get over here and look at this and tell me what it's doing at the bottom of my inbox."

Teresa lowered her head and came closer. Evana stood waiting. In slow motion Teresa took the sheet of paper and turned it so that she could read it. "It's, um, it's from the composition you did for Mr. Tropp last month."

"Yes, that's exactly what it is."

Teresa reddened and tried to sneak a glance unseen at Evana, but there was no escaping Evana's fierce gaze. "What . . . what's the matter with it?"

Evana scowled again, her lips tight with disapproval. She grabbed the paper. "The matter with it is that Calvin Tropp was supposed to have these changes and apparently he doesn't."

"How do you know he doesn't?" Teresa looked fearful and perplexed at the same time.

The top of Evana's head felt like it could explode. "Because I have a system—which you're *supposed* to know. If these changes had been incorporated into the final we sent to Tropp, there would be a note on this saying so. Right there in the upper right corner. That's the system, and it has worked without fail for decades. I don't see any note saying so. Do you?"

Looking mercilessly trapped, Teresa took the sheet of paper into her hands again and inspected it inch by inch. "Maybe there was a Post-it note attached that got lost."

Evana snatched the paper back, crumpling half of it. She abruptly returned to the other side of her desk. "I don't use Post-it notes anymore! Now get me Calvin Tropp on the phone."

In three swift strides, Teresa was out of the room. Within a few seconds, Evana's intercom buzzed. "I have Mr. Tropp for you."

Evana punched the speaker button. "Calvin!"

"Yes, Evana? How are you?"

"There's an important revision to the score for your ballet, and I have to find out somehow whether the final sheet music sent to you has it. I don't know how to find out unless I can see a copy of the final. Could you fax that over to me today?"

He paused. "You're talking about the sheets you sent over about ten days ago, right?"

"Yes, yes, yes. There's a change I made in the fourth bar from the end of the third movement. That change has to be in there. I'd never forgive myself if the musicians play it wrong in performance."

"I remember it."

"You do?" She was stunned and then confused. "How could you remember it?"

"Well, because for some reason your handwritten sketch sheet was in the envelope with the printed music, so I couldn't help myself. I had to check the music to see if your changes were there. They were."

"They were?" Even to her own ears, she was beginning to sound like Teresa. "Oh, well . . . well." Now the confusion was overcoming her ability to think. The main thing—the really important thing—was that the correction had been picked up in the printed music, but the details didn't make sense. "Well, then how did the sketch sheet end up back in my inbox, where I found it this morning?"

She heard him taking a sip of some liquid, piquing her annoyance and impatience. "I was pretty sure you hadn't meant for me to have it but would want to file it, so I mailed it back to you. I guess someone opened your mail and put it in your inbox."

Her brain buzzed. "Apparently so." She hung up the receiver despite hearing Calvin's voice coming back through the line in response. She sat in silence, one hand rubbing her forehead. Then she set the sheet in front of her, noted in the top right corner that the changes had been incorporated into the final music, and took the sheet herself to her filing cabinet. With a deep in-breath, she confirmed that the system was now completed for this correction. Returning to her chair, she punched her intercom.

"Yes, Mrs. Arthur."

"Can you come in here for a minute?"

"Of course." The child's voice was tremulous. Teresa stopped just inside the door frame.

"Come in, come in. Sit."

Teresa smiled then. After a few moments of silence, she changed the subject: "How did you ever get that window open?"

Evana looked toward the end of the room. "Frank loved having the windows open in here. I always hated it and wanted them closed. Now I think he might have been right. Except for the flies."

Teresa rose from the chair and moved to the doorway. But there she turned. "I just remembered. Martha told me you asked her to bring Charley to the cabin, and then you couldn't wait for him to leave! What made you think you wanted Charley there? I thought you'd always hated that dog."

"What a horrid animal! But Calvin's little dog—now there's a nice pet to have around. I could get some good work done with her there."

Teresa looked bewildered, but Evana decided she had shared enough for one day. She rose and reached again for the papers in her inbox. "We'd better get to work, you and I."

Teresa sobered. "Yes, Mrs. Arthur."

"It's *Evana*."

* * *

Two mornings later, the eastern sky grew lighter and lighter, beginning at least a half hour before the first burst of sunlight cleared the horizon. Alexandra did not see it though, because she was seated on her straight-back chair in her bedroom. A blanket was draped around her with an extra fold to cover her head. This morning, nothing in her day-to-day life siphoned off the purity of her attention, so she sank into the rhythm of the inaudible mantra, letting it come as it would and ebb as it would.

Some meditators refer to it as bliss, but to Alexandra, it was heart awareness: that spiritual space inside that made itself known only in meditation sessions, and only occasionally there, an infrequent gift. And this morning, here it was. Everything else had fallen away; it was as though Alexandra had no body, no life or being outside of this moment. But this morning, rather than being still in peaceful silence, the spirit moved to a new depth in her, pushing open a tunnel where none had been before and shepherding her smoothly down, down. There was at one point a sensation of negotiating a turn on the downward course, and then—pure wonder! The whole universe spread out before her, as if at a drop of many feet in distance, and she fell, floating, headlong into it. It was darkness but lit by a million points of light. There was no sound; there was no concern about heat or cold; there was no sensation of touch; there was no time.

At first she floated above the lights. Then she came to rest on their surface, not feeling them yet at the same time being supported by them. When her spirit began moving downward again she slipped through a surface boundary, deeper and further into the light, and eventually she was part of it. And there she remained.

Later, though she could not have said how much later, a shift began in reverse and the spiritual space receded into a background of unawareness, where presumably it resides all the time. There was no sensation of rising up out of one state into another. For Alexandra, there was only a returning of her mental awareness, a sense of returning to her body and the apartment she lived in, to the life she informed and inhabited. But that is not to say that she was unchanged. As she rested, letting her body resume a normal pace in heartbeat and blood flow, she was aware that a softer layer of peace now cushioned everything. Nothing really had changed, yet the ground of her being was at a new place.

It was only later, after a shower and breakfast, after making her way to the ballet studio, after ballet class, when she was in rehearsal for the *Prayer* ballet that the realization dawned. She was resting on her haunches, back against the wall, watching Cal work with Katherine and Matt on the choreography of scene 9. The scene marked the transition of Matt's character from a clumsy, angry, despairing human being into a person who learns how to dance with the Spirit of Prayer. The choreography Cal was unfolding and teaching to the two dancers was a depiction of how prayer reshaped Matt's attitude and moved him out of his self-defeating feelings into self-forgiveness and harmony. At the close of the scene and the end of the second movement, Matt is able for the first time to rise up out of a slightly stunted posture to stand tall and whole.

She felt her jaw go slack. *This moment is what the ballet is about: when the power of prayer transforms the human being.* Lightheadedness rolled over her. She had not grasped it when her own character, just two scenes earlier, had made a similar evolution away from fear, resistance, stubbornness, and frustration and become able to move and dance in a mirror image of Katherine's movements.

But that wasn't all. The greater realization that sat lightly on her heart was the recognition of the spiritual peace that now resided in Matt's character, which was the very same peace in which she had emerged from her morning's meditation. *Would I have found it without this ballet? Could I be dancing this ballet if I had not found it?*

She watched Cal work with Matt, her heart suffused with gratitude, and tucked away in her memory these feelings and what they did to her body so that she could dance them later.

* * *

Two Weeks

"So we thank you for coming out to tonight's fund-raiser for the Tropp Troupe," said Valina Davenport, the elegant early-seventies matriarch who was president of the Tropp Ballet Guild as well as of the company's board of directors. Tall and dazzling, she wore a gown of burgundy taffeta with matching gloves and shoes, the burgundy perfectly setting off her coiffed silver hair. Valina flashed her smile at the 250 people in the room, each one of whom had just consumed a five-course, $1,000-per-plate seafood dinner. She seemed to know everyone with money in a five-hundred-mile radius.

It must be admitted that not everyone was favorably impressed by Valina's success in raising money for the arts. One critic in a "letter to the editor" exposé had characterized her fund-raising method as "get 'em comfy then pinch 'em in the purse." But the truth was that Valina brought equal parts courage, heart, and common sense to her fund-raising, and it had worked extraordinarily well. She had led Cal's troupe to financial solvency every year for the last ten.

Valina's philosophy about money was that it was not doing the world any good just sitting in an account somewhere. It made no difference whose it supposedly was—it belonged to the causes that needed it, and to Valina, ballet was a cause that served every person in the world, directly or indirectly. What was even more remarkable was that she was able to convince her wealthy friends of this point of view, at least often enough to make a difference. Once Cal had been at a private dinner with her and a donor at which a check for $10,000 was written, signed, and handed over with a self-satisfied flourish—only to be gently shoved back by her dainty hand. With a warm smile, she had tipped her head just enough to look over the top of her jeweled glasses into the startled eyes of the wealthy man. "Really, Ed, I am counting on you for at least ten times that. To a man like you, what's one more zero?" She had talked a little more, and Ed had ended up coming through with the much larger sum.

Without her, Cal was certain the troupe would have folded by now, but with her, the ballets he had mounted had been supported in every detail required to put on professional performances.

Valina continued her speech to the audience of wealthy balletomanes: "I know you have all been hearing rumors about Cal's world-premiere ballet that will be performed this season. Just keep in mind that without your continued financial support, it would not be happening." She moved in closer to the lectern, and with the subtle physical shift came a corresponding shift in the import of her speech. The audience grew quieter. "I think it's important, every now and then, to review in our own minds why it is that we support efforts like this ballet company." Her voice became at once more intense and more personal. "It's no small thing, what you all have done, and I'd just like to take a moment to remind you of it. You're all exceptional people, because time and time again you have risen to meet the challenge of keeping this important troupe performing. These gifts go both ways. We expect high quality, extraordinary skills, and monumental dedication from Calvin Tropp and his dancers and everyone else who is needed to put on these ballet productions. We want a dance company we can be proud of, and I think you'll agree that they have come through for us. And in turn, they expect from us not only enthusiastic audiences who appreciate what they are doing but the financial wherewithal to keep on doing it. It takes all of us, and together we create something that is larger and more beautiful and more important than any of us could do alone. It's that bigger thing I'm talking about. It's big enough to be a reason for living. It's big enough that, no matter what else you do, your life counts.

"So when you go to the opening night performance, remember that you have had a critical role in every step you see on that stage. I am personally very proud of each and every one of you, and I congratulate you for bringing Cal's level of choreography to the stage."

She paused then, took a breath, and shifted back to the role of glad-handed MC. "So let's welcome Calvin Tropp. Who knows? Maybe he will even share with us a little more about this new ballet than what we have been hearing by the grapevine. Cal, come talk to us!" With that, she stepped back from the microphone and raised her burgundy-gloved hands in applause, joined at once by everyone in the room.

Cal felt the heat rise as the spotlights swung toward him and followed him to the podium. He discreetly touched his shirt cuffs to measure how much they emerged from his tuxedo sleeves. The room was designed for banquets, from the subdued lighting to the heavy dark velvet attached in waves to the walls, held at intervals by gold sashes. Numerous waiters were at work, making sure everyone's coffee or after-dinner liqueur was exactly as ordered. He stepped onto the podium and faced his audience. "I also want to thank all of you for coming tonight, and most especially for your generosity in building and maintaining what we do, and I hope you enjoyed the food and the music that went with it." He gestured toward the string trio. The audience recognized the cue and applauded with polite enthusiasm.

Taking a note card from his inside pocket, Cal looked at it for a moment and then tapped it against the lectern, gazing out at the crowd. "I had a very nice talk prepared for you. It had a few points about my own background that you've probably never heard before and something about the ballets we'll be doing in just a couple of weeks, including the world premiere." Here he turned to nod toward Valina. "I even had a Ballanchine story that I've never told before. You would have loved that talk." He smiled and some of his audience chuckled uncertainly. "But it's going to have to wait until another occasion, because that's not the talk I'm going to give tonight." Watchful silence settled over the room. After a pause, he slipped the note card back inside his jacket pocket and stood looking at his audience. "You all come back next time though, because that's a really good talk." A moment of fright hit him: *What am I doing!* Empty-handed, he felt his heart constrict with nervousness. He barely heard the shifting and rustling that went through the crowd. To regain his contact with the present moment, he wiggled his toes inside his expensive new shoes and rubbed his index fingers along the edges of the lectern. When he felt his heart begin to calm, he took a breath and began.

"I realized on the drive over here that there is something much more important that I need to share with you, and if it's a little rough, well, that's because it's coming straight from my heart, and that's one part of me that hasn't been civilized as much as most of the rest."

Good Lord it's hot in here. He unbuttoned his jacket and let it fall open, though it was the cummerbund he would have most loved to discard. The bowtie, he knew, would have to stay right where it was, too snug against his Adam's apple. He gave himself the luxury of a couple of swallows of the ice water someone had kindly placed on the lectern shelf for him and was soothed to feel the coolness descend inside him.

Next he looked over his audience and silently selected three people: a young man off to his left, a woman who looked to be about his age toward the center of the room, and an older gentleman seated in the right third of the room. What he had to say, he would say to these three people, holding eye contact with them, speaking directly to them, as though just those three sat with him at a coffee bar somewhere. He hoped to create not only greater ease for himself but also the illusion for the audience that he was having an intimate chat with friends.

"I—" He stopped and then decided to proceed along that route. "I work in an extraordinary world—maybe many of you do too and I'm just not aware of it, but the world in which I function is surprisingly full of people who not only *say* they are willing to give an arm and a leg and all of their heart to every single thing I ask them to do, but they actually *do* it, time and again, no matter what is going on in their personal lives." All this he said to the woman in the center of the audience, and as he had guessed she would, she responded by a deepening of the intensity with which she listened to him. Her engagement gave him courage.

He turned his head toward the young man on the left side and continued, "They seldom complain, and they don't keep reminding me that I am over the top, many times, in what I demand of them. They just keep on giving me everything they've got." The young man now looked squarely toward Cal.

Here and there, light reflected as if in sparks from diamond necklaces and bracelets and earrings. Women sat perfectly still except for their dangling earrings that bobbed back and forth, catching the light of candles and of the subdued light fixtures on the walls. At the table on the right side of the room where the older gentleman sat were a boy and girl who still worked at the remnants on their dessert plates. The older man held Cal's gaze easily, without looking away. Cal said to him, "Tonight, I want to talk to you about some of the extraordinary people who really are most responsible for the successful preparation of the art your contributions bring to the stage. Mrs. Davenport said that I might be cajoled into talking a little bit about the new ballet, but this talk is really *all* about it." Here, someone in the audience whistled and shouted "Bravo!" but Cal continued with only a slight smile in acknowledgment.

"I'm going to start with the composer. You'll see her name in the programs. Probably just a small line that reads, 'Music composed by Evana Arthur.' Five words." His voice coarsened and he paused, his eyes on the empty lectern. *What the heck?! Am I going to get choked up about this?* He cleared his throat and went on.

"The first moment Evana got wind of this new ballet—which needed a score—was nine weeks before our opening, coming up here in another twelve days. She of course assumed I was calling about an opening a *year* and nine weeks away, not a mere sixty-three days away. That would have made a lot more sense. And she could have rightfully told me to buzz off and call again when I could be reasonable." A soft rumble of chuckles came from the audience. "But she didn't. The accomplished professional that she is, she rolled up her sleeves, took time away from her professorship at the university, and got to work. She even took herself away to a remote place where I couldn't find her, because the work required the most intense focus and concentration."

The sense of choking came back. He cleared his throat again and took another drink of water. "I don't really know what it means, what I asked of her. I'm not a composer. I'm just a choreographer. I'm used to taking the hard, hard work some composer has poured his or her lifeblood into and seeing in my mind the dance movements that would go with it. But my sense of it is that composing is much harder work than what I do. I'm dealing with a few human bodies whose range of motion can seem virtually limitless but isn't, and after all these years I know pretty well what a human body can do. I was asking Evana to come up with something totally new, something never heard of before, and I was asking her to come up with it in an ungodly short period of time.

"But she did it." He stopped talking then, mostly because he knew his voice would come out in a squeak if he didn't pause for a moment until his throat muscles relaxed again. The audience sat in complete silence; even the children stared and waited. He made use of the moment by looking for a few seconds each at the young man, the woman, and the elderly man. Again, the older man held his gaze, appearing to bridge the thirty yards between them to give him support. Ever so subtly, the man appeared to nod, and Cal blinked in acknowledgment.

"So . . . so I hope you're all there on opening night because that is when I will ask Evana Arthur to come up on stage and be publicly recognized for what she did. It was an extraordinary accomplishment and one I hope never to ask of a composer again—not in that kind of time frame—because I think that's a well a choreographer can draw from only once in a career."

Not waiting until opening night, the audience began to applaud Evana on the spot, and Cal was sorry she was not in the room to receive it. But with the number of reporters on hand, he was sure that the word would reach her.

He widened his stance then and shifted his weight to rest more centrally. To the woman in the center of the audience he said, "Choosing the dancers wasn't hard at all. In fact, almost as soon as I knew what the theme would be, I had already chosen, by some mysterious process that I don't understand myself, who the dancers would be. There are three of them, and their names are names you are already well familiar with because they've danced with me for years. You've seen them in dozens, if not hundreds, of performances.

"One of them, Katherine Melton, has been one of the troupe's principal dancers for eight of the ten years she has been with the company. She reminded me recently that I have made fifteen ballets on her." He stopped himself to explain. "That's ballet jargon, and most of you already know what it means. Katherine has been the dancer I have used to work out the choreography for fifteen different ballets over the years I've been here in San Francisco. It means that when I see a new dance in my head, it's her body I see doing the movements, so the ballet inevitably becomes one she can dance more authentically than any other dancer in the world, you could say. Other dancers will learn the steps and movements. Over time—we hope—many other dancers will dance it in performance, but somehow when Katherine dances it, it will be at its most true, most faithful expression of the original vision.

"As soon as the first glimpses of this new ballet began to come to me, they came along with my visual memory of how Katherine dances, how she looks on stage and in rehearsal. Some would say that she has been my muse or my inspiration—and I would not argue with them."

He was silent then, realizing how much more his heart would like to say about Katherine as the woman he had so recently realized he was in love with. *Now is not the time.* Shifting his weight and turning his head toward the young man off to his left, he went on. "But nothing in life slows down or comes to a stop just because we're putting a new ballet together, even when we have only sixty-three days to do it and could really use the full cooperation of the universe. Some of you are no doubt aware that Katherine's mother died just over three weeks ago." There were gasps and murmurs here and there through the large room. "To say that the two of them were close is a significant understatement, and Mrs. Melton's passing was certainly the most difficult blow of Katherine's young life. Now how do you go on dancing when something like that waylays you?

"Well," he said to the older gentleman, "you go on dancing because you're a professional and dancing is what you do." The older man nodded visibly this time. "Katherine asked that she not be replaced in the new ballet. She kept learning the dance, kept working with us in rehearsal, overcoming the inevitable, pervasive distraction that grief brings." He paused and looked down again at the empty lectern. "Someone said that what she is doing is tabling her grief to deal with after the performances in October, and maybe they are right. But I think, instead, that what she is doing is dancing out her grief. Dancers know how to express emotion through movement, how to express the most powerful feelings in a captured, controlled way that comes across as the passion it is and the art that it can be at the same time. That's what I see Katherine doing, and I think that maybe she is making the whole thing a tribute to her mother." Once more the choking sensation came to him, but this time he knew that it would pass if he just gave it a few seconds.

"But she's doing something else too." He turned back to look into the eyes of the woman seated some twenty yards from him, over the tops of the heads of the people seated between them. "And here I guess it's time to say a little bit about this ballet." Cal cleared his throat and slid one hand into his pants pocket. The other rested on the lectern. "I've never been a man to pray." At once a sense of calm settled over him. His field of vision widened so that he no longer focused on his three chance colluders but saw the audience as a mass, as one person, one face with 250 subtly different expressions. "My son tells me that everyone prays sometime, but I have never been much aware of doing that myself. So maybe you can imagine my surprise when one morning before light, I was brought awake out of a dead sleep by the certainty that I heard someone talking *to me* about prayer."

The room was as quiet as predawn. Every face was turned toward him. "What this voice said was, 'We are going to make a new dance and the theme is prayer.' Now why I did not shake that off as a silly dream, roll over, and go back to sleep, I cannot tell you." He corrected himself. "Well, maybe I can. The reason is that it was so very real that I could not shake it off as not real, as something I merely imagined. Some things you simply know that you know, and this experience is one of them. That was exactly fifty-one days ago.

"But I was not exaggerating when I said that I have never been a man to pray. I was so little acquainted with the concept I had to look up the word *prayer* in a dictionary." More than one face in his audience formed a sympathetic smile. "There began one hurdle after another after another—just like in any ballet production, except this time with an extremely telescoped timeline—but, and this is the strange part, I never felt that I was leaping these hurdles on my own, and they never failed to be overcome.

"The ballet is about prayer coming into the lives of two people who are lost in their day-to-day misery, as so many of us are, I think. So lost that they encounter the world only in anger, fear, bitterness, distress, even blindness. We all know people that describes—I think we have all *been* these people, at some points in our lives. Those two dancers are Matt Wade and Alexandra Kreyling. You'll see that they do an excellent job, portraying every unhappy emotion in the book. But when prayer enters their lives—and in this ballet, my Spirit of Prayer is danced by Katherine Melton—that spirit changes everything.

"For the first couple of weeks, the three dancers and I worked on creating the choreography almost completely without music. That is something I had never done before and never dreamed that I *could* do. It was as though we were dancing on the whisper of God."

The hush in the room felt nearly electric—so much so that he paused without intending to, hearing again within his head the phrase that had slipped so casually out of his mouth. *The whisper of God—I guess that's what it was.*

He spoke then about Matt and Alexandra; he talked briefly about Rob Deinken and Amelie Boiroux; he described the supreme patience and trust shown by Ned Freedman and the costumes department. Then suddenly, after what had seemed a torrent of words, he was silent. He stared at the empty lectern, he looked up searchingly at the audience, and then finally he opened his hands in a gesture of surrender. "I guess that is all I have to say about it. But I'll be happy to answer a few questions, if anyone would like to ask."

Hands went up all over the room. They wanted to know how Katherine was doing, how her mother had died, whether he had thought he was risking the whole venture by agreeing to Katherine's request not to be replaced. He answered as he could. There were several questions about how the choreography was created, and someone wanted to know if the ballet would really be ready in twelve days. Then the young man off to his left stood up and asked, "So have you become a praying man through this experience?"

Cal thought a moment as the audience waited. "Probably not the way you might think, but I am becoming a man to whom prayer seems to come naturally."

"What does that mean?" someone at the back of the room demanded.

"It means that I more readily recognize when I've reached the limit of what I can do and am more willing to admit it when I've reached that limit, and it feels natural now to ask for help at that point."

The same insistent voice came again. "Help from whom?"

"From whoever it was who told me we are going to make a new dance. Whoever or whatever that was has been dependable. We have done this together. I certainly didn't do it on my own. I would never have even attempted it on my own." He took a step back from the lectern and raised a hand to signify the end of the evening. "And I hope you will all enjoy the result. Let us know what you think after you've seen it."

Applause began as a ripple and then grew to a standing ovation. As he made his way to the door, with Valina Davenport opening a way for him through the press of people, a light touch on his arm caused him to look to his right, where he saw the woman who had sat in the center of the audience. "I just wanted to tell you what an extraordinary speaker you are. I felt as though you were speaking directly to me, like it was just the two of us in the room!"

He smiled. "I'm glad you were here."

* * *

On Monday Ned called Cal to tell him that the lighting design was finished.

"That's great, Ned!" He hid his relief under a cover of humor. "How did you get it done so fast?"

"Amazing how not having enough time can build a fire under a design." Ned did not respond to Cal's chuckle. "There'll be lots of room for color changes and focus revisions when we get into the implementation, but I have the basic plot figured out and down on paper. When do you want to look at it?"

"Let's do it this afternoon. I'll stop by your office after two o'clock rehearsal."

Later that day, Ned—the sleeves of his dark blue flannel shirt rolled to his elbows—spread out the lighting plot across his drafting table. As he switched on the lamp overhanging his slanted table, the light caught the gold hairs on his muscular arms. A stranger seeing Ned out and about would not jump to the conclusion that he worked for a ballet company. Stevedoring company, maybe.

Cal bent over the plot. At first the paper seemed dense with a meaningless clutter of music bars, indications of libretto scenes, and icons representing automated light fixtures and standard fixtures. But as always, Cal focused first on the music until he could hear it playing in his mind and then shifted his attention to the lighting notations. The libretto notes were not necessary—he knew his libretto by heart—but they had been critical for Ned, and as he progressed through the plot, he periodically checked the libretto notes to make sure the package tracked correctly. As he worked his way along the music bars, he saw in his mind his three dancers on the stage and watched the lights change with the choreography according to Ned's design. From time to time, he murmured, "Uh-huh" or "Hmmm," and once he said, "This might turn out to be a little too red, but we can adjust it when we see it." Another time he pointed to the first scene of the third movement. "I see Katherine here with more lavenders than blues. Try that and see what you think."

Ned marked the plot with a pencil notation. "Yes, I could see that in lavenders."

Cal bent closer over the plan for scene 9 in which Katherine, as the Spirit of Prayer, danced with Matt. "I think you'll need a following spot here and also one at the end of the ballet, where Katherine is walking the two of them upstage."

Ned agreed.

When Cal had gone through it once, he turned back to the beginning and patiently began again, this time commenting about color variations in the early scenes as Matt and Alexandra danced their misery. Ned, meanwhile, was making clean notes on another copy of the plot draft of all the revisions.

Finally Cal put his pencil down and stood straight. "It's looking really good. Of course you'll use that young fellow Jeffrey as the spot operator. He is the smoothest I've ever seen."

"He's good." Cal knew that Ned had trained Jeffrey and continued to work closely with him. "This is a copy to take with you," Ned said, rolling the lighting plot into a tube. "I know you'll be going over it again, so just let me know as you find places that you see differently." He snapped a plastic cover onto the end of the tube. "I've been meaning to ask you, what made you want to do something on prayer? I didn't know you were a spiritual man."

"No, not too many people have ever accused me of that."

"So then—?"

"You're asking me how I explain this?" Tension tightened his throat. *Why am I clenching up? What do I have to be afraid of?* He flexed his shoulders, knowing that Ned would see a shrug when what he was really doing was releasing the tightness. "Don't you ever wonder about spiritual things, Ned?"

"Not a lot anymore. I still remember a class I took in college when the professor told us that God is dead." He lifted his cap long enough to smooth a hand over his balding head and then put the cap back, settled it, and rubbed the back of his neck. "That was something of a shock. In fact, he held up an issue of *Time* magazine, and right there on the cover in big letters it said, 'Is God Dead?' Everyone in the room went stone silent."

"Did you believe the professor?"

Ned averted his eyes. "What was funny about it was that none of us—the students, I mean—discussed it among ourselves. We went out together like we always did for beer and hamburgers, but nobody wanted to talk about whether God was dead or not. I guess that was because none of us believed it—or we didn't want to believe it—but we mainly didn't want to be pressed into talking about it." He laughed without humor.

"Pretty heavy thing to put on a bunch of college kids. Did you grow up religious?"

"Well, it'll surprise you, but yes, I did. We were a nice Midwestern family, and part of what that meant was going to church every Sunday. And I was not one of the kids who sat in the back and talked and giggled and made fun of the whole thing. It was serious business to me." He paused. "You?"

"No, no. My father was proud of saying he never darkened a church door. My mother was interested in it, read her Bible a lot, that kind of thing, but I grew up pretty much unfamiliar with all of it. Even so, you can't really be part of this society without hearing a few things."

"So what happened? Did you have some sort of conversion here recently? I mean, is that what led to this ballet?"

Conversion? "Hmmm." Cal laughed uncertainly. "If that means what I think it means, maybe what I'm having is a slow conversion right now as this thing comes together." He made a show of looking at his watch. "In any case, we both have to get back to work." He took a step backward toward the door. "But I *can* tell you that I'm pretty sure God's not dead." He didn't wait for a reply.

At his desk, Cal sat with his shoulders pushed into the chair and his hands behind his head, fingers interwoven, part of his mind still amazed by the unexpected conversation with Ned, another part thinking about the lighting plot Ned had put together. The thing about working with professionals like Ned was that he could tell them what was in his mind, but what they did with it nearly always surpassed his imagination. Ned's lighting design—and the same with Evana's composition—was equally as crucial to the success of the ballet as his choreography and the skills of his dancers. It all had to work to create an effective ballet.

From his desk drawer he drew out the list he had made two weeks earlier in a desperate effort to calm his panic—the list of items to be accomplished for the new ballet. Many of them already had checkmarks, but he read through the whole list, pausing longest at the items "choose the two musicians" and "get sheet music to the musicians." Both were checked off as completed, but something bothered him, an intuition pushing into his awareness from deep in his gut. He brought his chair forward, reached for the phone, and punched in a number. When there was no answer, he called the studio receptionist.

"Cindy, find Chuck Good for me, would you?"

"Sure thing, Cal."

"Thanks. I'll hold on." He continued to pore over the list while he waited.

A deep, melodic voice, obviously that of a singer, came on the line. "Cal? Chuck here."

"Yes, Chuck. I'm wondering about the musicians for the new *Prayer* ballet. Do you have them in rehearsals?"

"They're on it."

"How's it going?"

"Interesting that you should ask. I've been surprised at how rocky it's been."

Cal's brain flipped to hyperalert. "Rocky how?" But before the troupe's music director could form a response, he was already on the next page. "I'd like to come listen. How soon could I do that?"

"Uh, let me just confirm . . . they're scheduled for ten thirty tomorrow morning. Will that work for you?"

"Absolutely. I'll be there." Cal sat with the nagging feeling in his belly. He had been at this too long to ignore it when his stomach told him something was going awry. It was exactly the sort of thing he would have overlooked as too insignificant to worry about in his extreme youth and from that cavalier attitude had sprouted more than a few of the gray hairs on his head. He spoke aloud to the empty room. "Whatever it is, we have just nine days to get it fixed. I hope that's enough." He waited, expecting some reassuring feeling to come over him. When none came, he spoke a little louder. "You know, it's really only eight days. It would be nine if that rehearsal were today." Still nothing. The qualm persisted. Finally he opened his palms in surrender. "We've come too far for me to start doubting you now. I'm just going to show up at that rehearsal tomorrow, and we're going to sort out whatever it is that's wrong."

Just before ten thirty on Tuesday Cal opened the door to the soundproof practice room where a well-postured, middle-aged woman sat at the piano and a young man in a stretched-out T-shirt was hunched over a synthesizer. The latter wore earphones and was busy adjusting dials. Cal's stomach tensed. The young man's face looked red and strained under a few days' growth of beard. Cal waited and watched for several minutes more, during which time Dr. Charles Good also entered the small room, and now both of them stood watching the fellow tinker with the box of dials, switches, and sliders. It was hard to believe anything resembling music could come from such a contraption.

Cal could stand it no longer. "Something wrong?"

The young man looked up and pulled one ear free. "Pardon?"

"I asked if something is wrong."

"Uh, yeah, yeah. The LFO is off."

Cal looked at Chuck, who waved his hand. "Something's going on with the low frequency oscillation."

"Well, let's hear what it sounds like," Cal said. "The piano too." He nodded to the pianist, whose hands went to the keyboard, fingers spread. Cal pointed out where in the score he wanted them to begin and then folded his arms across his chest as though to defend himself from whatever might be coming.

It was terrible. Almost excruciatingly terrible. After enduring several bars, Cal turned to Chuck. "Has it been sounding this bad all along?"

"Not *this* bad! Sounds to me like the pitch envelope is off too. We'll get another synthesizer in here to replace this one."

"Go ahead with that, but I'm going to talk to Evana too." *Why didn't I realize this before?* "We might have to go with something else—other than the synthesizer, I mean." *Why didn't I even think to check on this!* What Evana had produced for him had come to his ears through the phone line as ethereal, even otherworldly, and at the time, he'd thought it would fit his Spirit of Prayer perfectly. But now he realized that it didn't. From his own experience of prayer, he now understood that it was not something of another world; it was something here in *this* world that made all the difference for how *this* world went.

On top of that, the synthesizer he had just heard produced a harsh, brassy sound that was the very last thing he wanted.

The music rooms were housed in a separate building some five blocks from his rehearsal studio. Cal walked as quickly as he could, striding hard in an effort to beat back panic. *Keep moving. Just keep moving. If you stop you might become paralyzed.* He struggled not to think about how few days remained until opening night.

Back in his office, he dialed the composer's number from memory. "Evana?"

"Mrs. Arthur is here. Would you like to speak with her?" It was the child secretary.

"Yes, please."

"I'll put Mrs. Arthur on the line for you, Mr. Tropp."

He blinked, realizing that the girl—was her name Teresa?—had recognized his voice. He remembered the cool distance she had maintained when Evana was on the Oregon coast composing the piece.

"Calvin? Is there a problem with the score?"

For once he was not the least put off by Evana's brusqueness. Instead, he was grateful for how no-nonsense she was. But he needed her now, and he didn't want to set off a panic. "Well, I don't want to call it a *problem* yet."

"Just tell me what it is, Calvin. I don't have all day to dance with you."

"It's the synthesizer. I don't think it's going to work." His mouth twisted in a flinch, and he waited for a vitriolic onslaught. She had every right to throw back in his face that it was *he* who had not only approved using the synthesizer but had been extremely enthusiastic about it.

Evana was silent for only a second. "I've been wondering about that too."

His eyes opened wide. "You have?"

"It seemed just right when I was putting the piece together, but as I've lived with it since, the synthesizer seems a little strident for what you're trying to do." He mumbled something, but she went right on over the top of him. "I tried it the other way, swapping the two instruments, since you seemed to like the synthesizer idea, but that didn't work either."

"No, the piano is perfect for that side of it. But—" He stopped himself before he could vocalize the obvious. If he could just stay mindful every second that he was talking with her, maybe he could avoid wasting her time and spare himself her awful scorn.

"Nothing formal, of course," she began again, confusing him because she seemed to be in the middle of a thought.

What did I miss?

"But I've given a little thought to another instrument. The best I've come up with that I think might work for you is a pan flute. What do you think?"

"Pan flute?" For a stomach-rolling few seconds he couldn't remember what that was.

"I know an expert on the Romanian pan flute who could do a good job with this."

"Romanian?"

"Well, *she's* not Romanian, but the Romanian-style pan flute—you know, that's the one that's curved. It has a good sound and lots of capability for the *Prayer* composition in the hands of someone who knows what she's doing."

Suddenly the choke point in his vocal cords broke open, and he flooded the phone line with questions: "Is she local? Could she get here to do this? Is she available for the next few weeks? Does she—?"

Irritation made Evana's voice even rougher. "Take it easy, Calvin. I can't answer anything yet. Let me get in touch with her. I'll give you a call as soon as I've reached her." She hung up without saying good-bye.

Just as well since I am reduced to sputtering anyway. Cal sat trembling as adrenaline continued to course through his veins.

At the end of the day, he could barely wait to get home. His habit lately, on a normal evening as he left the studio, was to pause to breathe in deeply and check the color of the sky before trotting down the steps to the street level, but on this evening he couldn't lift his eyes as high as the sky, so he almost didn't notice the lone woman who stood waiting beside the covered bus stop across the street from the studio. At first barely glancing at her, he looked back when he realized she was staring at him. The bus was less than a block away. *Don't people waiting at a bus stop normally watch the approach of the bus?* He turned his head to check on the bus himself, and when he looked back, the woman had moved so she was no longer quite visible, almost hiding now, it seemed, under the cover of the bus stop. One hand, fussing with the scarf on her head, shielded her face from view.

Then the bus rolled up, compression brakes blasting air, and when it rolled on, the woman also was gone. But the image of her staring at him was frozen in his mind. *Anne! But how could that be?* He shook his head, knowing that he had to be mistaken. *This thing really is getting to me. Besides, after this many years, would I even recognize her?*

Pulling into his driveway he heard Miss Agnus barking from within the house. Her welcome-home touched his soul with the first peace he'd felt all day, and the moment he swept her into his arms, he felt as though he were enveloped in a sacred shroud. "Did you have a tough day too?" He kissed the top of her head, deftly dodging the tiny pink tongue that darted over his chin.

He set her on the floor and stretched out on the sofa, trying to force his breathing to slow down so that maybe he could relax a little. His back felt like a board against the soft surface. Warring images of the kid with the awful synthesizer and the face at the bus stop took turns testing the stability of his stomach.

Miss Agnus bounced on her hind legs, attempting the jump onto the sofa despite the added inches of his body. With one arm over his eyes, Cal reached with his other hand and scooped her off the floor and onto his chest. Her five pounds felt surprisingly noticeable, concentrated into four tiny points of contact. He lightly pressed against her back and she lay flat, her breath coming in quick, gentle puffs against his throat. He peeked at her from under his arm, knowing that from her position it would look as though his eyes were closed, and she watched intently. From her earliest puppyhood, she had been remarkably respectful of his sleeping time. Suddenly she yawned widely, her tongue emerging in an upward curl from between little sharp teeth. The deep yawn forced her eyes shut for an instant, but then she resumed staring at him. Nothing in the world was more interesting to her than her master.

In spite of his weariness and his disquiet at seeing an apparition of his ex-wife, he smiled at the Pom and felt his back let go of some of the tension, easing by degrees into the contours of the sofa. He took a deep breath, aware of the small dog rising with his chest and falling slowly with his exhalation. *Somehow Evana was already thinking about the synthesizer problem before I brought it to her—before I was even aware there was a problem*! Even more amazing, she had been working on a solution! A wave of gratitude swept over him, with something else too, something that made his heart feel strange: tender yet not sentimental, vulnerable yet not fearful. *I don't know if I have ever felt so humble before.* Never in his experience had problems been solved before he'd even addressed them. Or had they? Had this actually happened to him before and he had simply not noticed? Was spirituality merely a matter of becoming aware of what has been there all along? He stroked Miss Agnus, letting his hand linger in the soft warmth of her hair. He was overwhelmed by the kindness that he felt enveloping him. As his eyes came open, Miss Agnus's ears came forward, and her head tilted in anticipation. "Thank you," he murmured to the unseen presence in the room. Miss Angus tilted her head at the opposite angle as he whispered it again.

When, after several moments, he had said nothing more, Miss Agnus let her head ease down to rest on his chest, and soon she was snoring softly. Cal lay listening to her. Now he thought about the woman at the bus stop. The longer he held the image in mind, the less he cared whether Anne was in the city or not. In any case, it wasn't likely. But if she *had* come and had waited across the street to catch sight of him—he waited for the pain of memory to take hold of his heart. Nothing but mild sadness arose. His memory of her felt far away and long ago.

Cal stirred, noticing now that the room had grown dim with the evening. At once, Miss Agnus woke up, jumped down, and began spinning in circles to make sure he did not forget to feed her.

Later still, the phone rang. "Okay, we're set," Evana was saying when he got the receiver to his ear. "She'll do it, and I'm getting the score over to her tomorrow. I don't have time to talk, Calvin. I just wanted you to know so you would stop your incessant worrying. You've got to get hold of that before it kills you." And she hung up.

Within seconds the phone rang again. "Something else," Evana said. "The end of scene 12."

"That's the very end of the ballet."

"Yes. I'm thinking we need to cut the music entirely for, maybe, five or six bars' worth."

"But that would mean—"

"Yes, it would mean that your Spirit of Prayer is escorting the other two upstage in total silence."

He felt stunned. *Of course!*

"Silence is a big part of spirituality, isn't it?" Before he could answer, she went on, "Well, you think about it. I'll do the arrangement for the pan flute that way, and you can see what you think. We can always go back if you don't like it." Then there was a click and the dial tone.

To the empty room, Cal whispered, "Pretty soon I'll have to be running to keep up!"

* * *

One Week

Matt Wade sat in striped boxers on the end of the weight bench and rubbed a white towel over his blond hair, front to back, in long, slow strokes. His gaze moved about his small apartment but without seeing, as his memory went from one recent conversation to another, one past experience to another. Finally he let his face rest in the damp towel. His biceps and triceps tingled and pulsed from near exhaustion, but the muscles across his back and chest felt satisfied. The loosing of his body's tension had released an ease of thinking.

Is it because I grew up with no father figure maybe? I mean, Stephen as much as said that was a possibility. His face grew hot at the memory of his therapist suggesting that he might be attracted to Ricardo Vitale because he was so much older than Matt himself! In spite of his wishes, his heart thumped a little quicker at the memory of his hours with the dark-eyed Italian dancer. He could not deny the impact his one experience with the older man had had. *But that was one night! How can one experience mean that I'm gay?*

Just asking himself the question caused a clutching in his throat. He swallowed, trying to breathe easier, and then reared to his feet and moved to the dancer's barre. In places, the wooden bar was stained darker from his own sweat and rubbed smooth from the hours he had gripped it to steady his practice sessions. There, by reasserting control over his muscles, he regained a little control over his emotions.

It was Sunday morning. He was due at Stephen Marksman's office in a few hours. He didn't want to go, embarrassed now for showing up at Stephen's in a panic after that horrible phone call in which Ricardo had hung up on him. Stephen had said he should be prepared in case Ricardo called him again—but no such call had come. *Good thing!* He was having trouble enough in the aftermath of one; he didn't want another. Not just yet anyway. And he couldn't think of what he would say if one came.

Then there was the question Stephen had asked him: "What's the alternative?" So cold and abrupt, it had shocked him out of his swamp of misery, and now his memory unreeled the shattering session. Truth was, he could not see what Stephen was getting at.

"Well, shit! Then he can just explain what he's asking." He wadded the white towel into a ball and threw it across the room. For the first time in his life, Matt felt uncomfortable in his body and out of sync with his perception of himself. He stripped quickly in the bathroom doorway, where he didn't have to see his face in the mirror, and went to take a shower.

Two hours later Matt sat in front of Stephen. "So," he said as though they were in the middle of a conversation, "I tried to think about your question, but I don't know what you mean by it."

Stephen looked at him blankly. "Refresh my memory."

"You don't even remember?"

"I want to hear what *you* remember."

Matt's forehead tensed in a frown. It wasn't like Stephen to pretend that he was up to speed if he really wasn't. "The question was, what's the alternative?"

Despite Stephen's bland expression, comprehension lit his eyes. "And you don't know what the question means?"

Matt shook his head.

Stephen took a moment before restating the question. "What did you do before your experience with Ricardo?"

"What did I do?" He shrugged. "I danced. I went to the studio every day. I dated some." He shrugged again and opened his palms. "Just life, man."

"And now that you've been with Ricardo, how do you think it will work out for you to just continue going to the studio every day and dating some?"

"Well—" Matt couldn't finish. He remembered the intense aliveness he had felt with Ricardo and with no one else, ever.

"You don't get the option of living someone else's life, Matt."

He felt gutted by the simple statement. He rolled it back and forth through his mind. "Is that what you think I'm trying to do? Live someone else's life?"

Stephen's voice came out gentle. "I think that a gay man who wants to convince himself that he's not gay is trying to live someone else's life."

Just as before, there was suddenly not enough air in the room. Matt cleared his throat and struggled to breathe. "Is that such a bad thing?"

Stephen tipped his head to one side and then back, as though weighing the relativity of badness. "Maybe not bad but probably unhappy."

The two men fell silent. Matt writhed on the chair and then lurched to the window, where he stared at the pane of glass. The window itself might as well have been opaque. Ancient dust filled the corner, its smell becoming more noticeable as he stood staring at it. "You make it sound as though there is really no choice about this."

The therapist drew an audible breath and let it out before he spoke. "I've never met anyone who was gay who could make the choice not to be gay, Matt. As I said, some people do make the choice not to be happy. I suppose that is the choice you have, but I don't recommend it."

From a distant place a memory flashed, a strange fact that he had learned somewhere: A dolphin must breathe on purpose if it is to breathe at all. When its life becomes no longer worth living, it can choose to stop breathing and will sink to the ocean floor and die. In that moment, Matt would have given anything for this miraculous power of self-annihilation. Stephen's voice came from behind him, sounding much farther away than it was.

"Matt, you're acting as though this is some huge tragedy that you alone of everyone in the world must face. Don't you know that there are millions of gay men? I happen to know quite a few who have decided that being gay isn't a bad thing at all."

"Ha!" Matt's voice sounded hollow. "Maybe you should introduce me to some of them."

"As a matter of fact, there *is* one I would like you to meet, if you want to. It's entirely up to you. He would be quite willing to meet you."

Matt turned from the window. "I can't believe you would try to fix me up with someone!"

"Oh, I'm not doing that." Stephen laughed. But his attention was on his open desk drawer as he rummaged through a rubber-banded stack of business cards. "This isn't any kind of date—but it puts together this issue you're dealing with and the other one you brought up in our last session."

Now it was Matt's turn to blink, uncomprehending.

"Here is his business card. This is not an assignment, and I really want to emphasize that you are under no obligation to talk to him, but if you feel like it, give him a call. There's no charge to you for going to see him."

Matt crossed the room to take the cream-colored business card from Stephen. Curiosity compelled him to read it. It was imprinted in brown lettering with a phone number and what was apparently a name: Fr. A.R. Brandigan. He looked at Stephen. "I don't understand. Is the F-R for Frank? Is his name Frank Brandigan?"

Stephen looked amused. "No. F-R is short for *Father*. Andy Brandigan is a priest."

Matt's jaw dropped open, but no words came out of his mouth.

* * *

Father Andy Brandigan was a revelation for Matt and an introduction to a world he'd had no connection with before. Equally blond as Matt was, and not a whole lot older, Father Brandigan had the clean, sharp look of a man who was careful what he ate and worked out at a gym regularly. The black shirt with the priest's collar did nothing to conceal the trim, athletic build.

The priest reached out to shake hands with Matt and invited him into a study that was well lit and lined with books. It took a moment for Matt to realize that the lamps in the room were not turned on. A skylight directly over the square where they sat illuminated the two stuffed chairs, a low rectangular table, and the deep blue carpet at their feet.

"What would you like to talk about?" Father Brandigan asked.

Matt was aware that he liked this man and felt comfortable in his presence but that their lives had probably nothing whatever in common. He opened his hands. "To be honest, I don't really know. I've been seeing Stephen Marksman for a couple of years now, and he thought it might be good for me to talk to you, so here I am."

Father Brandigan nodded. "I know Stephen well. Good man. Good therapist too. Well, why don't we start by telling a little bit about who we are. Is it okay with you if you start?"

"Sure. Let's see. I'm a dancer with The Calvin Tropp Ballet Company. Been there for five years and I'm a principal now." He glanced at the other man. "That means that I've been with the company for a while and worked my way up so that I manage to get my share of the lead roles for men."

"You're one of the stars."

Matt laughed. "Well, we don't use terms like that, but I'm not a beginner, that's for sure. Have you ever seen the troupe perform?"

"Yes, I have. Not that I can get to the ballet often, and it hasn't been for a couple of years, but I've been to a performance or two, and the more I recall it, the more I am certain that I have seen you on stage. That's an extraordinary career you have."

Matt was surprised at how pleased he was that the priest had seen him perform. "Well, your career is somewhat extraordinary too, isn't it?" He smiled broadly but toned down the smile and looked away. The last thing he wanted was for Father Brandigan to think he was coming on to him. But even breaking off eye contact didn't diminish how comfortable Matt felt with the priest.

"Oh, it's pretty ordinary in the circles I run in. I was ordained, hmmm, about twelve years ago now. It's funny—I've never questioned that this is my calling, but then I doubt that you've questioned yours much either, have you?"

"No. No, dancing is what I do."

The priest nodded. "And who are you when you're not dancing?"

For the first time since he'd shaken Father Brandigan's hand, Matt felt himself sobering. Now when he lifted his eyes to the priest, he knew that it was apparent that he was troubled. He hated to spoil the camaraderie, and he couldn't think how to start.

Obviously noticing the sudden change in Matt's mood, the priest invited in a patient, kindly voice. "Why don't you tell me about it?"

"It's just . . . uh. It's just—" Matt's gaze bounced around the room. When he finally was able to meet the other man's soft brown eyes again, he was relieved to notice that no judgment, no irritation, no impatience was evident. Matt cleared his throat. "It's just that lately I've begun to think that I'm . . ." *You're not really going to say that out loud!* He looked at the other man again. "That I'm not the person I thought I was."

The priest nodded and waited.

"I mean, I thought I was—well, for one thing . . ." Matt knew his face had reddened and that he was going to have to blurt it out or it would never get said. "For one thing, I thought I was straight." He felt like he was drowning. For several seconds he watched an airplane through the skylight, watching to see just where its trajectory would hit the south side of the skylight casing. When it had finally passed beyond the skylight frame, he forced himself to look at the priest.

Father Brandigan was calm and at ease. "That wasn't easy to say, was it?"

Matt was flooded with relief at the absence of condemnation. "No, it wasn't."

"It gets easier."

Matt began to calm. Apparently the other man was not going to throw him out or scream at him or tell him he must be mistaken or insist upon who he should be or be anything but accepting. Then he realized what the priest had said. "It gets easier? You would know that?"

"Yes, I know that. There are some situations in which it will always be tough the first time you have to say it, but for the most part, it gets easier."

A throng of questions pressed into Matt's mind. "But you're a priest. How can you be gay?"

Father Brandigan's voice remained patient. "My sexual orientation didn't come to an end because I took a vow of celibacy, any more than the straight men who are priests stopped being heterosexual when they became clergy."

"But do the other priests know?"

"About my orientation, you mean? A few of them do. It's not a huge issue because we don't act on it. That's what the vow is about. But yes, there are some who know that my orientation is gay."

"And they don't—?"

Father Brandigan shook his head. "I don't hold it against them for being heterosexual either." He continued to speak calmly but his smile eased away. "The position of my church is one thing, and I am obliged to respect and honor it, which I do by keeping my vow."

"You seem—I don't know—you seem pretty easy and peaceful about the whole thing. How can that be? I mean, was it always easy for you?"

"No, it definitely was not easy coming to terms with this. There has been nothing else in my life that I have prayed about as much as this— you know: Why me? Why did I have to be born with this? How will I ever tell my mother? Has my father already guessed? Will they kick me out? Will I lose all my friends? What will my coach say? What does this mean for becoming a priest? The questions were endless, and I spent hours and hours praying and worrying about every one of them." The old emotions kicked about on the priest's face with the memories, but none of them stuck. At the end, his eyes were again clear and untroubled.

"And now? How is it that you're so calm about it now?"

The priest shrugged. "What's the alternative?"

Matt's alert level snapped higher. *Are people going to be asking me that for the rest of my life?* "What do you mean?"

"Well, it's always looked to me as though you have to find a way to accept who you are, because if you don't, life is going to be a whole lot rougher than it has to be, and that's an alternative I didn't want to live."

Matt made a face. "Yeah, I guess that's what Stephen has in mind too, but what I'm not getting is *how*. I get it intellectually what you're saying, but my emotions on this subject are pretty strong. How do I just overcome that?"

"The truth is, Matt, I couldn't have come to this place if it had not been for my faith. It may seem to you that I talk this way because I have this collar around my neck, but I say the same things even when I'm not wearing it. I trust God, and anything I don't have strength enough to do, God helps me to do."

Matt stared at him. "You're suggesting that I take a vow never to—?"

"Oh, no, of course not!" Father Brandigan laughed, clearly surprised. Matt laughed too, longer than might have been needed. The priest went on, "No, I'm not encouraging you to try to be celibate. I'm encouraging you to accept who God made you to be: a dancer who happens to be gay."

There it is. Matt struggled to keep his mind from being pulled down under the sudden crushing weight in his chest. A gay ballet dancer was just what he had never wanted to be, had been certain that he was not. How could it possibly turn out that he was exactly that after all? He tried to breathe, but the intolerability of the idea prevented air from going deeply into his lungs. "But you had to go into the priesthood to deal with it."

The kind, peaceful man across from him was shaking his head. "No, I didn't make myself clear. I didn't go into the priesthood to deal with it. I just have to deal with it the way I do because I became a priest. Matt, I always knew from when I was a little boy that I would become a priest. Truth is, I was a priest then too. I tried to baptize every kid on my street and about half the dogs in the neighborhood if I could catch them." He stopped long enough to grin. "I'm a priest first before everything else."

A stretch of silence followed. Matt surprised himself by not fidgeting during the lull. He wasn't itching to leave. His thigh muscles didn't hurt from being pressed against the chair. He didn't rack his mind and let tumble out of his mouth the first thing he could think of. In a subtle shift, his awareness expanded to take in two contradictory truths: he had never felt so vulnerable, and he had never felt so safe. Staying with this awareness, he found that he could breathe again.

A glance at Father Brandigan told him that the priest was not restless to continue. Matt used the silence that held between them to go back in his mind over what had been said so far. And where his mind landed was a second surprise. "I want to hear more about this thing you said about if you don't have strength enough to do something, God helps you. That sounds pretty spiritual."

"It *is* pretty spiritual. Nothing rational about that, but it works, I can tell you that."

"What makes you believe that? How did you get to that place?"

Father Brandigan stopped to think. "Well, it's biblical, to start with."

"That really—I don't know what that means."

The other man nodded. "But second, and probably more important, I've proven it to myself time and again just by praying and asking. God has always come through with the strength I needed to do something when I knew it wasn't in me by myself. Dealing with the gay thing was just one of hundreds of things."

"So you don't ever feel alone—is that what I'm hearing? You feel like God is always there."

"Yes, I could put it that way."

"I can't even imagine that."

"It's something we could explore together, if you want to. Coming to imagine it could be very helpful to you."

Matt nodded. "You need to come see this new ballet we're doing in October. Opening night is the sixth. We've been working on it for a few weeks—not nearly as much time as we normally work on a new piece—but it's about this very thing: how people can find a spiritual way of dealing with life."

"And you're dancing in it?"

"Oh, yes. Me and Alexandra Kreyling and Katherine Melton, just the three of us. You'd probably understand it a lot better than I do, and then you could explain it to me." He grinned and was pleased when the priest nodded, but something that felt like sorrow overcame him again, and he felt the grin disappear.

"What's worrying you?"

Matt looked from one side of the study to the other. "I'm not sure I can put it into words." In his distress, he rubbed his palms up and down his quadriceps. "I guess I'm uneasy about who I am as a dancer now. Will I always be wondering if people can see it on me somehow?"

"You will look no different to anyone else. The only person you look different to right now is yourself, but that will pass. Remember that you are first and foremost a dancer—that was the very first thing you said when I asked you to tell me about yourself—and you will just go on dancing as you always have."

The two men agreed to meet again and Matt left the presbytery, carrying the sense that he had crossed a threshold into a new phase of life. He knew what he needed to do next, and all the way back to his own neighborhood, he planned what he should say. Once home, he grabbed the phone and dialed his sister's number. "Laney?" It brought him instant joy that she sounded so thrilled, as she always did, to hear from him. "Laney, there's something I need to tell you. Have you got a minute?"

* * *

Alexandra Kreyling sat in her bedroom on a straight-back chair, her feet on the bed, her hands at rest in her lap. The blanket she had draped first onto her shoulders, and then over her head, had kept her body warm as her internal temperature had fallen during the meditation session. She was unaware of the blanket or the bed or the chair or the room but resided at a depth inside herself that was indistinguishable from the universe. There was nothing about her body that she could feel, nothing in her mind that she noticed.

Then a ringing began nearby, jolting her with a sudden increase in her heart rate, which poured heat through the inside of her body. Her mind didn't know what the ringing was; it was focused instead on the nausea that came with the precipitous plunge upward from a deep meditative state, the ripping away of peace, and the dizziness that made her certain that she would faint if she stood up. She lifted her knees and let her head fall to rest upon them. The ringing persisted, but now she knew it was the telephone in the next room. *I must . . .* She tried to think how to get to the phone without falling but knew it was unlikely that she could. With tremendous relief she remembered that her answering machine would pick up the call; there was no need to get to the next room to answer. No need for her to move at all. The flood of gratitude for this salvation eased the nausea, and she noticed that her heartbeat, which had felt at first like boulders tumbling down the inside walls of her chest, began to calm—now not so loud, not so painful. She began to believe that her chest would withstand the pounding without cracking.

Then into the receding chaos came an unwelcome spurt of adrenaline as she heard her mother's voice enter the next room via the answering machine. Her forehead still snug against her knees, Alexandra closed her eyes against the sound, but that didn't make it go away.

"Honey? It's Mom. Honey? Are you there? I was really hoping to catch you before you left for the day." Alexandra listened as her mother mumbled, "Maybe you're in the shower—maybe if I just hang on . . ." Never one to remain irresolute for long, Mrs. Kreyling shifted her tone and took charge of the situation. "It was just so nice of you to buy the ticket for me to come out to San Francisco for your opening—and of course I will reimburse you—but I'm not going to be able to make it, sweetheart." Now she began to speak in a rush, expediting one of the hundreds of small duties she would dispatch that day. Even so, she managed to sound regretful. "I know you were counting on it."

Alexandra already knew the next line. She threw off the blanket and pushed her feet to the floor. Steadying herself against the walls, she reached the phone just as her mother said it: "It's just this time of year, honey. We're so busy at the office now."

She grabbed the receiver, clunking the side of her face in her eagerness to respond. "No, it's not that, really, is it, Mother?"

The line went silent. Then Mrs. Kreyling, nonplussed, said, "I don't know what you mean, sweetheart. And hello, by the way."

No longer nauseated but still feeling as though her legs could collapse beneath her, Alexandra sat down on the sofa. She could take a moment now to catch her breath and let her body finish stabilizing. There was no way that Mrs. Kreyling could permit herself to hang up now until the conversation had smoothed into a semblance of civility. There were family rules, after all, and Alexandra had not been away for so long that she had forgotten them.

But the next move was hers, and they both knew it. Each listened to the other's breathing. Finally Alexandra echoed her mother's small laugh. "There are worse things we could be doing, you and I. Being silent together on the phone isn't such a bad thing."

Mrs. Kreyling, a veteran of thousands of business parties and therefore an expert at small talk, fell into line. "No, you're entirely right. Much better than, say, screaming at each other."

"Screaming never accomplished anything for us before. I don't know why it would now."

"I'm so glad to hear you say that."

Alexandra blinked with her realization that there had been a time when even that simple statement would have been enough to send her into a fury. *It sounds like she's baiting me.* But now she realized, *No, probably not.* Screaming had been the primary tactic Alexandra could think of to use when she was a teenager. Now she saw how ineffective it had been.

After some moments Alexandra asked, "Have you heard from Daniel?"

"No, honey. I never hear from Daniel—well, maybe once or twice a year. I don't even have an idea where he is. Have you heard from him?"

"I doubt that he even knows that I'm in San Francisco now."

"Well, he knows that much from me, but he wouldn't know how to contact you."

With that, they had exhausted the thread of conversation about Alexandra's brother, unless they were to go back over the history—and it was the history that Alexandra intended to discuss, even though she knew her mother would hate it.

The moment that flashed into her mind then was from the funeral. A half dozen of Ricky's friends had attended, wearing an odd assortment of punk clothing, strange hair, and more makeup on the boys than on the girls. Most of the attendees were friends and business associates of Mrs. Kreyling, all solemn in their business black. This motley assortment had gathered to remember a boy most of them had never even met, and probably all of them spent more time sneaking peeks at the others than contemplating the casket at the front of the church.

Already at the funeral, the coping mechanisms chosen by the four remaining family members came into evidence. Mrs. Kreyling devoted herself to the people from her office circle, making sure they were comfortable and had whatever they needed, even if that was as simple as not sitting alone. Those co-workers with whom she was cultivating more advantageous working relationships she seated in the rows right behind the family. Alexandra's father had arrived at the service late, with alcohol on his breath, though he had never been an excessive drinker. He chose a seat in the back, as far away from his wife as he could get, but the funeral-home ushers came, took his arm, and urged him forward to sit, reluctantly, within a few feet of his son's dead body. As for Alexandra, to keep from crying hysterically, she spent the duration of the service withdrawn into herself, focused on dance sequences, surreptitiously marking steps with her fingers held low in her lap. Daniel did not attend.

"I was hoping you would make time to come for the opening," an emboldened Alexandra said into the phone now to her mother. "But even more than having you see the ballet was that I wanted to spend some time with you. There is so much that needs to be said between us." In recent weeks, those things that needed to be talked about, spoken of out loud where family could hear them, had been surfacing in Alexandra's memory.

Ricky Kreyling had been only thirteen years old when his life began to veer off track. Up to that time, he had been a good student, a polite young man, if somewhat quiet, and given to reading books and playing with the Commodore 64 computer his father had brought home for him. It wasn't that he was socially inept, but he was unprepared to know how to respond when he was befriended by another boy from school, a boy named Bradley. Who could say what drew them to each other? At first glance, Bradley appeared so unlike Ricky. A disinterested student, Bradley was known to interrupt his lethargy now and then with spurts of violent loudness, after which he would retreat into a quiet that was frightening because of the feeling of darkness that he exuded. His most appealing feature was his very dark eyes, which didn't always look angry but usually did.

On the phone line now, her mother was silent, perhaps bracing herself, so Alexandra went on, surprised that she felt no storm of emotion. In fact, it was as though such a gulf of time had passed that the raw hurt was gone and what was left was only the desire to befriend her family again after the nine years since her brother had died.

"I just think that we need to talk about Ricky. All of us need to talk about it, but if you and I could at least make a start, maybe eventually we could reach Dad and Daniel too."

Her mother's unwillingness was like static on the line, causing her voice to recede and stutter. "I-I don't think . . . I don't really want—"

Alexandra forced her voice to become gentle. "I know it's hard, Mom. I understand that it's really easier in some ways to just keep it all buried and never talk about it, but look at what it's doing to all of us. We're a family, aren't we?" She was silent to see if her mother would answer. Finally she did.

"You're my daughter—" But here she faltered.

For the first time Alexandra felt concern. *Maybe this really is more than she can do. Is she going to break if she has to think about this?* "Mom?"

Ricky had first abandoned his interest in books and the computer, because now his free time was spent with Bradley, and what had been merely a quiet nature turned by quick increments into a sullen silence. Finally he no longer spoke to members of his family, and if they spoke to him, they were rebuffed by the increasingly hostile glare with which Ricky regarded the world. His mother and father spoke of it between themselves, as parents dealing together with the difficulties of having another teenager in the house. "Do you think it's best to just leave him alone?" asked the mother. "Making a fuss about it might antagonize him further." The father agreed, "I went through a period when I couldn't stand my parents. I got over it. He'll outgrow it too. It's teenager stuff. He'll be okay."

"You're my daughter, but you're a grown woman," Mrs. Kreyling said now. Again she stopped, and a heavy silence lay on the phone line between them.

What does that mean? Alexandra tried to think what her mother meant to communicate: That she was old enough now to put her brother's death behind her? That after their children reach a certain age, parents no longer bear responsibility to them? That she should be smart enough by now to figure this out without help from her mother?

Alexandra, two years older than Ricky, had never been particularly close to him, feeling that the two boys were aligned against her, but his older brother, Daniel, had once been his hero and was stung to be so summarily rejected for the likes of Bradley, whom Daniel considered a nasty lowlife barely worth anyone's time. "So much for you," Daniel had told Ricky. "Call me when you get back to this planet." So Ricky's attire had become more outrageous, and his family could see, when they passed him in the hall, that he was smudged with the remains of black nail polish, black eye makeup, and a look that was increasingly haggard. He would appear in the kitchen in the middle of the night to eat from the refrigerator hours after everyone else had left the table. His mother had hidden her worry from him, continuing to pray that he was only in a phase that would pass, and his father had continued to reassure her, "If we force the issue with him, things will only get worse. Better to let this run its course."

"It wasn't your fault, Mom," Alexandra began.

With a sound like strangulation, Mrs. Kreyling hung up on her daughter.

The finality of the broken phone connection rang like a struck bell. Alexandra's eyes opened wide, her pupils dilated, and something like coldness washed over her shoulders. One of the family rules had been broken. *Is this how it ends then?* For an awful moment she contemplated the possibility that there would be no further contact with her mother ever, that she had, by her own act, caused the final unraveling of her family. The weight of this possibility crushed in upon her.

Finally when Ricky's school quarter report card had showed up, with almost all his grades plummeted to failing, his mother had confronted him. She had rehearsed her confrontation, practicing tact and motherly concern, but he had been so cold toward her—not the least abashed—that she had been overcome by her terror and had found herself screaming at him, demanding that he straighten up, that if he wanted to be a member of this family, he had damn well better act like it. After that, Ricky had stopped coming home altogether.

Alexandra sat staring at the phone as though it had slapped her. Eventually she caught sight of a clock and realized that if she did not get to the studio, she would be late for the morning classes. She stumbled through the day, somehow present and not present at the same time at her rehearsals, relying entirely on body memory to step through choreographies.

That evening she reached for the phone to call her mother's number but could not bring herself to dial more than the area code. She put the receiver back into its cradle and sat staring into her small living room. Finally her gaze came to rest on the end table beside the sofa, and for the first time it seemed empty with only a lamp atop a small knitted mat. She got to her feet and went to a closet where she stored boxes she had never unpacked, never since her move from New York. There were three boxes, and in the second one, she found the family portrait.

The photographer had arranged them with the two boys in front: Ricky and Daniel, both in blue shirts, each on one knee. Behind them on stools were her father on the left, herself in the middle, and her mother on the right. It was the year before the trouble began. Despite how old-fashioned the frame and the photography were, the five people still looked like a happy family. She wiped off the frame and took it to the living room. Sitting on the arm of the sofa, she held the photograph close to the lamp and studied each face in turn: First Ricky, who, at twelve years of age, appeared to have the makings of a nerd. Daniel, the oldest child, would have been fifteen when the picture was taken. His face, despite a minor problem with acne, looked unclouded. Her parents, too, showed no clue of what lay ahead for the family.

The next morning, Alexandra's meditation session was again cut short, this time by a sudden onslaught of sobbing, as though an impervious membrane of which she had had no knowledge had been pulled back from a vast reservoir of grief. Bent double, she abandoned the meditation session, leaving the bedroom altogether to go open the windows in her living room, throw herself onto her sofa, and sit staring at the family portrait. Holding the photograph a mere inch from her nose, she stared into Ricky's young eyes but could detect no hint of the maniacal self-destruction and family destruction about to descend. His eyes were as clear and untroubled as an August sky.

On the following day her mother phoned again just as Alexandra was gathering her things into her ballet bag to leave for the studio.

"I'm sorry," her mother said at once. "I've been hating myself ever since we talked."

"Hating yourself?"

"Yes, for coming apart like that with you. I'm sorry, Alexandra. I hope you can forgive me."

"There's no need to forgive anything, Mom. It will probably take a lot of tears before we can all become ourselves again." She bit her lip, waiting for a response, knowing that her mother would despise the suggestion that there would be more tears.

But Mrs. Kreyling ignored the reference. "I know it's unforgivable that I hung up on you. I'm so sorry I did that."

"I'm just glad you called me back."

Then Mrs. Kreyling sighed, and as if she was changing gears, her voice lowered and took on an edge of determination. "What happened, Alexandra—" She stopped, swallowed audibly, and tried again. "What happened is that your dad and I blamed each other, and we couldn't make ourselves stop. After thinking about it these days since you and I talked, I think that's really the crux of it."

Alexandra said nothing, waiting.

"Back when it was all going on after—after Ricky died—I knew it would be better if we could face it together, but every time I looked at your father, I blamed him that my beautiful little boy was gone. He had promised me that it was something Ricky would grow out of. He *promised* me! I couldn't bear it that he was so wrong and I had trusted him with my son's life." She took a deep, ragged breath. "He blamed me too because I had confronted Ricky. He said I should have left things alone and not forced the issue with him, because that is what made him turn completely away from us. He kept asking me, over and over, 'What did you expect? What did you expect?' As if what I ever expected was to lose my son." Her voice was thick and low with old bitterness.

"Oh, Mom . . ." Tears seemed to boil up from the heavy hardness that filled her throat.

Ricky had been found dead by Bradley's mother, who had finally decided to check on the boys when for more than a full day they had not emerged from Bradley's room. The boys had intoxicated themselves to the point of alcoholic coma. Ricky could not be revived. Bradley had been taken by ambulance to the hospital, where he'd spent a few nights in intensive care. He might have been well enough to attend Ricky's funeral, but the Kreylings had asked that he not be present at the service for their dead boy.

"It was the most horrific time in my entire life," Mrs. Kreyling said. "I do my best to never think about it."

"But, Mom, it's not over."

"Yes, it is!" Her voice was fierce and rough. "Ricky's gone! It's over! We—" The strangulation sound was back in Mrs. Kreyling's voice.

"Mom, don't hang up! Don't hang up."

For some moments, a sound like gulping was all that could be heard. "No, I won't hang up on you again." But the phone line remained silent for some minutes in a fragile balance that Alexandra was terrified of tipping. She listened to her mother's breathing, monitoring as the gulping calmed toward normality. After some minutes she glanced at the clock under the lamp and realized that she would be late to the studio. At that moment, her mother—always an expert at picking up the faintest clues—sensed the change. "I've got to let you get to work."

"No, no! It's okay if I'm late. I won't get into trouble. I'd rather that we talk."

"No, I've got to let you go. You have things you must do and so do I."

"But we'll talk again soon, right?"

"We'll talk again soon."

As soon as she heard the click of the broken connection, Alexandra grabbed her ballet bag and was out the door. Setting off in a fast walk to the studio, she shook her head and breathed in deeply, trying to bring her attention to the work ahead of her. The family issue that she had barely given a thought to for most of a decade now held her brain hostage. She forced herself to visualize Katherine in the studio dancing a Spirit of Prayer sequence. Then she remembered the cassette tape. Cal had given each of them—Katherine, Matt, and Alexandra—an audiotape of the music for the *Prayer* ballet. Now Alexandra rummaged in her ballet bag for her Walkman, clipped it onto her jacket pocket, and put the earphones in place on her head. Gratitude poured over her as the first chords brought her to the present, to the life she had built for herself in San Francisco.

Cal's idea was that each of the three dancers would play the tape every possible moment in their waking hours so that the composition became as much a part of their structure as their bones. Inevitably, as they listened, the movements that went with each phrase played in their minds, creating unscheduled rehearsals that moved the production forward. Within a dozen bars, Alexandra was caught up in the dance, entirely focused on the choreography.

Her fast walk to the studio served her warm-up so that by the time she entered the studio, she could safely shorten her usual barre routine and soon join dancers working their way through floor exercises.

"Did you catch the board on your way in?" Matt's blond hair was already damp, his blue T-shirt beginning to stain in splotches of perspiration.

"No, what did I miss?" Dancers—and everyone else connected to the troupe—rarely failed to check the company bulletin board for daily updates of announcements, assignments, and messages for individual members of the company.

"Cal has put in a couple of extra rehearsals for *Prayer*. I hope you don't have anything planned for this evening."

"No, that's fine. Thanks for the heads-up." Actually she *had* had something planned, without being quite aware of it: a call to her mother. She was hoping just to say, "I love you." But with a late rehearsal, it would be too late to call the East Coast by the time she got home. And she still didn't know whether her mother would reconsider and use the ticket to come to San Francisco for the opening. It was only five days away now. A flutter of anxiety started in her stomach. *Thank goodness for those extra rehearsals.* She forced her attention back to the ballet class just as Amelie was calling everyone to their feet. Alexandra drew in a deep breath. *I'll have to think about it all later.*

* * *

October rolled around. Cal turned the calendar page, his heart speeding up with the realization of how close now opening night was. His mind went to that list he kept in his head without even meaning to—the list of the multitude of elements that went into the production to track where the troupe was on all of them. He also had lists down on paper, of course, so did Rob, so did Amelie, so did Ned. It took all of them, constantly noting progress, to get everything ready on time. His heart rate slowed to normal as he worked through the list, satisfying himself of the status of the major elements. He wasn't quite done when the intercom buzzed and Cindy's voice came through: "Cal, there's a call for you from a woman named Anne Braxton."

The name meant nothing to him, and he wanted to continue his mental list. "Send her to Rob, would you, Cindy?"

"Sure thing."

But when he left the studio a couple of hours later for lunch, she was waiting for him. There was no ducking behind the bus stop cover, no fussing with a scarf to conceal her face. When his foot reached the bottom of the small set of steps down to the sidewalk, she stepped forward. "Hello, Cal."

It was a voice he would know anywhere. His head snapped up, and now he was staring into the face of his ex-wife. The years had altered her looks a bit, but she must have made an effort to look good for this encounter. The makeup and hair were perfect; no gray was visible in the dark brown hair, and the brown/gray eyes (Jon's eyes) rested squarely on him.

For a moment he couldn't manage a word, but when he could, he surprised himself by the calm and disengagement in his voice. "Long time, Anne."

Her mouth, the feature he had most loved about her so many years ago, formed the briefest smile, as though she was uncertain now when she had expected certainty. "It's . . . nice to see you," she said.

He found that he couldn't reply in kind and was glad to be spared having to reply at all by the approach of two women on the sidewalk. He nodded to them and stepped backward to clear space for them to pass. One of the women smiled broadly at him and had gone only a few feet on her way before she turned to her companion and said, "That was Calvin Tropp! Did you recognize him?"

"So," Anne said. "You've become famous here." Her tone was a mix of wonder, sadness, and mild ridicule.

He watched the retreating women and then turned back to face her. "Why are you here?"

She moved closer. "I always knew I'd come back to you someday."

Now he remembered his own tears, the gasping release of pain when he had finally—so recently—accepted her abandonment of him and Jon. He searched his heart, first with a sense of dread, and then with a feeling of surprise. "I think it's too late." The resolve felt solid.

But she had begun to speak rapidly, almost babbling. "I wanted to live, and there we were cramped in that tiny, ugly apartment in Houston. You must remember how horrid it was. I couldn't stand it. I just couldn't stand it. And you were so focused on ballet while my career was ending. You had a future and I . . ."

She stopped to take a breath as he stared past her at the passing traffic. *Are you going to even mention our son? Do you remember Jon at all? How could you not have thought about the impact to Jon, if not to me?*

"But I always knew I'd come back to you someday. I always pictured you just marking time, waiting for me."

He looked at her again just as she was lifting her eyes to take in the studio behind them. *Not marking time, Anne. Maybe not really living, by your standards, but certainly not just marking time.*

"I was always sure you would wait for me." She reached out and grasped his forearm.

Even through the leather jacket he could feel her possessiveness, thwarting his small start of compassion at the pathetic picture she painted of their earlier life. After some moments, he shook his head and said as kindly as he could manage, "I didn't."

He looked into the dark brown/gray eyes, still lovely but now impotent to evoke the response she wanted in his heart. Her incredulity gave way, her hand left his arm, and she turned to walk away. He remembered then that she had never been good at not getting her way.

* * *

"So how are you feeling, now that the final rehearsal is under our belts?" Cal asked Katherine. It was eleven o'clock on the night before the opening. They sat in a red-seated booth, having breakfast. Around them, the busy restaurant pace had settled down. Most of the patrons had left, so only a couple of tables were occupied. At one a female student sat hunched, writing earnestly into a notebook, and at the other, a young couple held hands even though they appeared to be in a frowning disagreement. Their joined hands confirmed, maybe especially to each other, that they were united despite the temporary fissure. The windows were dark except where streetlights cast a glare.

Katherine reached for her cup of coffee and drank a few swallows before answering. "I'm doing okay, but I have been realizing that this will be the first time in my entire life that I've had an opening night and she wasn't there."

He heard her voice catch, but she remained tearless. It was five weeks and one day since her mother's death.

Cal looked at his beautiful principal dancer, his Spirit of Prayer, and was struck all over again by how graceful and poised she was, how elegantly her long auburn hair lay against her shoulder. He could not pinpoint exactly when, in their ten years of working together, he had fallen in love with her. It seemed to be recently, but maybe it was only his awareness that was recent. He still had not told her. *Better to give her time. After the season, when her grief is not so fresh. At least after the premiere.* "Maybe she will be there after all. How do we know she won't be?"

Katherine lifted her eyebrows. "Well, then just in case, I will dance this for her."

"You know, the opening night performances are dedicated to her."

"Really?"

He nodded, smiling back. "I had it noted in the programs, because all of us in the troupe know what an important role she has played. We all miss her."

Her eyes took on a shiny look. "She always sat in the same seat, off stage right, within the area lit when the lights were up bright on us, so I could see her when I was on stage."

"I know."

A waiter came by with a coffee pot, but Katherine shook her head and Cal held his hand over his cup.

"How about you?" she asked. "How are you feeling about the opening?"

"Rehearsal was great today, but you and I both know that it's not always the best sign when dress rehearsal is perfect. But the strange thing is that I'm not nervous like I usually am." He saw a sly smile slide across her mouth. "I guess you know full well how nervous I usually am before an opening." He ignored the urge the reach across the table to touch her hand. "But this time, I mainly feel . . . excited, I guess would be the word, to see how the new ballet unfolds. It's been such a joint effort."

"Yes, with Evana Arthur coming through for you like that, and Ned with the lighting—"

"And the three of you willing to work with a whole new style of choreography." He paused and then decided to trust the instinct to tell her. "And that's not all. From the very beginning, there's been a spirit about this piece that I've never experienced before."

Katherine nodded, showing no sign that she found his comment strange. "I've sensed that all the way through. Like a divine overseer for the whole effort."

His heart jumped. "Exactly!"

But then she looked troubled. "Cal, I want you to be the first to know that—well, I know this could just be part of the grief process, but I'm starting to think about the time when I won't dance anymore. I'm really not sure how many more opening nights there will be for me."

Alarm constricted his chest, and he cleared his throat before speaking. "Grief changes how we look at everything. It must be terribly hard to do this opening without your mother beside you."

"And you know I won't make any firm decisions without a lot of thought and talking with you about it every step of the way. But I'm already seeing my feet start to go."

"Your feet are beautiful." He stopped, feeling like covering his mouth with his hands. He hadn't meant to say it out loud, certainly not with such passion. Her face wore such a startled expression that he scrambled to think of something to offset what he had blurted. "I've seen *thousands* of dancers' feet over the years! Yours look pretty darn good."

She squinted as though doubting his words. He knew as well as she did about her knobby bunions, the calluses, the scars where torn blisters had become infected, the ends of her toes permanently flattened. "They take such a beating. At least you men don't have to do the *pointe* work."

Cal straightened his shoulders to help regain his composure. "You're young, Katherine."

"I'm twenty-nine!"

"That doesn't even make you a senior in the troupe."

"It's older than the average—you know that perfectly well."

"Yes, but with your training and your discipline, you could dance another ten years, easy. That is, if you want to."

She gazed down at the table, but he knew she was trying to see far into her future.

A decision formed in his mind and as quickly came out of his mouth: "We'd like to keep you dancing as long as you want to dance, but when the day comes that you want to stop, there will always be a place for you with the company."

Her eyes widened and began to shine.

"Always," he repeated. He had not thought of her as needing a lifeline, but her face told him how relieved she was to have one.

* * *

Opening Night

On October 6, cars streamed into the underground parking garage and available street parking without letup for an hour and a half before the opening curtain. Some patrons came early for the talk Amelie Boiroux and Rob Deinken had organized to share background on the ballets that would be danced that evening. These comfortable chats gave those who attended them a feeling that they were seeing into the inner workings of the troupe—and they were. No details were held secret, and all questions were answered candidly. The preperformance sessions had grown in popularity over the three years they had been held, moving into larger rooms of the opera house as the crowd had grown. Women in gowns and stoles sat beside college students in denim jackets, neither appearing put off by the other as they took in the behind-the-scenes details of life as a dancer in Tropp's Troupe.

Meanwhile, the large foyer filled to bursting with people clutching tickets, eager for the tuxedoed ushers to open the three sets of wide, ornate double doors to the performance hall. Most carried coats because the evenings were cooling earlier and earlier now, and they anticipated needing extra warmth when the performance was over. They had no idea of the scurry of activity on stage as, curtain still up, the stage manager and crew members hurried back and forth to make sure that sets were lined up ready for cues, lights were all in working order, tall stacks of slick-stock programs were in place on stands beside the performance hall doors, and dancers were already in makeup and costumes. Most of the women dancers had arrived two hours before curtain, and each dancer put on her own makeup and ensured the perfection of her own hair. It was not acceptable for even a wisp to be out of place. In the orchestra pit, two musicians at opposite ends of the pit bent over their instruments, practicing the difficult passages of the evening's music.

A sense of excitement and urgency tinged the crowd. Men looked impatient to gain entry; mothers with young daughters (obviously young ballet students, with their hair in buns, wearing frilly dresses and patent leather shoes) looked pleased as they imagined the day when all these people would be waiting to see *their* children on stage. Those young female dancers old enough to appreciate the gravity of opening night stood primly, swallowing down the excitement and waiting in self-conscious, sophisticated anticipation; those too young were as apt to yank their uncomfortable dresses right and left and even over their heads in their overstimulation. One had pulled off and abandoned her tight patent leather slippers to walk around in her white socks. The very few young boys in the foyer mostly pretended that their attention was elsewhere, lest anyone surmise their interest in ballet.

Four men with six-foot-wide brooms made a running pass to remove all dust and debris from the stage, and then at exactly seven thirty the forty-foot-high curtain was drawn closed, and the ushers opened the three sets of auditorium doors. Patrons streamed noisily into the main hall of the opera house, faces alight with anticipation. Children could not be constrained from running down the aisles to peek into the orchestra pit and then dashing back to report to their mothers, "Mom! You have to come see this!" Older patrons sat down to read programs or talk quietly, heads tilted toward each other, as the rows and rows of seats gradually filled. The rest of the orchestra members, most carrying instruments, filed by ones and twos into the orchestra pit, and soon a cacophony arose, a clamor of warming instruments uniquely beautiful to musicians everywhere.

At exactly seven minutes after eight the audience cheered and whistled in recognition of Music Director Dr. Charles Good as he stepped briskly to the dais in front of the orchestra. Stiff with both a new tuxedo and the pomp of opening night, he turned once and bowed to the audience to acknowledge the applause, even waving a white-gloved hand. Then he turned back to his musicians and raised both arms. Quiet fell on the auditorium as everyone, patrons and musicians alike, recognized the cue. The tip of the baton flicked in a blur and the music began. When the massive dark maroon curtain opened again, the audience gasped to see all forty dancers of the Calvin Tropp Ballet Company arrayed on stage, perfectly poised and ready to dance their hearts out in the evening's first piece. Their concentration was so absolute that patrons sitting close up with opera glasses could see the strain in facial muscles contrasting with the elegant calm of their bodies. Another high and blurred flick of Good's baton and the dancers began the high-energy, geometric ballet they had practiced with Candace Bennington, daughter of the English choreographer.

The world premiere *Prayer* ballet was scheduled last on the program, after the clamorous second intermission. By this time in the evening, ballet patrons were feeling totally at home in the huge opera house, moving casually as with ownership out to the kiosks offering food and drink and calling across rows of seating to others they knew. Most of the advertising for the evening's performances had featured the *Prayer* ballet, so everyone expected that something special was yet to come, and their enthusiasm was undiluted. Soon the lights began to flash to indicate five minutes remaining to curtain, and balletomanes turned their eager attention back to the main hall, finding their seats again, this time with ease.

When the auditorium lights were dimmed, Dr. Charles Good raised his baton again and the crowd stilled at once when it heard the haunting sound of a pan flute, accompanied by a piano, offering a brief taste of the mood the audience was about to enter. But instead of the massive curtain opening again, a corner at the far left was drawn aside and the audience began to clap as Calvin Tropp stepped through, immediately recognized with cheers and whistles from the audience. He smiled and waved in response and walked to the center of the stage.

"There's something both thrilling and totally terrifying about a world premiere," Cal said with a smile, casting his gaze through the auditorium and up to the second and third balconies. An appreciative sound passed through the crowd. Most of the people in the audience had been patrons for as long as Cal had been in San Francisco and had carried on a sort of love affair with his presence in the city and his creativity on the ballet stage.

He mentioned that the *Prayer* ballet had been unlike any previous ballet he had ever made and commended everyone from Amelie, the ballet mistress, to the stage manager to the musicians for the speed at which they had pulled together the artistry needed for the production. "But very special mention must be given to the composer of the music, of which Dr. Good has just given you a first taste. I'd like you all to recognize Evana Arthur for an extraordinary effort in creating the music for the *Prayer* ballet in something like three weeks, which would be unheard of if we were not accustomed to heroic creations from her. Evana, would you come out and give the folks a bow?"

The diminutive Evana, almost birdlike in her gown and high heels, appeared through the parted curtain next to Cal as the crowd rose to their feet in ovation. He held an arm out toward her and the applause grew louder. Then he noticed that she was smiling. *Have I ever seen her smile before?* On an unfortunate impulse, he took her hand in his and raised it to his lips. Instantly he knew this was a mistake. When he looked up to meet her eyes, he saw that now her smile masked eyes narrowed in disdain. But Cal held her hand a moment longer before turning to again face the audience. The cheering ovation continued until Evana gave a final wave and slipped back through the parted curtain, leaving Cal alone. He wondered if his face had reddened, but it didn't matter if it had. What he wanted to do now was get to the wings and let his dancers take over. "We all hope you will enjoy the *Prayer* ballet," he said to the audience and then nodded to Charles Good and ducked through the curtain himself as the audience roared again, electric in its anticipation.

From the moment Alexandra and Matt threw their fists up in the rage and despair of the opening scenes, Cal was drawn in as he had not expected. It was as though his brainchild, his heartchild had grown into its own life, and he was seeing it for the first time along with everyone else in the auditorium. The mystery of performance is a commonly observed phenomenon, inducing an edge of excellence, a sort of miracle push not encountered in even the best practice session beforehand— but this felt like something different. This felt like something very large imbuing his dancers with skills he had not seen in them before. He could only stare as Matt and Alexandra staged and raged and coursed their way through a choreography Cal should have known intimately but found that he didn't. *How can there be surprises in this?* The intensity of his dancers overwhelmed him as they transformed into the running stream of emotions, from frustration and dissatisfaction to despair, grief, anger, hatred, rage. Using the entire stage, they raced toward each other, only to turn their backs at the last second, passing without contact.

When Alexandra was alone on stage, strife erupted from within her, equally as much as it had shown between the two, and Matt also, when he danced alone, revealed a depth of internal conflict. The audience sat hushed, as transfixed as Cal was, some rigid with tension, some with tears. When the fury of the two dancers was turned outward, against each other, alarm moved in a silent wave through the opera house, so real was the passion on stage. Gradually the anger expended itself and the gestures altered toward beseeching as each sought in the other the absent peace, only to find failure because there was no trust between them. But this supplication, expressed mostly in their hands, in motions that approached invocation, was enough to awaken a deeper level of interaction, and when it was finally—dear God, finally!—time for the Spirit of Prayer to emerge, a murmur of astonishment and awe came from the crowd with the realization that she had been waiting there all along, somehow unseen, upstage right. Lighting on the sheer scrim, now being withdrawn, had kept her hidden.

The music disclosed a similar secret. Evana had resolved her question of when to bring in the pan flute by having it present from the first piano chord but hidden under the other instrument so that only the most discerning ear could have heard it. Now the lighting tech brought up the pale lavender lights on Katherine so gradually that she seemed to melt into shape and form. The more she became real, the more the pan flute could be heard. And when she raised an elegant leg and took her first step *en pointe*, another murmur sounded from beyond the footlights.

Katherine, the Spirit of Prayer, moved serenely to Alexandra and began to remold her gestures, soothe her expression, and ease her suffering. Alexandra resisted and then yielded stubbornly, soon falling back into despair and needing to be coaxed again to peace. Matt, when it was his turn, appeared swamped in shame but found his resistance crumbling, not by an external force that invited contest and combat, which he might have surmounted, but by a force of love to which he had no defense. Raw anguish filled Matt's face as he lifted his bowed head, bringing his arms up and up in rudimentary surrender, only to crumble in clumsiness. With grace and patience, Katherine retrained their hands to form the prayer pose until their fright and grief and uncertainty were eased and their confusion dispelled. The two dancers moved out of inadequacy to self-forgiveness, and finally Matt stood tall and whole as he left the stage.

Watching from the second wing, Cal saw Katherine's preparation for her solo as she found her starting point opposite the landing light, lifted her arms, and rose *en pointe*. He had expected to feel his heart constrict at this moment, but instead he felt so light that he could not bring himself to worry. He knew, he simply knew, that she was in hands greater than his. He watched her dancing praise and thanksgiving, somehow stopping time as the grace of her movements created a paradise that embraced not only Matt and Alexandra but also himself and the stage crew and all two-thousand-plus members of the audience who sat seemingly oblivious of each other's presence, hearing only the wistful pan flute as Katherine moved over the stage in the simple movements of Cal's choreography.

She danced a running *pas de bourrée couru*, her steps *en pointe* so tiny and so quick she appeared to move supernaturally. At the end of her solo, with a last feathered whisper of the solo flute, Katherine leapt toward the wing, glancing with only lowered eyes at the last moment toward the seat, off stage right, where her mother should have been sitting, had sat for ten years' worth of her daughter's performances.

Next the piano returned, its melody familiar but altered, bolstered noticeably by the pan flute, and Matt and Alexandra rose to their feet to dance as two people who have rediscovered why they love each other. Echoes of earlier scenes between them played out, as the two commanded the entire stage, running toward each other on diagonals but not turning away now from each other, instead clearly celebrating. Finally they danced a *pas de deux* that ended with faces and arms raised, the hands— his right, her left—together in prayer.

At the conclusion of the ballet, Katherine was beside them, the pan flute dominating with piano chords underneath. As she turned toward upstage right and the two dancers turned to follow, the music faded out until she led them in perfect silence. It seemed that the audience barely breathed, so quiet was the auditorium. A stage board creaked as it accepted their weight and then creaked again as they moved on. Then the curtain fell.

When all three dancers had left the stage, Cal found himself holding onto a buttress and realized that he had been holding his breath. At the same moment, he heard the eruption of the audience, which sounded like the roar of a fierce storm but, he knew, was the overflowing of emotions and the tremendous urge to congratulate and prolong the amazing thing they had seen. He took several gulps of air as all three of his dancers swirled around him, visibly shaking with the remains of the performance energy and joy to have the premiere successfully danced. Mustering himself, he smiled and touched each of them. "Fabulous. You were all just fabulous. I am so proud of you." Their faces, sweaty and flushed, beamed, and he understood how crucial his approval of them was. "Let's get out there and take our bows!"

As soon as the massive curtains had closed for the last time, the stage filled with people—troupe members who had already changed out of costumes into street wear, family members, dancers from visiting troupes, members of the orchestra. Emotions remained at a fever pitch as the voice levels continued to rise.

For several moments, Alexandra failed to recognize the woman who stood passive and waiting just inside a stage left wing. Then a wave of disorientation spread over her as she realized that the woman's gaze was on no one but her. *Why? Who?* But then she knew. The hair was different, in both color and style; the face was older; now there were glasses. *But of course.* Her mother had come after all. She had used the ticket Alexandra had sent and come to see her daughter dance.

Numb, Alexandra began pushing through the throng of well-wishers, past people who fairly pranced in the irresistible pull of the energy behind the big curtain, keeping her eyes locked with the eyes of her mother. *How many years?* Reaching her now, she looked into her eyes, surprised to see the tears through which her mother looked at her. For some moments, neither seemed capable of speaking. Finally, she was able to say, "I'm so glad you decided to come after all." Her mother nodded. "Me too. I can't believe how close I came to missing this, to not seeing how beautiful you are and what a dancer you have become." She shook her head then, unable to say more, and Alexandra took her hand and led the way to the dressing room, sensing that for a few minutes more, it would be the quietest place in the building.

Once there, Alexandra pulled her mother into her arms, not seeking permission first, because she knew that her mother would not welcome the embrace. *This is for me, Mom. If you'll let it, it could be for both of us.* As expected, the stiffness felt like she'd taken a cardboard cutout into her arms, but Alexandra held on anyway, refusing to be put off until her mother's arms closed around her.

Soon, Mrs. Kreyling began to collect herself, loosening her arms, but she didn't let go. She cleared her throat, perhaps testing her voice to see if it would work. "I know you have a party to go to. I remember that. There's always a party after your openings, and it's important. You have to go."

Alexandra shook her head. "I've been to a hundred of those parties, Mom. I want to sit with you and talk. We have so much to say." Then she pulled back from the embrace. "But—you're probably . . . you probably won't stay long . . ."

On her mother's face, decisions appeared to shift and firm. Then Mrs. Kreyling lifted her shoulders and let them relax. "I'm here. I'm staying for a little while, maybe a few days, maybe several days. We'll see what we need." She smiled. "Besides, there was no return leg on that birthday-present ticket you sent me."

Alexandra laughed out loud. "No, there wasn't!" *She hasn't booked the return flight yet! She's giving us time.* Maybe she had come with an intention of talking, just the two of them, to try to heal some of the family destruction that had occurred when Ricky died.

Now Alexandra realized that at any moment the dressing room would be swarming with people, and she wanted very much for the two of them to be alone in her own apartment. But she noticed her mother's high heels. "I'd better call a cab to take us to my place. It's only a few blocks, but you can't walk in those things."

"Are you kidding? I haven't walked in anything but high heels for so many years I'd probably fall down without them! The nights are nice here. I'd love to walk."

* * *

Back on stage, Matt noticed that his calves had stopped tingling. What he really wanted to do was grab a shower. His damp costume felt clammy against his skin, and he itched to be rid of it. But just as he turned to leave the stage, he caught sight through the crowd of a familiar profile: Ricardo! For a moment, Matt's heart felt as though it had stopped in his chest, and then such a wave of heat moved over him that he didn't feel the clamminess of his wet clothing anymore. *Where did he come from? Has he been here the whole time and I had no idea?* Then a more sobering, exciting question arose: *And what is he expecting?* Matt might have ducked behind others in the crowd if he had been able to move. Instead he stood watching the dark Italian dancer. Ricardo moved then so that his back was toward Matt; he was bent toward someone. Even at a distance, Matt could see that the older dancer was focusing all of his considerable sensual charm on that someone. And then the object of Ricardo's attention came into view. *Oh no! Father Andrew!* Matt felt his eyes narrow. *Of course, another blond boy from San Francisco!* Matt began to move toward the two men. Whether he wanted to confront Ricardo or not, it was important not to leave his newfound friend in Ricardo's clutches. But before he could reach them, he saw Ricardo reach into an inside pocket, take out a card that he held between two long fingers, and slip the card suggestively into Father Brandigan's jacket pocket.

Oh no! No! Now Matt didn't know what to do. Should he charge up to them, rip the card away and tear it up? Should he tell Ricardo as coldly as he could that his mark was a priest, for crying out loud? Should he . . . For a brief but terrible moment, Matt wondered if Andrew might actually *want* to wind up at Ricardo's hotel room later. Flushing confusion poured over him. Then to Matt's relief, it became clear that Father Brandigan did not need his assistance. The priest retrieved the card from his pocket, glanced at it, and calmly handed it back. He wasn't smiling. But he said something—something that bent Ricardo's head and kept it bowed when Father Brandigan walked away. Ricardo, however, was only briefly chastened. Within moments he began again to scan the crowd of dancers. Matt backed his way toward a wing, and as soon as he reached it, he turned and walked quickly toward the men's dressing room to clean up. It no longer felt like a good idea to go to the after-performance party. He knew that Ricardo would be there, probably looking for him.

* * *

But for most of the dancers, the party *did* seem like a good idea, even though everyone knew that tomorrow night, the ballets must all be danced again. But that was tomorrow, and tonight needed celebration of a successful opening night. The energy level stayed at fever pitch in the move from the closing curtain to the banquet room. Only there did the adrenaline levels, noise levels, and emotion levels gradually ebb.

Jon Tropp kept one arm around Amelie Boiroux and the other around Miss Agnus, who seemed to assume that all these people had gathered in her honor. It was easy to see why she might think that, as everyone who saw her oohed about how cute she looked in her tiny tuxedo. She stared placidly from black-button eyes at each person, not the least frightened by the loud swirl of humans. One of the corps dancers remarked, "Hey, I thought that dog was a girl!"

"Oh, she *is* a girl," Jon said. "But she's never looked good in a dress."

It was a familiar observation to Jon—something his father had said many times—but the corps member laughed loudly and clapped him on the shoulder before moving on.

Miss Agnus had waited in her cage with a rawhide bone to gnaw on during the evening's performances. The well-trained pet of a ballet choreographer and dance company artistic director, she had known not to make a peep. But each time Jon came to check on her, she'd gotten to her feet, a rise of three inches, with anticipation that maybe it was time to be out with the people.

* * *

After the noisy celebration behind the closed curtain, Katherine headed for the women's dressing room in hopes of finding Alexandra, not knowing that Mrs. Kreyling had decided to come to San Francisco. Disappointed, Katherine painstakingly removed her makeup, showered, and dressed slowly, putting off the moment when she would have to leave the large room and accept that there was no one waiting for her. How very much she had taken it for granted, all those years, that her mother would always be there for her. Other women dancers came into the dressing room, most looking flushed and excited, happy to be going out. They changed quickly, a few not even bothering to remove the heavy stage makeup, so eager were they to get to the party. Nearly all of them either called a quick "Congratulations!" to her or gave her a smile and a brief touch on the shoulder on their way out.

Finally she was alone, sitting facing her mirror, her back to the room. She scanned the mirror, taking in as much of the room behind her as she could by moving only her eyes. She saw a Coke machine, which must have been there for years but she had never noticed before. It certainly didn't look new. She rose from her seat and moved toward it. Bottles of soft drinks stood ready, many of them dusty, and grateful for the diversion, she unlocked the drawer of her dressing table and took out her purse, finding the quarters for the machine. She put in three of them, pressed a button, and was startled by the noisiness as a bottle rolled, fell with a loud crash, and rolled again within her reach at the bottom. She carried the opened bottle back to her seat and began to drink, wincing at the acidic edge but glad to have a further delay of her departure, because now she had to finish the bottle. Around her, the building quieted.

There was no telling how long she had sat there, but the bottle was nearly empty when a door shut somewhere down the hall, and alarm prickled the back of her neck. *I'd better leave.* She'd never stayed so long after everyone else had gone. *What if they lock the building and I am stuck inside till morning?* With urgency now, she set the bottle aside and stood, gathering her ballet bag and purse, and went to the door, dreading the moment when she would have to see that her mother was not waiting for her. *Well, I'll just refuse to see it, that's all.* She kept her eyes downcast as she opened the dressing room door, stepped outside, and closed it behind her. She moved resolutely down the hall, watching one foot land in front of the other, again and again.

So it was from behind her that she heard her name called so gently: "Katherine?"

She was too focused on avoiding pain to be startled. She simply turned and saw Cal waiting for her. She dropped her things and ran to him, her face contorting as she closed the distance and threw herself into his arms. He held her as she sobbed out the grief she had danced through for the previous five weeks.

After some minutes, they slid down the wall to sit on the floor, but she still clung to him, and he stroked her hair and kept her close to him. When the tears subsided, she asked, "Aren't they going to lock up the building or something?"

He barely moved his head, unwilling to pull away from her. "I've got keys."

She made a small sound, embarrassed to appear naive, but she relaxed then, and he did too.

* * *

By the early hours of October 7, Cal had driven Katherine to her condominium and kissed her at the door, and Jon had returned Miss Agnus to Cal's house. Miss Angus barely waited for Cal to finish unzipping the crate before she clambered out, vigorously shook herself to try to set her hair right, and jumped into his arms. He removed her disheveled tuxedo and scratched her back where the straps had been tightest.

"We missed you at the party," Jon said.

"I didn't expect to miss it, but it turned out to be a rough evening for Katherine." He hugged the Pomeranian to his chest and then set her on the floor.

"I thought it might be something like that. What's the status?"

"Well . . . I'm hopeful."

Jon scratched the back of his head. "Aren't you worried that—"

"That she's jumping into something with me just because she misses her mother?"

Jon nodded.

Cal nodded too. "I know. Could be that's really all there is to it. I guess I'll know in time. All I can do is what you and I talked about before: take it slow and not expect too much." For a few minutes both men were quiet. Then Cal said firmly, "I'm not going to rush this, but I'm not going to miss it either."

Jon smiled at him. "Good for you, Dad." He reached for his jacket, which lay across the back of the sofa. "I'm going to get to bed now. I know you have another performance day tomorrow and I have to drive home to LA, so I'll say good night now."

* * *

Approaching two thirty in the morning, Miss Agnus lay asleep, stretched out against Cal's thigh as the two sat on the living room sofa. Both of her front paws rested in his palm. He had not closed the heavy drapes, so pale moonlight entered the room, filtered through fog. The community around them had become quiet; the room had grown still; most of all, within Cal, silence and peace had finally come. He was aware of a presence in the room with them, but instead of speaking, he waited, letting his heart listen and sensing the growing companionship, the strengthening relationship. When at last he felt moved to speak, the words that formed were, "I'm ready for whatever's next."

-0-

Acknowledgments

I'm not sure that it's possible to remember every person and every influence that should rightfully be acknowledged for contributions to a written piece that has taken years to complete. Next time I'll keep better records. But I could not have written this story if I had not fallen in love with ballet in watching the Pacific Northwest Ballet perform in the years when Kent Stowell and Francia Russell were artistic directors. A true balletomane, I went with the troupe to Australia when it opened an international festival in Melbourne and kept my season's tickets for many years until I could name dancers as they emerged from the wings. I was well into the manuscript when uncertainty about credentials in spirituality overcame me, and I resumed the writing only after earning a master's degree in the art of transforming spirituality from the School of Theology and Ministry, Seattle University. The discussions in spirituality have continued in a spiritual directors' supervision group, including, in recent years, Alegria Albers, Carol Kassner, Margaret Riordan, Maria Thompson, and Mary Ellen Weber. Another group that has mattered significantly in the forming of the text is a writers' group focused on spiritual subjects. The composition of the group has varied over the years; current members are novelist/physicist Roger Anderson, poet Lois Holm, poet and essayist Jacqueline Leksen, and songwriter (and fabulous singer) Al Roehl. My training in transcendental meditation was with Annie Skipper. My partner, Helene, a former mental health provider and chemical dependency counselor, contributed not only encouragement and patience but also important guidance regarding therapy sessions and alcoholic coma. My friend Cindy Riche unknowingly helped me stay on course by dropping me an encouraging e-mail after she read the sample chapter on my website (jeangilbertson.com). And my friend Linda Becker read the same sample chapter and advised naming sections by the week remaining till opening night, rather than by chapter numbers. Books consulted have been too numerous to cite but ranged from ballet instruction books, dancer biographies, spiritual and religious texts, books on musical composition and synthesizers, and books on writing and editing. To every influence and influencer, a heartfelt thank-you.

Reading Group Discussion Questions:

1. When he was a teenager, Cal's mother told him: "There's bigger forces at work than we know." Cal takes her words as gospel. How do you see that philosophy in relation to the rest of Cal's story?

2. When have you had to make a serious decision involving your personal or professional reputation? What were the circumstances and what happened?

3. Is there a place in your life where you are faced with such a decision now?

4. Talk about times when you have stepped out in faith. How did that go?

5. How about Evana's story—was her work any less an act of faith than Cal's? What were the main challenges she faced that Cal didn't face?

6. Talk about your experiences when Spirit spoke a message into your soul. Did you listen or ignore it? What was the result?

7. Why is there such a tendency to ignore the still small voice of God?

8. Of the three dancers, whose subplot story do you most relate to? Why?